SCOTT M. SWAINE

FORGOTTEN MASTERS X

THE LAST ASSIMILATION

Primix Publishing
East Brunswick Office Evolution
1 Tower Center Boulevard, Ste 1510
East Brunswick, NJ 08816
www.primixpublishing.com
Phone: 1-800-538-5788

This is a work of fiction. Names, characters, places, and incidents either are the product of the author's imagination or are used fictitiously, and any resemblance to any persons, living or dead, is entirely coincidental.

Published by Primix Publishing: 01/07/2025

ISBN: 979-8-89194-225-7(sc)
ISBN: 979-8-89194-262-2(hc)
ISBN: 979-8-89194-226-4(e)

Library of Congress Control Number: 2024911469

Because of the dynamic nature of the Internet, any web addresses or links contained in this book may have changed since publication and may no longer be valid. The views expressed in this work are solely those of the author and do not necessarily reflect the views of the publisher, and the publisher hereby disclaims any responsibility for them.

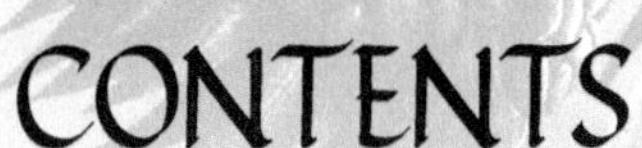

CONTENTS

Preface

In this book, which would mark the final chapter of the Forgotten Masters series, I feel I should offer a special tribute to those others who held similar dreams, and who wrote stories of legendary heroes crusading across far frontiers and performing extraordinary deeds. And in so doing, allowed me to dream a little for myself.

One in particular is R.A. Salvatore. He is a well-known fantasy author who wrote a number of stories relating to a society of elves known as Drow, which in his case is derived from the Forgotten Realms fantasy scenario. The name of my books, by the way, is purely coincidental and unrelated to the former, but admittedly with some elements of this and others borrowed for inspiration.

I once consulted with Mr. Salvatore relating to publishing my books, hoping to find a little confidence in myself. As a man of honor and wisdom, he shared his thoughts with me that I should not hold back, if I truly felt a desire to reveal my dreams.

The scenery I use here does not involve specific people or names to otherwise interfere with any other literary work, whether his or others. While I may use certain terms, it is largely to identify the universal concept of a bad guy, recognizable to the genre, and the seemingly irreconcilable conflict between two sides.

However, my books are designed to portray a progression of evolution, which I believe every society must follow, that they should not be perpetually locked in the past, and instead have the opportunity to develop, as all people must, eventually to solve their problems for the combined benefit of all. The rivalry of nations is unproductive. The persecution of the individual or the group is similarly wasteful, and these can only lead to conflict. Rather, a society must come together, a union of all bodies, if they are to achieve true enlightenment and prosperity. By combining our resources for a positive gain, rather than squandering them on so many destructive goals, we can accomplish miracles.

These books are as much a story of problem solving as they are my interpretation of mankind's failure to do the same in reality. In writing this series, I had hoped to describe a scenario of achievement, albeit with its inherent sacrifices, to signify a progression of labor to bring people together in harmony, such that they could redirect themselves to higher pursuits, rather than unraveling everything with renewed wars and repeated errors. A society cannot realize this if it is constantly at odds with itself, tearing itself apart with either political or social intrigue.

As I say in my books, the Seas of Creation are vast. But unless we grow up as mature adults with higher wisdom and calmer minds, we will never see it. Furthermore, we might find ourselves in need to share this wisdom with others who are themselves still growing up. We must set the example. We must demonstrate a higher purpose. And we must teach this to our children, that they will hold this dear above all other things.

In short, we must evolve.

Chapter 1

INFILTRATION

In a deep underground cavern, from out of a musty tunnel of cold stone and aged lichen, a lone figure emerges into view. The traveler was a young female, with her features concealed under a hood and a heavy cloak. She travelled with two companions, but these were not people, they were the four-legged kind, mammalian, with long fangs and sharp claws.

She was approaching a massive wall that closed off a large cavern behind it. Within that cavern was a city carved largely out of the native stone. The wall itself featured arrow slits and several windows, all well above ground level, and with excellent coverage of the grounds outside. A single portcullis, fashioned out of heavy grade iron, closed off the entrance. This was the only visible way in or out, although there was suggested to be a secret back entrance known only to the locals.

On either side of the gate were two towers overlooking the area, and from one of these came a shout barking out to the visitor arriving at the front.

"Halt! State your business or begone!"

The visitor stopped in her tracks and nonchalantly looked up at the guardsman.

"I'm a merchant traveler here to make a few coins in trades after a long journey to find this place."

"Unlikely! What are those…beasts…you bring with you? And where's your wagon with your trade goods in it?"

"First, these are my bodyguards. Travelling alone out here is not for the faint of heart, and they keep my skin attached. Second, travelling with a burdensome wagon is also unwise, as it tends to slow me down. So, I make my trades with smaller items of value that I can easily carry with me in my pockets. These are specialty items that only a select few of the more prestigious families might find of interest, and therefore I do not need a wagon for it."

"That's an interesting excuse, but I'm not convinced. I've never seen creatures like those before. Where did you find them, and how is it you are able to control them if they're so fierce that they can guard you against the sorts of dangers you might find in these caverns?"

"Aye, they are special, and it is precisely for this reason that they can provide their protection, as the dangers you might find around here would not know how to defend against their form of assault. As for controlling them, I have a special trick that I use, but this is a trade secret where I come from. Now, I desire to rest my weary legs and see about a few trades, and standing out here arguing over such trivial details isn't bringing me any closer to that. Therefore, if you are really so interested in seeing how effective we are at fending off the dangers out here, maybe I could demonstrate by casting this potion bottle against your walls..."

She now reaches into her cloak and pulls out a small bottle of a dark liquid to show the guardsman up in his window. He studies it apprehensively, even though from his vantage, he could not see clearly what it could be.

"What's that?" he asks tentatively.

"Oh, just a little appetizer. The basilisks are well-known for their love of rocks, but they're also well-known for their love of each other. And if that group of males I passed by a short while ago should catch wind of a female in heat...well, all I can say is they won't stop at walls for it," she chuckles mischievously.

The guard reeled back in his window at the obvious assertion. Basilisks were large and rather powerful creatures known to lurk in the caverns and tunnels. And being lithovores that consumed rock, as opposed to organic matter, they would just eat their way through the walls to find their goal. This, by itself, was enough to stifle the guard for any reply, feeling instead it might be a better course to simply allow this wandering 'merchant', or whoever she might be, entrance, rather than aggravating her further, especially if she felt confident enough to bring this up with those two other creatures at her side stated to be enough to protect her.

He glanced at his partner who was standing behind him in the tower window. The two of them exchanged stares for a moment before the other one nodded. The guard then returned to the window.

"Um, right. I don't think that'll be necessary. But before I let you in, we hold a policy to record the names of those strangers who pass through here. What name do you carry so we can record it in our ledger?"

"Fine, this is fair enough, I suppose. My name is Relissa of House Moonshimmer."

"Moonshimmer?" he winces. "What kind of name is that?"

"A fine and proud one, if you want to keep your tongue about it. Anything else?"

"Uh, no. That is all. Open the gate!" he shouts down below.

The portcullis slowly grinds upwards to allow passage, and the lone figure saunters inside, along with her entourage. She makes her way along the avenue to an intersection and turns down a lane in the direction of a tavern. The streets were mostly empty of foot traffic, as not too many people made it a habit of simply walking around town. Not unless they had business, and even then, they often made haste to get out and back home again to safety, as walking the streets was a hazardous affair, to say the least. Everyone was armed with at least a dagger, which was often poisoned for additional kill power, and no one trusted anyone…ever. Not even their own family members.

This was a Drow city, located somewhere deep in an underground region known as the Underdark. They were the last of the societies on Tae'Eladar that had not yet been assimilated after the unification of the population on the surface into the kingdom created by Lord Thaelyn and his wife, Lady Aerlie.

The Drow society was an exiled clan of elves, driven into these deep burrows after a violent series of wars once saw their kind banished from the surface world. They turned away from their native pantheon of gods, known as the Seldarine, and instead began to follow a sinister goddess who filled them with hate, lies, and murderous intent. As the result, the surface world had to endure a long series of what the Drow described as raids to prevent what was believed to be an imminent assault of a large army surely to find its way down from the surface to finish what was once started. But there never was any, and now the surface world has finally grown tired of the long wait for these people to come to their senses.

Relissa and her people were also dark elves, but from a clan that survived those wars and migrated to greener pastures to start new lives, only to be discovered in recent times by Thaelyn and his people, and then integrated into his population. This now gives him an opportunity to use them to help the others find their way back. But this would not likely be easy.

Relissa strolled along the block to a local tavern, which was one of the few places considered to be neutral ground, where people could go find relaxation without the possibility of having a knife planted in their back. She became familiar with this locality after several scouting reports came back from other agents in disguise to report on the general lay of the city and its amenities in order to prepare her for her mission. But before proceeding inside, she stepped away from the door into a shady spot for a bit of privacy. There, she began seemingly speaking to herself.

"All right you peeps… Earrings, pop into view here in my hands."

She holds out both hands with her palms open as mini surfaces. From underneath her hood, and concealed beneath her modestly short locks of white hair, what seemed like a set of gold earrings vanished from their former positions and reappeared as small insect-like apparitions in her hands. She peers down at them as she continues speaking.

"Good, now we need to call in our contacts. We're working with the two least-important Houses here in the city, but not all at once. It might draw too much attention if they both show up together. We'll go one, then the other, and I'll meet with them inside here," she nods in the direction of the door.

The two insect agents nod and take flight in their respective directions. Once out of sight, Relissa checks the surrounding area to make sure no one was paying attention before continuing to the door. She entered inside and halted to survey the room before proceeding to a lonely table on one side. She takes a seat and instructs her two companions to lay down on either side of her. The other patrons in the room eye her carefully, and especially her animal friends, unsure if they should stay as they were, or simply leave.

She sits there silently with her head down, fully hidden under her hood. Even though she was a dark elf, the same as the others, the long duration of time since her people diverged from the rest left its mark in the diversity of her skin and eye colorations, where she would now stand out if she were to reveal herself openly. Therefore, she was taking a risk simply to present herself in this environment, at least somewhat, unless she could find an excuse for herself, such as a traveler from a distant city where the locals might hold a different ethnic flavor. Nevertheless, treading around a Drow city was distasteful for her, as the Drow were regarded as a disgrace to her people for how low they sank since the time of those ancient wars. And yet, she had a job to do, and it was at least as much a noble effort to correct this as it was an offence simply to speak to them.

Several long moments pass until the first of her appointments arrives. It was a young man. He stepped inside and quickly took notice of the lone figure surrounded by the two ferocious-looking beasts. He almost wished to turn around and run away. But he knew from the other agents he had spoken to before that this informant had something important to reveal that could alter the Drow perceptions of the world such that it might change their whole way of life…one way or another. And so, he cautiously stepped forward.

The other patrons in the room studied the scene, many of them mumbling to themselves about this individual at the table and the sanity level of the man approaching her. But it seemed very apparent that this was an arranged meeting, which wouldn't be outside expectations, as many secretive and often subversive dealings could be found in places like this. However, they knew not to inquire about such things if they valued their own lives.

The man slowly approached the table, carefully watching the two animals on the floor, as they also studied him for his actions.

"Are you the informant I was told about?" he asks gingerly.

"Maybe. Are you from one of the lower Houses of the city?"

"I am. But what purpose does that actually serve?"

"It serves the purpose that you might listen to what I have to say, as opposed to those in the higher ranks. They can be a bit finicky."

"I see. Very well, and what is it you have to say?"

"The first thing I have to say is to sit down and stop shouting across the room."

"I'm not shouting…" he begins, but quickly stifles his response as it was obvious that simply speaking aloud was enough for the others nearby to hear him.

He pulls out a chair and gently sits down, still watching the two animal companions for their reactions.

"What are these…things…down here?" he asks softly as he glances at the floor next to him.

"They're called tigers, in this case white tigers. Rather lovely, don't you think?"

"Uh huh…sure. And what happens if they get hungry?"

"The same as anything else that gets hungry. Those teeth of theirs aren't just for show."

"As I thought. All right, so what is it you want to talk about? I was told by others that you bring important word about the surface world and the people who live up there, correct?"

"I do, but let me first ask what you know of it, from your own teachings and anything you might hear rumbling around the city."

"Fine. My teachings tell me that we must always be ready for an invasion or an attack of some sort, and that they could be marching on us at any moment. Then, I hear where some of the higher Houses send out bands of their best warriors to launch hidden strikes to reduce their numbers and hold them back."

"Right, this is generally what I thought. I hear this is a common story given out by those higher Houses, and not only in this city, but all the others as well. Unfortunately, it's all a lie, which shouldn't be too surprising, as most everything around here is a lie in one form or another."

"A lie…" he pauses in thought. "So, the rumors I'm hearing lately are actually true? And for how long?"

"Since the beginning. They never had any interest in crawling down into this hole to bother with peeps like you who essentially buried themselves out of sight and out of mind."

"Out of sight and out of mind?" he gasps. "Then just what are we to them?"

"A nuisance…a bother…a massive pain in the backside for all these so-called raids, which don't hit masses of warriors, but instead common peasants, farmers, merchants, and others who don't even carry weapons to fight with. And these are the glorious stories told by your esteemed warriors of great victory over a hard opponent who is so determined to advance on you that they would crawl around in the dirt simply to find you."

He glares at her for the apparent audacity of the statement. The rumors he had been listening to in recent times were part of a positive propaganda campaign launched by Thaelyn's kingdom to correct the errant stories passed down by the higher authority figures of Drow society and their goddess with her designs. It was a slow and difficult process to overcome the long-standing statements that had been circulating for so many thousands of years, but it had to start somewhere. Now, Relissa was here as part of a follow-up mission to nail home a few final pieces.

"Then what are they actually doing up there if not preparing to move on us down here?"

"Evolving, which the Drow are not. In the time since the Drow found their homes in this place, they have mostly kept to their original lifestyle, along with the tools they use, the weapons they wield, the knowledge they teach, and so on. But knowledge isn't limited to only that which you brought with you into this hole. It goes well beyond that. And if you have enough gumption to do so, you can grow and learn new things, even to evolve your society into a new Age, with new wisdom, new tools, and new ways of solving problems. Unfortunately, being stuck down here in this hole tends to limit just how far you can actually grow, if you don't have access to anything bigger. Up there, they came into new leadership some time ago, and that new leadership encouraged them to reach well beyond what the world had once upon a time when all this began, such that you wouldn't recognize the place by now."

"Really! And how would this reflect on the larger Houses sending their warriors up there? Because I know they do send them up. I've seen some of the raiding parties go out on occasion."

"Fine and good, and then they come back with these stories. But I'll put it to you that those stories are largely to save face in the eyes of the priests and their goddess. To do anything else is to ask for a quick lashing, or whatever they give on these occasions, just to speak their mind on it. There are garrisons at the exit points for each of the tunnels leading back up to the surface. Over the course of time, they learned where those warriors come out, and built walls to hold them back. Then, whenever one of these raiding parties comes into view, they simply shine a very bright light in their faces. Living down here for so long, the Drow have become very sensitive to bright light. To them up there, it's an everyday thing, but for anyone down here, it's painful to the eyes, such that you might crumple over from it. Then they simply order them to turn around and march right back to where they came from. That's all. They're not welcome up there."

"No attacks? Not even to fight them when they come into view, simply for appearing on their native ground?"

"Nope. First, I might say, simply to appear isn't a cause worth fighting for, if they can order you to turn around. Much like the guards at the gate out here, if you don't have anything to convince them to open the gate for you, they tell you to turn around and go home. They don't simply kill you for standing out there."

"All right. Got it."

"However..." she asserts with a finger. "This is where I come in. I know a few things, and you would be wise to listen to me. You, your House, and anyone else with the ears to hear it. It's been roughly ten thousand years since all this began with the old Ssri clan, which used to be our name back in the day, when those ancient wars took place that sent these people underground..." she discreetly waves her hand at the local crowd, "...now to call themselves Drow. And the people up there have essentially suffered these idiotic attacks, murdering their citizens, and causing them to seriously hate these peeps down here for the favor of it. But apparently not to the point of marching down here to take care of it. Once again, keeping a vigil to prevent this on their side was more convenient, maybe also more productive than coming down here for it."

"Incredible. So, we go up and kill countless numbers of their population, and they only care enough to build a wall in front of us?"

"The general idea, I think, was largely based on how much trouble it might be to map these crazy tunnels just to find you."

"All right, this much I suppose I can understand. I'm aware that the tunnel networks can change over time, as you have the activity from such like basilisks and other creatures digging new ones and collapsing older ones."

"This is true, to say the least. However, this is where we come to the good part...or bad part, depending on how you want to see it. This new leadership brought all the races together up there... Everything. And we're talking of elves, humans, dwarves, and others who are part of that big society up there...now all ONE big society. So, if you make war with anyone, you make it with everyone, and this is a society you really don't want to tussle with. Your warriors wouldn't stand a bloody chance at fighting anything, even down to the civilian level by now, as each of them is also trained in magic to a point where they might now be dangerous to you. Therefore, you'd be seeing corpses sent back home, not victorious heroes."

"I see. And therefore, I suppose, they regard us as so insignificant to deal with. Out of sight and out of mind, like you said."

"Insignificant, maybe, when you consider how far they've travelled up the knowledge ladder by now. But while you might be out of sight, you're not completely out of mind. You keep sending those parties up there, which continues to be a bother, even if they are turned away at first sighting. The simple fact that you keep doing it is already enough for them to eventually grow tired of the bother, and then WANT to do something about it, if only to put a final rest to it."

"Uh oh…"

"Aye! And this uh oh is serious, as they're at that point by now. You're afraid of a big military advancing on you? Well, keep up those nuisance raids and you'll see one, but this is a law enforcement move, not a hit to finish up some forgotten war. Murder is illegal up there. Any form of unjust killing, whether for personal gain or something else, is often punishable by death or similar. And the Drow have a long history built up by now. Furthermore, after uniting all the people up there into one big society, they're now looking at one final piece that is so far unresolved, if only for the inconvenience of its placement."

"A missing piece…and inconvenience of placement?" he winces. "What do you mean by that?"

"Picture this. This new leadership I spoke of came here for a reason…to unite the people of the world…ALL of them, so they might all go forward into a bright new future of wisdom and wonder, free from war, free from crime, free from persecution, and anything else that might otherwise hold a society back from the progress of evolution. By now, they have everything, except for one. So, who is missing, and where are they found?"

Relissa pauses and leans back in her chair as she allows this to sink in. The meaning was readily apparent, and the man drew back as he began to put it together.

"But that…would defy reasoning…wouldn't it?" he emits tenuously. "Us? They would want us, after everything else is said and done? Why?"

"You're still people, Drow or otherwise. You live here in this world no less than any other. And once upon a time, our folk were a part of that group up there until some fool turned them against their proper gods and started digging themselves graves down here."

"Digging graves…to which the others don't want to crawl around in…looking for us to finish…what WE started back in those old days. Is this why they don't actually come down here? Are they somehow hoping to, um, what word would we use here?"

"To redeem us. Aye. But the trouble is the Drow society of today gives their worship to the wrong goddess, one that is NOT part of our native body, but instead one who took possession of our people after they essentially defiled their old religion. This is one of our obstacles, and the reason why I might try speaking to someone like you rather than the higher Houses."

"Ah! Yes! This much I understand. They would simply balk at the idea. But then what? Are they hoping to convert us or something? And then, of course, what about those higher Houses who would otherwise protest against it…rather violently I would imagine."

"Here is where that military action might come into play. Listen to these words very carefully and come to your own conclusion. This world is owned by one goddess in particular. She ordered it to be restored from a dead condition to a living one, and then new life installed on it to serve a specific purpose of her own design. This was the human society. We elves intruded on this, not knowing the history or the reason. We were initially unwelcome, but later she reconsidered that we might add into this grander plan of hers, and in order to see the plan fulfilled, she installed a very special individual to govern and organize it, leading the world into the unity it has now."

"Sounds complex so far."

"Indeed! And so here we are, a world united, at least for that part up there, with only one piece remaining, the Drow, who don't like cooperating with anyone, and all due to that witch of a goddess you peeps worship."

"Um…" he nervously jolts back and quickly scans the room to see if anyone else heard the statement.

The man was suddenly very anxious. You don't go around calling your goddess by that word. At the very least, if she didn't do something personally, she would pass the word to an army of priestesses to do it for her. And punishment for something like this was harsh, to say the least. Now he was watching the door to see if anyone was rushing inside to contend with it.

Relissa knew he would carry this reaction. The whole reason she chose to use that word was to employ emphasis on her meaning. The Drow defiled their old pantheon and turned over to one of the worst members of the god society known as the Estelar. Their goddess was perhaps the least favored among the local group for her manners and methods. And she was especially disliked for occupying space on Tae'Eladar by its owner, Maker Kuroku.

The man studied her for her smug confidence, sitting in her chair as if she held no concern over the violation she made. As a female in a society ruled by females, she held a higher position of authority over a male, and the females were generally very devoted as the sole priesthood of their religious worship. Males didn't get personally involved in that at all, but they often found themselves subjugated by it. But her open defiance began to intrigue him.

"How can you sit there and speak such things when, um…"

"When every priest of the Spider Queen is female, and as one, I should be up there doing the same? Because I don't worship that unsavory wretch. I follow the Seldarine, our right and proper gods as elves…any kind of elves. So, if she has anything to say about it, she'll need to wade through that first, and I have numbers on my side, as well as the owner of this world, who is none too pleased to see her holding space here."

"The owner of this world? Meaning to say, she is not even supposed to be here to begin with?"

"You got that much right. Therefore, we come to the final bit…that military movement. For those of you wise enough to realize where this is going, we can maybe ask the Seldarine to take you back. Although, I suspect they might have you do a bit of work to redeem yourselves, but the final result will be worth it, I think. As for the rest, our own glorious military will see to it, once they actually do arrive. And then you, or maybe I should say those higher Houses that won't cooperate with us, as well as their witch of a goddess, will get their walking papers. And this will conclude the final piece of that unification bit. From there, we all go forward into a future we can only begin to imagine. But I'm sure it'll be a good one."

The man now finds himself glaring at her for the sudden turn of wording.

"Where did you actually come from that you and your House don't follow the Spider Queen? And what do you mean when you say 'us' and 'our' military?"

"I'm from a clan that escaped during those old wars that sent the rest of you running into a hole in the ground. We survived outside of it, still holding on to our ancient beliefs, and true to our old gods. Now we're hoping to bring back the rest of you, or what's left of it."

"What's left of it. Interesting. All right, I think I understand, but just for the sake of clarity, even with the threat of your military coming into play, where would that put us on the other side of it? If we are unable to follow this advice of yours, for instance the Matron Mothers of our Houses, who can be rather rigid in their opinions…"

"Right. We'll look for our openings where we can find them. Even in the most rigid of societies, there can be those who don't take wholeheartedly to it, and we'll try to bring them out. We also have the children, who likely haven't been as deeply corrupted as yet, and we might try rehabilitating them. As for the rest, unless they begin to see the greater direction, we might simply have to remove them as irredeemable refuse. If they want to go down fighting, so be it, but this world MUST come together, as a matter of divine mandate. It's not about you, me, your Matron Mothers, or your goddess. It's about Maker Kuroku who owns the show and has special plans for us."

"What sort of plans? Or do I dare ask?"

"She's called the Maker of guardian societies, and we're one of her creations. We are made to solve problems. And for the moment, you Drow are a problem that needs solving. After this, who knows where we may travel and what else is out there to solve. But we're building ourselves as the ones to do it."

"That sounds like a bold statement."

"It is, and we've already demonstrated ourselves able to rise to the challenge. Unknown to you peeps down here in this hole, we've already travelled to other worlds and solved the problems we found there. You probably don't even know what that means, living down here without even a sky over your heads."

This statement stifled the man, as he didn't even know what a sky truly was, let alone what it might mean to have something else like another world out there. Their local teachings were entirely absent of this concept, even from a historical perspective of what they might recall from the last time they lived on the surface. And their forays up there were not about stargazing or anything else intellectual.

He leaned back to contemplate these statements. He knew his purpose here was to learn something he could bring home and share with his family, or at least those who might actually listen, and possibly bring it up to their Matron Mother of the House, the one who governed the family dynasty. She would be the worst of it, but if he could convince her of these principles, she might hold the authority to convert the whole family. It would be but one step within a city full of situations like this, where each one would need to be processed independently, and with perhaps increasingly higher difficulty as you ascend the city hierarchy of authority, where the higher Houses represented the more stubborn of city officials.

And yet, even if he was not successful at convincing anyone in his family, by the sound of it, that fabled invasion the people spoke of so often, and for so long, if none was ever present in the past, now there would be, and largely due to the Drow posing as such a bothersome menace to the people on the surface that they finally grew tired of it. And unfortunately, they were advancing themselves with new knowledge and capacity whereas the Drow were not. This now represented a severe imbalance of power. But this also represented its own paradox. These were just words so far, and Matron Mothers were not so easily swayed by simple words.

"She'll want to see something in all this," he mutters softly. "Do you know that? She won't just take someone's word on it, she'll want someone she can trust to be her eyes and ears, maybe also her hands and feet to travel there and actually see it."

"Maybe so," Relissa nods. "And so, it looks like you might have a job ahead of you. There's a tunnel passage you peeps use locally to go up there for your little raids. But instead of sending another raiding party, who this time might not come back, try sending a political envoy and talking a bit. See what happens."

"The top Houses? They're the ones who govern the city. But I doubt they would listen to something like this."

"Probably not, but yours might. Then see about spreading the word around. Maybe it'll soften some of them up a bit. Or maybe not, but it might also give them a good heads-up that their goddess is about to go bye-bye."

"I'm afraid of what sort of reaction they might have to that. Ours is not high enough to be a part of the ruling body, and neither do we hold much power within the temple. We might do our part, but our role is minor as compared to the rest."

"It has to start somewhere. In this case, at the bottom and working its way up."

"All right, I'll see what I can do for my part. Am I to assume you will share this with some of the other Houses? It might make a difference with our Matron Mother if she's not alone, and has the support of other Houses doing the same."

"It might, and we are working this problem not only here in this city, but several others as well, so you're not alone."

"I see. Very well, I should be returning home with this."

He gets up from the table and once again cautiously glances at the two tigers lying contentedly on the floor. He then discreetly surveys the room and its other patrons, many of whom were attempting to appear not to be paying any special attention to the meeting, although it was clear by now something very revealing was occurring during the discussion. He turns and briskly leaves the establishment, then hurriedly trots home to find someone to talk to.

Relissa waits until her next appointment arrives, and she carries a similar discussion with him, another representative from another of the lowest ranking Houses in the city, hoping to build a starting point for what might ultimately represent a kind of rebellion against their authority so that the people could be rescued from their sacrilegious dedication to a false goddess and her malicious teachings.

At the end of the meeting, this newest contact departs in a similarly hurried, but careful manner, hoping not to draw any special attention that could interrupt his return home with this most precious news. Now it was Relissa's turn to leave. Her work, for the moment, was done.

She gets up from the table and calls to her pets, who both rise and promptly come to her side. They begin sauntering towards the door, once again under the careful scrutiny of the others in attendance, including one young female sitting at the bar counter quietly sipping her drink…one of several she had ordered by now, if only to extend her stay long enough to see the final outcome of this most curious visitor and her conversation partners.

As Relissa departed out the door, the female patron set down her drink, as she was essentially done with it by now, and rose up to follow behind. She had in mind to see where this strange visitor was going next, since she was clearly up to something. And in a city like this, or any other in Drow society, being up to something was never a good thing.

Relissa was strolling along the street searching for a convenient private spot that was out of view of anyone. She originally arrived through the front gate with the story of being a merchant selling trinkets, and to leave so soon might seem a bit suspicious. Furthermore, if she wanted to make any return visits, she wouldn't want to be seen coming and going so often through the gate, as this might also seem out of place. So, she needed her own private form of conveyance, and it had to be out of sight of anyone who might take notice. For this, she would search for a dark alley behind a building. Something that didn't stand out, and might not be of any interest for anyone else to pass through.

She continues along the street until she passes by a local shop. The shop itself wasn't the concern, as it was simply trading household items and utensils. But as she peeked around the corner of the building, she could see an alley running behind it, probably for utility, like trash disposal. She glances around the scene to see if anyone was following behind, but the coast seemed clear at the moment. Although she did take notice of someone walking along behind her at a distance a moment ago. So, before anything else happened, she chose to duck around the building into the alley.

Now that she was alone and out of view, she quickly drew up the sleeve on her left arm to reveal a strangely futuristic digital information cuff on her wrist. She then pulls open her cloak to find a bizarre attachment on her beltline. It appeared as a device snapped into a mounting bracket on the belt with a pale blue gemlike cabochon fixed in the middle. She reaches down to unlatch the fixture and holds it in her left hand, now snapping a plug attachment into the underside of her cuff. The unit engages with power as she begins programming the cuff for one of its primary functions.

Her two feline companions study her, somehow realizing the process she was taking and surveying the surrounding area for any intruders.

"Easy now, girls," Relissa coos. "We'll be going home in just a moment. I just need to mark this spot for later."

She engages the unit, where a soft beeping emits from the device in her hand, along with a series of small lights circling around the gem as it charges up. As the circle fills in, the gem begins to glow, then abruptly flashing in a lateral spiral of energy, expanding outward and collapsing back in on itself, leaving the gem glowing brightly for a moment before settling.

"Good," she muses. "Now we can come back here later. I just hope no one is standing here when we do. Wouldn't that be a surprise for these peeps, to see someone popping in by way of a portal. I'll bet they don't see that sort of thing too much around here," she giggles softly.

She returns the device back to the mount on her belt for common use, and then begins to reconfigure the cuff for a portal return back to her home base. But before she can finish selecting from the menu system on the data screen, a voice calls out from around the corner.

"You there! What are you doing back here?"

Relissa jerks up to peer into the face of a young female Drow, the same one who had been discreetly following her from the tavern. The two tigers also jerked around and took a quick defensive stand against the intruder, baring their teeth, but otherwise holding their ground.

The female stepped back a pace when she saw the reaction of the animals, realizing they were reacting defensively, but also that she should not press herself any further or else this could change dramatically.

"Control these things!" she states firmly. "I'm assuming you govern them, and they are only here for protection."

"Aye, generally speaking," Relissa responds coolly. "But that's only part of it. You've been following us, and we all know it. Why? Who are you and what do YOU want?"

"Don't use that tone of voice with me, young one. I'm the third daughter of House Deghym."

"Is that supposed to impress me? I serve a king, so whatever House you live in would fall beneath that. He owns a nation, not simply a House."

"A what?" she gasps. "What part of the Underdark is governed by a king, of all things?"

"That's a fine question to ask. But then, I suppose, if you don't get out much, the answer might not hold much meaning to you, unless you somehow know the full lay of everything out there."

"I don't think I like your attitude. No, I do not get out to visit the entire realm of the Underdark, but I think I am knowledgeable enough from my studies to know of the various cities out there, and none of them are governed by kings, or any other manner of…males," she sneers.

"Probably not, or at least not yet. But they will be, once he either convinces them to join up, or simply conquers them for all their belligerence of not joining up willingly."

"Hold! He, meaning a male, would dare offend the Spider Queen by presuming himself to be of such authority?"

"He, meaning a King, who doesn't give a hoot for the Spider Queen, has conquered more than that simply for the audacity of others to ask such questions. So you, Miss Third Daughter of House Deghym, should mind YOUR mouth, or else he'll silence it for you. You don't own him, you don't govern him, and you don't tell him what to do…and you never will. However, if you really want to know who I am and what I'm doing here, you, the third daughter of House Deghym, whichever one that is in this city, might find my answer very interesting…or very frightening, depending on how you like to see things."

The woman was clearly outraged by the impetuous attitude of this younger female, but the presence of the two large animals forced her to temper herself. They were both watching intently, and still baring their teeth. One of them was even growling softly. She delicately rolled her eyes downward to glance at them, and felt a subtle urge to back away further. But she also felt a timid sense that if she tried retreating now, they might simply give chase.

"All right, allow me to start again," she forces her calm. "My name is Malafay of House Deghym. As I said, I am the third daughter of the Matron Mother who rules that House, and in answer to your other question, as you are clearly not native to this city, it is the sixth house in the city hierarchy of authority."

"Six? Out of the top eight? Not a bad place to be in. Maybe not the best, but you can't complain."

"There are some who would wish for better, but generally, I would tend to agree."

"All right then, in fairness, I'll give out my name. Relissa of House Moonshimmer."

"Moonshimmer, this is a strange name. Where does it come from?"

"It's an ancestral name for a clan that managed to maintain a few principles the rest of you forgot. Therefore, you live in this place," she glances around her for emphasis, "so far removed from anything you should be properly acquainted with if you really want to know what's happening out there."

"You are speaking in riddles, and I don't like people who speak in riddles. What do you mean? I saw you in there speaking to two males, and I recognized them by their clothing as belonging to two of the lowest ranking houses in the city. Why them?"

"In short, because I doubt someone like you, coming from House Six, would be interested in hearing what I have to say."

"Is this to say, we would not hold value in it, that only such as Houses Fourteen and Fifteen might hold an interest? Or is this to say you hold something against a House like ours, being who we are in our position, that you might regard us as too proud for it."

"That's a really interesting way of putting it, and I suppose either or both might serve. No value, if you don't like what you hear, maybe thinking it's all rubbish and unworthy to consider. Too proud, meaning to say you tend to value your beliefs so much that you aren't interested in hearing anything else, rubbish or otherwise. Therefore, we have those others who might be more open to new ideas, whereas yours would probably reject them. Yours could simply be too set in your ways for anything else."

"I see. But as a daughter of the sixth House in the city political circle, I feel it is my duty to understand what you are doing. Those Houses might be well beneath my concern, but ranks can change, if you do not pay close enough attention to their ambitions. And I like ours where it is, if not also to move higher. I do not wish to see someone come up from behind with ideas of taking something away from us."

"I doubt anyone that low would hold any hope of that. And this is entirely unrelated to your city politics. It goes on the level of that king and HIS politics, along with that nation he owns."

The woman glares at Relissa, squinting her eyes at the hooded figure, even though she couldn't see Relissa's full face under her hood.

"That king again. All right, this sounds like something I would certainly need to know about. What ambitions does HE have?"

"Very simple, and perhaps the last thing you might actually expect to see around here, especially if you're one of those Houses that keeps sending those annoying raids up there to bother him."

The woman's eyes suddenly bulged at the suggestion, as hers was indeed one of the upper Houses who occasionally sent those raiding parties, and listening to their stories on their return home. She also reasoned this is where the notion of a king might come in, as no Drow society would be governed by a lowly male. They simply didn't hold this level of authority. But at the same time, it also defied that same reasoning as mentioned by the first male appointment Relissa spoke to, where the stories told of great victories, not of being described as a bother. This now demanded further explanation.

"Very well, I am listening. How could this affect us? We do send some of those raids, and they do return with their stories of defeating an enemy force up there. What of it? Do you know of what plans they hold for us next? And for that matter, if you actually serve this king, why would you come here to inform us of his plans?"

Relissa studies the woman for a moment, raising her brow as she finds this level of interest bemusing. Was this woman simply digging for detail, or did she hold a sincere interest in learning something new. She was part of one of the higher Houses, not a likely place to find a sympathizer. But as she said earlier, you never know where one would show up. She tentatively peers around the corner of the building to see if anyone else was out there listening. The woman follows her actions.

"This is not exactly the sort of place to carry a conversation like this," Relissa muses.

Malafay also turns to look out onto the street. It was currently empty, and being a local, she felt confident enough to be able to judge the sorts of traffic you might normally find there, and this would represent the height of it. But nevertheless, if secrecy was so important, maybe a more secluded spot would be warranted. She pans her gaze around the alley and sees an alcove nestled between a couple of buildings further along. She waves at Relissa to follow as she leads the way.

"Over here. In this corner. This should afford us a more private conversation, not that I would expect anyone to bother us even if we were on the open street. Now, why are you actually here, and what did you say to those two males?"

"Let me first ask you a question, to test the waters. If someone came along and told you everything you thought you knew of the world around you was a flippin' lie, would you accept it as fact, or at least a possibility, or boil them in acid for simply speaking about it?"

Malafay paused as she stared at Relissa under her hood, still unable to see her full face. She pondered the question, feeling a twinge of passion as it seemed to open up something old and nearly forgotten. Eventually, she came to her response.

"I think I would wish to see a demonstration of this statement before making that decision. It might also depend on who it was giving the statement, for instance if that person was reputable enough to listen to."

"All right, fair enough, and that's a good answer, the sort of thing

I might hope for in someone who might actually listen to what I have to say. Does anyone else in your House think this way?"

"I cannot answer that at this time. I have two younger sisters, both of whom I helped raise from birth. I also have my two elder sisters, neither of whom I can speak for. And then, of course, is our Matron Mother."

"And likely as anything, she would be the toughest to convince of anything that might otherwise fly against your common reasoning."

"Maybe. But it might again depend on the statement, the demonstration of evidence to prove it, and who is speaking. But now, what is it you have to say? Is there something being described as a lie here? And what is it?"

"You said your House occasionally sends raiding parties to the surface to fight those ever-present armies with their eternally perpetual instructions to come down here for whatever reason, right?"

"This is an interesting choice of words. Ever-present, and eternally perpetual. All right, and if these are the words you are choosing for this occasion, how am I supposed to see it?"

"As rubbish, all of it. There never were any armies, they don't hold any real interest in coming down here, and you are essentially out of sight and out of mind except for those raids you send up to make an occasional bit of noise just to remind them you're still alive and being a bother."

"Still alive and being a bother," she muses privately. "WE are being a bother to THEM. Then why don't they come down here and do something about it?"

"Like I was saying to those two men: One, you dug a grave for yourself in this hole. Two, they don't see a point in digging you out simply to bury you officially. And three, well, these tunnels you have around here make it a pain in their backsides trying to figure it out."

"The tunnels I can understand, but the rest..." she considers as her voice trails off. "Digging a grave? And then burying us officially. What about these raids we send up? What do they actually do up there?"

"You don't know? Do they actually report to you what happens?"

"Not to me. They might report to the Matron Mother, but I think she receives her notices from the Spider Queen directly, rather than from the males who return."

"This makes sense, as she's the one feeding you so many lies. Let me put it to you this way. Your men go up, get turned right around by a wall, and come back down here with great stories of tough fights against an eternal army of who-knows-what that was simply waiting for the right word to march on you. They know where you come out on the other side, and they have garrison posts there to block you. You're little more than a nuisance to them that never knows when to quit, and they're growing a bit tired of it by now."

"Growing tired?" her voice escalates. "They describe us as a nuisance, and with no interest in digging us out of our own grave, but now they are growing tired of it? They did not wish to bury us officially, so now what… Are they changing their minds?"

"Slow down a bit," Relissa cautions. "You want to know all of it? Fine. But it goes deep, and if you want to know the plans they have up there, you also need to know there are conditions to it."

"Conditions!" she huffs. "I cannot imagine what sort of conditions they might have if we were no more than a bother during this time that they lost patience in waiting for us to simply stop for the sheer futility of it."

"Right, futility is a good one. Do you know anything about the history of the Drow down in this hole? That is, where you came from, how you got here, and why?"

"Huh? Wait, um, let me think. This would be old history, right? I cannot be sure if I carry that with me. Most of our studies as children only teach of the more recent history, not the ancient lessons that seem to hold no more meaning to us. There was a war, I think. It was said our people were banished from the surface to fester in this…hole."

"Banished, sure. Fester, not so much. We were all once part of a larger society called the Ssri. And this was just one clan among the full elven body known as the Tel'Quessir. This was our name from the old days when our people, all of us elves, came to this world from the old Fey world of our home."

"Came here?" she winces. "But…we are not made in this world?"

"No, no one was…made…in this world. Everyone, and everything, was either brought here, or migrated here from somewhere else. When we elves first arrived, we found the human society already here, and naturally believed it was THEIR native home. But the elven societies chose to divvy up the land for themselves anyway. Unfortunately, this angered someone, first that we arrived here uninvited, and second that we might spoil her grander plans for this world, which SHE owns and put the humans on it to grow them."

"Hmm, interesting. So we are not actually meant to be here. But we are here now, and I do not personally know of anywhere else to go."

"This is fine, as she later decided to keep us and work the whole thing together into a bigger plan. Humans, elves, dwarves and more. Then, to make this work, she installed a special agent to bring it together. He would unite the entire world up there into one big nation…everyone and everything, whether they liked it or not, and some of them were as nasty as the Drow in their own way."

"How did he do this? Conquest and war?"

"Not entirely. He used politics and diplomacy whenever possible, for those who would listen, and military for those who didn't. But his purpose, which is literally a divine mandate by this goddess who owns the world, was to bring them together into one society, solving their problems and teaching them to like it."

"I see, so he forced it upon them."

"Forcing…" she muses briefly. "Aye. He forced peace on them, forcing war OUT of them, forcing crime OUT of them, forcing hatred and belligerence OUT of them, and forcing them to realize the incredible benefit of what true peace and prosperity was good for. Since then, that world up there has moved forward by great leaps and bounds, much more than anyone was doing before his arrival. But then we have you peeps down here, behaving in many ways like the elves of Old, except for you smoldering away for nearly ten millennia with your old hatred, and further fueled by your goddess, and with nary a mote of new inspiration to push you forward. She probably never told you what we were doing up there, especially if she still says you're fighting something, when in fact we could crush you like bugs for all we actually have by now. In those early days, you were killing peasants, unarmed civilians, not warriors who could fight back. You're described as murderers and criminals, and we have every right to enforce our laws on you for it."

"Criminals… Would this in any way reflect on that statement of festering? We are made to think we are festering because we were criminals once and still are?"

"Aye. You started some part of those old wars, and the rest punished you for it. They drove you off to find peace for themselves, and here you are now, still fuming for it, with your goddess driving the fuming part."

"Her again…"

Malafay paused suddenly as she felt a rise of tension for speaking of her goddess in such fashion. The Spider Queen was very authoritarian in her manners, and any outward mention of dispute or querying of her methods was often harshly punished, usually by torture and then death, or even worse, as they might use magic to twist and deform their victims.

Relissa continues, "And as I said to those others, their common civilians these days all learn magic, and by now, if not for that wall, a simple shopkeeper could probably defeat your warriors. And if our king actually did have in mind to come down here with a real military force, this city of yours would be reduced back down to the magma it came from. Now, how does your position as the third daughter of House Six feel at the sound of that, with your warriors and their false stories to please your goddess?"

Malafay gaped at the young woman for the wordy statement. Although parts of it sounded outlandish, if any of it was even remotely true, it would represent an astonishingly different view of things as compared to whatever she was taught as a girl. To begin with, if a single person, whether male or female, could successfully unite an entire world, and essentially force feed them a new philosophy that negates war and hardship, despite any natural tendencies, thereby bringing an Age of prosperity where they can experience a continual surge of progress, this in itself would represent a level of advancement that could possibly lead to any manner of new developments. And if even a simple shopkeeper could fight back against a raiding party of warriors, who by now might be seen as archaic in design, this was dangerous for her people. But again, these statements, as sensational as they might sound, were also unfounded without that demonstration her people liked to see. The Drow were no fools to simply take any fable passed along by a wandering bard.

She studied Relissa and her two animal companions, now asking herself if they also somehow mastered control of wild beasts, as she clearly held a firm level of control over them. And finally, Malafay recalled why she was here in this alleyway. She saw Relissa duck inside here for some reason.

"What is your real reason for being here?" she asks. "Simply to frighten us with these stories of yours?"

"The people up top are tired of waiting for you down here to realize your mistakes. So, I'm sent as part of a program to teach you a few things, maybe even to get a few of you to follow along and change your ways. Just like up there, we'll use diplomacy to see if we can work a deal, but for those of you who don't listen, it comes back down to that divine mandate to unite the world, one way or another, and you're a part of it, like it or not. One final piece we haven't gotten around to until now."

"So, if we do not give ourselves over to you, you simply attack and clean out this…grave…of ours?"

"Don't go putting words in my mouth with your foul manners, Drow. My folk escaped from this curse of yours, and you peeps down here disgrace us with your ways. You turned against the Seldarine, the proper gods of our people, all to turn to this witch you call the Spider Queen. She's not our god, and doesn't even belong here. Go and ask her if she knows the name Maker Kuroku and see what she has to say about it. And if you're still standing upright, you might want to ask yourself how much longer you have to pray to her once OUR gods come down here to set things right. So, you can join us if you want, and we'll put in a good word for you with our REAL gods, or we'll simply conquer you and wait for your next line of children to come out, and then teach them our way. And you and yours can go rot in a new grave. This world belongs to the Maker, not to you and your goddess. She's allowing us to live here, and she has big things in mind for us…all of us, and this might also include you, if you can bring yourself up to it."

"So you say, but how can I even be sure if I can believe you. You say you grew into something new and fantastic. But all I see is a lone female in a cloak with a hood. I can't even see your face. For all I know, you are just a trickster spreading bad stories."

Relissa knew something like this might ultimately come up. It was part of that demonstration aspect of things. So, she pulled back her hood to reveal her face. In the Underdark, there was not much visible light to actually show anything, save for a few braziers or other artificial sources reflecting in the streets and homes, but all of it extremely dim. The Drow were much more accustomed to using their infravision, which spread into the infrared spectrum more than visible light. But they also had an enhanced form of low-light vision, much like night vision, and she could see just enough to realize this girl was very different.

Relissa's skin was noticeably lighter than the average Drow. Hers was a medium charcoal gray with a soft hint of purple, as opposed to Malafay's which was much more a deep sooty color. Relissa's hair was a cleaner white as opposed to the dustier color of the Drow, and her eyes were clearly a lavender hue as compared to the reddish tone of the native dark elves. Malafay stared at the strange physique.

"Well, you certainly are different from the rest of us. Is this what you look like who still live up there?"

"My people were found on a completely different world, but aye, this is who we are. We call ourselves Night Elves for our colors."

"Another world?" she grimaces. "But wait a moment, what does that actually mean? There is ANOTHER world out there?"

"What was your name again? House Deghym, um…"

"Malafay, third daughter of the Matron Mother."

"Right, Malafay. Look, you peeps down here don't know half of what even THIS world has to offer, much less anything else that might be out there. We've moved beyond this world by now. Our kingdom covers five worlds in all so far, and I'm sure it's a safe bet to go even higher as we move further out. I'll bet you don't even know what the sky above looks like, or the sun at full daytime, not that your eyes could even handle it, living down here all your lives. You haven't changed since the time you first came down here, and you seem to think the rest of us are the same. Our armies all use highly enchanted adamantium armor and mithril weapons, the sort of thing that would break whatever you use. Every citizen studies magic, as part of their standard education, and they use it in their daily lives, whether as their profession, or simply for home use. We've invented science and technology of the sort I doubt you even have words for down here…"

Relissa now pulls back her sleeve again to reveal the cuff interface on her arm, touching a few menu selections along the way to demonstrate it wasn't just a fancy piece of jewelry.

She continues, "And now we're hoping to tidy up the last few bits of unfinished business with you down here. We would invite you to join back with us, but we won't tolerate any more of this funny business of yours sending those pointless raids up there just to remind us of how annoying you are. So, it comes down to a simple decision: go peacefully, or go hard, but either way, you're going. And somewhere along the way, whether with you, your children, your grandchildren, or anything else that comes after, you WILL learn to like it, and your goddess will be forgotten."

Malafay felt a bit overwhelmed by the strong declaration, and despite how young Relissa appeared in relation to her, she seemed very solid in her beliefs. This sort of fortitude in confidence doesn't come without training, conditioning, as well as a firm dedication to something irrefutable. It actually touched something deep within Malafay which once again stirred an old memory. At the same time, it also reflected on her own training as a younger priestess for her House and the dedication forced on them to follow their goddess. But this was a lesson she always had difficulty with, as she often had questions that went unanswered, except for a lashing simply for asking them. And still, she could not allow herself to fall prey to what could otherwise be a hoax to fool her. She would need to see something more than a fancy wrist adornment to demonstrate to her there was something more at work here.

"Very well, but how do you plan on this, um, diplomacy of yours," she wonders. "Do you think you can simply walk in the gate and propose this absurd idea of unification? I think the guards would have something to say about that, to say nothing of each of our Houses and their private armies."

"To be honest, your armies aren't the problem, it's your attitude. You don't like mine? Well, none of us up there like any of yours. So far, we're trying to spread a few rumors around town to open up a few minds from the lockdown your goddess has on things. This is to let you know you don't have a flippin' clue what's really happening out there. If you don't personally ask your warriors what they saw up there to hear it straight from their mouths, how can YOU say your story is better than mine? Stop listening to your bleedin' mother and her witch of a goddess, and find out from those who saw it with their own eyes, assuming they'll actually say something for all the fear you spread around here."

"All right, I will admit I did not ever do this before, as it was not my place to do this, and I also know of the fear you speak of. I have seen this enough in my own lifetime. But if all they saw was a wall barring the way, this does not tell of anything more than an obstruction to them fulfilling their reason for going up. What about the rest of it? You do understand that we will not simply take someone's word. Recall what I said about a demonstration."

"Fine, like I said to those two men, just go up yourself and see it personally. I'll even meet you there, if I can, and I'll give you a tour. There's a garrison post. Go up, maybe with a few others as support, and extra eyes to look around, and tell them you're there as part of a diplomatic effort to learn something new. They won't attack unless you start something wicked. So, don't start something wicked, or you won't be going home from it. Aside from that, if you think your Matron Mother might be willing to listen, go ahead and break it to her. But if not, and you feel your own pressure for this fear factor, I would instead suggest you keep your skin in one piece and not go making waves in a pond full of nasty buggers that'll eat you up. And this goes for anyone else in your family that might think the same. Got it?"

"Yes. I am currently thinking of who else in our family might be able to share this with me. After all, I, uh…would need additional representatives to assist me in this expedition. And I think this would be a necessary venture, as I would represent a House currently on the city council."

"This is a good one. Do you have much weight with anyone else out there?"

"Not a great amount with those in the higher positions, as they represent stronger Houses, although the Council must share equal authority between our members. But the Houses themselves are another thing. Still, if your plan is to start a movement of some sort, trying to raise this awareness of yours…hmm. I cannot be sure where this might lead, but I think it is certain you will experience many who would not wish to hear it. And I, um… I actually dread to hear the screeching in the temples if it should ever reach up that high."

"You're right, but at some point, it probably will. Even now, I would think if your goddess paid as much attention to peeps like me, she's already crying to them about me romping around making noise."

"Yes, and about that, how did you actually get in here in the first place?"

"I told the guards at the gate I was a travelling merchant with rare goods. But now that I'm inside, I don't need them anymore. And if your goddess really is watching, I'll bet she'd realize real quick that she can't do anything about it, either."

Relissa pulls away her cloak to reveal her portal gem device again on her belt, now making ready for her final departure. She makes a casual glance around the area, which was nicely secluded and private. No one else was in view.

Malafay studied her actions, and also the curious device on her beltline. It tended to stand out as a prominent feature. Relissa referred again to her cuff device and pulled up a menu selection for a portal jump. Malafay tried to follow along, but not only was the device completely alien to her, the language involved was also unfamiliar.

"What are you doing with that?" she asks.

"Do you know what a portal is? We use these often to travel around.

Nothing stops us from going where we want to go. And now that we have an index to your city, we don't need to bother with those guards outside."

"Oh no!" she lurches back. "Wait a minute, is this to say you and your people can use this to come directly inside here…without warning… an entire army of them?"

"Technically, yes, if you push us into it. Emphasis on YOU pushing US into it. We don't start wars, but we will finish them. We're law enforcers up there, all of us. And you are now on notice for these raids of yours. Meanwhile, I need to get back to report on what I've done today. I'll let you think on the rest for now."

She taps on her touch screen to engage a menu selection for her portal jump. The screen displays a confirmation box. Relissa then calls her two pets to huddle up close, and she kneels down to wrap her arms around them. She hits the confirmation button and grips her pets tightly in her arms.

Malafay steps back as she hears a strange beeping sound, although to her ears it was as alien as all the rest. She could see a circle of small lights starting to illuminate on the device on Relissa's belt, along with the gem in the middle. And in another moment, she is nearly blinded by the bright flash of the portal energies swallowing up Relissa and her two companions. When Malafay's vision finally cleared, she was all alone in the alcove.

Chapter 2
PREPARATIONS

"**M**y Lord! I'm just getting back from my little run down below."
"Ah, Relissa! Did you encounter any difficulties? I always worry for our people when they travel to those regions."

"Nah, I think you trained us well enough for it. It went smoothly enough. I got in the door using my story, then found that tavern, sent the spooks out to find our marks and call them in, one at a time, and had a little chat. I think I got the message out as we wanted it, so we might want to tell the guards at the outposts to expect visitors soon. But there was this one extra bit I didn't expect, at least not initially."

Relissa was returning back to the guildhall in the kingdom's capital city of Bya'an Tamoranth, where she was reporting in to Thaelyn in his personal office.

"An extra bit?" he muses. "What sort?"

"There was a dame apparently sitting in that tavern. At first, I didn't pay much mind to her, like all the rest. They're just peeps, after all, and with the two girls at my side, no one bothered me. I met with those two guys from the bottom two Houses, which rank as numbers Fourteen and Fifteen in the local hierarchy, too low to be much of a concern to anyone, at least not unless they start making a lot of noise, but let's hope they're wise enough not to do that right away."

"Indeed, Drow society is not known to tolerate any opposing opinions that rail against their primary faith."

"Primary faith… Jiggers, to worship someone like that goddess of theirs isn't much of a faith. More like a demand, 'do as I say or whap!'..." she giggles softly.

"Indeed! One would need a great deal of faith simply to maintain their composure. So, who was this extra person, and how does she fit in?"

"Her name, as it turns out, is Malafay of House Deghym, which is Number Six on the list."

"Six! Most interesting. This would be a good position for a contact."

"Aye, it would. She followed me on my way out, and found me in an alleyway as I was marking an index and making ready to leave. She started asking a lot of questions, which I suppose is to be expected of House Six, since they're part of the top circle of eight in the city council. I worked my way into it gently, first by asking how she might feel if someone said the world around her was nothing like she expected. She seemed open enough to hear more, but like a good Drow, and a lot of us up here, I suppose, she would need something tangible to go along with it. So, I went into my bit with her. Being a female, and the third in line under the Matron Mother, she was a tough sell to get the message across. But she did admit to a few things."

"Such as?" he raises his brow.

"Such as, she never personally interrogated her House warrior group of their tours up top and what they actually saw, if anything. She always assumed, either from word coming out of her Matron Mother, or their goddess herself, that they go up, fight something, and come back with a proud victory. Nothing about a wall or garrison turning them around."

"This is most unfortunate, and it simply proves, yet again, the virtue of any sort of communication to understand the nature of things. And unfortunately, as with so many other occasions, that aspect of communication is cut off before it can properly circulate."

"Aye, and how many times have we seen this before," she sighs. "Anyway, we might have another one. She said she has two younger sisters who she helped raise, so maybe, just maybe, we might have a couple more, but who knows what else after that, or what other influence they might have. I think we might need to play it by ear, like so many other things. But if they do turn it around, I'm already thinking we'll need to offer support, if only for that bit you mentioned about turning against that goddess and how she likes to carry things."

"Yes, I was thinking of this also. We might need to install one or more of our agents in there, along with perhaps a few safeguards to offer defense. In the past, I have heard stories of Houses that lost favor with the city hierarchy and temple authority, and the result was a vicious form of retribution, where conjurations of demonic creatures would be summoned to rend the House and its occupants apart. We certainly do not wish to see any of that occur to potential redemptions. That goddess of theirs needs to be made aware that this is her final moment in this world. I may have my own misgivings with her, but I think Adalon has it even worse."

"Aye, and knowing her like we do, jiggers, I don't want to see the end result of that. I still have visions of that final day on Azgarén," she giggles.

"Yes! That was certainly a day to remember. I still carry a few of my own memories, and that entire journey represented a rather grueling ordeal," he chuckles softly. "Very well, you might want to give this to Nemelle so she can make a few of her own preparations. I think she will want to meet with some of these people, at least as much to demonstrate herself in their eyes as to explain where all this might ultimately lead."

"Aye, then I'll go see her now."

Relissa makes a quick, but courteous bow before leaving the office. She proceeded through the guildhall to another office where another prominent member of Thaelyn's team relating to this project could be found.

Cardinal Nemelle, as she was properly known, was another Celestial, much like Thaelyn. An ascended being that was literally part god, being related to the Estelar. In her case, she was of Drow descent on the mortal side, and her divine Father was part of the Seldarine, the leader of that group known as Corellon Larethian.

As Relissa arrives, she knocks gently on the door before peeking inside.

"Cardinal Nemelle, it's me, I'm back with a few words for you."

The stately female looks up from her desk as she had been reviewing several papers during this time. She begins speaking in her habitual form of third-person speech.

"She bids her visitor to enter and present herself."

Relissa enters inside, almost feeling an involuntary compulsion to do so by the curious wording spoken by the Cardinal.

"Bloody hell, you're not doing that again, are you?" she grins.

"Doing that..." Nemelle pauses to reflect on herself. "Oh, my apologies, Relissa, I was lost in thought and simply fell into an old habit."

"Aye, and not just that, but you drove me to comply with it on this occasion."

"Oh no! I am so very sorry. My mind was drifting, and I guess it slipped a bit too far to affect the fabric of Reality again. I hope I did not disturb you with it."

"Nah, don't worry about it. It's just who you are. I just got back from down below. We might have a total of three reps coming up, plus whatever other peeps tag along for the knowing of it."

"Three? I thought we were aiming for only two Houses on this occasion."

"We were, the bottom two, but I was apparently spotted by someone visiting that tavern of theirs from House Six, and she got curious. Luckily, she was open enough to listen, and now she's a wee bit concerned for what it all means. So, she might also come up for a better look."

"Do you think she might be one we can offer greater wisdom to?"

"Well, she certainly stands out as a possibility, and maybe not the only one in her House. But we shouldn't jump too far ahead and play it by ear as best we can."

"Indeed, this is most certainly prudent. Very well, who was she? I should record her name so I can watch for her."

"Malafay, third daughter of the Deghym House. Like your typical Drow, she was a tough one, but not quite as bad as some, I think."

"I wonder what sort of reaction she would have to someone like me," she muses distantly. "Or any of them, for that matter. It will be a rather curious sensation to feel their emotional response to it."

"Aye, maybe so. Anyway, we'll pass the word to those outposts to watch for anything, and let you know what happens."

"Good. This project seems to be moving along nicely thus far, but this part is easy as compared to what will come when we more fully invest ourselves."

"I think you're right. This girl, Malafay, put up a good clue, and that being their guards and private armies might have a few things to say, along with those people at the top, and likely their priests in the temple."

"Yes, those will likely be the worst of it, as they carry a very strong association to that wretch of a Power they follow. I will personally be very pleased to see that cleared away from our sight. She is not very highly revered even amongst her own kind."

"And that's saying something," Relissa chuckles. "All right, I'm off to find a little rest. If you need me, I'll be around. I doubt you could miss it, not with those powers of yours!" she smiles brightly.

As Relissa leaves the room, Nemelle reflects on her final words.

"Indeed, Child, yours does shine rather brightly," she muses amiably.

✦✦✦✦✦

In the Drow city, Malafay was just returning home from her outing. Her mind was still spinning from her impromptu meeting with Relissa in the alley, and now she needed to consult with someone about it. Clearly, she needed to investigate these stories, especially as they implied a very serious turn of events forthcoming that no one in the city could ignore. She arrived in the house of her family dynasty and instantly began searching for anyone close. But in the absence of knowing where her sisters could be at this time, she instead found one of the house servants, who was part of the commoner caste of the city.

"You, chambermaid," she calls. "Have you seen either Rhyliira or Felynquiri?"

"Yes, Mistress Malafay. I saw Rhyliira earlier going down to the wine cellar to see about the choice for the family meal tonight, and I believe Felynquiri was checking a recent delivery just arrived at the stockroom."

"Good. Now continue along."

Malafay proceeded forward, first to find the stockroom, which was towards the rear of the family estate, where they often received deliveries of food and other supplies. She winds her way through the halls until she arrives in a large storage warehouse with many servants sorting through a recent delivery of goods, and Felynquiri overseeing the process to ensure the invoices were correct.

"Felynquiri, I need to speak with you for a moment."

The younger woman turned to find her elder sister waving at her from the doorway. She set the invoices down on a nearby table and rushed over to answer the call.

"Yes, Sister Malafay. What do you require of me?"

"Your ear for an important talk. We also need Rhyliira. I'm told she is down in the wine cellar, correct?"

"Yes, she was checking our stock to select the best choice for the meal later today. Is there a problem?"

"Yes, and I need the two of you to listen carefully, but you may not reveal this to anyone else…not unless you have my express permission. Understood?"

"Yes, Sister Malafay, as you desire."

The two of them now rush off to find the stairs to the basement. In the wine cellar below, they see Rhyliira studying several casks of wine being held in storage down there.

"Rhyliira," Malafay shouts. "Are you alone down here?"

Rhyliira was drawn out of her careful study of the age markers for several potential candidates when she heard her name called. She turned to respond and reflexively glanced around the area, even though she was fairly certain she was indeed alone.

"Yes, there is no one else here," she calls back. "What do you desire, Sister Malafay?"

Malafay and Felynquiri both approach for a close chat. Rhyliira studies her elder sister curiously, as she could see a marked expression in her face which did not bode well for any manner of casual conversation, not that any of the sisters often engaged in casual conversation to begin with, but the relationship between these sisters was somewhat better than most others in the family.

"I need to speak with you, as well as Felynquiri here. And as I already told her, now I will tell you. What I have to say is not to be repeated without my permission, and this includes the Matron Mother, unless I can make a firm decision on it first."

"Not even with the Matron Mother? How interesting…" she smirks demurely. "Are we planning something here?"

"No, we are not, and wipe that face of yours, this is serious. We have a potential problem in the city, and I have just been in conversation with someone who claims a number of details I am so far unsure of to be true. But if they are, it will mean trouble for everything we own here."

"Uh oh. All right, you have my ear, but if this is not to be shared with the Matron Mother…"

"Not until I can verify some of it, and then decide how to present it to her."

"I see. Very well, what are we speaking of here?"

Malafay pauses to take a deep breath and once again glance around the room simply to stall for time before going into it.

Rhyliira studied her elder sister, and although the rivalry between household members of the same gender was often enough to prevent any manner of true familial passion, she and her younger sister, Felynquiri, both held at least a subtle level of empathy for their elder sister due to their lifelong experiences together.

"You seem tense," she notes. "Are you alright?"

"Yes, it's simply what I heard today. But now, listen, both of you," Malafay asserts. "We'll begin like this, which is a similar manner to how my other conversation went. What do you actually know of the warriors when they go up on their raids, and then return with any manner of stories of what they saw?"

"Nothing directly," Rhyliira shakes her head. "Other than what might filter down from the Matron Mother or some other source."

"Same with me," Felynquiri adds. "I do not speak to them personally, and although I have sometimes wondered what they saw, they do not seem to speak of it in my presence."

"Naturally," Malafay advises. "No doubt, because we're all priestesses of the Spider Queen, and we all know what happens if you say something that might otherwise offend her. Therefore, if they have something bad to say, they'll simply keep it to themselves. And as such, the Matron Mother might be the only one to receive any kind of news, and often NOT from the ones who were up there to see it, but from the Spider Queen herself. After all, why would she lie to us about what they did up there, correct?" she smirks sarcastically.

The two younger sisters glared at each other for the obvious play of words, and suddenly felt a quiet hint of tension building up inside. They each cautiously glanced around the room to check for any visitors, or anything else that should not otherwise be there.

"Malafay," Rhyliira stresses softly. "I'm not sure if your words would be very appropriate, either. What do you mean by that?"

"Rhyliira, Felynquiri, I was the one to raise the two of you for most of your childhood. We all know the Matron Mother doesn't bother herself with such a menial chore as childrearing. None of them do, in any of the greater Houses. It's often left to an elder daughter, or some wetnurse she can pass it off to. And during our time together, although I had demands on me to teach you the ways of our people, I also shared a few of my own experiences and uncertainties along the way, if only to have someone to talk to."

"Yes, I recall this," Rhyliira nods. "You once mentioned your own childhood and some of the difficulties you experienced, and of course we also experienced much of the same along the way. Does this now play into it?"

"It could, and I may need your support. Something is happening outside our view, and we need to learn what it is."

"Very well, so what is it?"

"The warriors who go up to fight something, aren't actually fighting anything. They get turned away by a garrison post behind a wall ordering them to go home. It is said they are nothing more than a bother to the people on the surface."

"What?!" Felynquiri blasts impulsively. "A bother? A simple bother?"

"Worse than that. We're told they DO fight something, and then return home with great stories of cutting down whole armies of people who don't even exist. In fact, ALL of the stories are like this. In older times, they were killing the first thing they saw up there, apparently too lame to realize the difference between commoners and actual warriors, and THEN come back with their great stories of fighting hordes of vicious enemies to protect our people. And if it's not actually the males telling us, it must be the Spider Queen herself, if no one else is bold enough to actually speak out on it."

The two younger sisters glared at Malafay, and then at each other.

"There is something wrong with this," Rhyliira mumbles. "Cutting down commoners? But surely, there has to be something up there that can fight! And what about the warriors showing up AFTER we kill their commoners. Do they respond to anything if common people are assaulted?"

"Our people are probably on their way home by then. I doubt they stay long enough to find out. It's a quick hit and run attack, from what I make of it. They go up, hit simple civilians, and run home for a celebration feast."

"Yes, perhaps, but there is still something wrong here. Their warriors should pursue, especially if we have a history of doing this for so long."

"Rhyliira," Felynquiri interjects. "Could this somehow be related to us being a bother? Do they actually care if we hit their commoners? Maybe they care nothing for them."

"Oh, I'm sure they care," Malafay asserts. "I hear they are a society of strong laws up there, and this would be described as murder, which is punishable by death in some cases."

"Then they should be down here exacting that punishment, and THEN our warriors would have something to fight!"

"Yes, except for a few mitigating factors. To them, we ran off into this hole, as they call it, and dug ourselves graves in here. And it's too much of a bother to dig us out to exact that punishment simply to dig new graves for us. Also, the way the tunnels outside keep changing, trying to find a clear pathway through to us is also a bother to make the effort worth their time. So instead, they built a wall to block us."

"Uh huh, that might make sense. And we continue to go up, only to hit that wall, and then turn around and go home."

"But now, they're growing tired of us even making the attempt. We're described as a nuisance for all these continued raids, even if to hit a wall. The simple fact that no one around here even knows when to stop is enough to make them NOW want to come down here and stop it themselves."

"Oops!"

"Well," Rhyliira shrugs. "This would certainly give our warriors something to fight finally."

"Yes, it would," Malafay affirms. "But here we have our next problem. According to this person I was speaking to, and I'll simply say she was an informant for now, we first came down here as the result of an ancient war our ancestors started with the rest of the world up there and got punished for our insolence by being driven, not banished to fester, but driven as punishment into this hole. This is another story that is apparently false."

"Driven as punishment…for starting a war?"

"Yes, it would seem our ancestors must've been trying to take more than their fair share of things up there, and the rest didn't approve of it. After that, we were described as out of sight and out of mind, if not for our persistent raids simply to let them know we haven't learned our lesson for the punishment we refused to take."

"Um, Malafay," Felynquiri wonders. "Are you speaking in context for what this informant said, or your own interpretation of it?"

"A little of both, as this also reflects on some of my old feelings from when I was a child. We are described as criminals by those people up there, so it seems to fit with a little interpretation."

"Only a little?" she smiles tenderly.

"But it goes on. This occurred something like ten millennia ago, which is a long time, and I don't personally recall anyone teaching me it happened on this time scale."

"No, not I, as well. That is indeed a long time."

"And in that time, we, as a society down here in this hole, haven't progressed very far with anything new, like new knowledge, invention, or anything to improve our way of life. However..." she emphasizes with a finger. "They up there have apparently moved forward by incredible leaps, such that we would not stand a chance against them, even if we did find actual warriors."

"Uh oh, that sounds bad."

"This might also explain the part of being a bother and a nuisance," Rhyliira mentions. "If they've moved so far ahead of whatever wisdom we carry here..."

"Yes..." Malafay concludes. "Their commoners could probably NOW kill our warriors."

The two younger sisters flashed a sudden worried stare at each other as they tried to analyze this statement.

"Simple commoners?" Felynquiri winces.

"There goes the idea of commoners who can't fight," Rhyliira shakes her head. "This might then be the reason for that wall. They don't want to spend their meager efforts on us."

"But how would commoners fight warriors? Do they all now carry weapons to match us?"

"They all learn to use magic," Malafay admits. "Which might overwhelm anything we study down here, even for those of us who actually study it. Also, according to this informant, their military uses highly enchanted adamantium armor and mithril for weapons, which would surely be quite dangerous to us. And the whole world up there was recently united by one man who was apparently delivered by the OWNER of this world, a world where our ancestors, and in fact all the elven nations, apparently intruded upon uninvited. And he carries a literal divine mandate to unite everyone into one body for the future growth and prosperity of all involved. And he's doing it...up there at least."

"Hold on a second!" Rhyliira raises a hand. "I think you ran over something there. An owner of this world, and a man...a male...who united everything into one nation?"

"I'm not personally familiar with how their politics work up there, but my impression is males can hold a lot more power with them as what they have in ours. And I think I'll place this again on our goddess, who is very female-centric. As for the owner, she's a goddess who claims ownership of this world, where she intentionally planted the human population...you recall them from our studies, right?"

"Yes."

"Good, they were the original residents of this world, and the elven nations came in later from another world altogether. This isn't our native home…as we're told by our scholars. She later reconsidered our intrusion, and put this man in place to unite everyone into this one nation. From there, he has led them into a new era of some sort where they have developed things we might not even understand down here, since we live so far in the past by now. But now, I'm going to ask you a simple question. Who is responsible for us living so far in the past?"

"I think I would not dare wish to answer that."

"Right, because it's not me, it's not you, it's not the Matron Mother, or anyone else around here who might have a mind to think. Therefore, it's the reason why we don't have minds to think. But they up there DO have minds to think, and thinking is what they seem to be doing a lot of."

"All right, and if thinking is leading them into a new era of knowledge we wouldn't understand, what does this really mean for us down here? Because I recall you mentioning they were growing tired of our insolence for not learning our lesson of why we were driven down here, and then how we keep sending these raids up there to crash against a wall."

"Yes, and so here we come to that. They're coming to fix it, and they don't care about tunnels anymore. They apparently use portals to travel around, rather than simply walk."

"Oh great!" she moans. "And if they can open one of those in front of our gate…"

"Worse, to open one inside the city directly. This informant works for that king up there, and I saw her use one to leave and go back home."

Rhyliira was stifled for a response, and Felynquiri was stunned at the suggestion. They again glared at each other, but this time with deep worry.

"Malafay," Rhyliira offers gently. "What plans do they actually have for us, if they don't need to walk, and use such weapons and magic by now?"

"An offer. But the problem is, I doubt most people in the city would consider this seriously. They're apparently sending agents down here spreading stories in the streets, and recruiting members from the lower Houses, as they might represent easier targets than any of us in the higher rankings, to convince them to actually learn those lessons I spoke of and realize the Spider Queen is not supposed to be our native goddess. This person was a dark elf, like us, but from another clan that still survives up there and joined the rest. Our proper gods, according to her, is something she calls the Seldarine, which I guess must be from the time of our ancestors. We disgraced ourselves by turning to the Spider Queen and cursed ourselves into this grave. Now, they're offering us to come back, but we need to redeem ourselves in the eyes of the old gods and shun the one we have now."

"Oh, Malafay..." Felynquiri ushers gently. "You know, as well as the rest of us, to be careful when you speak of such things."

"Now I know why she said not to bring this to the Matron Mother," Rhyliira asserts. "This could turn bad very quickly."

"Listen," Malafay continues. "According to her, we are still regarded as part of this world population, despite the curse of this grave we dug. And this king she speaks of has this divine mandate to unite everything, which naturally includes us. They're only now getting around to it, and maybe also due to us being such a pain in their backsides, as she said. What this tells me is they did everything else first...that is, everything that was within easy reach, and now it's our turn. They will use methods of political and diplomatic talks to convince us to join. But for those who refuse, that military of theirs, which we never once actually encountered, will probably pop in right behind our backs and finish it for whatever is left. They will no longer tolerate our nuisance efforts with these raids, and will essentially force feed us to learn to be peaceful and respectful of their laws. But in return for this, we will then be free to think with our own minds and learn all the wonderful new secrets the rest of them are creating for themselves. But this is really all dependent on one thing I can't be absolutely sure of, other than she used a portal to depart the area."

"And what one thing is that, because if she used a portal inside our city, this is already bad news for us. It means they're already here behind our backs with these stories in the streets."

"Yes, it does. So, either way, we're in trouble, with the only true difference being to listen to them talk, or to feel their blades. The problem I'm having now is to believe any other part of her story... anything about the world above, like if the warriors actually do hit a wall and come back, or anything else she mentioned. If she can use a portal, this is bad, but if any or all of the rest of it is true, we lost ten thousand years of growth, and who do you think we should point our finger at for that misfortune?"

"Um, do you really want an answer, Malafay?"

"I think the answer is split between our own insolent ancestors who cursed us into this grave we're festering in now, as well as that goddess who stole us away from our ancestral gods. If not for these two combined, we might still be up there enjoying the sky and the sun we know virtually nothing about."

"A sky and a sun…" Felynquiri muses. "Those words are like fables to us down here."

"So, here is where I need the two of you. I need to go up there and investigate. If for no other reason than to confirm or deny any part of this on behalf of our role in the city council. These claims are too serious to ignore, but I need help. I know this woman was speaking to members of the lowest ranking Houses, so we might have them as part of the investigation. But for our House, I want to ask you to come with me."

"As for the wall," Rhyliira wonders. "Couldn't we just ask one of the males who've been up there what he actually saw?"

"We could ask Jhandril," Felynquiri offers. "He's the lead member of the House security."

"We could," Malafay suggests. "But he last went up with Alyraema, I think, and she's the second daughter, so probably under orders to conform to the Matron Mother's demands for silence in the name of the Spider Queen."

"Same as Alakaere would be, no doubt," Rhyliira adds. "The top two sisters of the House, and therefore closest to the Matron Mother. It's starting to sound like a conspiracy to withhold the truth, simply to give an excuse to occupy us with so much nonsense. We've been at this for thousands of years and never actually saw anything as a result. We never saw any recorded attacks down here, and if they were wise enough to realize we're attacking their warriors right outside the tunnel exit, they should move their training fields to somewhere else, and THEN bring them around in large enough numbers that our warriors, who don't number as many by compare, would be wiped away by it. THEN to follow those damnable tunnels to find the rest of us in our graves, and finish burying us."

"Yes, that does make better sense for the reasoning," Felynquiri nods. "But the story doesn't make it sound so neat. They're either too stupid to realize this and move their warriors to a safer place to train, or else too stupid to fight back in large enough numbers to actually win something, and maybe also too stupid to pursue us with even larger numbers to find us down here and bring the battle to our own front gates. How convenient."

"And we keep swallowing all this because, like Malafay said, we aren't allowed to think with our own minds."

"Oh yes, and I'm just wondering what those in the higher positions will do to us if they should hear any part of this conversation. We might need to start praying to those old gods if we should wish for any hope to actually survive this."

"That may be exactly the point. Felynquiri, what do you think would happen if the First House, for instance, were to hear us right now? You know what they do to Houses that disobey the Spider Queen. We've seen this once before. It wasn't pretty."

"No, it was not. The whole House, torn apart, and bodies stripped of their flesh. Nothing was left alive, not even the servants."

"You know," Malafay muses. "This might be the reason for this campaign of storytelling. If they can turn enough people, can the First House even fight back?"

"If they did," Rhyliira considers. "It would mean to raze half the city to the ground."

"And you know, if these people are actually trying to redeem us, I think they might step in the way of that."

"Maybe…hmm. Then this campaign might be as much an effort to rally enough people for this redemption to oppose whatever the higher authorities might offer to fight back."

"We'll probably see fighting in the streets regardless," Felynquiri reasons. "The First House will not likely go along with it. They love their position of authority too much, and we're speaking of submitting ourselves under someone else's authority, that king up there, which probably means no more council here."

"This is true. The top two Houses, maybe three. I can't be sure, but someone will oppose it."

"They can oppose it all they want, by the sound of it," Malafay notes. "I got a name from this woman, and I think it's dangerous, and not only for us."

"What name?" Felynquiri asks.

"I'm afraid to speak it, but it's the name of that goddess who owns this world, and I think she has something personal in it against ours, who is not even allowed to be here."

"Whoops!" Rhyliira chirps. "That goes on a level beyond us. If we're speaking of a battle between two gods, I want to be well and safe behind something solid."

"This is probably where we take refuge with those old gods," Felynquiri accedes. "Hopefully, they will offer protection."

"And so we have our final conclusion. We need to go back."

"First, we need to go investigate what's up there, if anything," Malafay admits.

In the grand Temple of the Planes in the city of Bya'an Tamoranth, an aged High Elf was making a visit to an old friend. She arrives at the door to an office in the rear and knocks gently before peeking inside.

"Aerlie? Are you busy?"

"Vonafel!" she sings as she rises from her chair. "Come on in. I got your note that you wanted to spend some time together. What do you have in mind?"

"Oh, maybe if we could find a nice little café and share some tea. Between your work and mine, it seems we can find so little time anymore."

"Vonafel, I think our work is not so severe that we can't find enough time for each other."

"Maybe you're right," she smiles softly. "I am mostly retired these days, but I feel my years coming upon me, and I find myself reflecting on so many past memories."

"Yes, I feel it too. We're the last two of our old group from the academy days. I feel like Thaelyn did once with that old acquaintance of his."

"Yes, but in his case, that old acquaintance came back for him," she grins coyly. "When I'm gone, you'll be all that's left of it. And how many more will you find after me? I feel for you, Aerlie. Yours won't be an easy life, no less than his for all the people you'll know and then see pass on, simply for being immortal."

"I know, and I've already known a good many. Do you recall Marelle Carronel? When I see the recent news of our new ventures into space, I think of her and the legacy she left behind. And now her daughters carry it forward in her honor."

"Ailene and Brianne, yes. And just like you, they're also Celestials.

Poor girls…" she shakes her head morosely. "There just aren't enough boys to fill all the gaps."

"Not amongst our kind, as each of us is unique. But Aristan and Aelwyn have two sons so far, though they're a bit young as yet. And it seems weird when you're trying to bring new life to a world only to fill in for the lack of a real population to find mates."

"I think the only solution to this is to ask those same Estelar who started the whole thing to finish it for us. We need more examples to work with."

"You know, that's not really a bad idea, if also a bit awkward. What are we speaking of here…enough for a colony base?"

"It couldn't hurt. It would provide for more selections and better numbers to play with. And speaking of which…" Vonafel raises her brow conspicuously.

"Oh no! You're not going to do that again are you? Vonafel…" she moans.

"Aerlie, you need to have something of your own, and we all know it. Before my days are done, I want to see a baby come out of you, so I'll know you have fulfilled one of the greatest joys in life."

"Oh, Vonafel, please. Thaelyn and I have tried so many times, but according to the med-techs, not that I actually need THEM to tell ME about this, our biologies are just a tad too different to effectively conceive of anything by natural means. Me being Avariel, him being a human base, Celestial or otherwise…"

"Um, Aerlie, do I actually need to remind YOU, of all people, that… science…" she flutters her fingers, "…can probably correct for that? You, being a Celestial, and the chief of our medical services to begin with, should know this much even from a few centuries ago, with or without our native sciences to help, as your own Celestial knowledge could probably do it."

"Yes! I know this, Vonafel, and so does Thaelyn. But it just doesn't feel, um, well…natural. And we both feel a bit sensitive about it."

"Is that sensitive for using a medical lab, or sensitive of saving face in the public eye that you're going this direction, as opposed to what everyone else does."

"Um, yes…?" she smiles shyly. "And being Celestial, we don't feel the same pressure of time to get it done."

"Oh! YOU don't feel the pressure of time, but what about the rest of us? Aerlie, how many times have I heard people speak of desiring to see an heir out of you two, if only to bring the pitter-patter of young feet to the royal house, to say nothing of actually requiring an heir out of a couple of immortals? It's simply natural to ask for this, to expand your family and demonstrate yourselves to be like everyone else out there and have children."

"Oh, please, Vonafel," Aerlie begs. "I know you're right, but I don't want to have another argument about this. Maybe we'll grow into it and take that plunge one day, but today is not that day."

"Aerlie, I'm going on five centuries soon. I have a daughter, a granddaughter, a great granddaughter…" she chuckles. "Need I go on? What about your mother? She's still alive, right?"

"Barely. And she's also nagging me about this. And I feel for her perhaps most of all. Oh, Vonafel, you're right, and I want to please her at least as much as anything else. Maybe I can have another talk with Thaelyn, and this time come to a conclusion of some sort."

Aerlie hangs her head and sighs solemnly. Vonafel steps in and wraps an arm around her long-time friend's shoulder to comfort her.

"Let's go out and find something to eat. There's that little place down the road. They have the best pastries in town. That'll make both of us feel better."

Chapter 3

SEEKING (FORBIDDEN) WISDOM

The rumors circulating around the Drow cities were escalating, although each city did not communicate with the others as often to realize it was universal to all of them. Distance, the difficulty of navigating the shifting and often hazardous tunnel networks, and a general sense of antipathy between them, often denied one to know anything about what the others were doing…not unless there was a disaster of some kind.

In the city where Relissa had most recently spread her message, the two lower Houses were assembling teams to venture out to investigate the stories and verify their nature. Although, so far, it was unknown what they might do about it. They didn't hold enough rank or authority to press for any political change, so they would simply account for a population body when the final movements came around.

Malafay and her two younger sisters were also trying to prepare themselves, at least as much psychologically as physically, for a possible expedition to conduct their own investigation. But before they could make any official moves, they would need the sanction of the Matron Mother simply to go out the door. And this might be the hardest part, as she would want to know the reasons behind it.

Malafay was leading her troupe, which now included the eldest male of the house, Jhandril, to the chamber of the Matron Mother for a meeting. An assembly had been called, which also included the two eldest daughters, Alakaere and Alyraema, to oversee the request. On their arrival, Malafay and her group each offered their proper respects on entering the room before beginning.

"Matron Mother Luariina," Malafay begins reverently. "I come before you with a request. You may not be aware of this, but in recent times, there have been some odd stories circulating around the city, and I suspect our city is not the only one. Where they come from is a mystery, but I believe either someone is passing these stories around to stir up unrest, or to reveal something unseen to us. Therefore, this may be to inform the people silently."

"Why would those who are passing these stories do so without first coming to us in the Great Houses? We are the authority here, not some rabblerouser in the streets."

"But of course, Matron Mother, this is the same as what I would ask. Unfortunately, who is doing it and what ultimate goal they have is still a mystery. However, I have listened to this, trying to understand what it is they are saying, hopefully to understand where, perhaps also why it was gaining so much attention, and I feel I have come to a conclusion, and therefore my reason to call your attention to it with this request."

"I see. Very well. And what is this you have found, and what request do you have?"

"As I said, my belief is this could be occurring in multiple cities, and this would naturally suggest it is external to any one city. If this is the case, I might then suggest someone, somewhere, is sharing knowledge of some sort, perhaps recently acquired knowledge, and this could potentially affect these cities, whether each one independently or all of them collectively. This might then represent trouble, as the stories tell of overlooked details and missed opportunities to learn something critical that could affect our lives here in the Underdark. I think something is coming our way that we need to investigate in order to understand what course of action we must take for ourselves."

"And is this your request, that you would wish to make this investigation?"

"It is. What I have learned in this time has pointed me in a direction I feel I should follow if I would learn the source of it, and then naturally I would bring this back to you and our House for consideration of what we should do about it. It might also be of value to the Council if this could affect the entire city."

"Yes, the Council would surely wish to know of this…assuming there is any truth to it. Am I also to assume these others standing here with you are your selection to accompany you on this journey?"

"Indeed. Surely, both Alakaere and Alyraema have better things to do than to chase down wild rumors, and I think it would be a good learning exercise for the younger sisters. As for Jhandril, he knows the tunnel networks out there well enough to assist us in finding our way, should we need to travel to any other city to find our answer. I feel we will be sufficient enough for this small task."

"The tunnels can be dangerous, you know. Maybe a larger body of warriors would be wise?"

"A larger body may be wise for protection, but I am also thinking of stealth, and having so many feet stomping around out there might draw more attention than a smaller group moving silently in the shadows."

"Ah, clever. Yes, you do carry a valid point. And how long do you suggest this journey of yours to take? Do you expect to travel far? The next city is a fair distance away from us."

"I am aware of this. I think the source of these rumors cannot be too far if they are so easily finding their way inside here. As for how long overall, this is hard to say. But we will make haste, and return as quickly as we can with our result. I simply need your blessing to begin on our way."

"I see. Yes, this would certainly require investigation, if for no other reason than to quell these rabblerousers and their wild ramblings so we can find our peace again. I will offer a prayer to the Spider Queen for your safe travels and wait anxiously for your speedy return."

"I thank you, Matron Mother," she smiles. "But somehow, I think even the Spider Queen might not take a personal interest to this trifle. Maybe we would not wish to bother her with it. Much like all the rest, I am sure she has better things to do," she chuckles disarmingly.

"How interesting. And perhaps you may be right. If this is nothing more than a simple fool with too many words in his mouth, perhaps you could assist in relieving him of a few."

"Oh, Matron Mother, I assure you, if that is the case, he will know his error."

Malafay then bows, along with her two sisters and one brother, as they back away out of the room. They turn and then proceed down the hallway and through the dynastic estate towards the front door.

"Sister Malafay," Jhandril emits tenderly. "That was a very careful play of words you made in there, and I am only barely knowledgeable of what you mean from our earlier conversation. Can you enlighten me further on what to expect out there?"

"Jhandril, I will enlighten you once we are outside in the tunnels. But your primary purpose here is your skills as a warrior. I will do all the talking if we should encounter anyone."

"Yes, Sister Malafay, I simply wish to understand what is expected of me before it comes to blows."

"Give us the time we need to get through the gates, then we will talk."

They emerged out onto the avenue, and began coursing their way along the streets towards a main boulevard that passed through the city. Most of the people walking around were commoners attending to personal chores, or tasks granted to them by their masters in the greater Houses.

They arrived on a lane that led towards the main city gate. In this case, the city was enclosed inside a grotto and closed off on one side by a massive wall. Outside were tunnels leading off in different directions through the various caverns and ancient passageways of the local region. Some were stable and didn't suffer from the activities of the local denizens digging out new pits and paths, while others were the collapsed remains of older tunnels leading to forgotten chambers.

Malafay orders the guards at the gate to open the portcullis for her to pass through. She then led her team outside, which would represent the first time she or her two younger sisters ever left the city. Her two older sisters, Alakaere and Alyraema, had both gone on expeditions in the past, at least as part of sending groups of warriors up for their raids. Once away from earshot of the guards, she turns to her group for a private conversation.

"All right, listen," she begins. "Jhandril, you know the way up there from the last time you were sent out, right?"

"Yes, Sister Malafay, although this causes me to feel uncertain, as you are essentially trying to do something Alyraema once forbade us to do."

"Forget that. If there is more to it, we need to know. Otherwise, it could find its way inside the city and destroy everything we have.

Now, what exactly did you see again? Repeat what you said to me so that Rhyliira and Felynquiri can hear it."

"Of course. And this is not simply the last time we went up, but each time during my life when I was sent out. I also recall my father speaking of the same privately to me when he was sent out in his time. We came to the exit of the tunnel that leads to the openness of the above-world. But before we could travel even a few steps further, a terrible blinding light erupted in our eyes, causing as much pain as it did prevent us to see anything."

"Did the light itself cause this pain?" Rhyliira asks.

"It was so strong, it hurt our eyes, but I think this is all. Then came a voice which seemed to boom out from somewhere behind the light. It ordered us to leave the area and return back to where we came from."

"What about this story of a wall of some kind?" Felynquiri wonders.

"Yes, on those occasions when we could get a glimpse of something before being hit by that light, we could see a tall wall blocking our way, curving from one side to the other. It appeared to be made of stone, but I have no idea what kind, and it was smooth, as if crafted by very fine hands."

"And this wall has been there for as long as you personally have gone up, even for your father. I wonder how long overall if all we have to speak for us is two generations."

"Probably a long time," Rhyliira accedes. "Just try to imagine, Felynquiri, if you are someone trying to unite a world, some parts of which might not go peacefully, how long might that take?"

"Not knowing how vast that world might be, I couldn't say, but surely, it might take a while, and this still does not answer the larger question of where that wall actually came from or how long ago, if for instance it predates that king of theirs."

"True."

"Excuse me," Jhandril interjects politely. "What do you mean by uniting something and a king?"

"Jhandril," Malafay responds. "This part is for you only, not to be shared with anyone else unless we can find sufficient reason for it, and I wish to be the one to make that decision. The world up there is coming for us, all because Houses like ours, whether in this city or elsewhere, keep persistently sending up warriors like you to hit walls like that, and they regard us as an annoyance for not taking the lesson by now."

"Uh oh…I was wondering about this a few times. We keep going up there, keep getting turned around, but to what end?"

"To the end that they have finally grown tired of us in this grave we dug for ourselves after all the old offences we laid upon them with earlier raids killing simple commoners, not warriors waiting to launch against us down here. There never were any warriors, but we have been made to think there were during this entire history of being in the Underdark."

"And who is it that makes us believe this if it is not true?"

"The one who drove us down here in the first place."

"I think you just lost me. My teachings might not actually include this."

"I'll give you a hint. It's the same one I told the Matron Mother NOT to tell anything about our journey."

Jhandril halted his rebuttal as he made a quick connection. He reeled back cautiously and glanced at the other two sisters.

"You mean…" he whispers.

"Yes. Our true gods, apparently, as elves of any kind, are supposed to be a body called the Seldarine. But we apparently defiled our old worship, and this resulted in a kind of curse, which leaves us down here, in what some call a grave. The surface world has no real interest in digging us out. They just want us to stop sending our warriors up there making further offences amongst their people."

"If they are so offended, why not come down so much earlier?"

"The changing nature of the tunnels from basilisks, elementals, and other creatures digging around makes it difficult to find an effective path, and I guess building a wall was easier."

"Yes, of course, it would be."

"But here is where we are now. The lands up there were recently united by a powerful king, so it is said. So, to offend anyone at all would be to offend the entire thing as a whole. He carries a divine mandate from a goddess who claims ownership of this world, all of it, and she is calling for the unification of all the people. Everyone. And this would likely include us if not for the fact that we became enemies to our old gods and cursed to rot in this grave we call the Underdark. Now, it's our turn to learn of our mistakes and make a decision on this. Those stories are to correct the errors of our teachings and raise awareness that we, as a society down here, have not made any sort of advancement of wisdom in this entire time, while they up there, and under the rule of this king, I suppose, have moved forward tremendously, such that if we ever did actually see one of their warriors, we wouldn't know what to do about it."

"Great. All my life, I trained to serve our House, and I thought I was a good warrior with a blade. But if they use something completely different by now…"

"Right, and they apparently don't care for the tunnels anymore, as they seem to use portals to move around now, which can grant them the ability to bypass those tunnels and appear directly on our streets without warning. And here we have our decision. To turn BACK to our old gods and join them in this new peace and prosperity they are pursuing up there, and it sounds like they are pursuing it rather vigorously, or be destroyed along with our goddess who is apparently seriously offending this other goddess who claims ownership of this world."

"Uh oh…that sounds serious, and I don't know who to worry about more at this point."

"I agree. But so far, this is a lot of talk. I met an agent of theirs, one of those who was spreading these stories, and she did in fact use a portal to depart back home. So, if she can use one to leave, others can use them to arrive. This much I think is certain. Therefore, if they really did want to finish us in this grave, they have nothing to hold them back."

"Ugh! Please don't tell me that!"

"However, they ARE holding back, if only to offer us a deal. For those of us who will listen, these other gods might be willing to offer us a form of redemption if we turn away from our existing devotion. This could grant us life, but it would not be anything like what we were accustomed to before, I think."

"Would they make slaves out of us, or are they offering something else?"

"I don't know the answer to that, and probably will not know until we go up there and see the world with our own eyes to understand what has become of it in this time. Until then, many things are uncertain. All except they are weary of this long wait."

"I understand, then we should be moving. Follow me and I'll lead the way. We should not encounter any trouble if we are silent and quick."

✦ ✦ ✦ ✦ ✦ ✦ ✦

"What about a blessing from Lathander?" Vonafel suggests. "Those seem to work some magic on occasion."

"Oh please!" Aerlie giggles. "You're not going to have me play that old trick, are you?"

"Hey, it's no trick, and you know it! Besides, you advertise it to so many other couples who want children, so why not try it yourself?"

"Because it's not as simple as that. His blessing is to strengthen the body to produce strong healthy babies, not necessarily to increase the potential of any form of conception."

"But those couples DO conceive right afterwards, regardless of any natural potential they might normally have."

"Well, yes, but you're also forgetting they're likely under advice to wait for that fertility period. And many times, we're speaking of humans who have those monthly cycles of theirs. We elves do it differently."

"True, but a little extra 'oomph' couldn't hurt," she smiles.

"Vonafel, just how much oomph do you think I need?"

"I don't know. How much do you normally get?"

The two of them let out a hearty laugh at the suggestion as they sat in a local café sipping tea and enjoying a pastry treat.

"We get plenty of that already," Aerlie grins discreetly. "No, it's not about that. It's just that we, um…"

"…Are stubborn as mules and afraid to appear ineffectual," Vonafel interjects. "Aerlie, you're like a sister to me…if you don't count the wings…and those topaz gem eyes…and the metallic gold hair…and the fact that you haven't matured a day in the four centuries I've known you…" she giggles. "But aside from that, I'm not going to let up until you break down and actually do something with yourself."

"All right, Vonafel! By the gods, I'll talk to Thaelyn and see if we can bring ourselves to a decision."

"A decision? That's what you call it? To have a baby… All right, it's a decision for most of us, but if you already want one, the only decision is to, well, do it…successfully, that is."

"Successfully. Yes. And this is where we have our issue. Maybe I'm just a little embarrassed."

"Ah! Now we see it. Aerlie, you probably brought forth half the population of this city by now, and YOU are embarrassed to have your own. Protector, help us, if ever I would see the day."

"Maybe so, but in order for us to do this, we would both need to go into a clinic and provide specimens. And this gets personal."

"Yes, I suppose it would, but it's not like you're baring yourself to the entire world out there. It's a private procedure, right?"

"Yes, but at the same time, I was never the one on the table."

"And this is the other side of it. You are the caregiver, not the care receiver. Being a Celestial, you're generally immune to just about anything and everything out there to go into a clinic for, and therefore you never had to give yourself to another person to treat you for anything."

"There was that one time as a child when Thaelyn first found me in that circus, but I think that was the only time."

"Yes, but I think that was a rather dire exception to the rule. All right, you'll just have to swallow a little of that pride and do it. I can't see any other way for you."

"Maybe so. But it sort of takes the romance out of the occasion."

"Oh great, she wants romance, on top of things," Vonafel tosses her hands up. "She's got an eternity of oomph to play with, but for this one occasion, she wants icing on her cake."

Again, they share a bold giggle as they finish their tea and pastry.

They turned their conversation to other subjects until they said their goodbyes and Aerlie returned to her work at the Temple. Vonafel continued sitting at the café, reflecting on the conversation and still silently disturbed that her best friend was being so reluctant.

"Oomph," she smiles privately. "Yes, I recall a little of that in my day. It doesn't come as often now, but such is youth. And she's embarrassed to be the one on the table. Great, but virtually everyone who required any sort of service has been on that table at some point. How many times have I been there? Hmm..."

She leaned back in her chair quietly pondering a myriad of subjects on how to encourage her longtime friend to take the plunge, while keeping the experience at least partially bearable.

"A blessing from Lathander. If he can help so many others, surely, he could add a little of his own..."

She suddenly halts her train of thought as an idea comes to mind.

"A little of his own oomph?" she wonders. "Oh, but of course! You don't want to be the one on the table, then ask for a little divine aid. And then you get your oomph AND a successful conception."

She spends a moment trying to envision the scenario, how Aerlie and Thaelyn might go into the temple for a blessing, like so many others have done in the past.

"Somehow, I doubt that would work. If they don't like appearing ineffectual, going in for a blessing, or going to a clinic for specimens, it's all the same…going somewhere and doing something that brings them into the public eye for simply doing it."

She continues searching her thoughts for ideas on how to manipulate the situation to give a viable result.

"It would have to be private, and needs to involve the famous oomph, so she can have her romance. But then what? Do we ask Lathander to go into the bedroom with them? Ugh, I don't think so. How do you get your romantic oomph with a god hanging over your shoulder giving directions?" she giggles softly. "And besides, this would need to be a special oomph to get over that hurdle of their biology. You need an extra kick to it."

Vonafel ponders for a moment how this might appear, trying not to think in so many dirty thoughts, but on a more practical level of succeeding, until she gets a curious flashback of a most extraordinary moment in the city's history. She begins grinning broadly.

"Oh yes, I recall that one. And it was him again, of course. Dear little Marelle and her husband. This is where we got Ailene and Brianne, by the way."

She begins reflecting on a moment that occurred almost a century before where a close friend, Marelle Carronel, and her husband, Sir Roderic Kholgard, had a most extraordinary encounter with Lathander where he blessed them so strongly that they nearly tore up a local inn with their consummation, and made headline news across the city for the noise they generated.

"Yes, well, that was special. And again, like so many others, it was supposed to be a traditional blessing. But if these two don't want to be known for it…um, hmm, wait a moment. Don't want to be known, so to keep it private…but they're so stubborn!" she scorns softly. "You would almost need to sneak it up on them simply to land a hit. How do you do that with two people who are otherwise so unwilling to do it themselves? To say nothing of these two being Celestials who would probably see it coming regardless."

She continues sitting there pondering this paradox.

"Unless you could slip them something, like a potion or a pill, something to distract them while they're engaged with that oomph. Then have him come in and hit them, but blindsided. But that's simply nasty…" she grins. "And I know someone who likes playing games like this."

She reaches down to her handbag and pulls out a device that resembles a cell phone. It was known locally as a shard-com. She engages the menu display and searches the directory for a number.

"I wonder if she's available right now," she muses. "I don't want to disturb her if she's involved in anything heavy. I know she's working that project in the Underdark these days."

She taps on an icon for a simple text message feature and types in a short line.

"Relissa, are you busy?"

She waits several moments to see if a response comes back. After a brief pause, the unit beeps softly and a line appears.

"Not right now. You want to talk?"

She replies with another line.

"Yes, hold on."

Vonafel now returns to the directory and touches another icon to make a call. After a quick ring, the line answers.

"Hey there!" ushers an enthusiastic voice. "I haven't heard from you for a while."

"I'm sorry, Relissa, I really should spend more time refreshing old times. Although lately, I'm trying not to bother you during this project you're working on. How is that going, by the way?"

"We're getting a few words out here and there. Those peeps down there don't like to socialize much, but I got a couple of their lower Houses sending up envoys, and one from a higher rank. That's the one I'm really waiting for."

"Which rank, in this case?"

"Six, so they're on the local council."

"Ooh! That would be a good one to catch if you can work it right. But do be careful. I recall from the old days the stories we had of those people. They usually can't be trusted."

"We're watching for that, but one way or another, it has to be done. We can't keep up this game of cat and mouse forever, either. So, what are you doing that you need to talk so suddenly?"

"Do I need a reason to reach out to an old friend?"

"Nah, hardly that, but your opening line tells me you have something bouncing between your ears."

"Oh drat! You and your scout training don't miss a detail, do you! All right. Although I am happy to speak with you, I do have a problem, and I could use a little help to resolve an idea or two."

"Sounds dandy. And how many marks will this cost us on Thaelyn's list, or are we hoping for a new edition by now?"

"Relissa! Do you honestly think I would suggest anything like that?"

"Yes! Especially now that you're going defensive on me," she giggles. They share the laugh as Vonafel continues.

"I swear, how the world changes. All right, listen. This is about Aerlie. We both know she and Thaelyn want a baby, but they're unable to conceive one in the traditional fashion, right?"

"Aye! Poor girl, I feel for her. I've got mine, you've got a few by now, but she and Thaelyn…"

"Right, and get this, they're both either too stubborn, or too embarrassed to go in for a medical procedure to do it artificially, or even to the temple for a blessing by Lathander to see if he can give a little extra into it."

"Grand! So, where do we fit in?"

"Do you recall Marelle back in the day, with her 'overdone' blessing?"

"Oh jiggers! Do I! The street out there was packed side to side and for a couple of blocks. All of us from the academy…me, Haran, Kaliya, and who knows how many more, all playing the looky-loo. And when they were done, everyone erupted in a big applause."

"Yes, I missed it, but I certainly heard about it from a lot of others. Wow. But now listen. Aerlie wants that special romance for the occasion, rather than just a visit to a clinic for a sterile procedure, then to go home and wait. They don't want the world to know they're having this trouble, although I'm sure by now a lot of people do."

"Aye, you got that one right. How long have they been together, and still nothing?"

"They've traditionally given the excuse, and this is what I call it, an excuse, that as Celestials, they have all the time in Creation to do it."

"Uh huh, I think I've heard that one before."

"Right, so my thoughts are, they want this the natural way, nothing outwardly artificial, maybe not even a blessing to kick it off, as it still shows itself, and most of all private, like most people. But if they can't do it the natural way for their biology being a little out of sync, we need something external to get in there, either like that medical procedure, or else some divine aid like that blessing."

"Uh huh, and how do you hope to slip this past their Celestial senses?"

"That's the problem. I have no idea. But if Lathander can sneak it in somehow and hit them while they're distracted with something, like that oomph moment, maybe we could get the best of both worlds."

"That's a wee bit tricky. If you're trying to compare this with Marelle, um…"

"Didn't I hear it said both she and her husband were in a dreamy state following that romp?"

"Aye! A bad one, too. Whatever he hit them with, it zonked them a good one."

"Well, do you think we could…zonk…these two with something, then maybe to hit them at a critical moment while they're engaged? But it has to be subtle to the senses."

"Aye, they're sharp, both of them. In the case of Marelle and Roderic, they were thoroughly dazed by it. But they were humans, and I'll bet you'll need a lot more to daze these two here."

"Yes, probably so. And even worse is to slip it past them unnoticed. What about a potion or something to put them into a really good mood first?"

"Oi! Vonafel, anything potent enough to hit them up would probably be illegal. And then you need to feed it to them."

"What if we say we have a new alchemical thing to set the occasion?"

"I'm no expert on the subject, not alchemy or biology, but I don't think they work like that. Not unless we can feed them a good line to go along with it."

"All right, so this is a stumbling point. Maybe we can think about this a bit. But meanwhile, I'm still wondering about that blessing. Surely, Lathander could get in there and kick things off to make that initial connection. If we can resolve this part at least, we might have one piece of it. So, what about this. He's Aelwyn's Father. Can she perhaps have a little talk with him to inquire about this and devise at least part of a plan for this side of it? Maybe she could also help with the other side if she has anything from her experience up there in Sigil. I recall now that incense they use in the Spirit test came from up there."

"Aye, maybe. I could certainly ask. Then, the next time I'm in the guildhall, I'll look her up and lay an idea or two on her. We might as well bring her into it, if we're aiming for a good mark on the list. I don't think she has one yet," she giggles vigorously.

"Good, and let me know if you come up with anything."

"Sure thing!"

They end the connection and Vonafel now gets up to leave the café.

◆ ◆ ◆ ◆ ◆

Malafay and her group had been hiking along a series of trails through the Underdark, following a maze of tunnels, both old and new, until they found their way up to what seemed like an ancient outpost ruin. She and her sisters stopped to examine the decaying buildings.

"Is this one of ours or one of theirs?" she asks.

"Personally, I don't know," Jhandril replies as he surveys the broken walls and crumbling roofs. "All I know is we pass through here, and on the other side is a stable passage that leads to our exit to the above-world. So, if I were to guess, this might be something like a watch post. If it's one of theirs, it's long since abandoned, maybe from some early moment before that wall."

"As I look at this design work," Rhyliira notes. "I can't say anything for what they use up there, but some of this might be elven, like what we use back home."

"It's old," Felynquiri observes. "This much is for sure. So, if it's ours, could it be from a time after we were driven into this hole?"

"That might make sense. An outpost to establish a base while we scouted the rest of it before pushing further in."

"Possibly. And then abandoned once we began building our cities down there. A piece of old history long forgotten, and perhaps with no record of it by now, if we are made to forget so many things."

"This makes me angry. I want to remember those things now. They are a part of us, who we were, where we came from, and why we're here. Isn't that important enough to remember?"

"That largely depends on who you speak to," Malafay accedes. "And not likely anyone back home."

They continued through the ruins to another tunnel that led along a winding path generally upwards. The ambient temperature along the way was changing, from the warmer climes down below, where the natural heat of the planetary core radiated up, to a much cooler region as they came closer to the surface.

"Is it just me, or is it getting cold in here?" Felynquiri wonders.

"It gets that way as you go up," Jhandril suggests. "I'm told the Underdark is warm because it's so close to the molten lakes further down."

"How do people survive in a place like this?" Rhyliira groans.

"Rhyliira," Malafay muses. "You might just as easily ask how people can survive in a hole like ours. Most of them are still up there."

"Granted. You are right, of course. We live in a grave...a rather warm one."

They continued along the winding path. The rock seemed old and unchanged for an untold measure of time.

"This tunnel is markedly different from those down below," Rhyliira mentions. "Too much activity down there changing the pathways, but this looks mostly untouched."

"Yes," Malafay nods. "And I think I feel a draft from somewhere."

"That's the exit," Jhandril replies. "We're getting close. Now, just so that I understand the plan, how do you wish to approach this?"

"Simple. We go out and try to talk to them. I have instructions from that agent I met to identify myself as someone to speak for our people using diplomacy rather than threats, as I'm sure we are probably best known for, if our history is such. She said they will not attack, but rather choose to explain a few things to us. That agent even said she might meet with me and give her own story."

"Do you know her name to ask for her?" Rhyliira inquires. "It sounds to me like she could be useful to find our way around up there."

"I believe I recall it. I just hope they recognize it, for instance if she came from this outpost or some other."

Malafay motioned for the group to proceed on the final leg of their journey. But before they could reach the tunnel exit onto the open land, a bright ambient glow was permeating the last segment of the tunnel. It was the glow of daylight, but to them, it was simply alien and unpleasant.

"Jhandril, is that the light you mentioned?"

"No, this looks different. It's everywhere, and a different color, I think."

"Do we continue?" Felynquiri wonders while shielding her face. "It's already causing my eyes to hurt."

"I don't know," Malafay responds, also covering part of her face. "We came this far, and I don't want to return home because of this. If there is something to learn, I want to learn it. Blast! Why do we have this now?"

She tried taking several more steps forward, but the light shining in from the outside only got worse. She peered around one final bend in the tunnel, and saw what looked like the source of the light. It was a hole, and outside was intolerably bright.

"Jhandril, can you see this? Is that the exit over there?"

He peeks around the corner to follow her direction.

"Yes, that's it, but it was never like this before. It was dark each time we came up here."

"Dark. All right, that might explain it. Sky, sun…this is daytime for them. You were here at night, and that is NOT supposed to have that infernal sun in open view. Wonderful. Now what do we do? Wait for it to vanish before we move on?"

"How long does that take?" Felynquiri asks. "I don't recall any teachings on what a day is for them."

"Yes, and whether or not someone would be awake in their nighttime to talk to. Well, we're here. Even if we have to cover our faces completely, we should at least try. We can still talk, even if we can't see who we are talking to."

"I don't like the sound of that," Jhandril moans. "If I'm talking to someone, I would at least like to know if I'm talking to a person, or their blade in my face."

"Granted, but like I said, they should not attack if we do nothing to provoke it. I think I need to trust this much, especially if they don't need to talk to us at all with those portals of theirs in play."

"Maybe. Or it could simply be a trick."

"Either way, I think I am willing to give it a try. Worst case, they tell us to go home, like they did with you so many times. Follow me. We'll feel our way through this last part, and hope we don't trip over something."

They each covered their faces with their arms, burying their eyes within the folds of their sleeves, and slowly crept along, feeling their way along the side of the tunnel, carefully stepping along the last stretch of rock until the light became so pronounced that they simply had to be outside by now.

They could feel a gentle breeze blowing by, along with unfamiliar fragrances. The echoes of the cavern were gone, now replaced by soothing chirps and buzzes of the native fauna. But soon after came an unnatural booming of a voice.

"You there! Drow. What business do you have here? Your kind is not welcome in our land."

The voice sounded like a person, but almost mechanical, and it echoed against something, probably the rock behind them, and maybe something in front.

Malafay and the others all turned to orient on what they thought to be the direction of the voice, but with the sunlight as it was, they couldn't see anything for their sleeves covering their faces. Then the voice boomed again.

"Your party composition is different than usual. Why do you come here?"

"Wait!" Malafay shouts, disoriented by the echoes and unable to focus on a direction. "We are here to talk. One of your people came to us and spoke to me about changes to the world above. I am here to speak with diplomacy, but I cannot see. This light blinds me...all of us."

"I understand. This is an odd time of day for you to arrive up here. You usually come at night. You are here as part of our work to educate your people? What name do you go by?"

"I am called Malafay of House Deghym. We come from the city of...well, I suppose it doesn't matter much. My impression is you are approaching all the cities of our people, is this correct?"

"This is true. Each of your cities down there is equally responsible for the atrocities you have brought to our people. And we desire to see a final end to it."

"Atrocities..." she mutters. "A final end? How would this final end appear?"

"That largely depends on how well you listen to our words. The more you listen, perhaps the better the outcome."

"I see. Is it possible for me to speak to that one I met before? She said she could possibly assist me in learning your story."

"I suppose. Do you have a name?"

"I think her name was Relissa of House Moonshimmer. She was a dark elf, like me, but her colors were a bit different."

"I know the sort you speak of. Give me a moment and I'll check on this."

Malafay and her group now need to wait, although for how long, it was uncertain. If this agent wasn't found locally, would she need to arrive from somewhere, and then, how far away was it, and would she walk the distance, or use another of her portals? They didn't know, and couldn't follow the action for the blinding sunlight.

Meanwhile, inside the guard post, the guard who was speaking on the intercom turned to a communications console. There, he pulled up an app on a terminal display to call in to the guildhall receptionist in Bya'an Tamoranth. A pleasant female voice answered.

"Order HQ, reception desk. How can I help you?"

"This is the garrison watchpoint at Pinewood Valley, Junction Six. I have a party of Drow out here trying to hold themselves upright in this unfortunate blazing sunlight, and asking for one of our agents, Relissa Moonshimmer. Can you check to see if she's available? We may need her to participate in a little parley."

"Very good, I'll check her line. Please wait."

The receptionist now pulls up a roster of their agents and searches for Relissa's contact information. She then selects the line item on her screen and directs her terminal to call the number.

"Scout Moonshimmer here," the voice answers.

"Scout Moonshimmer, we have an arrival at Pinewood Valley, Junction Six. A group of Drow who are apparently responding to what I'm assuming to be your work and asking for you by name. Are you available to respond?"

"Jiggers, if this is what I think it is, that'd be a fine bugaboo of a trick. Aye! Let me jump over to the office and I'll take the gateway out there."

"Very good, I'll let them know to expect you."

The link ends, and the receptionist refers the message to the outpost. From his office behind the large fortification wall, the guard goes on his intercom again. He had been studying the scene outside through a closed-circuit camera system, looking down at the ground where the tunnel opened up.

"All right, I have word on this side. Scout Moonshimmer will be arriving momentarily. I'll ask you to remain as you are until then."

"A scout?" Malafay retorts. "A simple scout? But wait, I saw her use a portal! I would expect her to be a mage, not a scout."

"Many of our scouts also study magic, especially portal magic as part of their training. It makes travel much more convenient."

"A scout also studied as a mage," Jhandril muses. "Well, that outclasses any of us."

"It does," Rhyliira offers. "And it also confirms the idea of many of their people studying this as a common feature."

"If a simple scout also studies as a mage," Felynquiri wonders. "What does a full mage study? Or do they even have such a thing as a full mage, if everyone learns some portion of it."

Relissa was at home at the time the call came in. She was taking a break from her work, but after receiving the call, she suited up with her usual Order scout uniform, including her portal gem, and used it to transit across to a military gateway node junction. This was a terminal facility that used the same technology, but with chutes for a traveler to step inside, as opposed to the portal gems. A person would request a specific destination at a counter, and a chute is assigned and programmed to send them away.

She gave the clerk her assignment and received her chute designation. She approached the tall alcove and stepped inside, then waited a moment for it to charge up. In an instant, she flashed away to the local terminal node near the outpost. From there, she proceeded up to the office to check in.

"I'm here, Scout Moonshimmer. What do we have?"

"We have a party of Drow out there," he announces. "They're in a bad way for the time of day we have now," he chuckles. "But if they're so determined to stick around, they must be desperate, or something."

"Aye, that's a good one. Do we have any names?"

"Yes, a Malafay of House Deghym."

"Jiggers, it's her. That's a fine catch."

"You know her?"

"Aye, third daughter of their House, which is Number Six out of eight for their city."

"Not bad. Well, I guess it's up to you now. Make us proud."

"Aye, and thanks."

Relissa turns and leaves the office, working her way around to a security door nestled in the wall. The guard follows her on his monitors and buzzes the gate to let her out. From there, he would simply observe the situation with the cameras.

Relissa exits outside into the enclosed space between the wall and the mountainside. There, she could see the four Drow visitors holding their arms in front of their faces in a desperate attempt to block the intense sunlight. She makes a careful approach to keep the situation calm.

"Well now. Third daughter of House Deghym, it's a funny thing to see you out here in broad daylight."

"Is that supposed to be a joke?" Malafay retorts uncomfortably. "This light is killing us."

"Right, I suppose it is. One sec, I have an idea."

Relissa turns to the wall and angles up into the nearby security camera, then shouts to the microphone.

"I could use a few deep-shade glasses out here."

"One moment…" the voice responds.

They wait briefly until the door opens again with another guard carrying several deeply tinted sunglasses. He circles around to hand them out to their visitors.

"Here, take these," Relissa offers. "Put them over your eyes. I'll show you how."

She assists them as they try putting on the glasses, which was an appliance entirely unfamiliar to them, but once applied, it allowed them to finally see something. They were able to take their arms away and look around.

The first thing they saw, other than Relissa and the guard, was a huge wall reaching well over their heads, and composed of what appeared to be, in their eyes, a single slab of smooth stone. The only feature was a metal door with no handles to it, and several attachments on the wall at various intervals of an otherwise unidentifiable nature.

Malafay studied the sight, as did the others. Jhandril had seen it before, if only briefly before being blinded by their floodlight. But now with more opportunity to actually see it up close, he could gain a much better appreciation of it.

"No way you could breach this," he muses. "Not without a hook and ladder. But what is it made of? I don't recognize this stone here, and so perfectly smooth."

"The stone isn't actually stone," Relissa explains. "Not in the normal sense of it. It's a substance called concrete. It starts out as a slurry of sand, lime, some gravel, and other things, then poured into a mold and allowed to harden. It comes out hard as any rock you can imagine, but customizable to the need."

"Liquid stone that hardens?" Felynquiri winces. "But is it hot, like the molten pools of the Far Deep?"

"No, you can touch it, and use tools to smooth it out, even to sculpt it if you have the artistic knack in you. We use it for anything that doesn't otherwise use wood or actual quarried stone, which is most of it these days. And using this, size isn't much of a bother for us. We can build sideways as well as up. You just need a good design plan for it."

"Who was talking to us a moment ago?" Rhyliira wonders. "His voice boomed like he was shouting through something."

"Do you see up there?" Relissa turns and points at the wall. "Those devices are called cameras. They can see us out here, and we have speakers where a guard in an office on the other side can see and talk to us from inside the building. He doesn't need to be physically outside to do it."

"Ah, wait," Malafay interjects. "I understand. We have something like this where we can peer into a kind of pool and see images of other places. Is it something like that?"

"Something like it, but the way it works is different. You're probably speaking of a Seer's Pool, but that's a magical study. This is a device as part of our science, which is the empirical study of how nature works. Still, the idea is similar. And then he speaks into a microphone, which he has on his side, and his voice comes out here. And it's probably a bit loud out here simply to make sure you can hear it. You peeps seem to be a bit dense for how many times we need to repeat ourselves," she chuckles.

"Thank you, but given what I see here, I think I may need to accept that. We are still told there is no wall, only a bunch of warriors who don't seem to know where to train themselves except right in front of this hole for us to find and dispatch them so conveniently."

"Aye, that's a good one. We certainly wouldn't want you to miss out on anything by walking too far for it."

"That most certainly WAS a joke," Felynquiri raises her brow. "And I think I'm almost ready to laugh at it, if only it wasn't a joke on us."

"Go ahead and laugh if you like," Relissa shrugs. "This is a learning exercise for you, and I want you to understand the philosophy we use up here at least as much as how we approach and solve our problems. And we do carry a very unique attitude where we look upon things in such a way that we might laugh in the face of challenge and adversity."

"By the depths of the abyss, you would laugh at such things? That, in itself, would be a bit frightening from our side of it, if you only laugh at us."

"I don't want it to seem demeaning to you, only that we are so confident in ourselves to solve our problems that we won't let them bother us."

"All right, I will consider this."

"But wait a moment," Jhandril interjects. "How would this relate to the long history of our raids and you apparently never following through to pursue us back down there? You only built a wall to block us. But if you feel so confident to solve these problems, as you call them…"

"Right," Relissa nods. "Our history up here tells us you were a bother with these raids for a long while, probably dating back to the beginning after the old Crown Wars. The nations didn't change in all that time, being independent from each other, and many times not cooperating on anything they had in common, like you and your raids hitting them from multiple directions across the land. Each nation had to deal with its own, assuming it had the gumption to actually do so. Some may have tried sending parties down there to find you, but they may have given up after a while, as trying to find their way through those deep tunnels proved too difficult."

"Yes, they tend to change from time to time, depending on what creature is digging a new nest for itself."

"In time, many simply gave up, and chose to post watch towers or guard posts in front of the suspected cave openings, hoping to catch you before you went too far. This proved useful in some cases unless you found another way around to foil things."

"This would make sense to me," Malafay agrees. "Surely, if we found a wall, we would look for a way around it."

"But then, something new happened in the world, and this would mark a big turning point for the population up here. It was maybe eight and a half centuries ago when a man would find his way here. His name was Thaelyn. No one knew who he was or where he came from, but he wasn't local, this much was certain. And he wasn't a common man. When the truth came out, we came to realize he was sent here by a goddess known as Maker Kuroku, and she had plans for him, and all the world around us."

"That's the name you gave me back home, when I spoke with you before."

"Aye, this world belongs to her, but she essentially donated it to the human population our kind found when we first arrived in this world many thousands of years ago. Unfortunately, at that time, no one knew the history of it, and she wasn't talking, instead simply letting things slide until they grew to a threshold where she would take more assertive action. This is where Thaelyn came in, to bring it all together and unite the world into one big kingdom under his rule. And he still holds it to this day."

"Um, hold a moment, you said eight and a half centuries. And he is still alive?"

"Yes, he is..." she declares confidently. "This is the trick. How do you get anyone, especially over such a long period of time, to follow a single focused philosophy that could unite a world like ours, and keep it that way? The answer: Not with any simple man. Therefore, Thaelyn. He's not a common man, and he's not a mortal like any of us. So, eight and a half centuries is barely a drop in the bucket for him. He's a Celestial, born of the gods themselves. Therefore, the reason HE was sent as opposed to anyone else."

"In all the..." Rhyliira wheezes. "This would certainly play a role. If the gods are getting involved in all this...that Maker Kuroku, those others you mentioned, the Seld-something...and then us with ours..."

"This world belongs to Maker Kuroku," Relissa asserts. "It was once her home before she ascended to join the Estelar."

"The what?"

"The gods. They're a huge society of people called the Estelar. After some untold measure of time, you have people, maybe a bit like us, who grow and evolve upwards so high, they can now be called gods. It might take billions of years, but it can happen. Yours would be one of them. The Seldarine are another set. But Maker Kuroku is a special case. She and her people, known as the Sarrukh, once lived on this world, but this was something like a billion years ago. Then a disaster hit, and the world froze. The Sarrukh saw it coming and had time to escape, moving off the world and seeking their fortunes elsewhere."

"I think I should've brought a journal book with me to take notes," Felynquiri chuckles softly. "I'll never remember all this to take back with me."

"Maybe I can give you something later. Anyway, Kuroku, as she might be known back then, was their leader. She made a special deal with one member of the Estelar to lift her up and become one of them, so she could oversee her people from on-high. But she also had other plans on her mind, one of them being to pursue an old rival from a time long before this. And HERE is where we come back to this world, which we call Tae'Eladar, in case you don't have a proper name for it. It was still frozen, so she called her children back to refurbish it and seed it with new life. This became all the plants and animals you see up here, and that human population it started out with."

"And then, the elven nations arrived sometime after?" Malafay inquires.

"Right. In the beginning, they weren't desired. It was a pet project the Maker had, and anything from outside was a potential problem to interrupt that. But after a bit, she had time to study the situation and realize she could fit it all together into a grander plan. But no one was cooperating with anyone else. This is where she needed a champion to bring it all together, and he had to be special, such that no mortal man could stand against him."

"Uh huh, and therefore uniting them whether they liked it or not, by the sound of it."

"True, some were compliant and reasonable to see the greater benefit. Others, meaning the powermongers, the tyrants, the despots, they wouldn't likely go along with it. But the plan demanded complete unity of all the people. She was creating what we call a utopian paradise. A perfect world, free from anything evil. She would not accept anything less. Then, once this was done, she would direct us on this grander plan of hers against this old rival I mentioned. This would be our trial to test the result."

"And the result of that trial?"

"We won in a grand way, and rescued another world out there full of people who didn't have a clue over what trouble they were in."

"You…rescued…a full world?" Felynquiri gasps.

The younger sister fell back a step at the insinuation that anyone could hold the potential to rescue anything on the scale of a full world, even though that concept fell considerably short on her as she really didn't even hold a proper perspective of what a full world might be like.

The others in the group felt a similar rush, with the elder members holding a bit more resolutely. But Malafay, being the leader of this expedition, felt it necessary to maintain her composure as best she could. While the story was intriguing, it was still just a story.

"And where does this put you now?" she asks. "How long ago was this test of yours?"

"Almost a century ago. The society of Tae'Eladar, in those days, was in what we call an Early Industrial stage. They were only beginning to learn how to use electricity on a large scale, only beginning to develop large-scale industrial centers to produce goods for the masses, and just beginning to use any form of mechanization, which is to develop machines to perform some of the heavier and more difficult labor, the sort of work that simple people wouldn't be able to do themselves. And yet, we found ourselves being pushed into new worlds, following a path of this old rival as it led back to his starting point, four worlds away from us, and all the mischief he caused along the way."

"Is this to say," Felynquiri wonders, "you actually had to resolve this…mischief…on each of those other worlds?"

"Aye. I was born on one of those, the first one Thaelyn came to. It's called Therinë. We're a spin-off of the old Ssri clan from the time of the Crown Wars. Our people moved on while the rest of you were here making trouble for yourselves. We, along with a clan of High Elves, and some humans, migrated to that one and set up new homes. Unfortunately, that old rival had his plans for us as well, and we fell victim to it in time. Then he tried making a move over here and caught Thaelyn's attention. Thaelyn would then chase him back across to ours, then on to another world, which we called Ruuki uy'Daan, at least back in those early days. It's been given a new name since then to better reflect the new ownership and how we choose to use it."

"Why do you say that?" Malafay asks. "What was it being used for before this?"

"For one thing, it was the home of the orcs. Do you peeps remember those? They arrived about that same time as the rest of us had our troubles here."

"I do recall some stories of orcs, but never down in the Underdark, that I can recall."

"But the name, as it was, actually came about from another set of people who arrived there once, after being chased away from home, and by that same rival, as it turns out. This was a term in their language, meaning to say, a place of exile, as they believed themselves to be in a kind of self-imposed exile from their old home."

"Interesting. But this was in those old days. And you say it has a new name now? Just for the sake of asking, what is this new name? Not that I suppose it would matter to any of us here…" she shrugs.

"Aye, maybe so, today, at least. We call it Ducalma now. We're describing it as a colony world. That rival made a mess of the place along the way, so there's not much left of our original population. Therefore, we have a long way to go to rebuild it."

"Ouch! That does not actually sound nice."

"Thaelyn then moved to the next one, called Morndindor, the original home of the dwarves, and finally to the home of a completely new society we call the Suuden-Aryku, and a world called Azgarén. This is where that one group originally came from. And that's the sort of guy we're speaking about here, someone who doesn't take no for an answer, and will literally chase you across worlds to find you. But he doesn't destroy people just because they're out there. He'll try to redeem them, if he can, and only destroys evil that can't be redeemed."

"Uh oh…and this is where we come in, I suppose."

"At the moment," Relissa nods. "Until recently, the Underdark was still a mysterious place, what with those tunnels changing so much. We chose instead to build ourselves a bit more before taking that one on. We sent spies down there to chart the place, locating your cities and spending a little time to study you. With my people involved, we could walk amongst you, within reason, and not be noticed as much. We would look for opportunities to see if anyone might be willing to listen to anything, and then carefully drop a few hints and clues here and there to break that shell of ignorance you seem so tightly wrapped up in, no thanks to your goddess and her ways."

"And this is where we are right now, I suppose?" Malafay asks.

"Mostly. You need to realize the world up here is NOT like you remembered it, assuming you actually remember anything by now, and not as your goddess seems to be telling you. There are no warriors out here simply standing around waiting for you to come up and stick knives in their backs. We have cities that would put most of yours to shame, with tall buildings and millions of people conducting their daily lives in the open air and sunshine, as opposed to you who mostly hide in your homes and barely go out shopping only if you have no other choice. No one is afraid of anything up here, as there is nothing for them to be afraid of. We don't have crime, so there are no people who want to plant knives in anyone's backs. Everyone worships Thaelyn's principles and beliefs as a type of religion, and each one will fight hard to uphold it. We spend all our efforts on upward growth, with nothing holding us back, like war and hardship. And in our modern day, we are recently entering what we call a Space Age."

"A what Age?"

"Look up there…" she points at the sky overhead. "The sky above us is only just the beginning. There's more out there if you know how to reach it. And that's where we're going now. Travelling to other worlds just got a whole lot easier for us. I consider myself very lucky to be alive right now to see it. When I was young, this was the last thing I would ever expect."

Malafay and her sisters, along with Jhandril, all gazed upwards. Even though they had to see the world through their deeply tinted sunglasses, it was enough for them to marvel at a sight they never imagined they would see in their lifetimes. But the glow of daylight obscured anything else that might be out there. So, the concept of other worlds still seemed far away to them.

"Now…" Relissa asserts. "We have a program to follow here. When we were putting together these plans of ours, we knew that if any of you were to fully realize the differences of where each of us stand, we need to take you on a little tour. You need to know what we've made of ourselves up here and how it relates to what you have down below. Then, with a little luck and a bit of soul searching, you might finally understand how foolhardy it is to send your raids up here to bother us with your incessant whining over old memories."

"Whining…?" Malafay winces. "This is how you might describe it?"

"Basically, yes. Your clan did a bad deed. The rest exacted justice on you, but you apparently didn't take the lesson. And you've been crying over it ever since."

"Wonderful. And this gives me a little insight to how you people think up here. We send raids up here to attack you, and you call it whining over old memories."

"When Thaelyn took possession of things, he built up a very powerful army, enough to literally conquer the world away from anyone else out there who might complain about it. We're not just warriors, but mages, priests, and scouts like me, and all trained in a long list of skills and talents. We do this because now, rather than simply fighting folks like you, we're expected to travel out there…" she waves at the sky above. "And deal with whatever strange new mysteries we find, and do so with enough wisdom and skill that nothing will stop us from seeing a way through it. You peeps, with respect, are small fry to us by now, but no less a pain in our backsides for these raids of yours, and you follow that witch of a goddess who is very soon to receive her walking papers."

"And so, you hope to redeem us away from her, as one way or another, this Thaelyn of yours needs to finish what he started and bring this last piece together along with the rest of it."

"That's right! And don't think he can't do it!" she wags her finger at them. "We have a history up here of fighting dragons, gods, and demons. Simple folk like you don't compare to that."

"How is it actually possible for you to fight all that?" Rhyliira asks.

"We're not simple people trained which way to point a sword. We're all augmented. We carry both magical and divine enchantments on our bodies, not just our gear."

Relissa steps in and pulls down the collar of her uniform to reveal a portion of her chest, where the group could see several glowing arcanic glyphs tattooed into her skin. Rhyliira suddenly felt her face turn pale. She reeled back as she studied this curious figure standing in front of them.

"What does that do to you?"

"It makes me a lot tougher than I look. They run all the way down in front here, a couple on my upper arms, and another set on my thighs. I'm stronger, faster, nimbler, and physically more durable than your average person. I can take several hard hits, and by this, I mean something to knock you through the air, but I'll just stand up and come right back at you."

"So, if a person were to actually try to plant a knife in your back, what would happen?"

"Depending on what the knife was made of; it might leave a mark. But after that, I would probably rip you apart for the favor of it. And that's assuming I didn't simply set you alight by magical fire, or something else."

"Seriously?"

"Seriously!"

"So, even if you did simply have a group of warriors standing around out here waiting for us to arrive, we wouldn't stand a chance against it."

"Some of us have considered that the only reason your goddess continues sending you up here is to give you something to do, to keep you focused on HER hatred for everything else. She would be a natural enemy to such like Maker Kuroku, as they come from opposite sides of the fence. The Estelar have this principle they call the Measure of Balance. All things in nature must balance, and both sides are necessary for this. They divide themselves on the polarities of positive and negative, where each has a different take on how they like to do things. We represent the positive side, and that..." she coughs softly, "...other one, would come from the negative side. Although it is also known to us that she is not very highly favored even amongst her own, as her manners tend to run into the extremes, and push the reasonable boundaries of their faith."

"What would this mean in relation to the others of her side?" Felynquiri asks.

"They barely tolerate her, from what we hear of it. We hold a very close relationship with those gods we associate with on our side. Let me see if I can put this in terms you can understand. On this world, which is generally alone in this universe, meaning everything else out there in the same space with us, we're isolated, so we might qualify for a special neighborly relationship with our local group of Estelar. Those other worlds we found are located in another universe, so they aren't found in the sky above in the proper sense of it. You need to go even further away, and you would need portals to do so. But this close relation we have grants us privileged knowledge of who and what they are, in a real sense of it, rather than the traditional mysticism that normal people might learn, if given their usual ways of teaching. The gods don't teach you everything, and won't teach you everything unless you grow enough to actually qualify for it. But again, we're speaking of extreme lengths of time for a society to grow into something completely new. We just got it early, and mostly because of Thaelyn. His father is one of them."

"So, he really is descended from an actual god. And he brought some of his privileged teachings to you here. And now your entire world society follows him to other worlds to share this with even more?"

"Those who might qualify, but only those lessons we are permitted to share. We need to follow those same rules. But then, we come back to you down below. We suspect your goddess should be well aware of us up here and what we're doing, if she knows what's good for her. I'm sure the Maker never made any secret of the fact that this world is hers, and someone like yours wouldn't be allowed. Although, why she took this long to correct it is another thing, but she's a patient one. It could therefore be suggested that your goddess has mostly been tagging you along, realizing that one day, the Maker would circle around and finish it, so there was no point in doing anything more. Thaelyn took control of everything else. What's to stop him from going down below and doing the same? He's simply too powerful to resist, so why bother, ay?"

"Uh oh..." Rhyliira moans. "I'm getting a picture here, and it's not nice."

"So am I," Felynquiri adds. "You can't fight it, so you're simply waiting for the end. Meanwhile, just keep them occupied with some nonsense until that end finally arrives."

"I don't like the sound of that!" Malafay retorts. "We are told to send our warriors up here to hit a wall and come back home with stories to encourage us to send up even more, only to hit that same wall. And to think, I actually listened to it so many times."

"Sister Malafay," Jhandril offers. "If I may, I have my doubts this will be accepted favorably with the other two sisters, or the Matron Mother herself. My last run up here was with Alyraema, and as with so many that came before, we are simply ordered to be silent."

"Yes, and unfortunately, I will be the one to present this to them, and then to listen to their screeching afterwards. But before we go into that, Relissa, you mentioned a program of some sort with a tour. Let's see about that, so we can actually see what you have. It might allow us to build a better picture of it, and maybe help me with a more solid foundation for my ultimate return home."

"Good!" she nods excitedly. "And speaking of pictures, maybe I can help with a few photos you can take back as visual evidence in case they ask for it."

"Photos?"

"Aye. Pictures taken of the places we visit. Here, look at this..."

Relissa reaches into a pocket and pulls out a curious device...or at least it was curious to the Drow. It was her shard-com unit. She holds it up for display, as the group leans in to examine it.

"This is called a shard-com, and like so many other things, it's part of our science, and therefore the technology we can build out of it. It's a multipurpose unit that allows me to talk to people I know, or anyone else I have in mind to call up. From where I stand right now, I can literally speak to anyone else, whether on this world or the others, so long as they have a similar unit like this."

"That sounds incredible," Rhyliira croons. "How does it work?"

"The operation is a bit complex, so to keep it simple, it sends a signal through a special network it links into. The network can then redirect that signal to some other unit, depending on the address I give for who I want to talk to. But in addition to that, it can also do other things, one of these is to take pictures of what we see out there, and these are called photographs, or photos for short. Here, let me show you. Gather up into a group and smile for the folks back home. You peeps do know how to smile, right?" she giggles.

Relissa moves back a step and waves for Malafay and her group to huddle together for a group photo. She takes aim at her target, then taps a small icon on the display to snap the photo. She then turns it around to show it off to the others.

Malafay and her group gazed at the image, feeling a subtle sense of awe at the ease and simplicity of capturing such a thing as a portrait, which to them might only be found with an artist and a canvas.

"This can be transferred to paper," Relissa notes. "That way, you can take it with you, if you like. We can do this with everything we see along the way, and therefore, if your Matron Mother needs to SEE something, rather than just hearing a tall tale out of you, you have a little more power to your words."

"That would be wonderful to have with me. Yes! If you could offer this to me, I think it would help greatly."

"Very good. So, let's get started. By the way, let me get to know the rest of your names."

"Certainly. These are my two younger sisters. First, we have Rhyliira, the fourth daughter, and then Felynquiri, the fifth daughter of our House. The male is Jhandril, first son of the House, and our best warrior to offer his protection during our travels."

"Did you have any trouble finding your way up here?"

"Nothing out of the ordinary. Once we moved out of the deeper tunnels, it was fairly easy."

"Good. Then come with me and I'll show you around. If you're here to learn something, you won't get it staring at a big wall."

"Speaking of a wall, can we take one of those photos of this thing? I think the Matron Mother might find it interesting to see what we were fighting all this time."

"Malafay..." Rhyliira cautions. "Are you looking for an early whipping with that suggestion?"

"Well, she DOES need to know what those 'warriors' were, right? And unless either Alakaere or Alyraema told her what they were facing, she might not know anything beyond what that...witch...is telling her."

"Uh huh... Just give me a moment of warning so I can hide behind a chair or something."

"Only a chair?" Felynquiri notes. "I think you may need to hide in the basement if she dares to use that word down there."

Relissa smiles at the exchange and steps back for a better view before taking a snapshot of the wall. She then waves them to follow as she begins on her tour.

✦ ✦ ✦◆✦ ✦ ✦

Somewhere in the Outer Planes, in a pocket dimensional domain dedicated exclusively for the Draconic race, Maker Kuroku was visiting her palace and her seraphim attendants to check in on the progress of her efforts, in association with Thaelyn and his people, on the conversion of the Drow. She was still in her Draconic persona, which she had been using for so long while residing on Tae'Eladar, assisting Thaelyn in leading the people there into the modern Age.

"Thaliel..." she begins. "Do we have any news... Regarding that wretch... Lolth... And her designsss...?"

"None as yet, Maker. Mine observations reveal no outward movements to the incursions of Thaelyn's people into that underground domain. Although I am quite sure she should know of it by now. I think she may be simply waiting to see their reactions before applying herself. But Maker, I do not trust her any more than thee. I would bargain a theory that she would wish to smite any who would oppose her, rather than permit their departure or conversion. Her vileness runs deeps, and her opposition to the Seldarine is unregulated. Why the rest of the greater Powers do not take action to bring this into alignment, I cannot say, but it disturbs me to think of where this could go."

"They are probably waiting... For me to take action... As Tae'Eladar is my home... And my persssonal domain... To police as I sssee fit..."

"And she being in thine own garden leaves it unto thee to pursue? Powers grace us for whatever result that might lead to," she chuckles ironically. "Very well, I will continue mine observations, and bring upon thee anything of special import."

Kuroku nods pleasantly as she turns to leave the operations center for her seraphim contingent. She makes her way to another part of the palace, a private section reserved only for her and her top-ranking assistants. It was a room where she kept some of her most private memories, including her original corporeal body from a time almost forgotten when she still lived on Tae'Eladar, once known as Khalen Ruuki, as a Sarrukh. She would visit here from time to time to reflect on herself.

She arrives in front of an array of bookshelves, cabinets, and other display cases, where she has accumulated so many mementos from a past life. And near the center was a stasis chamber with a sleeping body resting inside, held in perfect condition by the elaborate technology owned by the Estelar. She laid herself down in front of it and simply gazed into the inclined capsule at a life she once lived.

"Ssso long ago…" she moans softly. "I sssuffered under his rule. I ssstruggled with his demandsss. I ssspent… Every waking moment… To keep my children alive… Until that day finally came. And now I feel empty. How can thisss be… When I completed my tasssk… And fulfilled my purpossse…? I think I ssspent… Too much time… Dwelling on my passst… And fuming over my present… And not enough… To sssimply enjoy… Those precious momentsss… Of my sssuccess… To create sssomething… Extraordinary…"

She pauses to glance around the room at her collected memories in the form of old artifacts and diaries, journal books, and many volumes of memoirs. She then found her thoughts drifting to her final advance on her old master, Sargeras, and his servant, Darumon, as found on Azgarén during the final confrontation. This was the culmination of so many other efforts to lead the people of Tae'Eladar, and to bring a final chapter of an ancient story to its ultimate close.

"The challenge of Creation. Thisss is how he dessscribed it. And he felt thisss for himsssself… As he led his own into that Age… And watched his children grow. Yesss, Darumon… I know thisss feeling. And I felt thisss for myssself… As you did with yoursss. And though I may desssspise you… For all that you did… I feel worn… And weary… That I travelled thisss road… The sssame as you… Only now to find myssself… At the end. My children are growing up… And leaving their nessst…"

She holds her statement a moment as she reflects even deeper.

"More children… Growing up… Much like the firssst…"

She quickly jerks her mind back into focus, and shakes her head to clear her melancholy.

"Kuroku! You should know… Better than thisss! Look at you. You are a goddesssss! You are not limited… To jussst one plane of exisssstence… No lessss than you are limited… To that old body of yoursss."

She begins chuckling to herself.

"Sssentimental old lizard… You need a new challenge. Tae'Eladar is ssstill there. The people are ssstill there. It is not the sssame as before.

They may be growing up... But they only venture out. Perhapsss one day... They may move forward... But not for a long while. And then... You will sssimply make more. Yesss!" she huffs playfully. "Therefore I am called... The Maker."

She turns away from the stasis tube to angle at a wall of shelving with ornaments and old study projects she once kept as part of her early teachings after joining the Estelar. She passed from one to another as she tried to recollect where each one came from and what it represented. But she couldn't keep herself from peering back at the old body in the tube, as she reflected on her memories that she was using it at the time. And then, somewhere in the back of her mind, a voice seemed to echo out of the darkness.

"Thou dost miss those early moments, Sister Kuroku."

"Yesss, Brother Helm... From time to time... I do. Call it... Nossstalgia. I was not made for thisss... But thisss is who I am now."

✦ ✦ ✦◆✦ ✦ ✦

Relissa and her entourage were visiting a local children's school, to show where their society comes from and how it grows and learns the teachings of their people. It seemed like a good starting place to demonstrate how the society of the world gets its beginning.

"...And out here is where they come for recreation," she explains. "This playground. They have sporting events, where they divide themselves into teams to play games as part of their social development. The younger kids, like those in this school, usually play by kicking balls around, or maybe using the exercise equipment over there in that sandy area," she points at a location with swings and jungle gym bars.

Malafay and her sisters surveyed the playground area, unable to properly comment on what they had seen so far in the classrooms, with so many children quietly and attentively studying their lessons. Unlike in Drow society, there was no shouting and no whipping for asking too many questions. The children were happy and content, willingly taking their lessons from teachers who were polite and supportive. It seemed unreal, as if there was something wrong with the scenario. Now they looked out onto a large playground area with several large groups of children clearly engaged in an activity that seemed as alien to the Drow as the word 'play' itself. There was laughter, cheering, and shouts to direct the flow of the activity by teachers playing referee. In the sandbox, children were seen in open conversation, sharing personal stories and experiences as they played on the swings and bars.

Malafay gazed at it quietly, as did Rhyliira. Felynquiri reflected on her own childhood, which wasn't very long ago in her case, and felt a tear rolling down her face.

"I never had anything like this," she moans wistfully.

"None of us did," Rhyliira replies. "We can't even share ourselves with our own sisters, to say nothing of the, um…males," she glances tenderly at Jhandril, who stood stoically to one side.

"And you say this is only one part of your school system?" Malafay inquires. "What of the others? These appear as young children here."

"Aye," Relissa nods. "The different races mature at different rates, depending on what sort of lifespans they have and how quickly they grow up. These are the younger human children, since they make a good example. Now, I'll show you the senior youth academy for the older kids. It's across the way in another section."

Relissa now leads them out of the current compound of what was known locally as the junior youth academy, which involved the first seven years of childhood study, beginning at age four years for humans, and rising through their tenth year. The next section was the senior compound for the older generation.

"Here we are," Relissa directs. "This here is for age eleven up to seventeen, seven more years, and again for humans as they tend to grow faster than us elves. The elven school is elsewhere, as they need to calibrate the lessons to stretch over a longer time period."

"Interesting," Malafay considers. "So, you need to segregate them, if only for the vast differences in maturity rates."

"It's almost necessary. If you put elven kids in the same class, they would finish their lessons long before they could grow up and join a proper workforce, and you need to be a legal adult for that."

"How old is that?"

"In the case of humans, we currently set that at eighteen years when they are psychologically old enough to make their own responsible decisions. Physically, they might have another year or two, but by this time, they are wise enough to know better."

"Interesting. And for the elves?"

"Elves get it at seventy-five. By that time, we're mostly grown up physically, and even though we have a cultural habit to wait for that first century before we feel ourselves ready for any really big decisions, like marriage, children, and family, we're declared for that same level of, um…are you girls alright?"

Malafay and her two sisters were gaping at their host with shocked expressions and eyes bulging. Jhandril glared at both Relissa and his sisters, although more at the sisters for this point, and their reactions.

"A century?" Rhyliira wheezes. "You wait a full century before having children? Why so long?"

"Not simply to HAVE them, Rhyliira," Malafay notes. "That was simply before they feel ready even to make a decision on it."

"But Malafay! How old do you need to be before you're ready to have one, let alone to make the decision on it! I mean, look at you. Sure, you don't have any, but this is who we are. Only the Matron Mother is really permitted to bear any children in our House…or any House. How old was she when Alakaere was born?"

"Um, well, Alakaere is one hundred thirty-four, with Alyraema at one hundred twenty-two, and the Matron Mother is two hundred forty-six."

"Those aren't bad numbers," Relissa admits.

"Yes, but we need to consider what came before, as none of the daughters are permitted children in any of the greater Houses. The Matron Mother is the main body to govern the House, and everyone falls under her rule, HER children, no one else's. And this also leads us to the succession of her position, where…um…"

"Right, I know the deal. When she falters even a wee bit, bam, there goes her next-in-line, meaning the first daughter, with that famous knife in the back to take over. And this is sometimes followed by whoever is the second after that. Do any of you ever go long enough to see how long you actually live by natural means? My understanding is, you peeps might only last a few centuries before you kill each other."

As Jhandril reflects on this statement, he lowers his head in remembrance. He turns away, hoping not to be noticed, but Relissa's quick eyes see him anyway.

"Uh huh, you look like you have a story to tell."

Malafay turns to see him hiding his face.

"What happened, Jhandril?"

"My father… He was one of those."

"Who did it?"

"Her. I was the first born by his loins. Alakaere came second after me. Alyraema was third. But he fell out of favor with her after that. I was still young. I heard there was an argument of some kind, although I don't really know the reasoning, not that it probably matters. Next thing you know, he's taken away somewhere and tortured, then executed on the altar at the temple. I learned of this from one of the other men serving the house security alongside him."

"I, uh… I'm…sorry, Jhandril. I don't know how or why I'm saying that, but it just seems to want to come out now. Anyway, the Matron Mother didn't become Matron Mother without the removal of HER mother, or maybe an elder sister who did it… I don't know. No one ever speaks of it, and this was likely due to some trick she played to take the House seat. The rest of us would come after that."

"Uh huh…" Relissa shakes her head. "Jiggers, such a way to treat your family."

"What about your people? How does it work for you? Do you have Houses like ours and something like a Matron Mother?"

"No, not in ours. None of the elven societies up here do it that way. People meet each other, fall in love, get married, have kids, and they live long and usually happy lives together. We elves have a tendency to mate for life, and barring anything really bad happening, that's how it usually goes."

"And how long is that life, just for comparison?"

"Well, my Mum and Dah are still married after, oh…let me see. I came a bit late in her life, but I think they got married when she was just over a century, he a little more, and that was close to five centuries ago."

"WHAT?!" she screeches. "Five…five…"

She begins examining her fingers, just to make sure she understood the count.

"…And already a century even before that… SIX CENTURIES OLD?!" she screams.

Rhyliira and Felynquiri were both stunned and gasping at the figure. It represented a phenomenal amount of time as compared to any of their native experiences.

"And how old are you?" Malafay asks tenuously.

"I'm one hundred eighty-two by now," Relissa shrugs.

"That's…that's…that's…impossible! You look younger than me! How can that be?"

"Well, if I look younger, the only thing I can say is we live longer than you by some amount. Also, maybe if you involve magic, we tend to live longer when we practice magic on a regular basis. It has a kind of cleansing effect to add years onto you. And I've been doing it for nearly a century by now, so it might show a wee bit. But on the other side of it, we probably live longer anyway, if only because we don't go around killing each other as a habit and cutting ourselves short. As the result, we evolved, whereas you didn't. You might better represent where we were once upon a time back in the day when you first separated away from us. If given the chance, you might only go four or so if you're lucky."

"Wonderful. So that...witch..." she growls, "...not only denied us to learn anything new, but she also held us back from any form of natural growth."

"Malafay..." Rhyliira intones warily. "Your words, please."

"Rhyliira, my words are the least of the things to worry about. All right, Relissa, what else can you show us?"

"Let's take a wee peek around here first before moving on. You need to know something about a school like this."

"But this is a human school. How would this relate to people like us?"

"Basically the same, just stretch the numbers a bit. Over here, I think..."

Relissa leads them to a section of the classrooms where they have study labs. Malafay and the others peeked in windows and doors to check the lessons, not that most of it held any meaning to them on such a cursory observation, but it was clear this was a section of hands-on study in a laboratory environment practicing something. They eventually came upon one classroom where Relissa had them quietly peek inside. In this room, Malafay and the others saw what could possibly be described as the last thing they would expect to see children studying. They observed children in study conjuring up small cantrips, like balls of light and simple evocations of magic. Rhyliira gasped and rolled back against the wall as she pulled out of the doorway.

"Malafay, we're in big trouble. They teach their CHILDREN how to do it, and those look like they're still quite young."

"How old..." Malafay wheezes.

"These are twelve years old," Relissa notes. "Old enough to learn the very beginnings of what it is and how it works, plus a few simple, and otherwise harmless ways to use it, if only for the practice. This is the First Circle of mage craft here, out of a total of nine as you move into the adult courses."

"Are you saying this is all part of a standard educational course you give to everyone here?"

"The First and Second Circles are mandatory in the senior academy here. The Second Circle is at age fifteen. After that, you finish up here and go to a higher school, either a university or a technical academy for the others. Most people take at least some of it, likely due to a professional requirement, or simply to keep up with the general flow of society. This goes to Circle Six as a civilian study. Then we have Seven, Eight, and Nine as either an advanced civilian course, maybe for the higher, more technical professional applications, or for military use."

"Military, like you, perhaps?"

"I'm studied up to Circle Seven, which is where I need to be if I want to be fully functional as a scout."

"By the Sss..." she slaps a hand over her mouth as she cuts herself off abruptly. "No, I'm not going to call her name for this one. By... whatever gods are up there... Simply to be functional as a scout, you need seven of these Circles? Why?"

"To mark portal indexes and then use them. You need to be a Circle Seven mage to mark one in our training schedule."

"What does this mean for anything other than that?" Felynquiri asks. "I mean, surely they must teach more than just that if we're speaking of a full course of some kind, right?"

"Aye, I'm trained in elemental magic as a general study. Fireballs, lightning, ice showers, and so on."

"So, even as a scout, and forgive me for these words, but a lowly scout, as we might see it, we wouldn't want to see YOU up there outside that tunnel on any of our raids."

"You got that right!" she smiles brightly. "I could go invisible, and then hit YOU in the back. And if it was a properly arranged troupe, with mages and priests involved, the frontline warriors would be the least of your troubles."

"Thank you, but I think I would rather not."

"Good. But now, let's move on. I want to show you how our society has evolved our industry to produce things, so you don't get any funny ideas that you can just come in every now and then to hit something, then run away and come back later thinking you can hit it again to keep it in place, so it doesn't ever grow enough to bother you."

"All right, I believe I understand your meaning," Malafay nods.

◆◆◆◆◆

"Thaelyn... Are you busy...?"

The rasping voice ushered through the door of Thaelyn's office as he was reviewing several accounting papers. He quickly looks up to see a tall female peeking inside, adorned entirely in silver hues. She was slender, with long silver hair, silver skin, a silver gown, and silver catlike eyes.

"Adalon! Come in!"

He jumps out of his chair and steps forward to greet her, taking a hand and bending down to touch it with his forehead.

"Thaelyn... Why do you persssist... In demonssstrating... Sssuch reverence to me? I have never actually requesssted... And certainly do not demand... Sssuch a posture."

"Perhaps I simply want to annoy you with a level of admiration above and beyond any you would otherwise ask for."

"Uh huh... Sssuch a man. If only I could have found... One sssuch as you... During my early daysss... Back home. But anyway... I wish to relay... A few tender thoughtsss."

"Very good, and what thoughts are those?"

"They relate to Lolth."

"Oh dear. Very well then. Do we have any new information on her?"

"Nothing ssspecific... But she is a viciousss one... And not to be trusssted. According to Thaliel... There are no outward... Indicationsss... Of activity. But thisss only sssuggests... She is lying in wait... And thisss may be... To ssstage her act... Once a reaction occursss... Within the Drow sssociety. Once these initial... Diplomatic meetingsss... Are complete... We should be ready... For the repercussionsss. Thaliel and I both agree... Lolth might use... A sssscorched-earth policy... To deny the Drow... To return to the ssSeldarine."

"Indeed, we suspected something like this once. I have been trying to relay some careful instructions to our operatives on how to handle this, but in the case of a member of the Estelar being our foe, it becomes problematic, as they can peer into places not otherwise welcome."

"Yesss... Thisss can be... Problematic. We may alssso need... To be ready... To move quickly... If and when the time occursss... That we mussst act. We should keep… A large contingent of troopsss… On alert… With portalsss on hand… Ready to deploy… At a moment'sss notice."

"Of course. Very well. Do you think you will become personally involved in any of this?"

"I sssuspect I might… If she will not vacate her possst… Voluntarily. But I alssso sssuspect… She will have attendantsss… Of sssome sssort… To contend with… Alongssside her. For thissss… I may need… Reinforcementsss."

"Naturally."

Adalon bows her head and turns to leave. Thaelyn watches her depart and mulls several thoughts about his following actions. He rolls his eyes around the room, silently asking himself if anyone of the higher echelons could be watching them even now through their viewing pools. So, he casually returns to his desk and sits down. He picks up one of the reports and holds it as if he were intently studying the details. But rather than paying attention to the report, he had something else in mind. He brings up a hand to his temple and discreetly begins to apply his telepathic skills.

"Nemelle, I need to speak to you."

In her office, she senses his words echoing in her mind, and redirects herself to respond.

"Yes, Thaelyn, I am here. What do you need?"

"I just had a visit from Adalon. She reveals that she and her servants are concerned over Lolth's lack of response thus far, that it could be a wait-and-see delay tactic, only to respond once there is a reaction amongst the Drow proper, and it could be bad."

"As bad as we were suggesting once, to destroy them rather than release them?"

"Possibly. Therefore, I am going to place some of our people on alert standby for a rapid defensive move, if need be. But we might also need an information feed from the other side in the event we miss something from ours."

"I see. Very well, I am aware we have had a number of meetings already in several of their cities, and there is one taking place just now, which I am very hopeful of. Relissa is handling that one for us."

"Really! And who is it she is interviewing?"

"A representative from a noble House within the local city council."

"Ah, wait, could this be one she met recently?"

"Likely so. She called in a short while ago to report an arrival, and she was going out to investigate."

"Most excellent, I wish her well. This would also be a good example of an inside feed. I wonder if we could use them as a set of extra eyes for us. Being on their council, this would serve us well."

"I could give her a call to get an update, and then maybe see about providing something."

"Yes, do this, and if we feel confident in our position, let us take full advantage of it."

"Very well, I will let you know of the result."

They finish their link and Thaelyn continues pretending to read his report, just in case he still had eyes on him from above.

Nemelle pulls out her shard-com and brings up the text message interface, which was a bit more discreet than simply speaking. She begins typing in a line to Relissa's number using a custom encrypted language.

"Core here. Agent engaged?"

She waits for the response.

"Agent engaged."

She begins passing her instructions across, carrying an indirect conversation to her contact.

"Conditional instructions. Need inside link. Security critical."
   "Specify cause for inside link."
"Power response. Denial of release. Need local advisory."
   "Method of advisory?"
"Suggest comm tech, conditional of subject value."
   "Understood. Anything else?"
"Negative. Resume engagement."

They end the link and Nemelle puts her unit away, then returns to her work pretending nothing special had just happened.

On Relissa's side, Malafay and her group were intently studying the strange device she was playing with, and the odd form of communication taking place. The local language was lost to them, but clearly there was something happening, and it looked like she was writing very short notes to someone. When she was finished, Relissa also put her unit away. However, Malafay felt a need to inquire about it.

"Um, what were you just doing?"

"We have a little problem of being watched by you-know-who out here. If she pays close enough attention to her pets, she's probably aware of you being outside."

"Oh no! Dammit! Yes, it would be just like her, too."

"Malafay," Rhyliira moans. "This could be very bad for us. If she has any knowledge of it, simply going home..."

"Yes, and the Matron Mother would be the first to know."

"We have a couple of possibilities here," Relissa mentions. "We've tried to analyze this already, hoping to anticipate a few things. If she's paying attention to anything at all, we might see something already down below, simply to our stories. Some of us think she's playing a waiting game to see how it goes, which could give us time, but not necessarily as a good thing. She might be planning on something for later. Now, if this includes waiting for someone like you to go home before popping in on you, this is bad. But it might also wait for you to actually report in to see the reaction of your Matron Mother. Knowing the old girl as we do, she might wait for it to hit your whole family before she hits back."

"Oh please, not that," Malafay begs. "We've seen what happens to a House that disobeys the, um...her. I don't want that for our House."

"Right, and neither do we. Therefore, this little message I just got. We have to use some careful language here, so we don't relay our full meaning out in the open, but an idea was passed along, where maybe you can offer some help in this area."

"Us? How?"

"We might need eyes down there to tell us of anything wicked going on. You could serve this on your side."

"Um, all right, I suppose I could, but then what?"

"Let's finish up what we're doing, and then we'll go back to my office and talk shop. Now, back to this here..." she turns to face a sprawling industrial megacomplex.

Relissa had delivered the group via a local gateway transit to a huge industrial center. It involved several large manufacturing complexes all centered around a packaging and routing hub in the middle. The routing hub used a cargo delivery portal network to send shipments of goods to regional terminals, where they might be sorted and forwarded to cities and their local mercantile venues. It might function in some ways like a shipping port, or a trucking delivery network, but with some portion of it using portals for long distance delivery, rather than the ships and trucks, which may only be used for local routing.

Aside from the enormity of the manufacturing complex itself, the simple fact of using a portal gateway network to move things around, rather than walking or using wagons to travel, was in itself miraculous to Malafay and her kin.

They entered inside and found their way up to a visitor's booth with a balcony overlooking the expansive factory floor which stretched out of sight. They saw hundreds of workers at computerized stations, and rows of fully automated assembly lines transporting raw materials in rapid succession through stations that processed and packaged them into finished goods. She continued leading them through the facility to the shipping hub, where the final product, which was neatly boxed up and ready to go, would be bundled with other packages going out to the same destination, and then sent through a portal and out of sight.

"And that goes to wherever it needs to be," Relissa explains. "Depending on who ordered it and where in the world they're located."

"I swear!" Malafay gasps. "And how many of these go out in a single day? For as many as we saw rushing through that place, just how many people need things around here?"

"This world alone has billions of people on it. And they use up a lot of food and other things along the way. We might see a place like this that makes thousands of products an hour, simply to keep up, and this is just one out of I-don't-know-how-many to produce everything you might see in our shops and markets around the world, which is our next stop, by the way, to let you know how prosperous we actually are and what we consider fashion around here. But just for the sake of asking, how do you do it? Not that I actually need to know, but simply to bring it up."

"Uh huh, sure..." Rhyliira moans. "We may have a shop with a craftsman, who may have a few apprentices, and they hammer... And hammer... And hammer... And hammer..." her voice trails off.

"Yeah," she giggles. "As I thought. All right, let's go."

Relissa leads them back to the local gateway terminal and requests routing to bring them to the capital city of Bya'an Tamoranth. Here she would follow the local city gateway network to a downtown district and one of their larger shopping malls.

"Now listen up," she declares as they move through the downtown terminal hub. "First, you need to know, we have cities big and small, like most people. You down there don't tend to spread out much, probably because there's nowhere for you to go, so you cluster in tight spots and wall yourselves in."

"Yes," Malafay nods. "And one thing I've noticed is you have a lot of open space up here, and with no real walls holding you back."

"We try to limit how much we use so we can leave a fair bit for the native wildlife. After all, they need space too. But also, I've been showing you a few of the larger examples of things, if only to show you how high up something can go. There are smaller ones out there too, but if all you see are small things, what good is it for you to know how far we've actually come in this time."

"Of course, I understand."

"We have a lot of people moving around here…" Felynquiri notes as she studies a steady stream of pedestrian traffic passing through the hub and outside the windows looking onto the street.

Malafay takes a moment to realize this place was exceptionally busy, far more so than anything she ever saw back home, even in the best of times, like for festivals at the temple. Many of the onlookers were staring at the visitors as they passed by, taking special note of their unusual coloring, which was noticeably different from the more familiar Night Elves they had come to know in this time. Also, the archaic style of clothing tended to stand out, causing some to wonder if they were part of an acting troupe on their way to a stage play or something.

As for Malafay and the others, the local people also appeared strange for their clothing styles. There was everything from business suits to casual wear, and being summertime, there were many who wore short pants and T-shirts, which to the Drow was almost scandalous for the revealing nature.

Relissa now waves for them to follow her outside, knowing this would probably be one of the biggest shocks, as the city was a large metropolis, and far bigger than any Drow city.

They ventured outside into the bright sunshine, which had been getting on Malafay's skin by now, as her body was simply not accustomed to having actual sunshine beaming down on it. None of them were. But as they exited the terminal building, they halted in their tracks as they tried angling their gaze upwards to find the tops of the nearby skyscrapers.

"In the name of all that is holy..." Felynquiri wheezes. "What is THAT thing? How in all the nine hells can you even reach that high to build such a thing, let alone see that it doesn't topple over onto you!"

"Do people actually live in there?" Rhyliira wonders openly. "And how do they climb up there to get inside of it. The stairs must be enormous."

"Not unless they use more portals."

"And then what? Are those windows? No! There is no way you're getting me inside there if I have to look out of one of those."

"But what is it made of? I mean, I see what must be windows, like we've seen in those other places...glass, right? But it's all the way up? A full building made of glass? Is it truly so strong?"

"Girls, calm down a bit," Relissa soothes. "First, the glass is only on the outside so people can enjoy the view. And yes, they do like the view up there. That's an office building, probably for a lot of business professionals. We have lifts that run up and down inside, taking people to different floors, so walking really isn't the issue. And the structural framework of the building is based on steel, also concrete in a lot of areas."

"Steel!" Malafay shouts. "Wait a minute! You use steel on something like THAT? By the...you-know-who, how can you possibly make so much steel as to afford to use it in something that big?"

"Our industry is much more advanced, like what you saw before. Making steel, once upon a day, might have been a specialty thing that only a handful of peeps could do in small batches, and only for those with the coin to pay for it, but those days are gone now. The formula for making steel is old business for us, and it's a major industry that runs big now, with countless tons of it pumping out every day. We use steel for most anything that needs metal for the construction work. Simple iron isn't good enough, and stone is mostly for show these days, if you want a little artistic appeal on the outside."

"Countless tons. I don't believe it..." she emits as she again examines the tall building across the street from her.

Relissa then directs them to walk along the avenue towards a major city shopping mall. The multistory building was as broad as the skyscrapers were tall, and the display windows sported a myriad of current fashion selections arranged on mannequins, along with signs and advertisement posters. They stepped inside the doors and began walking along a central lane between rows of shops.

"Well…" Rhyliira concedes. "Here's where all that massive industry goes. If this is just one of them, in one city, and with all this, it would take a massive industry complex just to fill it and keep it that way."

"And with all those people outside buying it up," Felynquiri muses. "You must also have a massive source for the original materials, like farms or something. And again, like she said, large or small, it's everywhere, covering at least a good portion of all that open land out there to support billions of people living up here."

"This is unbelievable," Malafay shakes her head. "And look at us, all huddled in a hole in the ground. Yes, she was right, it's a grave. It certainly is small enough for one."

"And primitive, too," Rhyliira adds. "I was noticing a lot of those people back there staring at us like we were oddities. We probably are to them. We might belong in a historical archive by now."

"How do you suppose the Matron Mother would react to this?" Felynquiri asks. "Not counting the, um…her getting involved, just the Matron Mother. We're collecting these portraits to take home, although we still need them in a form we can carry, but how do you explain all this to someone who never saw such a thing, and has no way to understand it unless she is there to see it personally, like us?"

"I don't know," Malafay admits. "But it has to be done. Either that, or bring her up to see it herself, if she might ever come outside at all. She doesn't go anywhere outside the House except to the Council Hall for the occasional meeting. That, and the temple for their special festivals."

"That leaves us at a bad disadvantage. We are in a place we're probably not supposed to be, doing something we're probably not supposed to be doing, and hoping to bring it back to her so SHE can do something she REALLY shouldn't be doing. Ugh, my head is starting to hurt."

"And that's just the beginning," Rhyliira offers. "We still have the rest of the city…our city…and then everything else out there. This is going to be a battle, and it won't be pretty."

Relissa continues her tour of the shopping mall, or at least enough of it to gain an impression of the scale and clearly prosperous nature of life in the city. There was an ultimate direction to this program, and she had to build up a picture to explain it.

She then brought them to another tourist site, which was a tall needle-like skyscraper with an observation deck to look down and out across the city. This would afford them a better perspective of what one of THEIR cities might look like, as opposed to an average Drow city, simply to understand the scale of it. This too would hold meaning, once the tour was complete, and Relissa summed it up at the end.

Finally, Relissa brought them up to the front gates of the guildhall fortress for the famed Order of Tyr, the military body Thaelyn once created to bring it all together.

"And so…" Malafay muses. "This is where it all started. This one building, and then everything else built up around it?"

"Aye," she states. "Everything has a starting point, and this was it for Thaelyn and his young kingdom. Between this here for his military, and that down there for his religion…" she points at the large temple building down the road, "…this is where the people learned the meaning of true prosperity and peace. We solved every problem this world had to offer, up here at least, and even ventured out to other worlds, and helped them. But now, we have this one last piece, and it's you down there."

"I see, but let me ask you one thing. Why has it taken so long for you to find your way around to us? Is it only due to those damnable tunnels changing direction so often? If you can use portals, I would think you could bypass that a long time ago."

"True, we could. But it's not limited to that. Your society being as it is, your goddess being as she is, and what was necessary to correct THAT, slowed things down. We don't think she would let go of you without a fight. So, one thing that slowed us down was to make sure we had a good enough plan to fight a goddess in front of a lot of peeps who wouldn't know the difference between why we're fighting her and NOT the rest of you. We would find ourselves between two forces: One to fight for, and the other to fight against, with both of them hostile to us, and yet keeping people alive along the way. This is a liberation war we're speaking of here."

"That could be a problem," Rhyliira nods. "If you are fighting FOR us, but we are fighting AGAINST you, due to our devotion to our faith, you need to subdue that without actually killing us. That would be a bit difficult, I think. How would you do that?"

"We have a number of methods, some magical, others technological, to apply nonlethal forms of attack to stun peeps without killing them. Then, if it becomes necessary, we just take a lot of prisoners and hold them long enough to talk some sense into them."

"Assuming they would listen."

"This could be where those stories in the streets come in," Felynquiri mentions. "Soften them up with a few words so the rest sink in better."

"Yes," she admits. "But there are still going to be a lot of people who will not listen. And even those who might listen to those words might still find themselves on the wrong side if they do not realize who is speaking those words and why."

"Sister Malafay," Jhandril begins. "As the first son of the House, I feel it is my duty to offer a few words on the side of the defense of our House from any or all of that."

"Yes, Jhandril," she responds. "What do you have to say?"

"During this time, and with what has been said so far, my mind is circling around what we will expect to find once we return home. Will we simply be able to return home without incident, or will there be something waiting for us?"

"Yes, I must agree. I am also thinking of this."

"Next, if we assume we can return home, then to report what we saw, what will come to us AFTER that, as I'm sure the goddess will hear of it somewhere along the way, if she is not actually watching us at this moment."

"This is also true."

"And finally, how do we protect ourselves, if this is supposed to be a form of liberation against that."

"Naturally. And this also brings to my mind a few of my own questions, which I might wish to learn about as for what comes after even that much. Relissa, you have shown us many things, so let us speculate on a few items. First, if we make an assumption where you are successful in…liberating…us from our former lives. Where do we, as a society, go from there? What will your people actually do with us?"

"We will assimilate you as part of our own. Everything you see out here, everything I've shown you and talked about, will become as much a part of you as it is a part of us. You will be one with us again. And we will all go forward as a single united society into a future we can only begin to imagine."

"You certainly like to speak in big words," Rhyliira mutters.

"What is that out there if not something big," Relissa waves at the city skyline. "What is that industry, that shopping mall, those schools. We're not a bunch of tiny little villages with a mere dotting of farmers and a handful of guardsmen who can barely hold a sword. We're a civilization. And we're united, not a bunch of nations, or even city-states, that don't talk to each other enough to share ideas, much less cooperate to solve problems. We're a society with a philosophy to solve those problems at whatever cost, and we don't take no for an answer. Because the end result is to promote a lifestyle with so many greater benefits, the cost of doing it pales in comparison. What we made, we made for a reason, and that reason was defined for us by Maker Kuroku. We're a guardian society. This becomes our purpose in life."

"That grander plan of hers to refurbish this world?" Malafay wonders.

"Aye! We had to solve our local issues so there would be nothing to stand in our way of solving the same for others. The Measure of Balance is about the prosperity of life, that it must survive, grow, prosper, and maybe, with a bit of luck and a lot of hard work, it might one day find itself on the doorstep of godhood, just like so many others have done before, and like the Estelar did once to reach where they are now. This is where it leads. So, fighting each other isn't productive, and right now, you're in the way of that. Here we have two choices: Carry you along, or push you out. Which do you prefer?"

"Ouch!" Rhyliira winces. "I'm sorry for mentioning it. All right, if this is how you see it, I would certainly not wish to be pushed out. But this simply brings us back to the issue of protection if our goddess has in mind to fight against it. How would you do this? If to bring a military body into our city, for protection or otherwise, you would likely start a war simply for standing there."

Relissa nods silently as she realizes this is one of the known hazards of their work. But before she could respond, Malafay spoke up again.

"Who is in the position of authority of this project of yours?" she asks. "Maybe if we could speak to that one, we could come to a better understanding. Because Rhyliira is right. If we go home with any part of this, and regardless of whether something is waiting for us, as Jhandril mentioned, we will be opening ourselves up to retribution, if from no one else than by the First House. Do you know what happens to a House if the whole family falls out of favor with them or our goddess?"

"Aye, we do," Relissa affirms. "We've heard of this before. They call up a bunch of demons to ravage the place. All right, let's try it this way. I'm already under advisement to give you one of our shard-coms as a link to call in for help, just in case of something like this. But I suppose you do also carry a point, if that call is only as the result of hearing them busting down your doors."

"Yes, and that help of yours might come too late, even with your portals."

"Let's go speak to someone. Maybe she can help with this part."

Relissa waves them to follow inside the guildhall courtyard. On entering, the first thing the Drow visitors see is a large statue of two figures, a male knight kneeling in a thoughtful repose with his greatsword held in front of him, and a female who appeared almost priestly standing over his shoulder and pointing off in the distance. And while he appeared human, she was clearly elven, and bore wings on her back. The visitors stopped and gazed at it.

"Who are these two?" Malafay wonders softly.

"That's our Lord and Lady," Relissa replies. "Thaelyn, and his wife, Aerlie."

"Wait a moment!" Felynquiri blasts. "He looks human, like all those we saw out there on the street. But she's...well, I'm not sure what she is, with those wings of hers."

"I think I do," Malafay intones cautiously. "But this is at least as much a legend as anything I would expect to be true. They were once known as the Winged Folk...Arilerea, correct?"

"In the old tongue, yes," Relissa nods. "They're known commonly as Avariel elves, and part of our mother race, the Tel'Quessir. And yes, he's human, and yes, they ARE husband and wife. Humans and elves sometimes do that around here, although their lifespans are a bit out of kilter for a proper match-up. But still, they try."

"Why?" Rhyliira rasps feebly.

"It's called love, something you peeps should try one day. You might find fewer knives coming at you."

"Oh, thank you! Another joke?"

"She does that a lot," Felynquiri groans delicately. "But I suppose there is a lesson to be learned by it, as well. For all their prosperity, they laugh at our lack of the same."

"Yes, and we are seeing a lot of that today."

"In this case, however," Relissa continues. "Both of these are Celestials, and both installed by Maker Kuroku to lead the rest of us."

Relissa brings them further inside, now coursing her way through the halls to an office deeper within. They arrive at a door, but as Relissa prepares to knock, Malafay feels a strange sense of discomfort, leaving her feeling mysteriously ill at ease. She frowns at the unusual sensation, which suddenly erupted as they approached the door. She pauses to study the surroundings.

"Do any of you feel that?" she ponders distantly.

"Feel what?" Rhyliira responds. "I've been feeling a lot of things since arriving up here today."

"No, this is new, and sudden, just now as we came through the hall...up to this door."

"I can't be sure what you mean, Malafay," Felynquiri offers. "I'm probably too disturbed by everything else so far to feel anything new."

Relissa observes them, and although she felt subtly aware of what it might be, there was nowhere else to go but forward if they wanted a meeting with the director of this operation. So, she knocks on the door as she peeks inside.

"Cardinal Nemelle, are you available?"

She opens the door and calls the group to step inside. But as Malafay and the others come into view, there to see a strangely dark female rising up from her desk, a flood of conflicting spiritual energies rushes through them, causing them to cringe and fall back against a nearby wall.

The Drow visitors clutched at themselves, slapping their hands to their temples, and moaning as they tried in vain to stand upright in a shower of empathic sensations that bathed them in unfamiliar psychic emanations.

"Well now..." Nemelle coos. "What do we have here? Visitors, perhaps?"

"Nemelle!" Relissa teases. "Are you playing cat and mouse with them?"

"Perhaps only a little, but they will no doubt feel my polarity regardless. They radiate with the negative energies of the Malevolent One, so it is unavoidable."

"Aye, maybe so. But I think you're making it a wee bit worse for the wear."

"Very well, I will withdraw somewhat. I could feel their approach even from outside. This one, in particular," she points at Malafay. "She is perhaps the strongest. The others are still young."

"What are you?" Malafay wheezes. "And how are you doing this?"

"Calmly now, Daughter of a Noble House. My name is Cardinal Nemelle, formerly an adherent of the Guild of Sensations in the city of Sigil. But I doubt those words would hold meaning to you. I am a highly capable empath, meaning my mind is potent enough to feel, as well as to emit the sensations of empathy, emotions, and psychic influence upon other minds near me. But aside from that, I am an Eladrin, which is an ascended form of an elf beyond the mortal realm."

"A Celestial?" Felynquiri gasps. "You're one of them? And YOU are the one leading this campaign to liberate us?"

"My mother was a Drow, not unlike you. But she was betrayed by her House's Matron Mother due to a dispute they shared. The story she told me once described how she was tormented, and then given as a sacrifice to a baatezu her mother conjured up in exchange for some item. That creature, however, found little use for a frail mortal, so he sold her into slavery to a cult of illithids."

"Illithids!" Malafay ushers sternly. "I know that word. They are a devilish group of creatures. Some call them mind flayers."

"Indeed! And they most certainly live up to that name. But this group was later assaulted by a band of githzerai, who are their natural enemies. The githzerai liberated a number of slaves, including my mother. But without any firm solution as to their disposition, they were delivered unto others for caretaking. My mother was given over to the Seldarine, and the personal care of Corellon Larethian, their leader. He applied himself to rehabilitate her, until one day he bestowed upon her a special blessing of a child. And that child became me."

Felynquiri felt faint as she listened. She was still leaning against the wall when she felt herself compelled to speak.

"You? From him? And then her? Together?"

"He is my Father, yes. Therefore, I am a Celestial. And I have long desired to see the end of this fallacy of our people defiled by that wretch of a Power, and I use that term loosely, who would dare offend my Father and the others for stealing our people away."

"Uh oh…that sounds bad. And worse, coming from someone like you. Malafay, we have a problem, a big one. And I don't know who is the worse for it."

"I agree," Rhyliira winces. "We are trapped in a bad place, Malafay. If we have a Celestial directly on the other side of it, along with her Father, a member of these other gods, and then everything else we saw outside being governed by even more Celestials… This world has become a very dangerous place for people like us."

"Or at least for HER," Malafay concludes. "Yes, um, you said you are a Cardinal…whatever that is. We need to understand how this will play out and ask for a safeguard. We were speaking outside on this. If we should go home with any part of this, it is likely our goddess will learn of it, either directly if she is watching us, or indirectly through someone else. If you are aware of what happens when a House falls out of favor, we will need protection from that. Otherwise, I fear you will not win your redemption of our people. Not before someone else gets there first."

"Relissa," Nemelle asks. "Have you granted them one of our shard-coms yet?"

"Not yet," she responds. "We were on our way up to it when this came out, and I think she may hold a point. If we put guards on the street, it'll probably start a war with everyone else. But if we only wait for their call, by the time we get guards on the street, their House might be a smoldering heap. We need a compromise."

"Very well, I suppose this does hold merit. It must be immediate, but not as overt as to stir up the remainder of the city with our people inciting something we are not ready for. Not until we hit our threshold. This might also serve as a template for the rest."

Nemelle began circling around the room in deep thought. If it could not involve any of the local forces, it had to be from another source. But the only other source she could think of had to be something to directly counter the offending one.

"But of course," she mumbles coyly. "Ooh, that would be a vicious rub. I have an idea. And this might further provide an additional effect for us. Follow me."

Now Nemelle leads the group, first leaving the office and continuing out of the building back into the courtyard. She takes them out of the guildhall and down the hill to an intersecting boulevard, then turning towards the large temple building.

Rhyliira gazes at her younger sister, and then both of then turn to examine Malafay, as they all began to realize where they were going.

"Malafay," she whispers. "Are you sure you don't want to just stay up here? Maybe we could find a little place to live, something simple and quiet...um..."

"While the idea intrigues me," Malafay considers. "I think it would not work as simply as that."

They arrived at the front entrance to the large building, and Nemelle brings them inside. The interior of this temple was notably different from the design of their own back home, where the Drow mostly followed one primary deity, and the architecture was largely designed around things like spiders, spindly columns, spiders, cobwebs, spiders, burning pits…and oh yeah, spiders.

In contrast, this temple was ornate, with stained glass windows, a tall cathedral ceiling, marble pillars, and the atmosphere was light and airy, uplifting to the spirit. It was as alien to them as everything else so far, and up on the platform in front was a wide array of statues and icons depicting a great many deities for all the different races.

Nemelle strolls along the central aisle up to the platform in front, with her nervous entourage following loosely behind. There were several groups of people currently in attendance of a minor service, but on seeing the strange visitors, many turned their gaze to stare at them. Once again, Rhyliira and the others could feel their eyes watching them.

When they arrived near the altar, one of the elder priests came forward, and to Malafay's surprise, much like with her sisters and Jhandril, he was male.

"Cardinal Nemelle, so good to see you here," he smiles. "And you bring guests? How curious. And they do look a bit out of place in this setting. What is the special occasion?"

"We have a potential problem which might need addressing in our campaign to give aid to our fellows down below. Is Aerlie available?"

"I suspect, unless she is asleep, she likely already knows you are here…"

He turned towards the rear of the platform where they saw a door to one side. And through that door was emerging a graceful, winged figure.

Malafay and the others gaped at the image of the same woman they saw in the statue up at the guildhall. She briskly turns to her sisters.

"Show your proper manners, sisters. You too, Jhandril. If this is their Queen, we need to offer our respect."

Aerlie was arriving with the group just as Nemelle was finishing with the priest.

"Aerlie," Nemelle smiles. "We have a special need taking place here."

Malafay studies the interaction. The name was certainly that one representing their Queen, but Nemelle's presentation was more like a close relation than a subject under someone else's rule. She turned to glare perplexedly at the others in her group.

"Oh?" Aerlie muses jovially. "And what sort is that? Are we already trying to redeem someone?"

"It may be necessary to establish a few placeholders for us. Relissa was escorting this group, and they were just finishing up when a rather important concern came into play. As you know, this plan of ours is delicate, and we are working on two sides of a difficult situation, where neither of them will be friendly to our cause. If this group here should return home, and I would imagine this would be the same for any of them, carrying the sort of knowledge they have acquired thus far, and worse, we have examples of a ranking House within their city political circle, it will likely backfire with retaliation, either directly by their chosen Power, or one of the higher Houses taking this on her behalf."

"Indeed, this would certainly be a problem. We would need to offer something like a bodyguard layer to keep them until we could move forward."

"Precisely, but simply deploying guards in the area would stir up too much of a disturbance on their streets. Therefore, it needs to be something that is quickly applied, and secure enough to safeguard them. And I had an idea."

"All right, and what is that?"

"A little counter divine aid."

"Oh, Nemelle, that's not nice…" she giggles boldly. "How do you see this applied?"

"We introduce them to my Father. After all, he is not called the Protector for nothing," she smirks.

"Oh jiggers…" Relissa closes her eyes and shakes her head.

Aerlie cocks her head and smiles, then sets her hands on her hips and briskly flutters her wings.

Malafay and the others watched with at least as much curiosity as dread for the implications. She studied the faces of her younger sisters, and they both shared the sentiment.

Aerlie peered over her shoulder at the row of icons for the Seldarine along the rear wall. She then passed a quick glance at the group as she began strutting over to it.

"Now, let's see," she begins. "We need to decide on how we wish to apply this. Are we speaking of protection for individual people, or a location, such as the House itself, perhaps along with the surrounding grounds, like an aura effect?"

"The theory here is the retaliation of the higher Houses," Nemelle asserts. "Perhaps also of the Power herself, and this might involve an assault on the grounds, so the aura effect might be of service. And if this should serve our needs, we might wish to aim for this in other cases, perhaps to convert the Houses individually to curtail the advance of that retaliation until we can make our own."

"Yes, this is a good idea. Although if they do make this retaliation, one thing I can already foresee is a siege-like effect occurring on the streets outside. If you cannot go outside for any reason, even to resupply yourselves, you will need to stockpile ahead of time."

"This is true. Malafay?"

"Yes, I see it," she nods. "Our house often receives deliveries from outside, but this would be quickly cut off. And depending on how long it takes for you to collect enough other Houses before you make your move, we could remain this way for a long time. How would we survive in all that?"

"We can offer support," Aerlie suggests. "For instance, if we can gain enough confidence out of you and the other Houses, we could possibly establish an intermediary, perhaps with portal runes to import goods during this time until we can make an official movement. Then, if we can spread this around to the other Houses, perhaps we could create a kind of perimeter, converting some portion of your city to our side, and from there launch on the rest of it."

"Interesting. But does this mean we would need to convert ourselves to these other gods now?"

"Malafay," Rhyliira notes. "Recall what we said before when we were first deciding to do this. One way or another, and it seems very clear to me they CAN do this, we are either going back, or going down."

"Yes..." she sighs. "But I think this is going to hurt," she glares at Nemelle as she recalls that playful act in her office. "Then show us what you need us to do. And how do we apply this aura effect for our House?"

Aerlie waves for the elder priest to come back over.

"Yes, my Lady?"

"We are going to need some talisman charms, probably several of them. Oh, what the heck, bring a whole box!" she giggles. "We need to offer a kind of aura of protection for what I suspect will be a large estate home."

"Good gracious, that would be a fine sight to see. Very well, one moment."

"As for each of you, let me introduce you to the Protector, otherwise known as Nemelle's Father, Corellon Larethian..."

Aerlie now begins a hurried lesson on the local pantheon of gods and their philosophical doctrines, to introduce and at least partially indoctrinate them to their new religion.

Alakaere was visiting the chamber of the House matriarch to check in on the current events. As she enters, she offers her usual respects before she approaches to speak.

"Matron Mother? I am growing a little concerned about Malafay and the others. It has been a while since their departure, and none of them have been outside the House for this long before. I tried visiting the altar to offer a small prayer for them, but the altar seems silent, and I am unsure why. Have you heard anything since they left?"

"I have not visited the altar in this time, but I will admit how it seems unusually quiet lately. I was originally attributing this to the Spider Queen being distracted on other matters. But if you say she is not responding to Malafay and her sisters being absent for so long, I must wonder if she is indeed watching them, or if again she is distracted."

"Do you know if she holds any feelings for the younger sisters that she would choose NOT to watch over them? Did they do something that could perhaps offend her? And then, we also have these stories Malafay spoke of."

"Yes, I do not go out in the streets to listen to the commoners speak, but we do have a few servants in the House. Perhaps they know of something."

"I thought of this. I tried inquiring of a few if they would share anything. They seemed reluctant, claiming it would not be of interest to us as surely it is just commoner talk."

"Oh, really! That sounds like a ruse to dissuade the issue."

"My thoughts, as well. So, I decided to press for more. I brought one of them into the basement with me and forced her to speak. Nothing to cause true injury, mind you, only the threat of it to see if it would loosen her tongue. And it did, at least a bit."

"I see, and what did she say?"

"I suppose there is some truth to her original words. She says the stories going around suggest we are essentially rotting in this hole due to false beliefs and incorrect teachings that deny us to learn what is really happening out there beyond our view. And worse is that no one ever goes out there to correct it."

"Ha! That sounds to me like someone is trying to start a rebellion. No doubt this is what Malafay was looking for, to find the insolent wreck who is behind it."

"Maybe so, but it does leave me with a concern. According to her, the stories are drawing a lot of interest across the city. So, we cannot be speaking of ONE insolent wreck, but something bigger, and pressing it hard to make this level of an impression."

"Are we speaking on the level of the commoners alone? Or could this be affecting anyone else, like any of the greater Houses?"

"I cannot be sure, and I doubt she would know of it, if it is spreading beyond her personal knowledge. Furthermore, if this were affecting any of the other Houses, I doubt they would reveal it openly. This would surely lead to a cleansing."

"Yes, it would. And maybe Malafay is seeking her answers to prevent as much for our House."

"It does not help us to know who is doing it, or why, but I am concerned that if this is a movement of some kind, and potent enough to cause this much of a stir, simply discovering who is behind it might not be enough, by itself. And even worse, if they are successful, I dread to think of what level of discord they could bring if enough people begin to follow it."

"And this brings us back to a rebellion. But to what end? Are we speaking of going against...? Ahh, but that must be it. This is why she is so quiet lately. She IS distracted by something!"

"Matron Mother, if this is so serious that it could hold her attention on this level, it cannot be a simple rabblerouser making noise in the streets."

"No, it could not. We must be vigilant, Alakaere! Share this with your sister. She should know of it. As for Malafay, we will give her some more time. Perhaps it is a small thing, some other House pushing for an advantage. But if not, and if she is successful at learning something, I think we should listen carefully to what she discovers."

"As you say, Matron Mother," she bows and leaves.

Chapter 4

APOSTASY

"I'm feeling very uncertain about this, Malafay," Rhyliira moans. "I know we need to do it, but going back there like this is going to stand out. I'm not sure with whom, but it will."

"Relissa keeps speaking of knives in people's backs," Felynquiri intones warily. "I don't think they would give us that honor. They'll just come at us from whatever direction is most convenient."

"All right you two," Malafay whispers. "Hush. We don't want to give ourselves away before we even leave the alley. We'll simply stroll along the street as we might normally do, and make our way directly home."

"And if something is waiting for us outside?"

"Then we turn around and run like there's no tomorrow. We don't have that portal thing she was using to jump back and forth."

"That's the worst part of it," Rhyliira admits. "We can't escape out of here in a flash if we need to. Even if we run to the gate, would the guards simply open it up for us, or leave it as is, while whatever it is comes for us."

"Ugh! That's enough now! We got a blessing from the Protector before coming back here. We're also carrying this box of talismans for the House. We just need to hang them around the exterior to offer their protective aura. So, if anyone out there tries anything, well, this will hopefully block them."

"It does leave us to wonder how long it will last, if they are continually fighting against it."

"Yes, but Lady Aerlie said she would offer support in the form of food and other supplies, and also people to assist us. This simply leaves us to wait it out, maybe along with other Houses."

"But you know, it also brings to mind one last thing," Felynquiri wonders. "How many Houses might convert? And further, if just a few turn over initially, would this alert the rest to be on guard and maybe NOT convert if they sense something like a hostile takeover approaching. Would they turn against it, and not even try to listen to anything, therefore not convert at all?"

"This goes outside our ability to influence. This would more likely fall into the category of them with their military action to forcefully shove it down their throats. It will be enough for us simply to survive until then."

"All right, Malafay, then there's nothing else for us. Let's go."

The group had been returned from the surface world back to the alley where Relissa marked her portal index. They had been given a shard-com to make phone calls, along with a recharging unit, as the item was battery powered. They also had hardcopies of their photo album, a box of strongly enchanted talisman charms blessed with a protection aura, and a number of last-minute instructions on what to do in case of emergency.

They cautiously stepped out onto the street, looking out for anything that might be unexpected coming their way. As usual, the street was mostly empty, and while this might normally be expected, it now felt a little eerie. They pressed forward with a hurried step, hoping to make it home before anything actually could pop out of the shadows at them.

They coursed their way along the streets, passing taverns and shops, and other local citizens, none of whom seemed interested in paying attention to the group, at least as much as they didn't care to socialize, as well as to simply avoid a group of people who seemed in a hurry to go somewhere.

In the distance, they could see their dynastic House standing above many of the smaller commoner homes that would represent their servant quarters. Everything appeared normal from this distance, so they proceeded forward. They came into view of the front gate, with nothing unpleasant standing guard. The House appeared intact. There were no strange creatures lurking about, and no mercenary armies from any of the other Houses attacking the place, so they rushed to get inside.

"Do we put one of these charms on the door here?" Felynquiri asks.

"I, uh…" Malafay ponders. "I think we should wait to see what sort of reaction the Matron Mother has first. We might need these for ourselves, more than anything, if we have to leave quickly."

"Great, but whatever you say."

"Malafay," Rhyliira offers. "I have a thought. We need to bring this to the Matron Mother, certainly, but what about the rest of it? What I mean is, regardless of her opinions, and she can be rather strict in her opinions, we still have the rest of the family, and also the servants, and if the idea is to redeem as many people as possible, they should be included."

"Are you saying to approach them independently?"

"Probably so, with the only question being to do it before or after her. There is strength in numbers."

"Oh, Rhyliira, you have a point, but it's a dangerous one. To turn the whole House on her if she doesn't cooperate?"

"If she cooperates, fine, but if not, she might be condemning the rest to suffer the other direction."

"Possibly. All right, the two of you, gather up the servants and bring them into the basement. Jhandril, you take the males. Call a meeting down there. I'll go there now and wait for you. And try to stay out of sight of the Matron Mother, or the two other sisters. Surely, they'll start asking questions if they see us returning home."

The group splits up, each with their own task. Malafay rushes through the House towards the stairs leading to the basement, checking around corners to make sure no one important was coming the other way. The other two sisters do the same, searching for any servant they can find and giving instructions to call even more into a meeting down below. Jhandril hurries to the quarters with the males, and orders them to follow along. In several moments, a mass of people is assembling in the basement.

"I need everyone here to listen carefully," Malafay begins. "This is private, confidential, and dangerous if you should let it out uncontrolled. Some of you may be aware of strange stories going around in the streets, but do any of you know who is spreading them and why?"

The gathering glances around, but no one comes forward with a response.

"I need interaction here, people, not silence. If you have something to say, speak. There will be no punishment for the wrong words spoken. Simply bring what you know out in the open. But if you have nothing to say, I will continue. So far, I have yet to bring this to the Matron Mother. Hopefully, if she knows the greater wisdom of it, she will listen and realize the seriousness of what it represents. But you need to be told as well, and I cannot risk this being kept a secret by anyone, not even her if she chooses to bury it like so many other things."

"Bury it?" asks one of the males.

"Yes, bury it, assuming she is actually the one burying anything, or if it is a higher authority instructing her to do so. The stories speak of our people living down here as the result of us being banished by the above-world to fester in the Underdark. This is false, we were not banished to fester. It was punishment for our ancestors starting an unjust war and being cast out for it."

This statement raised a murmuring of oohs within the crowd. Malafay continued.

"They further say the world above has changed in this time, but we have not. And yet, we are told nothing about this, neither are we even suggested to advance ourselves for any reason. We are probably no different today than our ancestors who first came down here. And this was perhaps ten thousand years ago, which is a very long time NOT to advance our society with knowledge or wisdom."

These words resulted in another round of moans from the assembly.

"It also speaks of the warriors who go up to fight the surface people," Malafay states. "They come back with stories of great victories, but the part we do not learn is there were never any warriors to fight. And worse, there is a big wall we hit before we even have a chance to go out there looking for anything."

This startled the crowd, and they began whispering to themselves about the implications.

"Is this the part you mentioned about burying something?" the male asks.

"Part of it, yes. In the early days, the warriors may have gone up and fought something, but it was not other warriors. It was the first thing they saw out there, and it turned out to be unarmed commoners. So, you tell me, would you regard yourself a strong warrior if you killed unarmed people who wouldn't know how to fight, even if you put your own knife in their hand? We are described as committing crimes and atrocities, not fighting for our survival. Eventually, they built a wall to keep us out. It was simply easier than trying to find their way down here to bury us in a hole we already buried ourselves in."

"Then why do we continue to send our warriors up there?" asks another male. "I've been there and seen that wall. I heard a voice boom out of it telling me to go home. But when we return, the elder sisters tell us simply to be silent about it."

"By order of the Spider Queen, no doubt, as she is the reason we are down here in the first place. She is also the reason we know nothing of what they were doing up there in this time while we festered in this hole believing they were two steps away from marching on us. In other words, she lies to us, and worse, keeps us pinned down in this hole feeling as much hatred as she apparently feels for our true gods, the ones our ancestors once worshipped and then defiled, shaming us in the eyes of everyone else, and cursing us into this hole."

This caused the assembly to erupt in a bold series of cries.

"And now they are coming for us…for real this time," she continues. "We apparently keep sending our warriors up there to hit that wall, never once realizing the futility of it, because no one tells us there IS a wall up there. It is simply a distraction to fuel our hate. Meanwhile, that world up there came together under the rule of a powerful king who united the entire thing together and led them into an Age of Wisdom of a sort we could not recognize, let alone fight. Their purpose was to unite all the people of the world, and they did this. The only exception to this is us down here in this grave of a hole we dug for ourselves. Well, now they aim to correct that. They are offering to redeem those of us wise enough to realize there is another life waiting for us if we want it. But it does NOT involve the Spider Queen. We must return to our old gods, and learn the ways of the people up there."

"Um, Mistress Malafay," ushers one of the servants. "Mistress Alakaere was asking me about those stories once. She seemed very determined to learn about them, but I did not have much to say other than what I heard on the streets outside. I am aware that you and the others went out on a journey of some kind. Where did that journey take you that you might learn of this?"

"Up there, to those people we are never allowed to speak to, only to curse them for our misfortune that we were cast into this hole. We saw their cities. We saw their schools for their children. We saw their marketplaces, and that word almost seems inadequate, as half our city would fit inside one, to say nothing of the industry that fills it."

"You must be joking! How can they have such as markets the size of cities?"

"Because they have millions of people in those cities to feed and clothe. How many do we have here? I think not that many even during my full lifetime of people living and dying. And further, they are no longer limited to life on this one world. There are other worlds out there, apparently, if only you go to the sky for it. And we, down here in this hole, don't even know what the sky is, let alone anything beyond it. Now, who should we blame for these errors? Our ancestors for their mistakes, and that goddess who fails to inform us of anything. And here is where we are now. Those people up there are delivering these stories to teach us what we are missing. This is in preparation to come down here and try to redeem us, or else destroy us if we do not listen. But their purpose is to unite this world in peace, and we never once made ourselves peaceful in their eyes."

"Uh oh… Is this to say we need to bow before them now?"

"It is to say we need to rejoin our ancestral kin on the surface, as we once were. It is to say we need to go back to our old gods, as we once had. And if we do, we will become a part of what they created, and will go to those same places they are travelling to, and perform the same great deeds they are performing. But our goddess is not likely to approve of this. Therefore, these stories are to convince some or all of us to make a decision. The more who choose correctly, the better, as we can save more lives that way."

"And you are telling this to us so that we can make that decision?"

"Our entire way of life down here is apparently incorrect, as our goddess, being female, seems to hate males as much as she hates the old gods. This king is male, and HE is the one who rules up there, along with his wife and queen. We elves, or at least those up there, like so many others, have a history of marrying and creating families based on love and dedication. They bring children into the world, and nurture them as beloved treasures. They grow and prosper, and work together to build the world around them, carrying it one step forward with each new generation, based upon new knowledge, new inventions, and new discoveries. When was the last time WE did that? I certainly do not carry that same level of familial devotion with my sisters…well, not like we saw up there, and I doubt either of them do with each other.

And our people have a history, and a reputation, of planting knives in each other's backs more than anything else, and long before we can ever see the full length of our natural lives, and this is simply to gain an advantage for ourselves. This must end."

The room emits another round of vigorous mumbling.

"Now, I need to bring my report to the Matron Mother, and pray to this other god she doesn't blow her top. I have here a box of talisman charms I brought back with me. These are enchanted by this god of the old ways to protect our House. They need to be placed outside at various points to offer a warding effect, in case the First House, or anyone else, tries to perform a cleansing. Once I go to the Matron Mother, or even now, if anyone is watching, this is likely to carry repercussions, and we need to be ready. We will be changing our devotion here, and I will ask each and every one of you to join with us, to ask for this redemption and go back to the true gods of elven kind. But we may find ourselves coming under siege if the First House tries anything. We will need to stockpile food and other goods before then. You can help. Go out and begin collecting supplies, and store them in here. And if you need to find shelter for yourselves, come to us."

"What about any other Houses out there?" asks one more male. "This is supposed to be an offer for everyone, I suppose, correct?"

"Each House may be on its own, but yes. For those who actually listen, they can turn voluntarily. For those who do not, they may be captured by a military advance on the city, where they will be informed of it and given the choice. I'm not sure if we can do anything to help, but maybe some of you who live in the commoner enclaves can speak to others. Do so carefully, and share these words to see if they can find their way further along. Perhaps we can share a few ideas this way. But we will need to bring them together and do for them as we are doing here, possibly to give them charms like these, and idols to the old gods to call their names for protection. If we can bring some part of the city into this, we can stand together against the rest. And as I understand it, these people are doing the same in many of the other cities we own."

As Malafay finishes her sermon, she studies the faces of those in the room. Rhyliira and Felynquiri both watched and listened, along with Jhandril. Then, Malafay directs her sisters out of the basement and on their way to the Matron Mother's house seat.

"Jhandril," she declares. "See to the restocking, and anything else we need to prepare for this."

"Yes, Sister Malafay, I'll do my best."

She now joins the others as they continue towards their fated encounter.

"This will not be easy," Rhyliira mutters softly.

"No, it won't," Malafay admits. "But I know one thing, I want Alakaere and Alyraema present to confront them with the portrait of that wall…" she pats a handbag she was carrying which held the photos inside. "I want to see their reaction, as well as the Matron Mother, when that part of it is revealed."

"Are you trying to get someone killed?"

"Not killed, but to test a response. If the Matron Mother knows of it, and therefore the other sisters as well, we will know who is responsible for the order, at least within the family. But if the Matron Mother does NOT know, it's that…witch…again."

"Um, Malafay," Felynquiri ushers. "We're inside our own House again, right in the middle of what that…ahem…might be watching. Do you think it wise to use such words here?"

"If those people up there want to start a revolution, we need to sign up for it. So, we can't be afraid of what words we use any more."

"Well, all right. I was simply hoping for one more birthday, but maybe sixty-two was enough."

"I'm thinking of what Relissa said now," Rhyliira muses. "They have a legal age threshold of seventy-five up there. You're still regarded as a child by those numbers, and so am I at seventy-one."

They arrived at the door to the Matron Mother's chamber, knocking politely before entering.

"Ah! Malafay," the matriarch croons. "We were becoming concerned for you being gone so long. Did you learn about the source of those unfortunate rumors?"

"Yes, Matron Mother, I discovered a great amount of detail which I would now wish to deliver to you. And I think it would prove informative if we held a meeting with Alakaere and Alyraema as well, so they can participate in this hearing."

"Yes, naturally."

The Matron Mother rings a bell to summon the other two daughters. They wait several moments while the others assemble.

"Malafay," Alakaere asserts. "I am pleased to see you are still alive. Those tunnels can be hazardous, as we all know."

"They can be, but Jhandril knows the way through them quite well."

"We were speculating a bit on those stories you spoke of. We are concerned over what they represent, and if this could be more than a simple rabblerouser. They seem to be carrying a lot of influence out there."

"Yes, it would certainly appear that way. And no, it is not a simple rabblerouser. The source seems to carry a considerable amount of merit for the claims."

"Really! Then what did you learn?"

"Before I go into that, it occurs to me that I will need to use a number of terms and depictions that may not be entirely polite. Therefore, I think it would be prudent if I ask our Matron Mother if she would permit me the freedom to speak openly during this meeting, that I might be better able to describe what I saw without offending anyone, and in so doing, the entire purpose of my report may lose its focus within the flames of personal opinions."

"Such a fascinating request," the Matron Mother raises her brow. "And so carefully worded. Is this to say you have something for us that I might take exception to, and you simply want to keep your skin for it?"

"Yes, Matron Mother, as you need to know as much as any other, and it is not likely you will be pleased for it."

The elder female glared at Malafay, as the younger woman stoically held her stand, along with her two sisters, who attempted to feign their own resilience. She then glanced up into the eyes of her two elder daughters, who were on either side of her, and both of them similarly intrigued by the request.

"I see..." she emits flatly. "Very well, if the report you have to offer is so dire, and if it might affect such as to possibly cause more than a simple disturbance in the streets, then I may have no choice. I will grant you leave to use whatever terms are necessary to explain what you learned. But I should also caution you not to push this allowance too far."

"My thanks, Matron Mother, I shall endeavor to restrain myself. First, I have a few items to demonstrate as my evidence..."

Malafay reaches into her handbag and pulls out several photos. These were printed within the guildhall on paper, which was otherwise unknown to the people of the Underdark. After all, where can you find wood to make paper in a deep underground cavern?

The Matron Mother and her two elder daughters leaned in to study the odd artifacts.

"What are those?" she asks.

"These are called photos. They are essentially the same as portraits, but made by a device to capture an image of a place or a thing, and here record it on paper as the medium."

"What is paper?" Alakaere asks.

"A substance we would be unfamiliar with around here, but commonly used in some places. I suppose we could associate this with vellum, as we do have this here, made from the byproducts of the mushroom farms, but this holds a different quality to it. I was fortunate enough to meet with someone who was able to provide me with these to bring home."

"Who might have such a device that can capture an image of any kind and record it on…anything?"

"Someone who has spent a bit more time inventing things than any of us around here, it would seem."

"Uh huh…is this one of those statements you mentioned you needed to use?"

"One, but not the only. Alakaere, Alyraema, perhaps you can help our Matron Mother interpret this one here. I suspect one or both of you might have seen it before."

Malafay holds up the first picture, which was of the wall outside the tunnel exit. Rhyliira and Felynquiri exchanged glances as the others peered down at the imagery.

They studied the clearly perfect, if also strangely alien, photographic image. Alakaere simply gazed at it in awe.

"What is this thing made of?" she whispers. "And HOW is it made. I see no lines, no brush strokes…"

But as Alyraema viewed it, the picture hit a sudden note in her.

"What sort of trickery is this! How did you get this! Um…" she suddenly catches herself. "What I mean is, this must be some sort of trick! I mean, just look at it! How can you create an image so clean, with no lines, no, um…" she peers down closer at it. "No…anything, like paint or anything else. And that…thing! What could that possibly be!"

"Alyraema," the Matron Mother intones warily. "Do YOU know what this is? Maybe Malafay is right. There are terms to be used here that are not so polite."

"Matron Mother, I would never wish to offend you. But this here… This…thing! It simply must be a trick. After all, how could it be possible to create something like this? Paper? What is that? I've never heard of it before. And that image! If I were to look at that thing with my own eyes, it could not be any more perfect than what that image represents. And I've never seen anyone create an image like THAT before."

She turns and huffs emphatically, folding her arms and pretending to ignore the offensive presentation.

"Alyraema, I will ask once more, or perhaps I should simply have Malafay explain it to me. To me, this looks a bit like a wall, so why would you be so offended over a depiction of a simple wall?"

"Matron Mother, if I may," Malafay interjects. "Let us extend that blessing of yours to each of us in this room, as it may be necessary for this much. There may be hidden tidings that need to be understood, and that suggestion of personal opinions may cloud the end result."

"Now this is interesting. Are you trying to defend your elder sister?"

"I feel it may be necessary, as I suspect she knows something, but was forbidden to reveal it openly."

Alyraema turned to glare at Malafay, at least as much for the suggestion, which was true and accurate, but also that she would offer this on her behalf to diffuse the Matron Mother's suspicions.

"Malafay," she emits cautiously. "If you are holding this image, then you must know what it is. And if you know this much, you must know more than that. And then you would come before us with this…for what purpose? Clearly to expose it, but then what? If you are accusing me of withholding something, but then step forward to protect me…um…"

"Matron Mother, do you personally know this?" she asks. "Have you personally ever seen it before?"

"Me?" she relents. "No, not personally. But then, I have never actually been outside the city before. Where is it and why is this so important?"

"Alyraema, would you like to come forward with yours, or should I do mine instead?"

"Me? But… Oh curse you! All right, yes, I have seen this before, but I have always received instructions from the Spider Queen not to reveal it openly. Now, are you satisfied, Malafay?"

"Good enough, for your part. Matron Mother, this is the thing our warriors are sent up to fight. A wall, only to turn around and come back with their stories of fighting something."

"A what?!" she shouts. "A simple wall? Why are we attacking a damnable wall, of all things?"

"Well, we're not actually attacking it. We go up, get blinded by an intense light, then hear a voice shouting at us, telling us to return home, and that we're not welcome up there."

"Oh, we're not welcome, are we?"

"No. Apparently, we have a history up there of simply attacking unarmed commoners who never saw it coming. Then, before the REAL warriors show up, we run home with our great stories. And quite frankly, they're tired of it. So, they built a wall to stop us."

The Matron Mother glared at Malafay for the impertinent statement, with her face twisting in anger and confusion.

"One moment, let me see if I understood you. For how long in our history have we been fighting simple commoners who do not fight back?"

"My guess is forever, perhaps since we first came down into the Underdark. I can't be sure if there were ever any real warriors up there, but I would imagine if there were, we would have fewer of ours returning home with stories of any kind. Especially once they began to realize where we come from and move whole armies into position to face us, not simply a few lonely blindmen who can't see their own shadows. After all, if you are being hit continuously by something, would you simply allow more to come in and hit you again without improving your defense?"

"Indeed, this would make much better sense."

"And then to suggest there is anything at all up there to hit, like warriors who can't apparently fight well enough to win even once against us. We don't send that many up at one time, so if they're training themselves, you would think they should train somewhere else, where they have time to train up fully before exposing themselves to actual combat. Placing untrained people in front of a hole in a mountainside waiting for us to come out and cut them down before they're ready to fight is also a bit silly."

"Yes, it would be. And a bit too convenient for us."

"And yet, this is what we seem to be doing, if you listen to those stories we bring back. We go up, hit something, bam, it's dead, regardless of the fact it's supposed to be a warrior that ought to know how to fight, perhaps at least to cause an occasional injury, if not kill something, and our people come home to a feast. No, if it were me, I would build a wall or something to keep us out."

"Either that, or more aggressively pursue your attackers."

"Yes, if not for the difficulty of navigating these tunnels down here."

"Yes, point made. And what of the stories our people bring back?"

"Just talk to Alyraema. She already gave you THAT answer."

The Matron Mother glared at Malafay, then at Alyraema, as she began to connect the dots. Her face changed from the contortion of anger and confusion to now show disgust.

"You said you were commanded NOT to reveal this wall. And yet... well, no. YOU never said they did anything. You simply stated they did as..." the matriarch halted as she felt a conflicting set of emotions arising within her. "No, there must be something wrong here."

"Wrong?" Malafay asserts. "Yes. With her, maybe not. With the one who invents these stories, most likely, as none of US would tell such fascinating fables if we valued our honor. But then, I guess honor isn't the issue here."

"Honor... Malafay, I may have given you leave to use whatever words you felt were necessary to carry your point, but I also cautioned you..."

"...Not to press it," she interjects. "Yes. But there is no way to make my point without pressing the fact that we are lied to and told to invent even more lies about what we and they are doing up there... if anything at all...and then sending our people up to fight nothing more than a wall, as the result of these lies we are fed. There never were any warriors. Those people describe us as having already buried ourselves in this hole, which is as much like a grave for us, and we are simply not worth digging out to bury again. The only trouble they have now is us making a bother of ourselves by crawling out of this hole to kill harmless commoners, which to them is called murder and described as an atrocity."

"An atrocity! Malafay, according to the stories we are given in our lessons, they banished us into this hole they call a grave to deny us our space up there in the glory of the light. And now they call us murderers committing atrocities?"

"No, they banished us because we started a war to take more than we were due, and offending everyone else in the process, and they punished us for it by banishing us away from them. Our ancestors also defiled the old religions to the elven gods, and this essentially cursed us into this hole after we began to follow the Spider Queen, who led us down here to fester in it. That is our history, Matron Mother...nothing else. Everything else is a lie, simply to occupy us and maintain the hatred the Spider Queen has for everything else out there. And she uses us, much like sending our warriors to fight a wall we were never permitted to speak about. And much like the perpetual stories of warrior armies massing up there, so imminent to march on us to destroy us. They have no interest in coming down here, so long as we remain silent with our so-called whining about our misery for being banished due to our own impertinent greed. But we don't seem willing to take this lesson, so NOW they are massing to finish the job. And Matron Mother, they don't need to walk through tunnels to do so. Not anymore. They invented other means by now, much to our chagrin that we do not invent anything at all down here."

Malafay rests a moment to let that sink in, realizing her argument might normally cost her at least her skin, if not her life. But she had to finish it with that final statement in the hopes it would invoke further dialog, rather than retaliation.

The Matron Mother leans back in her chair, clearly outraged by the accusations, most of which were heretical, but for the evidence presented in this one photo, and the statements about the wall, this made them seem valid enough to warrant consideration. But the next part, about a real army amassing above, and with no further need to walk through tunnels, this left a new puzzle in her mind. However, before she could respond to this, it would be Alakaere who would take the next argument.

"What do you mean by that, Malafay? Are they now growing so impatient with us that this wall is not enough?"

"Essentially, yes. Alakaere, Alyraema, and Matron Mother, you need to know this. Regardless of your feelings on the matter, regardless of your feelings on me and my arguments, you need to know THIS... That world up there has changed tremendously, and we never knew anything about it, all because I suspect someone denied us to learn anything."

"Should I ask who that someone is, or simply take it for granted you are referring to the same one here."

"I will simply answer as yes, as I'm sure she is watching and should KNOW about this, but never gave it to us down here. All she ever did was say 'there are warriors up there...go kill...", and here we are fighting a wall. Then, if we go by Alyraema's statement, and that of such like Jhandril and others, who are denied revealing anything, the rest of us might have no other recourse but to listen to HER telling us of the result; therefore, to rejoice with a feast."

"Mother," Alyraema emits tenderly. "This is starting to make some sense to me, and the reason she might be so silent. She is realizing the others up there are preparing to correct this."

"She may be silent now because she knows her time here is short," Malafay asserts. "There is another goddess up there who claims ownership of this world from the beginning, and the Spider Queen was never welcome to come here to begin with."

"What? Are we speaking of one of the old elven gods?"

"No, this one is different. I went up there and spoke to that voice that chased you away so many times. They are the ones spreading these stories down here, and in every other Drow city out there. They are trying to break the circle of lies the Spider Queen has been feeding us, to make us realize the world up there is such that if their warriors ever did march on us, we would be doomed so completely that ours would faint dead away in their shoes. That's how powerful they have become, and we know nothing about it, all because we hit a wall before ever seeing it."

"Fine, but if what you say is true, why only now? Why did they not march on us earlier, or is this something new?"

"It's been developing for centuries by now, but the complexities of approaching us down here held them back until they could develop a proper plan for it. But to explain this…" she clears her throat briskly. "Matron Mother, relating back to that blessing of speaking out. The Spider Queen is described as a witch to these people, and responsible for essentially imprisoning us in this hole that others call a grave, then feeding us lies to make us little more than an annoyance in their eyes up there. So, here is the REAL story."

Malafay pauses to collect her thoughts and begins pacing around the room.

"In the old days, and we are speaking of something like ten thousand years ago, our ancestors started a war. It was one of several wars where we were the ones responsible for committing a number of offenses. As the result of these wars, our people were banished…driven out of the lands of the above-world, as we apparently had taken such beliefs and attitudes that we were no longer welcome to remain there. We also defiled the old elven gods, and this disgraced us in the eyes of everyone else. Here is where we apparently turned to the Spider Queen and followed her into this hole. We are cursed for this much, not banished to fester. I would imagine, during this time, our history has been muddled to disguise these facts with her lies to invoke even more festering and hatred, therefore we will send up warriors to hit whatever they see and call it a victory."

She turns and paces the other way as she continues.

"The people up there took to loathing us for these acts, and as I understand it, there WERE warriors marching on our cities on many occasions, but turned back due to such things like the twisting nature of the tunnels down here, and other hazards, and maybe also simply how deep we are that it became impractical for them to pursue it. Instead, they might post watchtowers and guard posts at those locations where we might come out. But then we changed our tactics to find other exits and try again. In time, this grew tiresome, and here is where I suppose they built these walls, or maybe tried to collapse those exits to block us."

"This would make good sense to me," the Matron Mother admits. "If I were on the other side of it, I might do the same."

"But we never took the lesson. We kept sending our warriors up to hit those walls, some of which were manned and guarded. They don't apparently have any real interest in killing us if all we're doing is sending a few warriors to hit a wall. Instead, they might order us to return home and not do it again. But it doesn't work, as we keep coming."

"Exactly as they did to us on so many occasions," Alyraema muses.

"And this would indeed grow tiresome after a while," Alakaere nods.

"Meanwhile, that world up there..." Malafay continues. "At one time, and for a long while, it was occupied by many nations, where they did not always cooperate on anything. Therefore, if one should take a hit, the others do not hear of it or care to assist. However, somewhere between eight and nine centuries ago, a king came to the land to unite everyone and everything together into one nation. So, NOW, to hit anything at all is to offend the whole thing. This, in itself, is bad, because that nation has a military numbering in the many millions of hard-trained veteran warriors, using adamantium and mithril as standard issue, and with many of them trained in magic and divine chants, such that they could melt our city to the ground with barely an effort."

The Matron Mother and her two eldest daughters all gasped and reeled back at the fantastical suggestion. It almost seemed too sensational to be real. But Malafay knew she had to continue, if only to nail it home. She reached into her handbag and pulled out the remainder of her photo album.

"What this means," she continues. "If to put it into very unfortunate terms for us, is we are simply not worth a full-scale assault, if only we would stop our crying about a forgotten war. But there is something else at play here which we are not aware of, and if you say the Spider Queen has been especially quiet lately, this could be the reason for it. They are coming for us...to finish what this king started up there. We are still regarded as citizens of this world, banishment or otherwise, and SHE is not welcome to occupy this space. They are offering us a chance to come back."

"Come back?!" Alakaere shouts. "After everything else? They would actually ask us to return back now?"

"Rhyliira, Felynquiri, and I walked amongst them in their cities and marketplaces, and we saw where and how they produce their trade goods for the masses, and the term masses here is an understatement. They have a population of billions up there. So, any idea of cutting short a warrior march is ludicrous. Simply take what we have here and multiply it many times over, and that might only account for one of their larger cities, out of many. They were remarkably helpful to us, and they gave us this wonderful tour of what they had built in this time. A civilization the likes of which would seem fantastical by our measure. All because THEY are growing, and WE are not. I have more photos here of what we saw with our own eyes. These were given to us along the way to bring back to you, so you could see it."

She steps forward to show off the pictures, explaining each one and what it represents. The Matron Mother and her two elder daughters all gazed in wonder and amazement at the strange sights of industrial complexes, shopping malls, metropolitan cities with their impossibly high skyscrapers, and masses of people just casually browsing the shops and walking the streets, as if they hadn't a care in the world for anything other than their personal chores and pleasures.

"They have studied knowledge that we don't even have names for down here," Malafay admits. "Look at this one…"

She now shows a set of photos of the schools.

"These are some of their children, human in this case. They each learn a standardized program of education, involving their history, culture, mathematics, science, and other things. They find recreation in play areas, to develop social skills and physical fitness. At age twelve for humans, a bit later for elves and others, if only because our kind tends to mature a bit slower through the years, they begin to learn the lessons of the arcane. So, Matron Mother, if our warriors thought they could fight even simple commoners once upon a time, now they could not. By the time these people reach adulthood, they are probably more skilled in magic than our own dedicated mages. And this is a common lifestyle study for them."

"You can't be serious…" the Matron Mother wheezes.

"They have vehicles coursing their way through the streets, which many people tend to use commonly to travel between remote areas of their cities. These use a form of power they call electricity, not people or animals pulling them along. And for everything else, whether travelling around the city on foot, or travelling from one city to another, they use a network of portals, Mother, to move around. So, walking for them is archaic. Therefore, we return to those tunnels outside. This might have been our first line of defense to hold them back at one time, but now they are moot. They don't need that anymore. They could launch an attack right here on our streets simply by going poof, here we are. And so…here we are. We have a choice to make, and the Spider Queen is about to be evicted."

"Malafay," she intones worriedly. "How do you mean that? Do they now think to assault us with this new army of theirs?"

"Assault? Only those who don't otherwise wish to take the age-old lessons we've been ignoring for so long. That king works for this goddess who owns this world. It's HER world, and SHE has plans for it. Here is the part of my story that might seem outlandish. But I was there, and I saw it, even felt it. Just ask these two, and Jhandril. We were all present, and all saw the same thing."

Again, she takes a deep breath and begins pacing.

"Centuries ago, when this king first arrived, and to remind you, we are speaking of between eight and nine here. He is not of this world, and therefore his lifespan is nothing like ours. In fact, I wonder how long ours might actually be, if we were not growing in this time. We have developed a reputation of planting knives in each other's backs long before we have a chance to see how long we can actually live by natural means. We're probably no different now than our ancestors from ten millennia ago, while up there, they have seen theirs increase significantly."

"Increase? Interesting."

"He came here as the result of this goddess sending him here. He and his wife, both of whom are beings called Celestials. This is a word we would not be familiar with, but I think we should become familiar with it, as there are several of them living up there by now, one of which is related to our kind, and the one behind this plan of theirs and these stories in the streets."

"Ah, so the one causing all this is actually up there."

"Yes, they are hoping to redeem us back to our old gods. This person in charge is related to one of them."

Malafay stopped her pacing momentarily to let this sink in and watch their reactions.

The Matron Mother glared at her for the ridiculous suggestion, and the two sisters simply gazed at their younger sibling for the statement.

"Related?" Alakaere emits tenuously.

"A Celestial is half mortal creature, like us, and half god, born directly out of one of them, and often for a special reason, such as to serve as an agent of some kind to solve a problem. And WE represent one of those problems."

"Uh oh…"

"As for this king, this world was another problem…all those nations up there that wouldn't learn to cooperate. Well, he was sent down here to TEACH them to cooperate."

"And another uh oh…" Alyraema moans.

"His wife came into it along the way, a member of the old Winged Folk, to join him. And in this time, they taught all those nations to join together in peace and prosperity. And anyone who refused was destroyed. Now, that world up there is launching out to OTHER worlds, as there is apparently more out there beyond that sky we forgot about, being trapped down here for so long, and they all serve not only this one goddess, but a wide assembly of others to teach anyone and everyone they might come into contact with how to learn, grow, evolve, and find peace for themselves. But this then brings us back down here, with our people."

"Um, yes, I suppose it does. What plans do they have for us? Because this is starting to sound like they have something other than simply conquering us."

"She mentioned something about redemption," Alakaere offers. "But if this means to turn away from…um…"

"Yes, to turn away, and she must already know this. Malafay, what you bring to us is very dangerous. If she is watching, and she probably is, we should expect something coming at us any moment now!"

"I know this," Malafay nods calmly. "And so do they up there…"

Malafay now pulls out her shard-com for demonstration.

"This is a type of communication device. It's on loan to me, in case we need to report in anything unpleasant, like a cleansing effort by the First House."

"Unpleasant!" Alyraema screams. "How can you call a cleansing by the First House as simply unpleasant?"

"Because we are going to box ourselves up tight in here, and place a series of warding talismans around us with a blessing by the one they call the Protector…one of the old elven gods…to keep us safe until they can come to our aid."

"Huh?!" she screeches. "What are you talking about?"

"I'm talking about the full conversion of our family, and perhaps our city, along with every other Drow city out there. And anyone who persists in following the Spider Queen after this will likely go down with her, once that goddess who owns everything arrives with HER army. Now, Alyraema, can you argue with THAT? They are tired of us festering down here. Now, it's time to rejoin them."

The elder sister felt faint by now, and she glanced around the room for a place to sit, but the only real chair was for the matriarch. So, all she could do was lean on it for support.

Alakaere was stunned at the revelation, and the Matron Mother sat silently pondering this seemingly disastrous turn of events for her House, if not the city in general. But at the same time, it was clear that Malafay took a precaution to protect what was left of it.

"Talismans," she mumbles. "Where did you find those?"

"They were given to me by this Queen up there, who is the leader of their religious worship, along with that other one, whose name is Cardinal Nemelle, an Eladrin, which is an ascended form of an elf with divine blood in her. It's all part of a plan to convert us back to our old gods for redemption…those of us who will actually listen. I'm trying to save lives here, Mother. No more planting knives in people's backs. That's called murder, and these people are very strong on laws and polite behavior."

"Laws and polite behavior," she snorts silently. "And we are expected to follow this now?"

"Yes, or be destroyed for your belligerence. They won't accept anything less. And I for one would like to live a bit longer. Along the way, they also introduced me to this same god. I spoke to him, and he offered me a small blessing, along with the rest of us," she glances at her sisters. "We are now under his watch."

"You turned against…" she begins heatedly, but quickly recoiled, rolling her eyes around the room as if expecting something.

"Yes!" Malafay responds defiantly. "I felt it was necessary, as I don't like being lied to and having my history buried under someone else's hatred for what that history represents in reality. Our ancestors made a mistake, and it shamed us for thousands of years. It's time for us to realize this and make amends. And the one who did this to us knows the time is near. Those stories out there are for a reason, to teach us what this is. They hope to convert as many of our people as possible before it grows so intolerable to the Spider Queen that she does actually take action with whatever she has left. And THAT is where this army goes poof in our streets to fight on our side. But we need to know WHY they are fighting, not simply to see them go poof, and therefore causing US to fight them as well."

"Matron Mother," Alakaere notes. "I see a certain amount of reason to this. If they are trying to redeem us, this means they want people to live through it, not fight and die for something unworthy."

"Yes," Alyraema chuckles ironically. "Like going up to hit a wall on command, just to give us something to do."

"I have already shared this with the servants and the warriors," Malafay continues. "I gave instructions to begin collecting food and other supplies, and stockpiling them for what could be a siege of our House, and to share these words with others out there who might also listen, possibly to help other Houses convert and survive this onslaught."

"Are YOU now trying to start a rebellion?" the Matron Mother growls.

"Mother, this has only two possible outcomes. We go willingly, or we go forcefully. They will no longer tolerate US, or HER, in this world as we are. That's all. So, either we realize this and join with them, or become prisoners. They might simply work on our children after that if the rest of us will not listen. This isn't a rebellion so much as it is a takeover and assimilation effort. And we will learn our lessons, even if it takes several generations of pounding to accept them."

"Incredible! Our entire way of life…"

"Our entire way of life is a lie, Mother. We are elves. We are supposed to behave better than this. There are six other major clans of elves up there, and we are a disgrace to all of them."

"There are also those Night Elves, Malafay," Rhyliira notes. "Tell her about those."

"Yes, then we have those."

"What are Night Elves?" Alyraema asks.

"A lost clan of our ancestors, once known as the Ssri. They escaped this fallacy and survived up there. Now they are trying to help the rest of us. Some of them are the ones in our streets spreading these stories. I met with one during this time. She explained to me who she was and what they were doing. She's the one who took us on that tour. She's a scout, but also trained in magic, up to the point where she can use portals, and probably compete with our best mages."

"A scout? Only that much?"

"Yes, and they use devices for many of these things. Whatever we might use in our craft is old school now."

"Very well, Malafay," the Matron Mother concedes reluctantly. "It would seem you have plunged us into this rather deeply, regardless of any inevitability it might bring to anyone amongst us. Where are these talismans of yours? As I would suggest we deploy them to guard ourselves against this OTHER inevitable outcome. Whether the Spider Queen is watching us right now, or will learn of it later, we need a defense against the First House, or any other she might approach. And what of this thing you spoke of to call for help? How does that work?"

"It's called a shard-com. It's a product of their recent development in science. It allows me to speak to someone up there, in this case that Cardinal Nemelle, and I can also speak to that same scout as an alternative, since she can use a portal to jump in and offer aid. We discussed several items of interest, one of these being for them to deliver someone, an agent, into our House to act as an intermediary between the two sides. They can offer such things as fresh supplies, additional guardsmen, and more if we need it. We are hoping to bring other Houses into this and create a line for ourselves. This might turn out to be as much a civil war as a liberation effort, but as they keep saying, one way or another, we're going."

"And what of the Spi…erm…is it even wise for us to speak her name any longer if we are expected to convert to the others?"

"Probably not. We need to turn away from her entirely. They will also deliver new icons for us to call on the old gods and reacquaint ourselves. If we can call on their favor, this will offer additional strength for us to survive this. And I would further suggest something else entirely atypical for our…way of life…Mother. To help others survive it as well. All our servants, and any others who might need refuge. We must offer this, as this would further deliver us into our own redemption."

Chapter 5

PROCREATIONAL CONSPIRACY

"Now, let me see if I understand this correctly," Aristan considers. "You, young lady, who are so well-known amongst us, wish to play a rather dastardly little game on those two darling individuals who so unfortunately have experienced such extreme difficulty in conceiving a child, that this plot of yours is to force the issue such that they can essentially have their cake and eat it too, by not exposing themselves to the public that they do indeed suffer this misfortune. Hmm?"

"Um, aye?" Relissa admits sheepishly. "Though it wasn't really my original idea. Vonafel is the one pushing for it."

"Of course. But it would seem she needs to enlist coconspirators along the way. Which simply leads us to this. Now, you would wish to involve my dear and precious wife here, along with her divine Father?" He directs them at Aelwyn sitting next to him as they shared a table in a sidewalk café.

"Aye!" she nods enthusiastically. "Lord Aristan, we all know they want kids, but the biology of a human and an Avariel seem a little out of whack to do it right and proper. Naturally, they could go into a clinic and get an artificial treatment, but you know Aerlie, she likes it, um, natural," she giggles. "Not that I can blame her, it's more fun that way."

"Oh dear Powers, help us for that aspect alone," he chuckles.

"She does hold a valid point, Aristan," Aelwyn accedes. "The natural sensation of childbirth, even from the moment of conception, is a blessed delight. And this would of course be her first, so it needs to be truly special. And I must admit, the clinical approach would rob her of some part of that."

"Uh huh, and how would your Father see it from his side? Or should I even ask, knowing him as we do?" he grins timidly.

"I would probably need to admit he would agree with some part of this. But the approach would be difficult. Just like she said, Thaelyn and Aerlie would surely feel the presence of a greater Power entering the room with them."

"Indeed, and this would make that aspect of it seem improbable."

"Unless we could hit them up with something to dull those Celestial senses," Relissa advises. "Something like a drug, or a potion, or something to distract them from feeling him in the full sense of it. And then, he would need to sneak in, real careful like."

"Oh, this much is certain. But to...hit them up...would likely require something extraordinary. And you know Thaelyn, he is a very savvy one to play the fool. It would have to be something unknown to him, which would leave many of the more common items out of play. And then, it would need to apply, at the very least, a kind of euphoric hallucinogen, if to dull those senses of his enough that a deity could then sneak in to apply a blessing of any sort."

"Aristan," Aelwyn considers. "Perhaps it would not need to be quite as potent as that, not unto itself. Rather, if to apply it for an initial effect, then to have my Father exaggerate it further, perhaps gradually as they engage themselves, and up to a point where they can no longer pay such close attention to his intrusion."

"Aelwyn," Relissa asserts. "Do you recall that time when Marelle had her rambunctious romp?"

"Oh, please. Yes. I saw part of that as they were finishing up, but I could feel most of it even as it first began. Wow, what I would not do for a little of that!" she giggles demurely.

"My dear!" Aristan mocks his bravado. "Do I not satisfy your most salacious wants frequently enough to maintain your contentment where you can focus on something other than more wants?"

"Oh, Aristan!" she beams. "Of course you do! On those wondrously rare occasions when you actually visit the bedroom."

"Excuse me! I visit that abode every evening when I require sleep. Do you not notice me?"

"Ah, that was you? My goodness, I thought that was the dog, for all the snorting it makes."

Relissa let out a boisterous roar of laughter at the play, while Aristan portrayed a visage of improbable defeat.

"Powers help me, I have been outplayed! Aelwyn, you are certainly in a chipper mood today. I suppose I will need to attend to that later, in order to bring you out of the clouds enough to set sights on your work again."

"But Relissa," Aelwyn resumes. "In answer to your question, Marelle received an especially intense dose of Lathander's energy…she and her husband. Before we could hit Thaelyn and Aerlie with this much, we would need to dull some of their other capacities first, and then likely apply it incrementally. But like Aristan said, it would need to begin with something unknown to either of them."

"Do you peeps up there in Sigil have anything to do the trick?" she asks.

"Um, I suppose I could answer yes, but this would again fall into something they might each know about, so we may not be able to use it here."

"Buggers. It's a good plan, if only we can get this one piece. All right, at least speak to your Father, and see if he can pitch in. Maybe something will come up later for this other bit, and then we can put it all together."

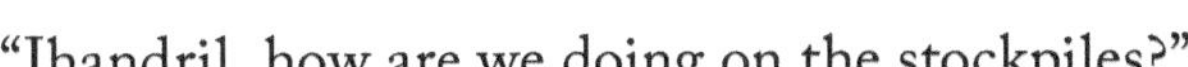

"Jhandril, how are we doing on the stockpiles?"

"The basement is filling up, but there is only so much we can hold. Also, I am aware many of the servants are telling their families, and word is now spreading to the servant quarters relating to several other Houses. Although I am growing concerned over whether the Houses themselves are listening, or if they might reveal the movement to the higher authorities."

"At this point, it might be more important simply to rescue anyone we can, as I'm sure some of those higher authorities are plotting their own actions. I can't believe the…ahem…would be so unspoken as to let it go this far before calling on someone to take notice. I'm expecting a messenger, at the very least, to come to our House from someone on the Council, if for no other reason than to investigate all this recent activity."

Malafay found herself in a rush to prepare the House for any repercussions relating to the abandonment of their old faith and the embracing of the new one, even though they didn't have any new icons to worship yet. But the old altar they used was now being discarded, and all the old tokens destroyed, to remove their influence.

The talismans she brought back were placed at multiple locations around the House, on doors and windows, and the walls surrounding the estate. But this would only serve as a first line of defense, and not necessarily a complete one, once the siege truly began…if one was coming at all. They would need to replace their old worship icons with new ones and begin praying full-time to reinforce the warding aura if the going got really tough.

"Malafay," Alakaere calls as she approaches down the hall. "The shrine room is clear, with the last of it removed and destroyed. I swear, if this doesn't make someone angry, I don't know what will. What do we do now? We need replacements, don't we?"

"Yes, I'll call in upstairs and see if they have that agent of theirs ready yet."

Malafay pulls out her shard-com and struggles to recall the instructions on how to use it, selecting the icon for the directory, then a line entry that was supposed to represent Cardinal Nemelle. She brings it up to her ear and waits as the unit rings. Alakaere studies her for the odd device and leans in to listen to the sounds.

"This is Cardinal Nemelle speaking."

Alakaere jerks back at the strange voice emanating out of the tiny handheld unit.

"Cardinal Nemelle, this is Malafay. We are ready to proceed on this side with the introduction of our new icons. I have the Matron Mother's support, although admittedly she was difficult. But we are following your instructions now and require something to reinforce our position. Can you help us?"

"Of course. First, we will need to establish a portal index inside your House. For this, I will send an agent we call a spook. He will apply a device to mark this initial index, and from there we can begin delivering our support. Give me a few moments of time to see this through."

"Very good, and thank you."

They end the link as Alakaere glares at her younger sister.

"You seem to have made a remarkable adjustment to their ways, Malafay. Perhaps you could teach me a few things?"

"I will, Alakaere. All of us will need this in time. But let's first focus on our most immediate needs. We should expect to see someone arriving soon. We should also decide on a room to use for our portal activity. It should probably be something out of the way and relatively empty, to allow space for it. I am also thinking of whoever they send us as the agent. He will likely be a surface dweller, and will require a lot more light to see by than anything we can tolerate."

"Great. All right, let me check on what we have and select something for you."

In Nemelle's office, she was calling in a special agent belonging to the Suuden-Aryku. As was typical of her kind, she was a tall female with blue skin, curved horns, hoofed feet, and a tail. She also had glowing pale blue eyes. She arrived in the office and came to attention.

"Yes, Cardinal, what do you need?"

"You are familiar with the recent work with Relissa Moonshimmer and her assignment, correct?"

"Yes, Cardinal. I've travelled with her on a few occasions by now."

"Good, we have another House down there converting to our side, and we need a portal index to that location. You will first need to identify it. It is the Deghym House. Use a map, if you must, to locate it, then get inside, find a suitable location, and return for a marking unit. I will assign an agent to follow behind once we have the index."

"Excellent."

The officer salutes and turns to leave the room. She makes a quick trot to a special room located in the rear of the guildhall that was allocated for private use among her kind. There, she takes a seat, which at this time was amongst several others already in the room, and relaxes into her chair. She then allows herself to fall into a meditative trance.

After several moments in this condition, she directs her thoughts to separate her mind from her body, a kind of out-of-body experience, but here to release her spiritual consciousness from her corporeal form and move about independently. Gradually, she begins to emerge as a ghostly incorporeal projection.

She steps away from the chair and her physical body, examining herself and applying her mental focus to manifest her metaphysical projection into a quasi-tangible apparition, capable of interacting with people and other objects in nearly the same way as her original body. Then, she begins to recall a familiar location in the Drow city where she would find her new assignment, and her image vanishes in a puff of ethereal vapor.

She arrives in the city, taking on a new form of a tiny insect, which wouldn't stand out nearly as much as her full body. She was already quite familiar with all the major Houses, so she simply flew over the rooftops in the direction of the Deghym House, landing on an exterior wall and searching for a window to peer inside. Once in position, she folds her image inside the room and begins fluttering about, looking for someone to talk to, although at this point unsure who her contact should be. As such, she makes her way to the ground floor near the front entrance. There, she reimagines her image to her natural form. She might as well use this as anything, as it's all the same for a new face inside the House. And they should be expecting something by now.

The foyer was empty at the time she arrived, so no one saw her making her impromptu appearance. She calls out to see if anyone would respond.

"Hello? I'm an agent sent from Cardinal Nemelle's office to assist with a portal index."

There was no immediate verbal response, but one of the servants heard the noise and came to investigate. However, on seeing the nearly eight-foot-tall female towering over her, she simply screamed and ran away.

"Well, that went about as expected," the officer muses silently. "I guess she wasn't the one who made the call."

The commotion drew the attention of several others, including a couple of males serving as House security.

"Easy now, people, I'm here on request," she soothes. "Who is it that made the call?"

"What is that?" asks one of the males.

"Looks like a demon to me," suggests another one. "Are they using demons up there now?"

Alakaere rushes into the room to find the rest, but halts cold as she finds herself staring up into the glowing eyes of something otherworldly.

"By the depths of the abyss..." she wheezes.

"Not quite," the officer declares calmly, hoping to diffuse the situation. "I'm just from another world."

Malafay shows up a moment later, also with a note of surprise to see the officer standing there with her head nearly scraping the ceiling.

"Wow, is that one of their agents? Where did they find those?"

"My name is Lieutenant Tawni Ven'Hagar. My people are called Suuden-Aryku, and we serve a special division of the military body up there called the Stormhooves. I was sent by request about a portal index. Who requested this?"

"I did," Malafay steps forward. "I've never seen one such as you before…none of us has. Where do you come from?"

"Our home world is called Azgarén, which is located rather far from here. We joined the empire only during this past century."

"Empire! Not a kingdom, but an empire?"

"Tae'Eladar sometimes still refers to itself as a kingdom, but this is mostly nostalgia speaking. We are an empire of five worlds so far, but I expect it to grow one day as we establish new colonies. This world is only beginning to reach into space, so we have a way to go before they become fully adjusted to it."

"They…this world. You are speaking in terms of the third person here."

"Yes, my people are substantially more advanced, but Tae'Eladar is rapidly catching up, much to our shock and surprise, and a little frustration," she chuckles.

"Why frustration?"

"Our civilization is two million years old, but in a mere fraction of that, they beat us to several key inventions, and are matching our own technology which we worked so long to develop. It really hits home when you see someone moving so fast."

"Is there a reason for this? This king up there, for instance?"

"He's certainly one reason, but the people of this world have a tendency to move quickly regardless. My people…well…" she sighs. "When your lifespans reach twenty thousand years, you develop a few bad habits," she shrugs.

Malafay felt faint, along with Alakaere. The rest were simply speechless.

"Anyway," the Lieutenant continues. "I was sent to establish a portal index. Where do you want it?"

"Uh, right. Alakaere? Did you find anything?"

"I did," she moans. "But I'm asking myself if she can even fit through the hallways to reach it. Still, it's this way."

Alakaere leads both Malafay and the officer through the House to a study parlor. There, in a corner, she had removed several pieces of furniture to clear space for the portal.

"Is this good enough? We don't have much without moving something to make space."

"This will do," the Lieutenant nods. "Just keep it clear, in case we need to bring something in, and then clear the space once it arrives."

"Good, so now what?"

"I need to bring in a marking unit. I'll be back in just a moment."

She now brings her focus to the guildhall requisitions office and folds her image out of the room, much to the continued shock of the people.

"I swear!" Malafay gasps. "She doesn't even NEED a portal. She did that entirely by her own will!"

"Is that what happens if you go two million years?" Alakaere winces.

"If it is, we are seriously outmatched."

The Lieutenant arrives at the requisitions office and collects the device, which was a unit mounted on a tripod stand. It had a portal gem device on top, and a control interface on one side with a display panel to configure the unit. She picks it up and then brings her mind back to the room in Malafay's House. She pops into view carrying the unit and sets it up in the corner of the room.

"How did you do that?" Malafay asks timidly. "Popping out, and popping back in?"

"My people possess a very special skill. This isn't my physical body. My body is up there, and this is a kind of mental projection of my spirit into physical space."

"Unbelievable! Such a thing is possible if you go high enough in your development?"

"It could be, depending on what sort of development you have. We got a jump start on ours as we have a very peculiar heritage. Our people are described as a young Celestial society."

Now Malafay loses it. She squeals and covers her face. Her sister gapes at the suggestion and steps back. The meaning was generally lost on the rest of the assembly, but on seeing this, it was clear to hold a meaning of some kind, so their reaction was at least based on the two sisters.

The Lieutenant sets up the device and configures the panel. She presses a button on the touch screen and steps back, not that it was actually necessary in her case, but out of habit. The unit charges up with a soft beeping, which Malafay instantly recognized with Relissa's unit. It then erupts in a lateral spiraling of energy radiating outward, and then collapsing back in on the gem in the middle. The gem glowed briefly before settling. She then approached to examine the data screen to confirm the marking.

"And that's it," she declares. "Now, from this moment, if we need to send anything to you, it will appear in this space. I believe we will be sending an agent to you soon, once we assign someone, and from there, he will assist further."

She picks up the unit and bows her head politely before flashing out of sight.

"They're quick, aren't they," Alakaere admits. "In, out, boom, thank you."

"Yes," Malafay emits softly. "I guess if you intend to go to other worlds, you don't wait for it."

"Cardinal Nemelle?" the Lieutenant calls as she arrives back at the office. "I have the mark. I sent it to your vid-mail."

"Good..." she checks her terminal for the recent delivery. "I will pass this along. Relissa was also curious as to our progress, so I should give her a call. Maybe she can make a visit to check on things for us as we assign our agent and prepare to deliver a few items to them."

"Excellent. Is there anything else?"

"That should be all for now. You may return to your other assignments."

The Lieutenant nods and salutes, then leaves the office, while Nemelle makes a quick call on her shard-com to report to Relissa.

"Scout Moonshimmer here."

"Relissa, we have a new index inside the Deghym House. Would you like to make a quick visit to investigate the situation for us while we set things up on this side?"

"Aye, that sounds dandy. Send it over and I'll go take a peek."

"Very good, I am sending it now."

Inside the Deghym House, Malafay was reporting the recent events to the Matron Mother, showing her the room and the corner where they should expect to see arrivals from above.

"We need to keep this area clear," she asserts. "So they don't stumble over anything when they arrive. I'm told we should expect someone soon. Then we can begin to arrange ourselves with their support."

"How many Houses do you think are doing this by now?"

"I don't know, and I probably don't dare go out and ask. I suppose we may learn of it in time, and then I would suggest we band together for our mutual support."

As they held their conversation, it was briefly interrupted by a bright flash in the corner of the room that almost blinded them. They both screeched and shielded their eyes until the effect settled, and they could focus again.

Relissa arrived in the room, and instantly found herself squinting, as she tried to see anything.

"Jiggers, you peeps need to turn on a few lights around here. A girl could find herself in a pinch if some lonely guy was hiding behind her."

"Uh huh…figures," Malafay smirks. "Mother, this is her, that one I told you about. Watch her, she's a jester."

"Really!" the Matron Mother muses as she studies the new arrival.

She steps over to examine the strange figure now standing in her home. Relissa was clearly a dark elf, but unlike any she had ever seen before.

"You are one of those my daughter spoke of that survived up there during this time?"

"Aye, but surviving is a bit of a relative term for us," Relissa replies. "My people migrated to another world, one we call Therinë, along with some others. But that world got hit by some nasty business, and our people got reduced down quite a bit. Still, surviving is surviving, and we'll rebuild."

"You sound like you are holding strong, even with all of that. And then you became part of this new kingdom?"

"Once they found us. We were so happy to go home, we couldn't wait for a formal invitation."

"Most interesting. It was that favorable?"

"More than that, in our case. We were struggling to uphold our old culture and religion. When they found us, it was a chance to rejoin our heritage. You just can't pass up something like that."

"And now you are coming for us."

"We don't want to leave anyone out. We're all part of the same mother race, and as people who hold this as our special legacy, we need to stick together."

The Matron Mother gazed at the exuberant young woman and felt a silent fire igniting inside. This was a strange and unknown sensation to her, but it signified a dedication of principle where some things were just too important to discard. She sighed as she glanced around the room at the other people still assembled in conversation.

"Well, then I should welcome you to my home. What is your name?"

"Relissa of House Moonshimmer. My Mum and Dah are both nobles, once part of our native Council, but later taking up positions in Thaelyn's government."

"You come from a noble house...but you work as a scout?"

"We still hold a responsibility to serve a role, regardless of where we come from. I chose this because I liked running the open fields."

"I see. And your parents, they serve in this Council now?"

"For a time, they did, but they're both retired now."

"Wait. Retired?"

"Aye..." she chuckles. "That's what happens when you live your full life without any knives in your back, and then you find time to simply sit back and reflect on all the grand things you did with yourself."

"Uh huh, is that supposed to be a rub?"

"Maybe a wee bit," she grins.

The Matron Mother turns to glare at Malafay, and then feels a very curious sensation welling up inside of her, which was nearly as alien as that fire she felt a moment before. She then burst out laughing.

"This is truly amazing! How is it possible to see such as this here in our House? Well, I should give you over to Malafay, as she is the one managing many of our efforts. I must...retire...to my chamber for a while."

"Good enough. I'm mostly here to check on things to make sure all is well as we move forward. Malafay, how are the preparations coming?"

"The basement stores are nearly full," she declares. "But we never really stockpiled so many goods before. We sent word out with our servants, to share with their families and anyone else they can reach, to prepare themselves. We are trying to do our part to help others realize this transition, and will open our doors to anyone who needs shelter. But this does also present a potential problem, if we see too many people rushing at us for help. Our House is large, but not so expansive as to take everyone."

"Right, I get it. We might need to offload a few here and there to some other holding area, at least until things settle for us. I'll pass this along to the Cardinal and see if we can find some temporary shelters."

"Just keep in mind the issue of light. It needs to be sufficiently shaded for our people to find comfort."

"Something indoors, without windows perhaps? Or maybe underground? I know dwarves like to live underground, but they also use more light than any of you. Maybe we can find an old settlement or some such…"

"An old settlement?" Malafay reflects as she recalls her journey through the tunnels. "We found something as we were coming up. It looked old, like from a bygone era, and maybe elven, as if it once belonged to us."

"Yes! We are aware of these in a few places. Old outposts, probably from the early days of the migration. I wonder if we could refurbish any of them. They'd be really old by now, though. We would need to conduct a careful inspection, and probably a bit of construction work. Good, this might work for us. It would also be a bit ironic. We'd be turning something once used to send you into exile, now to bring you out of it."

"Yes, that would be a good rub. Maybe even appropriate."

They begin a tour of the estate, with Malafay now showing Relissa around, peeking into rooms, peering out balconies, investigating the basement storerooms, and finally the old shrine room which was cleaned out and waiting for a new altar.

"That temple of yours out there will be tough, I think," Relissa muses. "That's where your priests will surely be calling your old goddess and holding a showdown of some kind. By then, I hope we have enough people in safekeeping to bring you through this."

"I suppose, much like you, we can rebuild, if it gets too bad."

"Maybe so, but I hope not to let it go that far. My peeps got dusted down to one surviving city. Rebuilding for us involves making a lot of babies to fill up the numbers again."

"Oh no. What happened?"

"War, four centuries of it by invaders who didn't let up. They just whittled us down to the last, and held us there. They didn't want to kill all of us, they were hoping to use what was left for something. Then Thaelyn came in and rescued us. Now we're building new towns and having a wee bit of fun with ourselves."

"A wee bit of fun?" she raises her brow. "Making these babies, I suppose. Yes, I've heard this can be enjoyable…somewhat. Although I often wondered how."

"Let me guess, you're a virgin, ay?" she grins.

"Well, yes, but in our society, only the Matron Mother brings forth anything new within the greater Houses. We daughters need to wait our turn for it… if we get one at all."

"That's just not right. And worse, I've heard a few stories about how you do it."

"Yes, and this is one part I never really agreed with. The priestesses of the temple lay themselves out on the platform, then call in a group of random males to attend to their desires. And this is how you produce a child which you so promptly delegate to some caregiver until it's old enough to go into an academy for that tortuous learning exercise our instructors lay down for them."

"And you call this bit enjoyable?"

"Well, the engagement act itself is enjoyable, so they say. Probably the only thing in our society that does NOT plant a knife in someone's back," she chuckles.

"I suppose. But if all you're doing is calling in a bunch of males and say, here it is boys, make sure you're good and ready for it," she giggles. "The thing of it is, how do you get a guy, even if you have a bunch of naked girls laid out for you, to go at it on command. They don't quite respond like that, especially if under a lot of stress."

"Ah! Well, yes, I suppose I do understand this part. This is where that enjoyable part comes in. Both sides are tense at this point. It's a ritual they carry out at times, and different groups are invited to participate at different intervals. The females regard this as a mandatory act to create a new generation, at least as much, I suppose, to replace those previous ones with the knives in their backs."

"Oh jiggers, I wish you didn't put it like that."

"I know, but this is often how it seems. Sometimes they are called by name, other times it might be voluntary for any family looking to expand. But the impersonal nature of it means you are pairing up with whoever happens to be standing next to you. So, to make it a little easier to actually engage each other, they use a special incense to relax the senses, releasing the tensions and relieving them of the inhibitions that would otherwise come from not holding any personal interest."

"An incense?" Relissa perks up. "What does it do?"

"It's a special formula to place one's mind into a mildly incoherent state, a bit euphoric, but still with enough control to perform their actions. For the males, they find it easier to become aroused to serve the females. For the females, they find it pleasing to allow him to enter her body and satisfy her desires."

"Jiggers, I wonder if this could do it…" she muses privately. "Do you have any here I could look at?"

"Um, this would go to the Matron Mother. She might keep some in a private stash. Sometimes each House might have its own supply for the Matron Mother to choose her own timing."

Malafay turns and leads the two of them back into the House and up to the Matron Mother's private chamber. The matriarch was absent at this time, so Malafay sneaks inside to show Relissa a small ornately carved box.

"Here, these sticks of incense," she pulls a few out for display. "You burn a few of these around the room, give it a moment to settle in, and you won't have anything to hold you back from enjoying your moment. Why, are you interested in someone back home, and want to try a little?" she smiles mischievously.

"I'm actually thinking of a friend…and I know that might sound like a line, but it's true. They're having a bit of trouble lately, and maybe could use a little extra help."

"Well, if they're having trouble relaxing into the experience, this will relieve them of it."

"What about actually conceiving a baby out of it. Does it do anything like that?"

"I think this is an unrelated issue. You should know this well enough as an elf, but we need to take that special ritual preparation to make ourselves ready for conception. Then we take a man with us and boom…baby. Is this friend of yours elven?"

"Yes, but he's not, and they're having just a wee bit of trouble making it happen."

"He is not. Would he be human, as you mentioned once before?"

"Yes, but she… Well, all right, you didn't hear this from me. It's Thaelyn and Aerlie, and with her being an Avariel, they're having a tiny match-up issue."

"A match-up issue…"

"Probably due to her wings. It's part of a science we call biology. She has an extra set of appendages, so this throws the numbers off. Therefore, between the two of them, the matching of pairs is a bit tough. Maybe not impossible, but certainly tough enough to make it frustrating."

"This is actually a fascinating principle."

"We have a medical procedure we could use to solve this artificially, but these two buggers are too hardheaded to use it. We could also have one of our gods offer a blessing, and some folk use this for an extra hit to ensure healthy babies, but again, they don't want to be seen in public doing something that might tarnish their royal image."

"Ah, I see. So, it's a matter of image, and they want to be seen as infallible. This could be a problem."

"Therefore, a few of us are planning a sneaky little hit to get them going. But the problem is to sneak it in such that they don't see it coming. If we use that divine blessing, a Celestial will feel it too quick. But if to use something like a drug, or maybe this incense, it might offer us just what we need to put them out of their full senses so we can do it unnoticed."

"Well, this could possibly do that, but it also depends on how strong their senses are."

"All we need is something unknown for them to play with. We'll use that divine hit to put them the rest of the way under, and then bam, royal heirs," she giggles.

"Uh huh, and this is your king and queen. Do you do these sorts of things often up there?"

"Well, I have something of a reputation, but it's all in fun, and for a good cause. And they know me, so I'm not worried about it. If it gives them their privacy, and a baby, that's all we need."

"All right, well, here, take several. That should be enough to put them into a starting condition."

"I don't want to steal anything away from your mother. She might get angry, and it's better to keep her happy."

"Not to worry. I seriously doubt she'll be using this anytime soon, not with all that noise going on outside, and I'll simply replace it later. Give this to them with my special blessing that they are helping my people. And I hope you are successful with this little play of yours. Let me know if it results in anything."

Malafay takes several sticks of incense out and gives them to Relissa. She studies them briefly, carefully sniffing them, and then puts them into her pocket. Relissa then smiles warmly and wraps an arm around the unsuspecting Drow to give her a hug.

Malafay had never received a hug before. But the gesture was clearly one of sisterly passion. She felt a warm fuzzy feeling inside as Relissa pulled away, causing her to smile reflexively. They then continued their tour of the House.

✦✦✦✦✦

"Aelwyn, I got something for you…or rather, Aerlie. Now we need to meet and plan our approach."

"Got something?"

Relissa had returned home and was calling Aelwyn to report her new discovery. She was sitting at a sidewalk café not far from the guildhall on the main boulevard down below.

"Aye, are you free? Where's Lord Aristan?'

"I believe he is in his office. They had a session over in the High Council chamber earlier, but they finished almost an hour ago. Where are you?"

"At that little café we all like to visit. Our usual table. I just called in to Vonafel, so she's on her way over. If you can join us, we can get to figuring out how to make a new baby together," she giggles.

"You know, Relissa, you are incorrigible. All right, I will be down there in a few moments, and I will call on Aristan to join us. What about Nemelle? Maybe she would like to participate?"

"Fine and good. Why not get everyone on the list. See you soon."

They end the call and Relissa relaxes in her chair at the café. Soon, an elder High Elf arrives and sits down, and they begin some light conversation until Aelwyn and Nemelle show up, and then later, Aristan.

"Ah, so the conspiracy circle is now complete," he announces jovially. "Shall we call the authorities to collect you as a group, or would you choose to give them a bit of exercise and a happy romp around the city?" he grins.

"Aristan!" Aelwyn smiles. "You are as much a part of this as the rest, and YOU work in the High Council. Dear Powers, what 'authority' we have simply within this circle."

"Indeed, and this will certainly go down in the books if it should ever get out. Very well, what sort of mischief do we have today?"

Relissa leans forward and pulls out a small rolled-up kerchief and sets it on the table.

"This may be our ticket, and hopefully good enough for the job. But I think we'll only get one shot at it, so we need to make it count."

She unrolls it to reveal the Drow incense sticks.

"This is a type of incense, given to me by that girl, Malafay, the Drow I'm working with lately down below. She says they use this in that ritual of theirs in their temples, or sometimes at home, to pair up the boys and girls for their mating rites…and in this case it really is a ritual, as there isn't any true emotion to it. So, they use this to set the mood and help everyone go to it."

"I have heard of this…" Nemelle reflects.

"But Powers help us," Aelwyn shakes her head. "It sounds so mechanical. What does it do?"

"According to her," Relissa explains. "It's a type of hallucinogen to create a euphoric lift, relaxing the senses and relieve the tension that ordinarily goes along with ordering peeps to lay themselves out on a temple floor and work each other."

"Indeed, mechanical is right," Aristan muses. "No wonder their society is so rough, if they cannot even produce children without a divine mandate."

"Laying down on a temple floor and working each other?" Vonafel winces. "A group session? Oh yes, I can certainly see how that might play out in the eyes of a goddess commanding it. You, male…" she mocks. "Perform for this woman, and make it good!"

The group emits a tender chuckle as Relissa continues.

"Now, where the royals are concerned, this might not do anything as for actual conception, but it would dull their senses just enough that maybe we can get in there with our own bit. And best of all, this would be unknown to either of them. But we need to make it work the first time."

"Yes," Aelwyn nods. "I must agree. We could attempt this once, maybe to entice them to partake in a new sensation during their next act. But this act should not only provide a result, as I think we should also provide a make-up for all the lost time, and satisfy the need for some time to come."

"Such as?" Aristan raises his brow. "What are you suggesting we, erm, place inside there?" he smiles impishly.

"I would say no less than twins, much like Marelle once got. This would provide for an instant family to make up for the centuries of effort."

"Um, Aelwyn…" Vonafel notes. "She's an elf, and an Avariel at that. And we don't normally produce twins."

"Well, this will be an enhanced effort from the beginning, so we cannot describe it in the usual tradition. We will simply take whatever repercussions as they arrive. It is, after all, to overcome this handicap, so she cannot possibly complain about it."

"Probably not, and she'll get her famous oomph and romance, without going out there displaying her vulnerability. Very well, we need a timing for the event."

"We also need a good excuse for the incense," Nemelle adds. "A sensation, yes. But surely, they will ask where it came from and WHY they should explore this sensation at this time. We do not produce anything like this here, and if Thaelyn uses his logical analysis, as he so often does, he might suspect Sigil as a potential source. But if he is as knowledgeable of their agents as Aelwyn and I, for all of our experience, this might also raise controversy."

"Do you ever produce anything new up there? Surely, you people must invent something from time to time."

"We do, and in this time, you might think there could be something new, but we should also involve his Celestial senses and his experience within his Father's court. He was trained to detect the truthfulness of another person's statements. And while I do not see how he might normally suspect any of us of foul play, the suggestion of taking this, for a new sensation or otherwise, coupled with the necessary suggestion of Aerlie preparing her body for a conception event, might stand out with all our recent hounding."

"Oops! Yes…" Vonafel giggles. "And especially out of me."

"Aye," Relissa blushes. "And if my name is attached to it…"

"Oh, that'll throw up a red flag in and of itself."

"So, here is what I might suggest," Nemelle leans forward. "If we simply come out and declare it to be Drow, and used in a mating act to enlighten the senses for a more pleasing experience, this is true, and will ring out in Thaelyn's mind as correct, if he is using any of his senses at this time. It is also a new sensation none of us up here has experienced, so it might be rather interesting to experiment, simply for the sensation itself. Aelwyn and I both know the virtues of experimenting with new sensations from our time spent in the Sensorium up there in Sigil. This was our study, after all. So, between the two of us, we hold a solid foundation to suggest this."

"This is clever of you," Aristan nods. "It adds credibility to the offer."

"And naturally, as this IS another act to enjoy the lovemaking process, she should apply herself in preparation for it, if for no other reason than, as she likes to say, to play that lottery of numbers until the lucky one comes up."

"Ooh, Nemelle!" Relissa croons. "You're a wicked one. It must be a wee bit of your Mum coming through."

"Yes, I suppose it runs in our blood," she smiles timidly. "We do run a bit towards the chaotic side of the spectrum."

✦ ✦ ✦ ✦ ✦ ✦ ✦

"You want us to…experiment?" Aerlie raises her brow inquisitively.

"Oh, come now," Aelwyn asserts. "It is for the sensation of it! And you know this is, or at least was, a part of my study up there in Sigil. We recently came upon this from one of our contacts among the Drow. They say they use this commonly in their mating acts, for instance to help relieve tension and to enhance the experience. This is new to us, and I am curious. So, I am ordering a few experiments amongst certain control groups I know, and being someone who would understand how to evaluate something of this nature, you would be perfect for it."

"How interesting," Thaelyn considers warmly. "Not that I am one who would normally indulge in such as therapeutic or stimulative agents, but I suppose if you would desire a control group to examine this, it is not too much to ask, even if only to quantify it."

"You know, there are a number of oils and rubs people use during their acts to stimulate the senses. There is quite a market for this."

"Yes, I have seen this, but we tend to bypass most of that."

"But then again, Thaelyn," Aerlie suggests. "Maybe she's right, we should indulge a bit more, if only for the experience. The same old thing can become a bit routine after a while."

"Indeed, I suppose you are right. Very well, and how do we use this?"

"It comes in the form of an incense…" Aelwyn declares.

Aelwyn was carrying the kerchief Relissa gave her, and held it up for display, where she unrolls a corner to show the contents.

"According to our information, you might use several of these distributed around the room, for a broader effect. And as with any incense, you breathe it in deeply to saturate yourselves as you prepare for your engagement. It should not carry any long-term effects, and

145

it will make you feel a bit lightheaded, but do not let this distract you from enjoying the sensation."

"Truly!" Thaelyn nods. "I suppose I can do that. Aerlie, what do you think?"

"Certainly! I'm willing if you're willing. And then what, Aelwyn? We give you our results in the morning?"

"That would surely be adequate," she affirms. "Oh, and Aerlie, let us not forget to prepare ourselves appropriately. After all, you do not want to miss any opportunity for that magic moment to occur," she smiles disarmingly.

"Um, is that a hint of some kind, Aelwyn?" Aerlie eyes her suspiciously. "Have you been talking to anyone lately?"

"Aerlie, how many times have I heard you speak of this concept of a lottery? Well, one does not win a lottery if they only play the bet once in a long while. You need to run that spin each time, and do so frequently if you want to achieve success. Well, this is one of those occasions."

"Yes, Aelwyn, I will admit, you are right, but to tell you the truth, I am growing tired of that spin."

"Please Aerlie, do not give up. Go at this with all the vigor of your first time, and make it sensational!" she grins brightly. "That lucky number will one day be yours, and then we can share a few mothering secrets."

"All right, Aelwyn, although I suspect you are trying to apply your dominion over Reality on me to make me do this, I'll concede and give it my best shot. When should we do this, tonight perhaps?"

"Yes, I suppose tonight is as good as any other. That way we can find our results. Who knows, maybe this could prove itself a new market for the sexually deficient."

"Uh huh... I can see it now in the advertising campaign. Tested and approved by the royal family, try it for yourself and enjoy the experience of a lifetime!"

They share a laugh together as Aerlie takes the bundle of incense. They offer their goodbyes and part ways, with Thaelyn and Aerlie returning home to their manor on top of the hill behind the guildhall, and Aelwyn returning to a noble estate home a short distance down a private road further along the hillside and overlooking the city. And along the way, she made a clandestine call on her shard-com.

"Scout Moonshimmer here."

"Relissa, this is Aelwyn, the package is delivered."

"Good to hear. Did they argue over it?"

"No, I gave them a very clever line that it is part of a study effort to evaluate a new stimulative enhancement with a potential for further market value outside of a closed test. And they bought it."

"Oh buggers, girl. You're at least as bad as that other dame. Right. So, now we wait. Are they going to do it tonight?"

"Yes, once I suppose they relax a bit, maybe have something to eat, and then retire."

"Good. I'll get together with Vonafel and Nemelle. I was also thinking of calling in a few other peeps to share the moment. This one should be special, so we might as well invite the gang. Then maybe to take up seating in that café, since it has a nice view of the place up there. What are you and Lord Aristan going to do?"

"He suggested sitting by the window in the study, which can afford us a view of their home up there, if just barely. This should be sufficient, as our Celestial senses can feel it just as much as to see it."

"Aye, fine then. And your Father?"

"He is aware and watching. He will know what to do when the time is right."

"Great. Now we just wait for a bit of fireworks. I just hope the house is still standing afterward."

They laugh as they finish the call, and Aelwyn returns home to enjoy a relaxing meal with her husband, while Relissa gathers together with her friends.

Later in the evening, in that same sidewalk café down the road, Relissa, Vonafel, and Nemelle were meeting with two other friends, Kaliya and Ayene, both of whom were Suuden-Aryku and long-time friends of the royal family. They all took up seating with a view of the street outside, where they could observe the people walking by, the guildhall on the hill above them, and the manor home above that.

"And how many marks are we aiming for on this occasion?" Kaliya wonders.

"And what category would this fall under?" Ayene asks. "This would be a new one, as compared to all the rest."

"Aye, it would," Relissa nods. "But we all know it's for a good cause, so I'm willing to gamble on it."

"At least it's not me this time," Kaliya chuckles. "For all the times I got on his list, you might think he's running out of space by now."

"Didn't he once promise to start a new book for you?" Ayene grins.

"Yes, actually, and I dread to see how it reads so far. That biography they wrote once on our efforts on Azgarén was already sensational."

"Yes, but if you ask me, it was necessary. At least as much for the historical value as anything we did. You can't just hide from all you did to that place. And neither can I, really."

"That was hard, though. So many little details, and most of it on-the-fly."

"We're looking at a lot of the same down below right now with the Drow," Relissa accedes. "Those peeps are stuck between a rock and a hard, um, goddess," she grins sheepishly.

In the royal manor house on top of the hill, situated above a long flight of ornate marble stairs rising out of the guildhall courtyard, Thaelyn and Aerlie were just finishing up their evening meal and a glass of their favorite wine. They had some soothing music being played for them by one of the house servants on a piano, to further relax and set the mood for their bedroom engagement later on.

As they wrapped up their meal, they withdrew to a parlor to sit a while, sharing some light conversation, and further trying to psych themselves up for the intimate moment soon to come. Eventually, as the evening became late, they decided to retire to their room, feeling a little uncertain about their impending moment, but directing themselves to explore the possibility with the aid of this new incense.

They began to set the incense sticks in various locations around the bedroom, on tables and nightstands near the bed, and lighting each one.

"Well, so far, it smells interesting," Aerlie notes. "Maybe this might hold some value yet."

"Perhaps," Thaelyn offers. "We might wish to allow it a moment to build up. Let us prepare ourselves in the meantime."

They each make a visit to the washroom to check their appearance and general presentation. They change out of their evening clothes and set themselves on the bed, sitting on the edge at first as they continued to enjoy the aromas of the incense.

"It's a little pungent," Aerlie suggests. "But I feel a bit exhilarated. Maybe this will work after all. I'm feeling like I'm coming into the mood."

"Yes, I must admit, I was uncertain before, but, um…" he glances down at himself. "I feel as though we might have some impromptu activity occurring in the nether regions."

"Well, don't let it go to waste, my dear. You should know what to do with that!"

She smiles playfully as she throws herself back on a set of pillows on the bed, pulling him down with her. They first begin with a bit of foreplay, involving tickling and caressing, teasing the body parts as a couple of teenagers exploring each other for the first time. The incense subtly worked its way into their minds, as they felt a new vigor arising to indulge their playful act like never before. The centuries of boring routine seemed to melt away, and they found themselves stirring up new passions, the youthful excitement of interplay borne out as if it were a new sensation. And as they delved deeper into their carnal delights, the sounds of their moans began to echo around the room.

Down the way, in the house belonging to Aristan and Aelwyn, he sat by an open window attempting to read a book, while she sat nearby at a vanity combing her hair, not that she actually needed it, as she had been at it for a couple of hours by now. Suddenly, her senses began to pick something up, and she halted her actions, turning towards the window and peering off in the distance.

"Something is happening…" she mutters softly.

Aristan pauses to gaze at her for a moment, then turns to peer out the window.

"All seems calm from this vantage, so far. No burning villages, no fire and brimstone, no volcanos or tidal waves…"

"Oh, Aristan!" she jests. "You KNOW what I mean!"

"Ah, perchance your little play on our dearest friends up there on the hill? Hmm…"

He orients his view on the manor house, which stood out with one corner that happened to be the wing with the bedroom in it. But so far, nothing outwardly visible has occurred.

The moans in the royal bedroom began to escalate, as the couple became more engrossed in their consummate act. The pounding on the bed was now thumping against the wall, and this naturally drew the attention of several attendants from other parts of the manor. A couple of them advanced partway through the hall to investigate.

"That sounds serious," ushers one housemaid.

"Aye," responds a butler. "They must be having a good romp in there tonight! We should move back and give them their privacy."

The groaning from the bedroom continued as the couple was now deeply involved in each other. But it was no longer simply the incense working on them, as now there was another force being applied.

It was subtle at first, and had to disguise itself behind the aromas of the incense circulating around the room. It had to involve itself gradually, slowly building up to augment the incense with an additional effect. One that was so far unnoticed, and designed to discreetly overwhelm the natural senses of the two people in the room. As it approached a threshold, the engagement on the bed increased in vigor, and although the couple still felt it was the incense acting upon them, they felt a sensation like they never had before.

"Oh! Gods above, Thaelyn!" Aerlie screams. "Yes! More!"

"This is remarkable!" he groans. "I can feel so much of you!"

"More, my love, don't stop!"

The sounds of their cries were now echoing out of the window and around the courtyard outside. Aelwyn was leaning over Aristan's shoulder as the two of them stared out the window.

"He's doing it!" she smiles expectantly. "Do you feel it?"

"My dear, while I suppose I must answer yes, this feels a bit like voyeurism."

"Well, maybe. But it's fun."

"Fun, perhaps, but now I am wondering about those sounds. Can you hear it?"

"Yes, actually. Oops!" she grins.

"Wait a moment. Oops? What do you mean, oops! What precisely did you tell your Father to do up there?"

"Oh, just to give them a good time to make it worth the effort."

"Oh! Truly! Is that all? By the Almighty..." he huffs playfully as he returns to the window.

The boisterous shouts and screams resounding out of the royal bedroom were now echoing around the full manor house. Both of them were now engaging their Celestial voices in their lustful delight, and the booming was now carrying as far as the guildhall itself.

"Bloody hell, man!" emits one guard at the gate. "Where do you think that's coming from, ay?"

The other guard pans around the street below, and then the courtyard behind them, only to see several people coming out of dorm rooms into the courtyard as they also tried to locate the source.

On the street crossing down below, Relissa and her friends were still in conversation when the booming effect began to travel down into the city. They all turned to look in the direction of the manor house.

"Jiggers, not another one of those," Relissa moans.

"Well, there goes the privacy part of it," Vonafel giggles. "Marelle, you've got competition!"

"Look there!" Relissa points. "Bloody hell, peeps, that'll stand out a bit."

They all leaned forward to look up at the hill. They could clearly see the manor house, but in addition to that, the faint glow of a pillar of light was shining down on it from somewhere above.

Relissa and her friends stood up and stepped out onto the sidewalk for a better look. There, they took notice of several other people gathering from the café, and more still who were just passing by, now all collecting and gaping at the sight on the hillside.

Inside the house, the thumping had turned to thrashing, as the sounds escalated to rattle the walls. The booming of their voices reverberated across the hillside, now clearly evident of where they came from, such that a large portion of the guildhall student body had come outside to investigate.

"In all the blazes!" issues one student. "I hope that's nothing contagious up there!"

"Contagious!" shouts another. "Better to ask if it could bring the hill down on us."

On the street, people were gathering from nearby restaurants and night clubs, several inns, and a few late-night shops. They were all staring up at the royal house with blank stares and mouths agape.

A call came in to one of the local news stations, and a young reporter was rushing out to the site. She and her cameraman arrived through the local gateway terminal and hurried outside, where they were greeted by a growing crowd of onlookers. She quickly called her cameraman to position himself and start recording.

"This is Hana Laurens for the B.T. edition of the Imperial News Network. I'm here, live on the scene, on Providence Boulevard in front of the Guildhall of the Order. Out here, I'm looking at a growing crowd of people who all seem to be collecting from the nearby venues, and every one of them is oriented on a sight that can only be described as magnificent! Up there, at what is clearly the royal manor house, is a tall pillar of light from an unknown origin. At this time, due to where it is and how it appears, I simply must suggest it to be divine in nature, as we have seen this sort of thing before, if only on rare occasions. And by the sounds booming through the streets right now, I can barely imagine the riotous affair that might be behind them, but surely this must be one for the history books."

Inside the house, the attendants were rushing in all directions at once.

"You there!" shouts the butler. "Grab any loose articles and set them on the floor. And you, bring those paintings down and lean them against this side. And we need more people in here! Line them up along this wall and put your backs to it!"

The moans and squeals coming out of the bedroom were now at full power for their Celestial authority. This allowed them to be heard for blocks away in the city. The sounds were frighteningly loud to those inside the house, such that some thought it could blast the walls apart.

"Yes! Oh yes! Please! More! Harder!"

"By the gods people!" the butler shouts. "How much harder can you get!"

From the street, Relissa and the others all gazed disbelievingly at the sight.

"Well, there'll be no secret about this one. She'll be coming away with something big this time."

"So much for that idea of a lottery," Nemelle muses. "I think she just hit the jackpot!"

"Buggers to you, but aye!"

"She's right…" Vonafel shrugs. "And I suppose I can rest now knowing I've been thoroughly outmatched by my best friend in the game of bedroom bouts."

"I hope this doesn't become a habit," Kaliya shakes her head. "Before you know it, everyone will want one. It'll destroy the city!"

"I'm going to have mine on Azgarén," Ayene nods contentedly. "It's much safer there."

The pillar of light seemed to grow in intensity as the spirit of Lathander turned more of his focus on the couple in their bedroom. The two of them were now deeply entrenched in the act, such that they should no longer take notice of a divine spirit entering the mix.

From their window, Aristan and Aelwyn watched as a glowing orb seemed to descend through the pillar towards the house.

"There it goes," Aelwyn smiles.

"Oh dear…" Aristan moans. "And here go the windows."

On the street, the people gazed at the apparition of a divine hand coming into view and orienting at the house.

"Jiggers!" Relissa winces. "Brace yourselves!"

The news reporter had her camera on the house above as she followed the movement of the hallowed body.

"People, we look like we might be receiving a new arrival here!" she announces excitedly. "It's a little hard to refute what they're doing up there, and if that's who I think it is, by the gods! This might finally be the day for us!"

The hand touched down on the house and penetrated into the room. And on contact, the rhythmic shouts and moans escalated into a final scream of ecstasy. The two of them combined their voices into one harmonious cry that shook the air and rumbled through the streets. The bedroom windows exploded onto the grounds outside, and the reverberations resounded halfway across the city.

And as once before in the city's history, the assembled audience erupted in a tumultuous round of cheers and applause.

"Oh, please, not again," Relissa moans and covers her face. "This is it for me, I'm sure of it. I should probably retire after this one."

Kaliya simply patted her friend on the shoulder as the scene settled down for the evening.

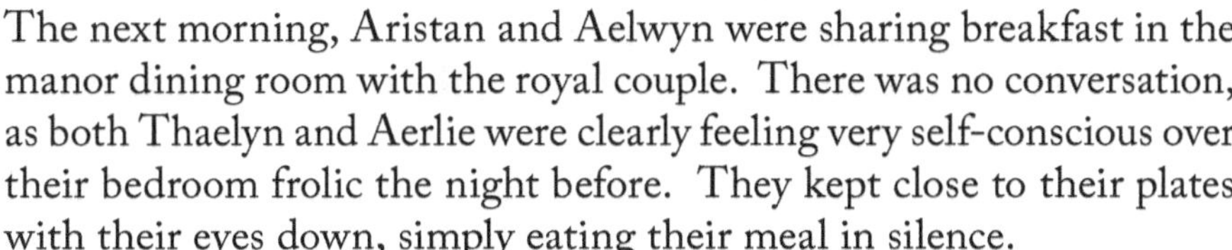

The next morning, Aristan and Aelwyn were sharing breakfast in the manor dining room with the royal couple. There was no conversation, as both Thaelyn and Aerlie were clearly feeling very self-conscious over their bedroom frolic the night before. They kept close to their plates with their eyes down, simply eating their meal in silence.

The royal couple sat at opposite ends of the table with Aristan and Aelwyn sitting opposite of each other on the sides. The butlers and maids lined the room, waiting for any occasion to offer their service. But although they were all well-trained for their professionalism, there was still a hushed level of grinning and snickering ushering up. Then Aristan decides to try livening things up with a bit of light conversation.

"Such a curious thing, this past eve. I think we had a pack of wild animals roaming through the yard. I have no idea where they might have come from, though."

Aerlie rolls her eyes up from her plate to glare at him, then back down again.

"They were a rowdy bunch, as well," he continues. "Yipping and howling for a fair length of time."

Now Thaelyn rolls his eyes up to view him, then further to observe Aerlie at the other end of the table before returning to his plate.

Aristan continues, "They sounded like they must have been attacking the lawn furniture, as well. I heard all manner of thrashing sounds out there. My goodness, I wonder what sort of damage they caused."

Aerlie felt a giggle coming out. She tried stifling it, but it was getting past her, even if she tried covering her mouth.

Several of the butlers and maids glanced at each other and grinned widely.

"I felt sure they were after the trash bins," Aristan continues. "For all the ruckus, I would imagine they must have dragged those completely around the grounds."

Aerlie was unable to continue eating. She was now covering her mouth with both hands and convulsing with hidden laughter. Thaelyn also tried desperately to conceal his reaction, setting down his fork and turning to the side as he tried hiding his face.

"Was it a full moon, perhaps?" Aristan continues unabated. "An entire pack of them baying at the moon, maybe also chasing each other around in a frisky little romp to enjoy the warm summer evening. But of course, that must be it."

Aerlie was nearly losing it by now. She was laughing uncontrollably, turning in her chair, and ducking down into her lap. Thaelyn was silently following suit, leaning an elbow on the table, and covering his eyes.

"But in the end, they must have moved on," Aristan concludes. "I wonder if there might be anything on the morning news. Aelwyn, have you seen anything yet?"

"Oh no! Please!" Aerlie shouts. "Oh! It'll be the death of me if they put that on the air."

"Put what on the air?" he wonders innocently. "A pack of wild animals romping through the royal garden? Why, I should say so! Just where do you think such as that might actually come from! Certainly not from around here, I will tell you!" he huffs playfully.

"Aristan! It wasn't wild animals, and I think you should probably know that!"

"Me?" he retorts harmlessly. "Oh, heavens no. I think I am much too young and innocent to imagine anything else it could be."

"Gods pay pity! Aelwyn, I think you and I need to talk."

"Talk? About what?" she raises her brow sweetly. "Oh, I recall now, you were going to tell us about that incense we were speaking of. By the way, how did that go?"

"Aelwyn!" she growls. "Just what was in that stuff?"

"Well, actually, I do not have the precise formula. It belongs to the Drow, you know. Something proprietary, no doubt. But I suppose I could find out for you if you like."

"I swear! If I didn't know you as well as I do…"

"Aerlie," Thaelyn interjects. "I think we may need to reconsider that aspect. For both of them. Drow formula or otherwise, there was at least some minor amount of mischief in that presentation."

"But you did enjoy yourselves, did you not?" Aelwyn wonders.

"I, uh…suppose the answer must be an unqualified yes. But we may need to examine the dosage a bit, if you are hoping to market the stuff."

"Good, so long as we have a result. By the way, I hear they are having a sale on windows this week. For some odd reason, there seems to be a sudden run on them."

Aerlie slumps in her chair as she glares at Aelwyn. But before she could say anything, a muted round of chuckling ushered out of their attendants, who could no longer hold onto it.

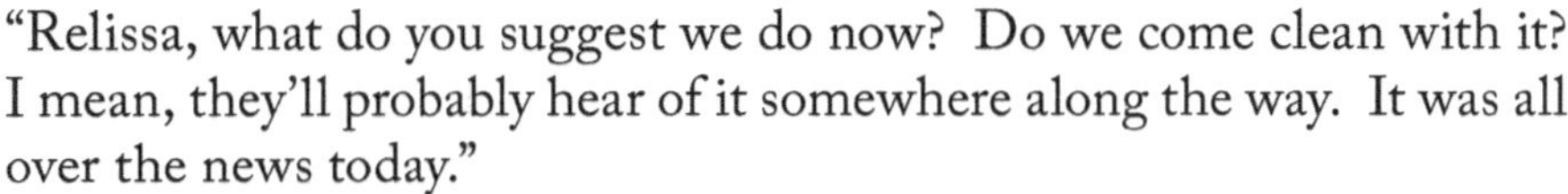

"Relissa, what do you suggest we do now? Do we come clean with it? I mean, they'll probably hear of it somewhere along the way. It was all over the news today."

"Do they actually listen to the news?"

"Um, I don't know, personally."

"Vonafel, she's your best friend, and you don't know if she watches the daily news?"

"Well, she might on occasion, but THIS one…"

"All right, here's what I'll say for it. If she does, she might say something to one of us, or to Aelwyn. And if so, all I can say is, she wouldn't go into a temple for it, so it came to her. And buggers to the idea of no one knowing about it. It's done now and the world is almost celebrating. So, there's your answer."

"All right, I suppose you can't argue that much. This takes the stress of that decision out of their hands. What's done is now done."

"Now, on the other side of it, if the people around her don't otherwise say anything, and I'm half thinking they might just keep it quiet, then she simply won't know. So far, she only thinks it was a hefty hit from something wacky."

"So far...all right."

"I think most people know she is very sensitive, especially those close to her. So, likely as anything, the people will simply assume it was arranged, probably BY her, so why bother saying anything TO her."

"Interesting. Yes, you do have a point. They would NEVER suspect someone like YOU to get involved. Nope, never that."

"Um, just a moment here. I only found the stuff. It was Nemelle to come up with the idea on how to present it, and then Aelwyn to actually lay it on them."

"Yeah, and that just makes it worse. A conspiracy on multiple sides. All I ever did was, um, suggest we need to help somehow."

"Uh huh, sure," she giggles. "Anyway, we'll all just lay low for now. How long do you think it will be until she gets the first sign? For me, it was a bit more than a month."

"You mean, the morning sickness? Yes, that sounds about right. She's Avariel, but I would imagine it should be fairly similar to the rest of us. My question is what she'll say to it once she realizes what she's got. Oh, I would love to be there when she makes that realization."

"I think a lot of us will. Good! We'll just bide our time until then."

They ended the call, and each returned to their work.

Aelwyn was back at her office in the guildhall reviewing a series of classroom schedules, while Aristan was in his political office at the High Council building. Relissa was busy with her military duties, and Vonafel was at home, relaxing with an artistry hobby.

Aerlie was back to work, trying to keep her own low profile after the embarrassing tryst she enjoyed, along with most of the city, the evening before. The priests of the temple all kept to themselves, giving her space and privacy, and life tried to carry on as usual. And she was most certainly NOT interested in reviewing the news to see the result of her escapade. Neither she nor Thaelyn cared to experience the further embarrassment of reviewing the world broadcast of their intimate moment, simply assuming it was a romp in the sack, and that was all. So, the report of the divine hand coming down passed by unnoticed.

Chapter 6

GUARDED REACTION

"Cardinal Nemelle? This is Malafay."

"Yes, how are you today? Do we have anything new occurring down there?"

"I'm fine, and surprisingly, no. I was expecting hordes of demons circling around our House by now, but I think someone must be holding back. Most of the commoner houses in our area are on our side, and I'm hearing from a few who speak to those in other areas of the city that there are several other Houses also converting. Are you aware of this?"

"Yes, actually. I have been keeping a tabulation of our progress, and I am pleased to say, we have seen a number of the larger Houses in several cities converting over by now. But our people up here are becoming increasingly concerned over the delay in the response. Therefore, we are placing more of our troops on alert, and in some cases deploying a few squads into position for the defense of some of these Houses. We were thinking of doing the same for you."

"It's a good idea," Malafay surmises. "But I think perhaps we can survive for now. I'm also thinking of the rest of the commoner homes. The greater Houses have their own security forces, but the commoner homes do not. If anyone wanted to cause any havoc, they are very exposed."

"Indeed. Do you think it could be possible to gather them up into a tighter space, and then place a defensive line in front of them?"

"We would almost need to divide the city in half for that. But it may come down to doing just that. I will speak to those we have here and see if we can gain a better impression of who is on our side and who is not. All the greater Houses have their individual servant's quarters, and depending on how firm they are in managing things, some may be getting the message and others may not."

"Naturally. But in the end, I fear we may have a mad rush as the retaliation we are all waiting for begins to flood the city with those demons you speak of, and then, almost anything goes after that."

"That could leave a lot of bodies in the street. Meanwhile, we have those new icons for the Seldarine set up in our shrine room. My sisters and I, and also the Matron Mother, have all been spending time in there. I hope this is worth it, and we have a chance to get out of this in one piece."

"Patience, and faith. We are with you."

They end the link, with Nemelle returning to her work in her office, and Malafay to her duties in her home.

Behind the guildhall, inside the mountain it backed up to, and deep within a series of large carved-out chambers, was a mature silver dragon and her adult son. Adalon made her home here on Tae'Eladar, as part of her duty to oversee the development of this world and its people. It was part of a process extending back almost two millennia by now since she first took up her position in this form.

She was Maker Kuroku in an alternate persona, and this management she was undertaking was part of her reason for engineering Tae'Eladar in the modern day. But today was special, as she was preparing a note to go out to the Royal Archives and the office of Casarolyn Whiteriver, Vonafel's granddaughter, and the current senior archivist in charge of a special memorial section of the Archives celebrating her grandmother's work on Adalon's prophecies. The tribute included memorial plaques and displays exhibiting Adalon's two books of her prophecies and the quatrains depicting the history of Tae'Eladar from the moment of Thaelyn's arrival, through to Aerlie's involvement, and finally up to the culmination of their travels to Azgarén and their pursuit of a lone Primordial and his servant, who were leftovers from an ancient time and the origins of the Estelar.

An attendant was visiting Adalon's chamber inside the mountain, having arrived through a special passageway from the guildhall above. He collected the note she prepared and offered his respects as he left.

He travelled back up the way he came, which at this time used a lift system, rather than in the old days when they arrived through a long stairway leading down from the guildhall. He exits the compound of the guildhall and strolls down to the cross street, then along the sidewalk for a pleasant saunter along the boulevard.

The streets of the city were lined with planters of trees and shrubs, to celebrate their love of life and an abundance of greenspace. The people of Tae'Eladar, and indeed all the empire, were very environmentally conscious. Their cities often involved lots of lush vegetation, and the aromas from herbs and flowers created an uplifting ambiance for the people.

He approached the Royal Archives building a few blocks down the road. It was a large cultural center and museum, filled with many old literary artifacts and ancient texts. He goes inside and finds his way to Casarolyn's office.

"Ma'am?" he announces as he enters the room. "I have a delivery for you."

The mature High Elf was at her desk studying several transcripts from some old Elven lore when he arrived. She redirected herself to greet him.

"Yes? What is it?"

The man steps over and delivers an envelope into her hand. He then steps back and offers a polite bow before turning and leaving.

Casarolyn examines the neatly sealed envelope. But almost immediately she recognized the seal, and it was not one she would normally expect to receive mail from.

"Gods above...it's her again," she whispers.

She gingerly opens the flap and pulls out the note, then unfolds it to read the comparatively short message. Her eyes begin to bulge as the words settle in.

"Oh no! Not another one!"

She now hurriedly searches for her shard-com and dials a number.

"Hello? This is Vonafel speaking."

"Grandmother! This is Casarolyn over at the Archives. I need you here promptly. She's at it again!"

"She...wait, you can't mean..."

"Adalon! I just got a note. She's pointing at that blasted Book Two again."

"Oh no, please. I'm getting too old for this now. Do we know what it is?"

"Not yet, I need to pull it out first. But I'd like you to be here to go over it with me."

"All right, I'm on my way. But these old legs can't run that distance anymore."

"I'll pull it out and wait for you. See you then."

They end the link and Casarolyn calls several assistants to her side as they go out to the large display on the floor of the museum. There, they gathered around to examine the two prophecy books in their glass cases and the plaques on the walls depicting the stream of prophetic verses that led them through their recent cultural history.

"This might need updating before we're done here," she muses softly.

She pulls out a keyring from her pocket with a large number of keys on it, and selects one to unlock the case. The commotion they were causing drew the attention of several visitors who were browsing the displays. Now a small crowd was assembling as Casarolyn opened the case and her assistants hauled out the oversized, and heavy tome. They set it on a nearby table and examined the binding.

The book was very nicely preserved for its age. It was bound in thick leather which was embroidered with silver scroll work and writing. The pages were not traditional paper, but again thin sheets of leather specially treated to preserve them. The writing was in an unfamiliar form of ink, generally believed to be a formulation borrowed from the Maker's point of origin in the Outer Planes, especially for several of the latter verses which only appeared after certain events took place to unlock the arcanic encryption and make them visible. But before Casarolyn was ready to open the book, she wanted her grandmother to arrive first.

Vonafel was hurriedly working her way through the gateway terminals to the Palace District, where she would make that same stroll along the boulevard towards the Royal Archives. She wasn't as young as she once was, so she needed to take this slow, but as she arrived in the lobby, she quickly noticed her granddaughter and several others gathered around the table with the book on it.

"All right, Casarolyn, let's see it. What is she doing to us this time?"

Casarolyn carefully opened the cover of the book and gently turned the pages to the last one, where previously there was only one quatrain at the top, and the rest of the page was empty.

"You know," Vonafel nods satirically. "I often wondered about that. You have the whole rest of this page, so why not fill it with something."

The page now showed not only that one verse at the top, but now a dividing line separating it from a new section following below it. Vonafel and her granddaughter, along with the others, lean in close to read it.

A time of change, the Dark Ones come;
The last assimilation.
When Son and Daughter find at last;
Their blood amalgamation.

"Blessings of the Seldarine," Casarolyn gushes. "They're going to have a baby."

"Yes," Vonafel smiles pleasantly. "It's about time. But let's not go shouting it in the streets just yet. Aerlie is already embarrassed enough for that little disturbance they made up there. It'll come out when it's ready…once she realizes she's actually pregnant."

"Wait a moment, she doesn't know? Well, I mean, it is only just now that it happened. But that hand that came down…"

"That's right, Casarolyn. She doesn't know. That hand was a little surprise. Those two were simply too stubborn to do it any other way," she giggles.

"Grandmother! Are you playing games on them?"

"I, um…have no idea what you're talking about, Casarolyn," she emits innocuously. "I mean, I'm much too old to be running this sort of thing these days. No, I would probably need help on something this big," she grins and winks, then turns to leave.

✦✦✦✦✦

Deep underground, in the Drow city, an especially aristocratic Matron Mother was convening a meeting with her two eldest daughters. They were members of the First House, the topmost dynastic member of the local authority.

"Matron Mother," the first daughter begins. "Has She revealed anything new to us?"

"She is being very elusive, but She is suggesting a conspiracy is afoot. She does not specify who is behind it, so I am interpreting this as a test of our faith. I feel it may be time for a Council meeting to investigate who else might hold any information."

"A test of our faith," the second daughter muses. "This must be due to those rumors we have heard so much of lately. It seems to be growing in severity. At first, we thought they were simply wild ravings, but they are not settling. Instead, they seem to be gathering pace."

"This would suggest an outside influence," the Matron Mother alludes. "If it were simply a local agitator, I think they would not hold such sway, and likely they would have been dealt with by now. And this further suggests a test of our faith. We must find the cause and put it down. But we may also need to know if anyone important has been moved by it."

"Meaning any of the other Houses?" the first daughter asks. "This would be unfortunate, and likely would require another cleansing."

"If they are taking up such positions that might offend the Spider Queen, they will receive their just deserves. She will not abide such disobedience. But I will choose to approach this gently, to feel my way through it. I will test them for THEIR faith, and see who falters in their response. I am developing a plan, and it will begin with a conference. Let us call a meeting of the Council. Send word out to the other Houses. Have them join with us in the meeting chamber promptly."

"Yes, Matron Mother," the first daughter submits politely and then leaves, along with her sister.

A series of messengers were sent out shortly after to the other seven top-ranking Houses as part of their governing Council. This naturally included House Deghym and Malafay's mother. On receiving the note, she calls her daughters into session.

"So, we finally have a response out of them?" Malafay asks.

"I think this must surely qualify," Luariina responds. "An immediate and quite sudden demand for a meeting of the Council. Normally, if she were to call a meeting, she would give us a bit of forewarning. Also, this is outside of the normal scheduling. Therefore, this tells me there is an emergency, and the only thing I can imagine to prompt this would be the one we are all hiding from."

"Wonderful. How do you hope to approach this? You cannot decline this demand. That would be a sure indication of our House turning its focus."

"I know, and I'm sure this is the reason for the sudden nature of the demand, to impose a threat of a possible usurpation. And, of course, this would require an investigation of who is on what side. I will need to choose my words very carefully."

"Matron Mother, choosing your words is, of course, an obvious need. But if the First House is under advisement of the, um…her…I think choosing words will not be enough. The Matron Mother of that House may already know what is happening out there, and this could be nothing more than a trap to corner you."

"While I would agree with you, I think maybe not…at least not entirely. If she did know this, we would know of it outside our doors. This could be a test, and if it is a test, it could also be the…ahem…is not speaking openly. This might then suggest to me SHE is testing even the First House, although I think they should represent an obvious result. But you know…" her voice trails off as her thoughts drift away.

Malafay and her sisters lean in attentively as they see their mother's face alter with a devious twist.

"Mother?" Alakaere wonders with a soft smirk. "What do you have occurring within you at this time?"

"This would be a nasty rub," she admits. "But if the First House is testing people, what if we could turn some part of this against them? I will need to watch for my openings, but if any of the other Houses are holding doubts, or simply confused as to the meaning, I wonder if I could draw them aside and suggest a few things privately."

"Oh, Mother!" Alyraema giggles. "But which ones? Maybe some of the lower ones, as I think the upper ones might be too dedicated."

"Possibly. Nevertheless, I need to respond to this quickly. They will be expecting us right away."

The Matron Mother rises from her chair and rushes off to her room to prepare herself for a hurried attendance on the Council. The others returned to their various duties, although their thoughts continued to circulate around the implications of the meeting and what it suggested. They had been waiting for this moment, and now that it had arrived, the tensions were rising.

Luariina arranged her appearance with a ceremonial robe. She checked her face and hair to ensure it was neat, and when she was satisfied, she made her way outside. A small carriage was waiting at the door, hauled by a strange reptilian beast used locally, rather than the traditional horses used on the surface. This would carry her across town to the Council Meeting Hall. On her arrival, she met with several others who were also convening. She studied their faces carefully to see if there was any hesitation due to the nature of this summons. She then attempted some casual conversation before entering the building.

"Such a curious thing, to be called on such short notice, do you think?"

The offhanded announcement caught the attention of the others in the area as they exited their carriages.

"Yes," responds the first one. "But I suppose it is to be expected by now. Have you heard any of the commotion occurring in the streets lately?"

"I have certainly heard of it, and one of my daughters even inquired on some portion of it, only to hear it might be nothing more than a bit of malcontent amongst a few of the commoners. Why, did you hear something more?"

"Possibly, but like you, my opinion is nothing more than malcontent."

"One thing is for certain, however," another one offers. "It seems to be gaining ground since it first arrived. If this is malcontent, it must be striking a very deep note with some people."

"Perhaps it is at that," Luariina admits tenderly. "And surely the reason for this meeting, to see what the other Houses have to say about it, perhaps also to see what each of US has to say about it, if anything."

"Each of us, meaning to say, we who speak for those Houses, correct?"

"Meaning to say, if the First House, or anyone else out there, has something to say, to see if we actually agree with it. If this is a simple bit of malcontent amongst a few commoners, so be it. But those are commoners, not any of us...yet. But as you already said, it seems to be gaining ground, and therefore to learn how much ground. And if it involves malcontent in any form, where could THAT lead?"

"Yes!" the first member nods. "I had this thought on the way over here. If this should pollute any of the greater Houses, we may have a new problem, one of corruption."

"Indeed," the second one adds. "And this could lead to a cleansing, like that last one we saw. Ugh..."

"That was an ugly sight. I would not want that for my House."

"None of us would, surely. But I think this is what Luariina is speaking of. Is it a simple run of malcontent, or if it is gaining so much ground, could there be a deeper cause of it?"

"But we are speaking of simple commoners here, right?" offers a third arrival. "Surely, none of us in the greater Houses would succumb to such folly as that!"

"Succumb to it?" Luariina balks conspicuously. "Of course not! Not unless there was really any truth to it," she continues more cautiously. "And I'm sure the First House knows this."

She then turns and promptly struts towards the door, leaving the rest of them nearly speechless in their response. They all gaze at each other uncertainly, until the first member speaks up briefly.

"This is a trap," she whispers.

Luariina enters inside the building, followed shortly after by the rest. They pass through a foyer into another room. It was a large circular meeting hall with a central table and many chairs. At the table, already seated and waiting, was the Matron Mother from the First House, along with two others who had already arrived. Luariina and the other three from outside took up their seating. This left only one seat unfilled.

Luariina and the others all glanced around at the attendance, but it was clearly evident that one person was missing. This would be Matron Mother T'rissae of House Arabarn, the Fourth House on the Council. Hers was an important member in the local community, being number four on the list, and her absence was quickly leading the Matron Mother of the First House to suspicion. But rather than launch accusations, she instead forced herself into interrogation.

"Where is T'rissae?" she inquires determinedly. "Was she outside with the rest of you?"

"I did not see her," Luariina declares as she glances back at the door. "Only these others, and we all arrived together. House Arabarn is not that far away, so she could not be too far behind us. Perhaps she was delayed?"

"Perhaps, but she should know this demand for an audience is to be responded to promptly."

"Absolutely! Could she be ill, and unable to respond?"

"While I suppose this is also possible, I would then expect the messenger to return with this missive to inform me personally."

"Yes, I must agree. Then I must fall back to the original assumption, that she is delayed. Do we wait for her, or begin without?"

"I wish to be on with this meeting, so let us begin now, and if she should arrive late, we will simply continue from that point."

"As you wish, Faerryna. Where do you wish to begin?"

"As I am sure many of you should know by now, if you are paying any attention to it, there seems to be some manner of unfortunate business occurring in our streets in recent times. Stories, by the sound of it, circulating around and stirring up unrest among the commoner caste.

I had some of my daughters investigate with our own house servants, as well as to dig for more detail outside, but it would seem either no one is speaking to us, or else there is nothing to say. But this still does not resolve the fact that someone, somewhere, is stirring things up, and it seems to be spreading. My concern now is to find out where it is coming from, who is doing it, and how far it has spread, because this could represent a disruption to our way of life in this city, to say nothing of our ability to control it."

Luariina casually glanced around the table at the other faces, rolling her eyes towards each of them, not simply to see their reaction to the statement, but also trying to gauge their impression after the talk they shared outside. So far, they seemed very cool in their demeanor, and none of them seemed interested in speaking up first, so she decided to take the lead.

"I, for one, will admit to hearing of these stories. Word has a tendency to travel on occasion, you know. And, in fact, my second daughter did try to interrogate one of our house servants to learn more. But much like your example, I suppose, she only got something about lost opportunities to learn something and concealed knowledge…as if a commoner might hold such privilege to possess any in the first place," she chuckles demurely.

The other women who arrived with her all passed furtive glances at each other for the statement, recalling her mention outside of something carrying truthful intent. This was clearly a clue to something, and she might know what it is, but was cleverly disguising it in front of the First House.

Faerryna, however, was not as easily placated. In her mind, any or all of them could be a suspect, and she was watching each of them the same. She was not aware of the discussion outside, but it didn't matter, as she needed to evaluate them for her own opinion. She pressed forward with her investigation.

"Only one daughter? Is this to say none of the others participated? What about other house servants? Perhaps this one was simply too feebleminded to offer anything."

"I feel rather confident in the loyalty of my servants. If one of them had nothing of special interest, I doubt any others would, as they all tend to travel in the same circles. As for my other daughters, they do not tend to go out and speak to commoners. That would be a bit unbecoming, don't you think?" she smirks cutely. "But in answer to your question, one of them did, in fact, have an idea to investigate further. What she found, however, was probably no different from what your own might have discovered, and that being the people are becoming restless due to something they otherwise are not receiving enough of."

"And just what could they desire that they do not receive enough of?" she huffs. "Taltyrr, what about you and your House?"

"House Godendar is largely disinterested in the random musings of the commonfolk and their wants," she asserts. "If they are unsettled, it is not my doing. My servants seem quite content in their duties, and do not complain to me or my daughters. Therefore, if there are stories of any kind going around, it is generally outside my view, maybe also my concern, as this is, after all, the wants of commonfolk. However, if the Council feels this is such a serious issue, I suppose I could pay closer attention to it as part of an investigation to discover the source and the reasoning behind it..."

She glances inquisitively at the other women in attendance, but settling on Luariina to meet her eyes before returning back to the table.

Luariina could see in the other woman's face a silent suggestion of curiosity, and much like with her own hidden portrayals, Taltyrr was trying to hint at something, but hoping not to show it openly here at the table.

Faerryna then turned to the next in line.

"And you, Zarraema? What opinion does House Alesek hold on this matter?"

"Our House," she begins, "being the seventh ranking in the city, may hold its influence within certain circles, but clearly this is not one of them. Like most others, we have heard a few whispers here and there, but also, like many others, those whispers, in and of themselves, do not carry enough detail to raise my suspicion of anything more than this unrest you speak of. Some of us were of the mind to simply disregard them as a passing fancy for something new to talk about. Life in a city like ours can become somewhat routine after a while."

"Oh, routine, is it? And what is it those peasants desire to break them out of this routine? Maybe a little more discipline to remind them of their place?"

"While I would not be one to argue this, my experience tells me an injured peasant is far less productive than a healthy one."

Faerryna glared at the woman for the statement, but Zarraema simply held her head high and stoically glared back. There was a clear dislike between the two of them for their perspectives on the so-called peasants, with Faerryna being overly punitive. But this was nothing new between them. Therefore, Faerryna moved on to the final member for her opinion.

"Dirzeari…" she clears her throat softly. "What does your House know…or do they know anything at all?"

"House Hlatlar may be the lowest ranking on the Council, and I realize we might not carry as much prominence within the city and its social affairs, but for that part we do afford ourselves, we would not succumb…" she briskly rolls her eyes around the table to the others, including Luariina, "…to such frivolous nonsense as what might be going around the streets. Surely, as you and others have said, they, being commoners, could not hold any such privileged opinions that would threaten our position…now, could they?"

"Very smartly stated, Dirzeari," she muses dispassionately. "But I think this carries more than that. While commoners, by themselves, cannot hold much against our authority, it is more my concern where it might be coming from that it is stirring so many of them up in the first place."

"But surely, Faerryna, given any of our Houses, yours especially, for our private security forces, any sort of uprising, if this is what you are suggesting, could not possibly succeed, could it?"

"I suppose that largely depends on how many there are in total, and who else might take up sides with them, if not only the commoners. We still have that hidden cause behind it, and it must be a prominent one, not to have faded by now, or been removed by any of those security forces that are otherwise serving the greater interests of our city."

"Faerryna," Zarraema offers. "We sometimes have mercenary bands that pass through. Could one of those be causing this disturbance?"

"I don't recall hearing of any recent arrivals, but if someone is intentionally stirring things up in our streets, I suppose we should consider a hidden arrival."

"Then this should be one of our possibilities. I could hardly believe this could have originated as something local."

"Do you actually believe this, Zarraema? My opinion might differ, but then, who am I to say, being the Matron Mother of the First House," she smirks.

"Faerryna, while you may be the Matron Mother of the First House, each of us on this Council is supposed to be guaranteed an equal opinion while at this table, and I will stand by mine as a fair offer. At least, not unless the Spider Queen bestowed upon you some privilege that she did not share with the rest of us."

Faerryna frowned and leaned back in her chair at the mention. While the statement, by itself, did not carry anything subversive, it did invoke that earlier speculation of a test. The Spider Queen did NOT give her anything privileged on this matter, and now she was being called on it. She paused in her rebuttal as she glanced around the table, and once again falling upon the empty seat.

"Where is she..." she mumbles agitatedly. "She should've been here by now."

Luariina turned to examine the seat for the Fourth House and Matron Mother T'rissae. It was clear by now she was not arriving.

"Perhaps one of us could investigate?" she suggests distantly. "I would hardly believe anything foul could have occurred out there... well, mostly."

"Mostly?"

"Yes, mostly, meaning to say...accidents...can sometimes occur outside one's house. This is the reason we have our private security forces, remember?"

"Yes, of course...accidents. Hmm..." she grumbles. "Very well, when we are finished here, perhaps I could send another messenger out to inquire about it."

"Or..." Luariina interjects with a finger. "Maybe one of us could do so."

"One of us? What do you mean, Luariina? Are you now demeaning yourself to a meager courier?"

"No, I am not demeaning myself to anything. You wanted to see who else out there is siding with anyone, and I suspect we are all here as part of that investigation. But where House Arabarn is concerned, if there is a true cause for it, do you think they would speak to YOU, Matron Mother of the First House? However, me being of the sixth House, while not as low in rank as Dirzeari over here, I might serve nicely to inquire on this matter. It might even serve as a kind gesture on behalf of the Council for how much we missed her..." she smiles naughtily.

The obvious play at words tickled a curious laugh out of Faerryna, a sensation she had not felt for a long time. She first smiled, then erupted in a hearty chuckle at the suggestion.

"Yes, Luariina, this is a fine offer. Perhaps you could take a box of candies over to her, as well, just in case she is ill. After all, we wouldn't want to see anything…bad…happen to her for the next time we call a meeting."

"Oh, naturally. But now, we still haven't heard from the Second or Third Houses. Do they have anything to offer in our discussion?"

"Ah, but of course. They arrived sometime before you, and we were speaking to ourselves briefly. Both House Despana and House Torduis generally agree with ours that this is a problem that needs to be corrected. Someone is intentionally invoking this unrest in the streets, and whether it could be internal or external to the city, it needs to be found and quashed, so we can return to our usual sense of containment."

Luariina studied the three of them, as they all sat close together on one side of the table, like a trio of old-timers sharing their personal interests. She expected this much, as they were rather closely associated, and all very intimate with the temple rituals.

"Yes, indeed," she begins coolly. "Then, this is to say the three of you are very much in agreement on the issue that it is a serious threat to our way of life, rather than a passing fancy or some other temporary fetish. But do you hold any specific opinions on where to begin?"

"This is what we were hoping to decide during this meeting, but it would seem none of us is able to offer anything definitive at this time."

Luariina nods gently, but at the same time carefully studying Faerryna for her expression. The elder woman was known for her opinionated perspectives, and like with most Matron Mothers, and even worse for those in the top positions, she couldn't be trusted. The woman gave the mild impression that she wasn't satisfied by the outcome of the meeting. The statements given by each of the attendees, at least those of the Fifth and lower Houses, were too cleverly formulated to offer anything to justify retaliation. Although this never stopped any House from aggressively disposing of another one if they fell out of personal favor. And the First House had an army to match most of the others combined. Therefore, if she should decide no one was telling the truth, she could try a unilateral takeover. This would demand Luariina to make her own move if she hoped to rescue the situation.

"Well then," she announces. "If this is the case, it would seem our work is clear, and that is to discover the root of it…"

She pauses a moment to consider her words, as this would need to propose a clue to those who needed to hear it, meaning the other women who arrived with her. She wanted THEM to know there was trouble coming.

She continues, "But if we then return to this notion of taking sides, we should be sure who is on the other one. After all, this body, whoever or whatever it is, if it has not been brought down already by someone's individual security forces, my first suggestion is this body must be very clever. Maybe too clever to allow themselves to be seen."

"Are you suggesting that idea of a mercenary body again?"

"While this is certainly a good suggestion, I might also ask the reason why. Why would anyone, like an external mercenary force, try to disrupt life in OUR city. What do they hope to accomplish by it?"

"A takeover, perhaps?"

"Under who's authority? Are we coming under attack by another city? Has our entire society fallen out of favor with the Spider Queen that she would allow others of our own kind to do this to us?"

This statement caused both Zarraema and Dirzeari to lean forward in their chairs and listen more intently. Just like with House Deghym, they too have not heard as much coming out of their goddess during their prayer sessions. This could be one of the clues they were suspecting Luariina was dropping.

Luariina continues, "And here you are suggesting it to be one of us, maybe even House Arabarn. Maybe they already fell victim to it, and we just don't know yet."

"That…accident, perhaps?" Faerryna now leans forward, along with her two cohorts.

Taltyrr was also listening closely, and was starting to piece together a few of her own ideas.

"Maybe…just maybe…Faerryna…" Luariina states. "If there is a body out there brazen enough to go up against everything we believe in, they might just hold a good enough cause to do so, if they held the belief that they could succeed. Not everyone holds such opinions as yours that simple commoners, or lesser Houses, could be so inferior that they couldn't start a war. But…" she wags a finger for emphasis. "I might also put it to you, a House with such attitude that nothing can harm it, might underestimate something that can."

Luariina leans back and studies the faces of the assembly. They all seemed impressed by her words, in one form or another, with Faerryna appearing repulsed by the notion.

"Are we finished here?" Luariina concludes. "Because if we are, we should be on our way to discovering some of this. Sitting at this table won't bring us any closer to the answers."

"Yes! You are right," Faerryna asserts. "Very well, session adjourned. And if anyone here should learn of anything, I will expect an immediate report of what it is."

"Oh, I think that is obvious, Faerryna. Whatever is out there will no doubt show itself, once it is ready. So, we need to be ready first."

The meeting breaks up, with Luariina and the other three women she arrived with leaving together. Faerryna and the other two lingered behind as they watched the others leave. Once the room was clear, Faerryna began to speak again.

"I don't trust any of them. Taltyrr is questionable for her loyalty. Luariina is surely trouble. I never did like Zarraema, and Dirzeari… well, she seems rather soft."

"What are your plans, Faerryna?" asks one of the others.

"Baeffyn, I think I cannot make a definitive move without one more test. My original plan involved the temple, to see who might still be loyal to the Spider Queen. Although, being as silent as she has been lately, I cannot be sure how effective it might be by now."

"Should we consider any of Luariina's words at all?" the other one wonders. "Like an outside authority trying to usurp our own in here. It might hold some credibility, or at least something we should not overlook."

"This may be true, Vierryne. It may also be true about House Arabarn, but until I see it with my own eyes, I think I will not take it as seriously. We may be looking at a group effort to usurp our positions by something that thinks itself bold enough to win."

Outside the building, Luariina and the others arrived at their respective coaches, which were grouped together just offside of the street. But before returning to their individual rides, Zarraema calls the rest to divert for a close huddle with Luariina.

"All right, Luariina," she asserts firmly but quietly. "I think you just got yourself on the list, and maybe the rest of us along with you. Now, what did you mean back in the beginning when we first arrived, and then in there by those hints you were so clearly shooting at us?"

"You're a clever one, Zarraema. It's no wonder Faerryna doesn't like you. You're too smart, and she doesn't like that in another person. You saw how she so clearly put down anything that doesn't meet up to her personal standards?"

"Yes, but that's nothing new. She does that each time we go in there."

"True, but on this occasion, she is in for a surprise she cannot counter. It has to do with the real cause behind those stories, but we can't speak here. If you truly want to know what I know, you will need to meet me at my House. But do so quietly. Go home, change into something atypical for your normal dress, and then come to me. We can't afford spies to see you travelling around anywhere you shouldn't be travelling around. Meanwhile, I'm going to send one of my daughters to check on Arabarn, hopefully to find out the real reason she didn't show up."

"Do you have any suspicions?"

"Suspicions are one thing, but accident or illness, I think word would come back somehow. Complete silence suggests she is hiding something, and I can't think of too many things she could be hiding at this time. Therefore, before Faerryna gets to her, I want to be there first. She may be in trouble, or soon might be. As for me, I'm already protected, and I'm going to suggest each of you do the same. On a list? Zarraema, you have no idea what sort of list I'm on, and I'm going to recommend you join me, if you're really as smart as you look," she smiles and winks before hopping into her carriage and pulling away.

The gesture was completely alien to the other women. No one ever smiled and winked like that in Drow society. Something clearly abnormal had gotten inside Luariina, and she apparently felt herself so confident that she no longer held any true worries, or at least wasn't showing them as outwardly. They glanced at each other briskly, and then returned to their coaches to hurry off home.

On her arrival, Luariina calls up her daughters for a quick meeting.

"Something is wrong with Arabarn," she declares. "And I need someone to go over there to investigate. Malafay, I'm going to suggest you on this occasion, since you hold the closest association to the people above."

"Wait," she issues briskly. "What do you mean? What happened at the meeting...as if I couldn't guess."

"I'm sure you can guess. Faerryna is calling us traitors, but without actually speaking it out loud. I'm sure she suspects most of us, maybe all of us, but she didn't specifically announce it. She claimed there must be someone out there starting these stories, and that someone may be trying to usurp power for themselves. She also spoke of people taking sides with whoever is passing these stories around, further that no one is apparently using their local militias to put it down, therefore this might suggest collusion."

"All right, this much I suppose I can expect. Did she suggest anything like a counteraction?"

"Other than to essentially declare her personal superiority over anything not of House Oussund, she seems to think this to be something you can control with better public discipline…meaning to beat it out of them. And even though I tried my best to redirect her to one or more alternative culprits, I doubt it worked, not on her. She loves her position of authority too much to give it up. So, we might as well expect trouble out of her, as well as the other top three. You know how they are. They're like a group of bed buddies sharing personal favors."

"Uh huh…and House Arabarn? What happened to them?"

"No show. Also, no word on why there's a no show. Did she take ill, did she have something occur on the way over, or is she hiding in a closet. I need to know…before Faerryna gets to it. T'rissae is no fool, and surely, she, like all the rest, understood the nature of that immediate summons. If she didn't show up, it must be because she's hiding something. Therefore, Malafay, I'll ask you to go find out. Be careful, but if she actually is holding back on something, see if you can work it in our favor. Otherwise, she might be in trouble from the other side."

"Got it."

"Meanwhile, Alakaere and Alyraema, Rhyliira and Felynquiri, we should expect company soon. I invited the other Matron Mothers from Houses Five through Eight to our House. We need to join together for our mutual defense. They'll hopefully be arriving soon."

Aerlie had been feeling a little under the weather all day since waking up. It had been just about a month since her boisterous bout in bed with her husband, but by this time the feelings of embarrassment had settled, and she had returned to a normal routine. And much like any other day, she was in her office sorting through some paperwork and accounting sheets. But her stomach had been nagging her off and on since breakfast.

She mostly tried to ignore it, thinking it was simply something she ate that didn't settle right, and trying to place her mind on her work. And then it would return sometime later. It was becoming annoying. But still, she felt it was simply something common that was returning to bother her, even though she generally never experienced a true stomachache or nausea.

She was a well-seasoned healer and specialist in the medical arts, but she had long since grown weary of the effort to actually conceive a baby. Therefore, the idea that she may have finally succeeded seemed like a distant dream by now. She generally avoided the news relating to her special moment, as it was simply a reminder of the spectacle she made, and she tended to be a bit more private than that on such personal matters. Furthermore, no one around her spoke of it, thinking it was prearranged and there was nothing else to do but wait for it now.

Her stubborn determination to focus on her work generally denied her to actually realize she was feeling a true form of discomfort that wasn't the result of muscle strain or bad posture. She adjusted herself in her chair, hoping to find a more comfortable position, occasionally to lean back to give herself a break, take a few deep breaths and glance around the office at the various furnishings. She even got up and walked around the temple several times, hoping to stretch the legs and walk it off...whatever 'it' was.

She wasn't especially hungry for lunch, with her stomach feeling upset like it was, but she tried to eat something anyway simply for the nourishment. She didn't feel such a strong need to rush into a restroom, but the sensations did rise up to the point where she had to stop and try some meditation to settle it back down again. She eventually broke down to apply a little healing touch to calm herself. This seemed to finally clear the condition...for now.

Malafay was arriving in front of House Arabarn. Much like her own House, this one was a large estate home, with an equally large yard and wall around it. And much the same as hers, it had many rooms, including those for the local militia. Some of the more immediate house servants also had their personal quarters inside, while others lived in their own homes in the surrounding area.

The manor home was imposing from the street, built from the native rock, like everything else in the city. The Drow held their own unique architecture, but artistry wasn't their specialty. Deep underground, where there is no natural light, who cares about pretty colors. It's all a drab gray.

She approaches the door. There are no windows in the immediate vicinity, although she feels as though she is being watched. She carefully knocks on the door, which is something most people don't generally do, as no one has any interest in visiting their neighbors. In several moments, a sound ushers up from the other side as the door is unlatched and slowly pried open for a servant to peek through.

"Who are you and what do you want?" she asks tersely.

"I'm Malafay of House Deghym. I would wish to inquire of the Matron Mother if I may."

"Why?"

"Well, firstly, there was a meeting of the Council today, in case she missed it, but the general belief is, unless she is either ill or injured, she intentionally avoided it. This raised a bit of concern with the First House, and if you know Matron Mother Faerryna as we do, she is not one you want to raise concern with. Therefore, my Matron Mother chooses to be first to inquire about this before that…concern…arrives here at your door officially. She would wish to learn of the reason for the absence and if there is anything of deeper consideration that we might need to know about before the First House comes to its own conclusion."

"Wait, are you actually suggesting you are here to help, or simply to take advantage of an opportunity?"

"I suppose I could say yes to both of those. Opportunities can come in many forms. But standing out here isn't the sort of place to discuss those forms. Would she be willing to speak to me? Or maybe one of her daughters, if not the Matron Mother herself?"

The servant was clearly surprised to see someone offering anything that vaguely resembled help, so she turned back into the foyer and began whispering to someone who was obviously hiding in the shadows back there. After sharing a few words, she returned to the door.

"You may enter inside here, but our House is not generally accepting visitors now. So, I will ask you only to enter just inside if you wish to discuss something that should not be heard outside. Mistress G'eldithra is standing here. She will speak to you. But she cautions to mind yourself while inside this House."

"Of course."

Malafay stepped inside the foyer and the servant closed the door behind her. The room was neatly furnished, with corridors leading off in both directions. A type of chandelier with exceptionally dim mini braziers illuminated the area just barely enough to see by for a normal person, but for the Drow, it was adequate. And standing a short distance behind the door was the eldest daughter of the House. Malafay turned to face the woman, but could see in her eyes she did not trust anyone entering the House. Likely not from any other House, and especially not with word from the Council.

"I will give you only a few moments to explain yourself," G'eldithra cautions. "After that, unless I feel what you have to say is worthy, I will ask you to leave and not come back."

"I understand. All I ask is enough time to actually say it, as what I have to say cannot be spoken in only a handful of words. First, may I ask why your Matron Mother did not attend the Council? It is my understanding this was an emergency summons, not the sort of thing you simply say no to."

"She is feeling unwell for this occasion. She was not in the mood for it."

"This does leave one to ask why she could not at least offer an excuse to the messenger who came with the summons. The First House may suspect something inappropriate if she does not at least excuse herself."

"Did they say something to this effect?"

"Not in so many words, but if you know Matron Mother Faerryna, she doesn't use so many words."

"Yes, so I have heard. And you? Why are YOU here speaking this to me?"

"To see if MY words might carry greater value to you than what few she might offer…if any."

"If any? Does she hold designs on us?"

"Probably no more than on mine, or any of the other Houses, save for the Second and Third. They tend to follow together."

"ANY of the others?" she intones warily. "What is she planning over there?"

"A counter to whatever the rest of us might be planning, at least in her mind."

"Uh oh… Maybe the Matron Mother had to join that meeting after all."

"I doubt it would really change anything. Mine thinks she probably had her mind set even before this."

"Oh great! But now, what is it we are actually speaking of, and what do we do about it? And what is this offer you spoke of…an opportunity?"

"Do you think you would be willing to hear it, or are you still of the mind my words are not worthy? Because my Matron Mother mentioned, before I departed, that she called Houses Five through Eight into a private meeting. So, I think, if you have the right mind for it, you might also be interested to hear what we have to say."

"Um, hold on…are you actually planning on something against the First House, or is this YOUR counter to HER counter?"

"The best way for me to answer that is probably no, on both counts. We do not have anything in mind to directly oppose the First House. We MIGHT, however, have a need to defend against her, therefore a need to secure ourselves. But that need is not something we, specifically, can control ourselves."

"You are speaking riddles to me. What is occurring that you cannot control, but might need to defend against if SHE goes out?"

"Maybe you already know…maybe not. Let's examine this closely. Why…exactly…did your Matron Mother not go to the meeting today? Mine thinks if she was ill, she would send an excuse to explain this. If she was injured, or something else bad happened along the way, some other form of missive might have arrived for that reason. But in the clear absence of anything to the contrary, it might seem she is intentionally hiding. Therefore, we might want to understand what she is hiding from and why. The First House is not a part of this, only mine. So, we might as well be open to each other, otherwise we cannot help each other."

"But why would your House, or ANY House, actually want to help ours…or any OTHER House?"

"Because we learned something, and it has to do with the reason the First House is upset. That woman seems to think the only way to solve a problem is through brute force. At the very least, to beat people into a better condition of behavior. At worst, a cleansing to remove an eyesore. Now, G'eldithra, would you like to come out with it, or should I simply go home?"

"Um, wait, I'm a little surprised, as well as confused. Too many strange things happening around us, and we're having a hard time trying to interpret them."

"Then tell me, and let's see if we can interpret them together."

"All right, but I'm warning you, if this is a trick…"

"G'eldithra, does it involve the stories going through the streets right now? Where they come from, who is spreading them, and why? This is what the First House is angry over. No one is apparently trying to stop it, and this might suggest compliance with what they are saying."

"Oops…"

"Yes, oops. So, how much of that oops kept your Matron Mother at home?" she raises her brow inquisitively.

"Um…" she glances around the room nervously, settling her eyes on the servant, who was standing nearby. "Well, she was uncertain as to the reason of this meeting…that is to say she felt it might hold a hidden agenda, and likely due to those stories…"

"And Faerryna is looking for who to blame," Malafay concludes. "Meaning the rest of us, and yours chose not to expose herself to it. Yes, my mother was right, T'rissae is a clever one to see this coming. And she was right to think this way. But unfortunately, not showing up at all could be just as bad as showing up and failing the test."

"A test… So, it WAS a test of some sort."

"Yes, and likely to see who among us is still faithful. Let's see how much you actually do know. What have you heard of those stories and how much do you actually believe?"

"Um, this is our problem. Some parts we can confirm, like our warriors going up and hitting a wall. And then the Spider Queen orders us to hide this fact, so we simply go back up and do it again. This is ridiculous."

"Agreed, ours do the same. But do you know anything else, like what is on the other side of that wall?"

"I, uh…" she turns to the servant woman. "You tell her. You seem to know those things better than I do right now."

"Yes, Mistress G'eldithra," she issues politely. "Aside from that wall, it is said, in the old days, our warriors went up to kill commoners who were both unarmed and unsuspecting. They then returned with these stories of culling powerful warriors up there as part of their duty to protect our people from what surely would have been a slaughter if they had marched on us down here. But excuse me, I do not know what sort of commoners they might have up there, but if they were both unarmed AND unsuspecting, where were the actual warriors we are supposed to be so afraid of?"

"All right, this is a good question to ask," Malafay nods. "One might also ask why they have warriors who cannot fight back, or at least to cause an occasional injury, just standing around up there waiting for our people to slaughter them. That's also a bit ridiculous. You might think someone would either train a proper fighting force and hold it in wait for us, or…oh, I don't know, build a wall to simply keep us away," she shrugs innocently.

"Um, right, to build a wall. I suppose this is what they did… Eventually. Then, it is said the people up there have apparently grown by a great amount, while we down here have not. However, this is one thing we are unable to speak for as that wall apparently keeps us back from seeing it."

"Yes, that would be a problem. Even worse is someone keeps telling us to go up and hit that wall, even though a voice screeches at us to stop doing it. You know, if the most they are willing to do is to build a wall to keep us out, we might take the hint after a while. After all, this might suggest we are little more than an annoyance to them. Rather, if they were growing so much in this time, and we were not, you might think our warriors wouldn't be as much of a bother to their commoners by now, to say nothing of their actual warriors. And THEN, here we are, making such a pest of ourselves by continually hitting that wall, without ever taking the lesson."

"This is reasonable," G'eldithra surmises. "You might think, at some moment, they would grow tired of this."

"Absolutely! To the point where either they would finally march on us, if for no other reason than to teach us, right up to our faces, to be silent with all of our groaning for living in this grave we dug for ourselves, or else to teach us the REASON why we dug this grave to begin with."

G'eldithra and the servant woman both glared at Malafay for the clever insinuation. They glanced at each other, and then at her again before G'eldithra responded.

"Living in a grave… Such an interesting term. Do you speak like this often?"

"Only when I'm hit with so many ridiculous ironies that I can't keep myself from laughing."

"Uh huh… All right, I suppose I simply must inquire about this. Why would you describe them as ironies?"

"First, that we spent the better part of ten thousand years down here thinking a bunch of fools upstairs would march on us, but couldn't train up a decent fighting force who could stay alive long enough before they learned how to march."

G'eldithra frowned at Malafay, and almost felt a giggle rising up. The servant woman, however, did release a tiny one, but quickly covered her mouth to stifle it.

"Ten thousand years?" G'eldithra wheezes. "What do you mean by that number?"

"That's how long we've been in this hole, which seems as much like a grave as anything else, for how we seem to treat ourselves down here."

"Wait, you're moving too fast. You answer one with a question for another. Like that grave thing again..."

"Let me give you a hint, G'eldithra. Knives in people's backs... THAT is who we are. We treat life like it can be traded at a trinket stand, such that I doubt any single person even knows how long we could live if given our full years. We were banished into this grave ten thousand years ago; did you know that? My teachings didn't use that number, so I doubt yours did either. It would seem someone forgot to count the numbers all the way. And more, they also forgot to remind us of WHY we were banished down here...the real reason. Assuming anyone really paid attention to it to begin with."

"Why would you say that?"

"Call it arrogance. Call it belligerence. Call it a demented ambition to want more than they were entitled to. If they held such a belief that they were denied this for any reason, they might hold a grudge, truth or no, for what they did in the eyes of all the rest."

"So, we think we were banished here for one reason, but it could be false, and either we did not wish to believe in it, or perhaps not accept it for our arrogance to want more?"

"Likely as much. And because of this, we're told to go back up to hit whatever walks or crawls on the ground, and return with grand stories of victory over hordes of enemies to protect our people. More knives in people's backs simply for the pleasure of telling stories. Well, that wall is their way of saying, no more. If not for the changing tunnels down here making it so hard to track their passage, they would've probably finished us thousands of years ago."

"Oh dear. So, what are we saying about them today? The stories say they grew in this time, and all they do is yell at us to go home when we reach that wall!"

"I suppose building that wall was simply easier than trying to march down here to bury us in a grave we already dug for ourselves. And if not for the fact that we kept sending our warriors up there to make any sort of noise, they might have forgotten about us. The only trouble here is, we never were allowed to forget about THEM, and with such stories as they were imminent to march on us; therefore, to go up and hit something, no matter what it is. But here we have another problem, G'eldithra. They apparently grew into something, all right. It's called a civilization. And what are we? We're a lonely little city that doesn't even go outside to meet all the other lonely little cities."

"Which means they're organized now. That sounds dangerous."

"And worse, we spend most of our time conniving and backstabbing each other, while THEY grew into something completely different, and so much more prosperous than we down here that even a shopkeeper could probably defeat our warriors. Now, ask yourself why they would build a simple wall as opposed to marching on us for any reason, even if they could NOW possibly navigate those tunnels."

"I honestly don't have an answer to that, especially if you keep saying we like to stab each other in the back so often, and were doing the same to them up there for so long. Wouldn't they want a little revenge?"

"Probably. I might also suggest they are well-deserving of it, especially if they hold any laws or other policies that forbid backstabbing, or any other form of...murder. But that word, to us at least, is almost unknown, and more often synonymous to finding yourself an advantage to move up in rank."

"More backstabbing..." she muses softly. "And as a civilization who has learned better policies... But this would simply exemplify the reason to march on us, if we hold this history with them, tunnels or no tunnels."

"It would, unless something else held them back, like maybe the cooperation, or lack thereof, of an earlier form of civilization that didn't share their knowledge any better than we did...and still do. This might bring us back to that growing aspect. They grew into something new, and likely just recently...or reasonably so. This might then be where that wall came from, if it is part of this new level of cooperation that they know where we come out and want to put a stop to it, as a convenient alternative to marching down here for it. But THEN, here is where it gets confusing for us down here. We go up, hit that same wall, hear a voice saying to turn around and go home, and with no other repercussions following, no matter how many times we do this."

"Right. And this would follow with us asking that question of them getting tired of it by now."

"It would! Unless…" she muses conspicuously, "…they had something else in mind."

"Uh huh. And I think you know something, and all of this is another test, in this case leading up to what YOU think. Am I right?"

"I would answer that you are a gift to your mother for her wisdom, G'eldithra," Malafay smiles.

The woman glares at Malafay for the clearly pleasant expression, which was not something you would normally see on any Drow, to say nothing of from a rival House. But even more surprising was the comment.

"Did you just complement me?"

"Yes, although you might want to perk up your decisiveness a bit. You're moving the right direction, but you need more confidence in your approach."

"A complement AND constructive advice. What happened in your House that you would do this now?"

"We know what is behind that wall, and we know what we must do to prepare for it, as they are NOW coming for us, all because we keep listening to someone tell us to do things that sound ridiculous."

"Uh oh… And let me guess. THIS is what offends the First House so much that they are looking for anyone who sympathizes with it, and why YOU, among others, are taking up defensive positions. But wait, you said defensive against THEM. What about those from up there?"

"They want to take us back, G'eldithra. After all this time, they are willing to forgive our past mistakes and reunite us with our ancestral brethren, whom we insulted once with all our backstabbing hatred and greed. And NOW that civilization, that has moved so far ahead of us, wants to see us have our own chance at it. They came together into one enormously powerful nation, but we're still down here festering in this grave thinking we need to kill something."

"And they want to put a stop to it. So, they built a wall to hold us back until they could organize enough to make this new movement. And THAT…" she snaps a finger, "…is where all these stories are coming from, I'll bet. They're trying to break us of that same backstabbing hatred, and all the ridiculous lies and storytelling we make."

"Very good. And they don't care about tunnels anymore. They clearly found their way down here to spread a few of their own stories. But G'eldithra, I should point something out. If they finally found their way down here and ONLY shared stories, this might also afford them a way to return with that army…for anyone who is not listening to those stories. So, HERE is where we come back to the First House, and anyone else who doesn't care for it. NOW, you and your Matron Mother need to make a careful choice. Whose side are you going to join? Because, as they say, one way or another, we are going back. They won't tolerate us in this hole anymore, festering or otherwise. We're people, a part of this world, and that nation wants ALL of it united in final and absolute peace."

The elder daughter suddenly found herself in a pinch. The story now made sense, but it also represented a problem, and likely a big one, with her House smack in the middle of it. She nervously glances at the house servant, who also seemed stunned over the revelation. G'eldithra then turns and marches out of the foyer, waving for Malafay and the servant woman to follow. She leads them through the House and into the Matron Mother's chamber, where two other daughters were standing by waiting for G'eldithra to return after answering the door. But on seeing Malafay arriving, they all perked up in surprise.

"Who is this, G'eldithra?" the Matron Mother asks tensely.

"This is, um, I'm sorry, what was your name again?"

"Malafay of House Deghym," she announces proudly. "And Matron Mother T'rissae, I find this a special honor to meet with you. I would not normally have this privilege under most other circumstances."

"Interesting," she responds cautiously. "Are you trying to soften me up for something?"

Malafay simply smiles and chuckles privately.

"Yes, more of the same. We are going to need to work on that perhaps most of all."

"Work on what?"

"Attitudes, Matron Mother T'rissae, where no one trusts anyone enough to offer the time of day, much less a genuine greeting."

"Is that so. All right, I will accept your greeting, even if it did seem a little unusual for how you presented it. But more importantly is why you are here."

"Um…" G'eldithra interjects. "Mother, she is here to help our family, as strange as that may seem…much like that greeting, I suppose, but this is who they apparently are now. She knows about those stories out there and where they come from. Also, why they're here and gaining strength. And further, the First House doesn't like it, or anyone who might otherwise listen to them. And unfortunately, we might be on the list after your skipping out on that recent meeting."

"Wonderful. I knew it was trouble at first sighting of that notice. But first, tell me of those stories and what you know of it. I want to understand where they come from and why so many people seem to be falling behind it."

"Right. Malafay, I'll need your help for the details, but let's skip all the little circles you made with me and go straight at it. She's already tense, as it is."

"Fine by me," she nods.

The two of them begin again to bring up the Matron Mother with the full layout of the stories circulating in the streets. They began with the wall, the reason for it, the nation up on the surface and how they came together, and how and why the Drow were called Drow festering in the Underdark. They eventually finished with Thaelyn's military force preparing to take final corrective action on a long-duration injustice on their people by a goddess who wasn't even allowed in this world.

"Not allowed?" T'rissae winces. "But she is a goddess. Can't they just go wherever they want?"

"Not entirely," Malafay states. "This entire world is owned by another one, who is a natural enemy of hers, and this world was intended for something else, to which she was never invited. And then we have us, and what she did to our people along the way, further disgracing us in the eyes of our fellow elven kind AND our native gods. This represents multiple offenses to us, and not only for what she did, but also what our ancestors did that essentially started the whole thing. So, we must take part of the blame for our greed and inherent hatred over things we were never supposed to have in the first place."

"But here we are now. And as a result of this, we are expected to be a part of this larger body, to grow and travel as they do? Do we have any real choice in this?"

"Not if we want to stay in this world. This world has a purpose, and everyone who lives here will follow this purpose."

"And what purpose is this?"

"To be a guardian race, to solve problems and bring peace to any others we may ever encounter along the way. And there are apparently many other worlds out there waiting for us to find them. It is perhaps THE most noble effort a society can take for itself. But we need to prove ourselves ready by rejoining the old gods and redeeming ourselves for our past errors."

"I see, and now I think I can see where your attitude comes in… and why you complain about mine," she sighs. "And it would seem, one way or another, we might not have a choice by now, as this goddess we have been offering ourselves to is likely to be very displeased, much like those who still follow her. This is probably why she isn't talking to any of us lately. She already knows the outcome, so she is waiting for it to fall fully into place so she can come in and perform a very special cleansing."

"And it is for this reason we need to take up our side before the First House takes theirs. I can call in help from up there and provide your House with a level of protection to guard against attack. We are using talisman charms as one line of defense, and replacing our worship icons with new ones, to call on THEM for help. My family is already offering ourselves up to them, and we would encourage everyone else who wants to survive this to do the same. And when that time comes for the real fight, we must know to stay out of it. Let the people up there do the battle. They use full adamantium and mithril equipment, and I understand their warriors are highly enchanted, by both arcane and divine means."

"Both?" she grimaces. "In all the abyss, that would make them very dangerous…to anything that got in their way, to say nothing of our warriors…who never encountered them."

"I know. This is one of those little ironies I would like to laugh at, if it were not for the fact it reflects on our own errors."

"Indeed. All right, I suppose we really do not have a proper choice by now, especially after that meeting today. I think we must take action as quickly as possible. How do you normally communicate with them?"

"With this…" she pauses.

Malafay pulls out her shard-com, and shows it to the gathering. The unit was typically alien to them, but Malafay demonstrated how it worked, within reason. She then dialed in a number to Cardinal Nemelle.

"Hello, Nemelle speaking."

"Cardinal Nemelle, this is Malafay, we need a quick delivery of aid to House Arabarn. They just came over to us."

"Arabarn? Wait, which one is that?"

"Four on the list for us here. And my mother is calling a special meeting of Five, Seven, and Eight at our House. The First House called a surprise council meeting on us today, and it's clear they're getting anxious. We think they are losing their patience."

"Powers help us, but at least this is progress. All right, are you at the Arabarn House now?"

"Yes, I am."

"Good, give me a moment and I will call a spook to your location to set things up for us."

They end the link, and Malafay finds she now needs to explain what a spook is.

✦

It was morning in the city of Bya'an Tamoranth, and the royal couple was enjoying their morning meal. Or at least, they were trying to. Aerlie was still having difficulties with herself. She already had a close call with a toilet, as her morning sickness started up early today. Now, although she was trying desperately to enjoy her meal, it was going down slowly.

"Aerlie," Thaelyn notes concernedly. "You seem a bit sluggish today. Is there something wrong?"

"Oh, Thaelyn, it's my stomach, for some odd reason. I started having some sort of weird upset inside there. It was recurring a lot yesterday, even though I didn't really eat that much. I'm almost thinking I picked up a bug of some kind."

"That would be rather unfortunate. Perhaps you should seek assistance at the Healer's Ward?"

"Yeah, wouldn't that be a cute first," she chuckles softly. "ME, laid out on a table inside THERE."

"It would not necessarily be the first time. Recall when we first found you," he smiles tenderly.

"Yes, but I think that was a rather gross exception to the rule for someone like me."

"Nevertheless, we should not presume anything. If this is bothering you over the course of two days now, you should not dally with an appropriate review."

"All right, Dear, I'll go. Maybe it's nothing, and it'll clear up later in the morning."

They continue their meal, and then tidy themselves up for the day.

Thaelyn went down to his office in the guildhall. He would first review several enrollment reports, and later he was scheduled to visit his favorite exercise, the combat training hall, where he would sometimes offer a few personal lessons from his own experience. It was a special pleasure he took for himself from time to time to bond with the new recruits.

Aerlie continued back to her office in the temple, although technically this wasn't her only office, as she was also the chief administrator of their medical and health care system. But since part of that came out of the temple services, as their priests doubled as medical professionals, and she was also the Matron Pontifex of that aspect as well, her favorite office was inside the temple.

As before, she tried desperately to settle herself into her work, once again falling into her old habit of trying to ignore her personal condition in favor of her duties. Even after the conversation she had with Thaelyn, she felt as if the condition would likely clear up with the opening of the new day. It was just a matter of allowing herself to drift into her duties, and before you know it, the rest would disappear.

Well, it didn't.

Late morning was coming around, soon approaching lunchtime, and her stomach was still nagging at her, if only subtly for her concentration to oppose it. She would pause to reflect on herself, asking if she really did need to visit the Ward for an exam. But she resisted being the one on the table. She finally pulls away from her desk and glares at her midsection.

"What is wrong with you down there?" she scolds and jabs a finger at herself. "Can't you just go back to sleep and leave me to my work? I swear, whatever got into you, you just won't let go of it, will you!" she huffs. "All right, fine!" she tosses her hands up. "We'll see about you, even if I don't like being the one under the microscope. I suppose a quick little scan won't kill me, and THEN we'll see who's boss around here!"

She jumps to her feet and begins marching out of the office and around to a hallway leading from the temple portion of the building to an annex that was the local Healer's Ward.

The Ward, in this case, was much like a hospital. It was neat and clean, pleasantly appointed with wall art and relaxing imagery, and numerous examination and medical care rooms, most of which were empty at this time, since their health care system was so efficient. There were hardly ever any long-term patients taking up beds.

The facility had a main entrance from the street, but also a connecting corridor from the temple side, and a person could easily walk from one side to the other, perhaps to use the temple as a type of waiting room to offer prayer for their loved ones who might be in service for a major incident.

She arrives at a connecting junction, where she finds a reception desk to admit herself into care. The receptionist looked up at her and instantly rose to offer a polite bow.

"My Lady! What brings you in here? Are we making another review already?"

"Not quite," she concedes reluctantly. "I have a little personal issue I need to examine, so I need to find an available intern to take a look at me."

"Oh dear! Well, all right, I suppose it can happen even to the best of us. One moment, and I'll call someone up for you."

The receptionist returns to her seat and makes a quick call to an intern's station. A few brief moments later, and a young woman emerges through a door into the room.

"Yes, my Lady, how can I help you?"

"I need a quick look at something. I've been experiencing a bit of stomach upset lately, and I'm growing worried that I may have picked something up...although, for the life of me I can't possibly imagine what."

"Well, that's what we're here for," she smiles sweetly. "Follow me. We'll take up this first room just down the way here. It's been a slow day for us...and week...and for that matter most of the month..." she sighs.

"Well, we certainly can't have THAT, now, can we?" Aerlie chuckles.

They proceed to the nearest examination room, which included some of the latest medical scanning technology, portions of which were recently borrowed from the Suuden-Aryku and their much older technological designs, including an overhead positron emission scanner to visualize the biological processes occurring within the body.

The intern directs Aerlie to sit on the table, which was an experience Aerlie knew from so many moments where she did this to others, but this time, she was on the other side of it. She suddenly felt a tinge of nervousness, being the one on the receiving end.

"This is so silly," she mumbles to herself. "I should know better. It's just a little exam. How many times have I done this to others?"

"Are you nervous, my Lady?" the intern muses gently. "Good gracious, that's a new one."

"I know! This started up yesterday, but I didn't pay much attention to it, thinking it was just a little stomach upset. But it's with me again today, and of course Thaelyn suggested I take care of it, no matter what it might be."

"He is a very nurturing one. But then, this is who he is…and you as well. I suppose it is no wonder you feel so unsettled to be the one on this side of things."

"It's sensitive for me, but I suppose, at the same time, I must've grown into this image of complete invulnerability, being a Celestial with so few of my own personal concerns."

"Ah, but my Lady, perhaps this is your error. Would it not be by your own teachings never to take anything for granted?"

"Oh please! You're not going to pull that one on me, are you?" she chuckles. "All right, fine, so be it, here I am."

"Good! Now, let me ask you a few questions as we begin. You say it started yesterday. Did you eat anything abnormal to your usual diet?"

"Not that I can recall. The food we have at the manor is all very fresh and specially prepared for our needs. My personal diet tends to be a little more vegetarian than Thaelyn's, but I don't recall anything that goes outside the norm."

"All right, what about travels. Did you travel anywhere, perhaps to partake of anything local that could alter your condition?"

"I've been in my office most of the week, with only a few small outings, like to local cafés for snacks. But again, those snacks are things I've had before, and they all tasted fine to me."

"Interesting…"

The intern begins checking the usual features, such as eyes, mouth, pulse rate, and body temperature.

"You seem a little elevated," she notes. "Not by much, but it's a tad above normal."

"Really! Yes, I'll admit, I have felt a little warm lately. But I think I simply attributed this to the warm summer air this season."

"Possibly, but this isn't due to the seasonal temperatures. You are definitely showing your own, in this case."

"All right, so it's not just my stomach. This is starting to worry me a little."

The intern continues with a cursory examination of Aerlie's remaining body, checking for marks on the skin, the arms and legs, the neck and face.

"I would ask you to remove your gown for me so I can check your midsection."

"Yeah, and here it goes," she sighs. "I have to get naked."

"Oh, come now. How many times have we each done this? We're all the same underneath. Now, perk up and let's see what you have to show for yourself!" she announces buoyantly.

Aerlie smiled at the witty pep talk as she unhooks her gown from around her neck and slides it down to her ankles. She then steps out of it and takes up her seat on the table again, now only in her underwear.

The intern proceeds with another superficial examination of the body, still looking for anything that stood out externally, such as insect bites, rashes, and parasitic infections. Even though most of their major diseases had been taken care of by now, there were still a few hazards to be aware of in the natural world around them.

"No, nothing to be seen here," she admits. "So, we'll have you lay yourself out, and I'll run a full body internal scan."

Aerlie nods and repositions herself to lay flat on the table. The intern then sat at a console with the controls for the overhead scanning arm, bringing it to life and causing it to move into position over the patient's body.

Aerlie gazed up at the apparatus, recalling on so many occasions where she was the one at those controls and reviewing the monitors for the color-coded output that showed the intimate details of the person's internal workings. Now it was her turn. A part of her was curious about the result, as she had never actually seen her own body in this way.

The intern orders the scanning arm to pass a wide beam over Aerlie's body. This resulted in a detailed image of her biochemical processes, including such things as her internal organs, circulatory system, and bone structure, all as a 3D image that could be rotated for different viewing angles.

Aerlie turned to peer over the intern at her image on the monitor.

"Fascinating..." she muses softly. "That's me."

"On a cursory review," the intern notes. "You seem very typical of an Avariel. Your internal organs all appear normal… Lung capacity, for an Ariler, seems normal…"

"Yes, but in comparison to a normal elf, mine is a bit larger, since we tend to live at higher altitudes as a natural habit."

"Yes, and being flighted, you tend to spend a lot of time up there anyway."

"And the bones," Aerlie points. "That image shows them as hollow, just as it should be. To reduce our mass and make flying easier."

"Indeed, much like an average bird would have."

"I guess the Winged Mother knew what she was doing when she gifted my people with all this," she smiles.

"Absolutely, but so far, I don't see anything outside of normal for your health condition. The computer doesn't show any infections or unwanted guests…thank the gods. But this leaves us with a bit of a mystery. What could be causing your stomach to be so upset? This simply brings me back to something you ate, or…um…wait a moment. What about… How long has it been?"

The intern perks up, as a sudden thought flashes through her. She rises from her chair to make a personal inspection of Aerlie's abdomen. Aerlie watches her, unsure of what she has in mind, but keeping silent to allow her time to work.

The intern engages her special Healer's Sight, which causes her eyes to glow softly, and thus allowing her a kind of x-ray vision to see inside the body directly. She then studies the lower abdomen for any visual signs.

"Oh wow…" she wheezes expectantly. "My Lady, would you mind if I take a blood sample for a quick test?"

"Um, sure, I suppose I have a little extra to spare. But it goes at a premium, you know."

"Oh, but of course!" she giggles.

The intern hurries to a nearby counter where she finds a hypo-spray extractor. She inserts a small vial into it to receive the specimen and returns to Aerlie. She presses it against an arm and engages the unit, where it painlessly extracts a small amount of blood into the vial. She then takes this to an analyzer unit, placing the vial into a tray and closing the device. The unit powers up and makes a microbiological scan of the blood within the vial to reveal a chemical analysis.

Aerlie observes the action, curious as to what the intern was doing, but until the computer could make its full report, she could only lean back on the pillow and wait. She allows her eyes to drift off into the distance as she tries to settle herself for the result. If it now involved a blood test, it must hold something special. This, combined with the elevated body temperature, was beginning to point at something other than a simple stomach upset, although there did not seem to be any other recognizable causes.

Meanwhile, Thaelyn had been in session in the combat class up at the guildhall. He was demonstrating the proper stance for swordplay, which was his favorite style of combat art.

"The placement of your feet is especially important," he instructs. "How you balance your weight and use it to your advantage could mean the difference between an effective blow to your opponent, or one he could make against you, which could then destabilize your stand and make you vulnerable to another."

He took up a posture with a two-handed sword, showing it to the class with his feet spaced apart, one to the rear of the other, and also with his knees bent slightly and his weight shifted to offset his leverage. Within the classroom, the local training sergeant contentedly oversaw the lessons while the students all mimicked Thaelyn's posture as he led them through several attack swings.

Elsewhere, Aelwyn was in her office, while Nemelle was in hers, each attending to their associated work. Aelwyn was reviewing a series of report cards for a selection of classes she oversaw relating to the Suuden-Aryku and their special metaphysical teachings, which was a unique study made exclusively for their native capabilities. Nemelle continued with her work relating to the Drow, now assembling a collection of recent reports where Malafay and her people were concerned. She was also cross-referencing this with other reports relating to other Drow cities, hoping to borrow from her successes here to use as templates in the others.

Down the road, in a large parliamentary complex, was the home of the native Imperial High Council, where Lord Aristan worked as the House Speaker. He was currently in session with the other council members reviewing a new piece of legislation.

"According to our early studies," he proclaims to the meeting. "Our recent excursions into the Katharian Galaxy seem to be opening up a few possibilities for us. If to consider that Galactic Council, which we discovered in that one our dear brethren describe as the Milky Way, according to some of their cultural depictions, it has suggested to us that such a governing authority could be applied elsewhere, should we ever find anything else to apply it to. Although we have not yet found any other sapient life in the Katharian Galaxy, and those examples we have found still surviving, um…" he coughs softly, "…yes…still surviving in the Ikir'Raalu Galaxy, home of the Suuden-Aryku…"

There was a gentle moaning at the mentioning of this factor, as it hit home for certain members. The resident Suuden-Aryku all ducked their heads as this brought up memories of their oppression under the Primordials, Sargeras and Darumon, who once drove them on a revenge effort against the Estelar. In the process, Darumon created a powerful military force, and to test it, in part to ensure it was up to the job, and also in part for his personal pleasures, he aimed his pet society at a lot of training targets, which resulted in a lot of devastation around the local galaxy.

Aristan continues, "…The idea of us perhaps applying the same elsewhere might prove one day to be as beneficial as the one we are currently observing. Therefore, we would propose this as a starting point, even though we do not have any other members to join into it, but for that occasion when we do find someone, and can convince them to cooperate in such an endeavor…"

Back in the examination room, the blood test was nearing completion. The intern studied the monitor as the progress meter ticked down, until finally a report flashed onto the screen. She ran a quick filter search on the results to test her theory, and the report came up with a positive confirmation flag.

"Great gods!" she whispers. "My Lady, we have our result. You are with child!"

Aerlie had been leaning back on the pillows, trying to relax. But when these precious few words came out, her eyes popped open so big, they almost shot across the room. This was followed by her mouth falling to her chest, and whatever air she had in her lungs blasting out. And in that brief moment when she still had any presence of mind, she struggled to pull just enough back in to gasp out a few words.

"What…did you say?"

"Here! It's right here!" she rejoices. "You're pregnant! It's nothing more than morning sickness. This also accounts for the rise in body temperature."

Aerlie leapt off the table to gaze at the monitor. The indicator was clearly evident. In a result box in an upper corner of the screen, it highlighted a pregnancy condition as positive.

She started panting as it settled in. She stumbled back against the table, with her face aghast at the unexpected revelation. And as it further manifested itself, her empathic emanations began to seep out ferociously.

Up in the guildhall, Aelwyn, being especially empathic, was one of the first to feel it. In Nemelle's office, she also being very empathic, felt it the same. The two of them, each in separate rooms, jerked their attentions away from their work to gaze out into the open space. They each then rose up from their chairs, and Aelwyn telepathically communes to her longtime friend.

"Nemelle, do you feel that?"

"Yes. Dear Powers, Aelwyn. Three...two...one..."

In the examination room, Aerlie was ready to explode. The extreme emotional shock and delight, and after so many centuries of trying, to finally hit that famous jackpot, simply overwhelmed her. She pulls in a deep breath, slams her hands to her temples, and screams with the Celestial force of a thunder strike. The booming of her voice blasts through the temple and onto the street.

In the combat hall, where Thaelyn had been in his session, and he not being quite as empathically sensitive as Aelwyn or Nemelle, NOW he feels the hit. He halts in mid-statement from his lecture and nearly drops his sword as he stumbles back a step and slaps a hand over his brow. An instant later, the shocking boom of Aerlie's screams rumbled through the building.

The sergeant jerks to attention and nearly ducks for cover, much like the rest of the class, and glances around the room to find the source of the commotion.

"Gods above!" he shouts. "What in all the nine hells is that now?"

In the High Council chamber, Aristan is also hit by an unexpected jolt, forcing him to cringe away from it, just as the remainder of the booming reverberates around the room. Several of the councilmembers jump out of their seats, including a young Suuden'kai named Latena Ta'yeen, and an elder member, Santari Vankkar.

"In all the nether-space!" Latena blasts. "What just happened out there?"

"Cu'Nar help us!" Santari moans. "Are we under attack?"

Aelwyn and Nemelle were first to react, as they had the benefit of their empathic forewarning. They were rushing out of the building into the courtyard. Outside, they found a chaotic morass of students and teachers gathering from other classrooms, all searching the grounds, as well as the skies, for whatever it was that shook the place.

By this time, the scream had run out. The guards at the front gate were on alert, and generally directing their attention at the temple down the road.

"Gods be blessed, man," announces one to another. "That bloody well better be a good thing. Because if it wasn't, we're in for a dastardly time of it."

In the combat hall, Thaelyn was trying to pull himself back upright.

"My Lord!" calls the sergeant. "What the bloody hell was that about?"

Thaelyn was now trying to focus his Celestial senses to find the cause of it, and it seemed to center on the temple and his wife. His face grew unnaturally pale.

"Powers behold... Aerlie!" he gasps.

He now drops his sword and goes rushing out of the room.

"What?!" the sergeant blasts. "What do you mean? What happened to her?"

"She is with child!" he shouts back through the hall.

"Bloody hell..." he wheezes. "And she needs to scream over it? Class is adjourned!" he shouts. "Everybody, outside!"

Aristan was also trying to focus his Celestial senses, and like the others, they directed him at the temple. He then attempts to commune with his wife.

"Aelwyn, what just happened?"

"I believe Aerlie just found out she is pregnant."

"Oh! Is THAT all. Well, I suppose the window merchants should have a new supply in by now, so we might as well use it."

He then turns back to the assembly.

"My friends, I believe we have a bit of a commotion down at the temple. Perchance I could offer to take a brief recess to go investigate."

"Oh, only a brief recess?" Latena blurts satirically. "Are you sure we don't need to evacuate the city?"

"I believe those portions that are still standing might suffice for now. Although, I imagine the inspectors will be quite busy for the rest of the month. Come along now!"

Aristan waves for the assembly to follow him as he leads them out of the room.

Aelwyn and Nemelle waited for Thaelyn to catch up in the courtyard. Meanwhile, Aelwyn had been on her shard-com to call in a few friends who might want to share the joyous moment.

"Jiggers!" Relissa yips on the com-link. "She did what? Is the place still standing out there?"

"I do not see any significant damage to the building, although this is only on the outside. Hurry over, and call the rest. This will surely be a special time for all of us."

"And what about the, um, you-know part of it."

"So far, this is still a secret, so we will simply offer our respects."

"Aye, fine. I'll be there quick as a lick. I'll call the gang, also."

Inside the temple proper, the priests were scrambling to catch their breath and find their feet. Some of them made quick inspections of the holy icons and statues, while others rushed through to the Healer's Ward. The first of these arrived at the reception office, only to find the poor girl huddling under her desk.

"What happened?" he asks urgently.

"You're asking me?" she whines. "It came from back there... Somewhere... If there's anything left of it."

He continues to search the other rooms.

Inside the examination room, Aerlie had broken down to sobbing. It was emotional sobbing, in this case, both delight as well as stress. The intern, however...

On the other side of the room, blasted into a corner, along with the chair she was sitting on, was the beleaguered intern, trying to pull herself out. She glanced around the room to make sure there was no serious structural damage before crawling back out in the open.

"Gods be blessed," she mutters to herself. "I hope next time, she'll be better able to handle the news."

She pushes away the chair, which was partially covering her, and pulls herself back to her feet. She then picks up the chair and tries to return the room to normal. At about this same time, the first of the priests arrives to check on things.

"What happened here?" he demands.

"It's alright..." the intern tries to soothe. "Well, other than the disarray of things in here, and probably everything else outside. The Lady was visiting to see about a small trifle that was bothering her, but apparently, for all her experience in helping others, she didn't recognize the simple conditions of pregnancy in her own body."

"Pregnancy? Pregnancy!" he shouts. "By all the gods above!" he praises. "But you are right, a little restraint would've been in order," he chuckles softly.

"I'm sorry," Aerlie moans timidly. "It was so unexpected. I tried so hard, and for so long, both of us. And I was so frustrated that it didn't work for me."

"My Lady, not to worry. I'm not aware of any other occasions of an Avariel and a human coming together, so yours would be a first. And whether or not this might be as pleasant as we would desire, it is still an experience for us. Perhaps we could even learn from it to see about others...if they should ever arise."

"Yes, that's a good point. But now what? How much of a new sensation did I just make?"

"Um, I cannot offer an immediate answer, but I feel safe in saying, you might want to return your clothes to your body before it arrives just behind me."

"Oh no!"

Aerlie jumps off the table again and dives for her gown, quickly stepping into it and pulling it back up around her. The intern assists with the hooks at the neckline, and then straightens the appearance for what was surely to be a horde of people coming through to investigate.

"Maybe we should go back into the main temple," the intern advises. "I would imagine, at the very least, His Lordship, and probably half the guildhall will be arriving in a moment."

"He's not the problem. It's the INN people who will no doubt be showing up soon," she sighs.

"Did you happen to catch that report on your little excitement up there last month?"

"No, and I do not care to see it, thank you. It was enough simply to be in the room at the time..." she grins demurely.

Outside on the street, a mass of people was assembling in front of the temple, and among them, once again, from the Imperial News Network, was Hana Laurens.

"There's still no official word from inside the building," she announces to the camera. "I think the general consensus is for the people to keep outside, in the event we have something cautionary with the building itself. I'm seeing a large body of people coming along the street, some of them from the guildhall, and more from further away. Wow! Whatever it is, it's calling in some big names! I see His Lordship arriving just now, along with Cardinals Aelwyn and Nemelle. Let me see if I can get over to them for a few words."

Back inside the temple, the priests were bringing themselves back into order as Aerlie and the priest accompanying her returned to the altar.

"What was it?" asks another priest. "Where did that scream come from?"

"From her..." he points downward over Aerlie's head. "This sweet little lady, whom we all know to hold such poise and perfection, went so grandly wild at the mention that she is with child, that she had to scream it to the heavens above...in a literal sense of it."

"With child? Incredible! Oh, what a wonderful day! We should announce it to the world!" he shouts. "Sound the bells! Let us rejoice!"

"Oh dear..." Aerlie mumbles. "Well, all right, I suppose this is to be expected by now."

Hana was trying to push her way through the gathering crowds to find Thaelyn, as he made his way in from the other side.

"My Lord!" she calls. "Can you spare a moment? I don't see any emergency people out here yet, so can you tell me what happened to send that blazing ruckus halfway across the city?"

"Yes, actually. That blazing ruckus was my dear and lovely wife, who apparently just realized she is finally with child."

Hana gaped at the suggestion. She rotated towards the camera with her reaction, before squealing in delight.

"Ooh! I'm so happy for you, my Lord!"

She excitedly jumps up and wraps an arm around him, smacking him with a quick kiss on the cheek.

Thaelyn smiled and began to laugh.

"Thank you most kindly, but let us remember, I am, in fact, still married."

"Oh, of course, but this is such a special occasion. Ever since that day with the two of you up there. Ooh! I just knew we were in for something special to come out of it. But what about the Lady herself. That scream sent rattles all across the city. Is it actually safe to go inside?"

"I believe so. This building has stood against worse things. Let us go investigate."

He now leads the gathering through the doors, there to see Aerlie sitting on the steps with her hands covering her face for the clear display she made, and now with so many people who will be observing her. He approaches the steps and sits down to comfort her.

Relissa, Kaliya, and Ayene were all arriving through the Gateway network and now crossing the street to make the visit. Vonafel was already on her way, after she heard the scream, as she suspected it could only be one person, and only for one reason. So, she was halfway there by the time the rest of them were moving.

The rest of the people were slowly filing in and taking up seats within the temple to pay their respects to the Lord and Lady sitting together, with Thaelyn reaching his arm around his wife to support her.

Hana came around with her cameraman to position themselves for a hopeful interview.

"Lady Aerlie," she begins. "I hope I'm not bothering you too much with this, but to be perfectly honest, a lot of people out there have been waiting nigh an eternity for this most extraordinary moment to come out of you."

"Which one? The pregnancy, or the scream that brought down half the city," she smiles tenderly.

"Um, well, I'm sure the scream wasn't a part of the plan, but all things considered, I suppose it's deserved by now. After all, how long have the two of you been trying for this? But aside from that, can you tell us how you feel right now?"

"A little weary for the shock, but overall I can't even begin to say how happy I am. I'm also a little embarrassed, too. After all, I'm supposed to be the premier expert on medicine around here, and I didn't even recognize my own symptoms!"

"Oh dear Powers, Aerlie," Thaelyn chuckles. "That aspect alone might cause me to send you back to medical school."

They shared a brisk laugh together as Hana continued.

"But now that you know, do you have any special plans for yourself as far as your work schedule goes? If I understand correctly, you tend to place yourself rather deeply into it."

"Yes," Aerlie nods. "I developed a few bad habits where that goes. Clearly, like I would suggest to any other mother, new or experienced, I will need to place myself in a traditional program of diet and exercise, meditation, and regular visits to the Ward here to make sure everything works out well. I'm apparently the first example of an Avariel to bring this around with a human mate, so it's going to be a little curious to see where it goes from here."

"But speaking of that, one thing we CAN say is you will bring forth a half-elf child, even if the elven part is Avariel. This would surely cause a few of us to wonder how it would appear. For instance, would it inherit your wings, or go without. And then you have these most exquisite features of your elven physique. How would that play out?"

"I honestly don't know. So, only time will tell."

"I could possibly answer a little of that..." calls a voice arriving from behind the camera.

Hana and the others turn to see Vonafel arriving, with Relissa and the others of her group following shortly after.

"And your name, please?" Hana asks as she redirects the camera.

"Vonafel Windsong. I used to work over at the Royal Archives, but I'm also an old classmate and longtime friend of the new mother-to-be. So, Aerlie, you finally did it. Congratulations, now we can share cookie recipes...if you would ever learn to cook," she laughs heartily.

"Hey, I can cook!" Aerlie argues playfully. "I made tea for myself once. Of course this was after I burned the water," she grins brightly.

"Yes! And this is being said on global news. Thank you, Your Most Exulted Highness," she bows gracefully.

Relissa and the others came into view and gathered around the happy couple, offering hugs and well-wishes. And as the initial friendship circle opened up, the rest of the gathering made their respectful approach to give their individual offerings.

Chapter 7

DISSENTION

The next day, Nemelle was presenting herself in Thaelyn's office. But on this occasion, she was not alone. She brought with her a rather unusual accomplice. She knocked on the door before peeking inside, and as the two of them made their entrance, Thaelyn suspected something serious was approaching.

"Nemelle…and Adalon?" he announces. "This must carry a special burden if you are now travelling together. What is happening that the two of you are joining forces for the occasion? Or perhaps, I should simply guess?"

"I think guessing is not as necessary here," Nemelle offers. "I am here with my most recent report on our efforts down below, but on this occasion, I believe time may be running short on us with this one city where we had our recent acquisitions due to Relissa's work. As a result, I consulted with the Maker here," she directs to Adalon standing next to her, "and we are coming to a similar conclusion together."

"Very well, what do we have?"

"First the report, to bring you up to date. Not long ago, I received a call from Malafay of House Deghym, that one which represents number six on their local council. She informed me of several things all at once. One is the First House is getting anxious. They called a surprise meeting, and although they did not use the specific words for it, they essentially charged any and all others in the city, who are not otherwise actively trying to put down those stories of ours, to be instead conspiring with them. This would include any of the commoner society, as well as any other Houses not using their local militias to bring back control forcefully."

"I see, and this does hold an element of expectedness."

"The First House seems to be especially authoritarian, in this case. The Matron Mother there, known as Faerryna of House Oussund, is particularly despotic, believing that force is the one best way to gain control of a situation. Commoners are best controlled with beatings, and other Houses that do not comply are to be cleansed instead. This might give you an idea of the situation where THEY are concerned."

"That is simply deplorable, but so typical of Drow…with apologies, Nemelle."

"I am not offended, as I would feel the same for this much. Houses Two and Three, known as Despana and Torduis, respectively, and with Matron Mothers Baeffyn and Vierryne, are also known to be closely associated to the First, as the three of them tend to take sides together in so many matters of city politics and their local beliefs. So, we cannot, and perhaps should not, expect anything at all out of them except trouble."

"Indeed. This is unfortunate, but such a membership as this might behave this way."

"This meeting called for all eight of the top Houses, but House Four was absent. This one is called House Arabarn, with Matron Mother T'rissae. Her absence, even though Luariina, which is House Deghym again, tried diverting the situation by suggesting something innocent, like illness or injury that might pose a cause, did not set well with Faerryna, who is generally suspicious of everyone regardless. The remaining Houses, and let me list their names for you, simply to ensure you are thoroughly confused," she smiles mischievously.

"Perhaps I should start taking down notes…" Thaelyn muses distantly and he glances around his desk.

"House Godendar, number five, with Taltyrr. House Alesek, number seven, with Zarraema. And finally, House Hlatlar, number eight, with Dirzeari."

"Very good, now I have no idea who we are speaking of…" he chuckles boldly.

"Anyway, Malafay explained to me her mother shared a few private words to prime the situation before they entered the meeting hall. She apparently had a plan to use this as a kind of weapon against House

Oussund for their suspicions, thereby possibly turning additional Houses on them intentionally. And it seems to have worked. All three of those lower Houses held private meetings with House Deghym and are converting as we speak."

"Incredible! Nicely done, Nemelle."

"You should offer that to Luariina and Malafay, not me. They are the ones working this magic. But I will surely pass the word along. After the meeting, Malafay was sent to House Arabarn to investigate the reason for their absence. Apparently, it would seem, T'rissae is a savvy one who actually listened to those stories, rather than refuting them. She compared her own experiences, and those of her daughters where that wall was concerned, and the rest of it forming up an image of contradictory nature to what they are made to believe locally. This raised doubt in their minds, and the surprise summons to that meeting only nailed home the trap-like circumstance of what House Oussund might be attempting."

"How interesting."

"Here is where Malafay conducted a little of her own magic. She managed to sweettalk them with further details, until they realized the larger picture, both where we are concerned, and where House Oussund is apparently travelling now. This compelled them to make their own decision, and T'rissae, being a savvy survivor, chose to side with us. So, we have five out of eight Houses in that one city now."

"Most excellent!"

"This will serve me as a nice template to apply elsewhere, if we can manage a similar situation, but it also brings us to our next problem."

"And let me now guess... This is where Adalon comes in."

"Yes. Between these five greater Houses, they have accelerated the spread of our stories now that we have a critical mass to work with. The remaining lesser Houses in the city are also converting by now, along with a large portion of the uncommitted commoner society. But...here is where House Oussund and its partners come in. Collectively, they possess more military power than the rest combined. An uprising, if left to their own devices, would not go well. And this, so far, does not include whatever divine aid they call upon, or any conjurations at the temple. However, relating to that divine aid, the Maker and I had a thought."

Adalon now steps forward to make her own presentation.

"According to Thaliel... My chief ssseraph... Lolth is not resssponding... To our effortsss... In a predictable manner... For thisss example. Therefore... Our thoughtsss are... She is letting thisss one go... As a sssacrifice... Perhapsss to tessst usss... And to observe our waysss. According to our contactsss... She has gone largely sssilent... And thisss indicatesss to me... A departure. Thisss city is sssmall... And perhapsss expendable. But the othersss... Ssome in particular... May hold greater value... As they are larger... And with more population. Thisss is where... We might experience... Our greatessst challenge. We may find fewer alliesss... And more resssistance. Therefore... We should move on thisss one... To sssecure it. She may be watching... But we can do nothing... To prevent that. However... If we withhold... Ssome of our forcesss... From obviousss view... We can maintain... An advantage for later."

"Spoken in true form, Adalon," Thaelyn nods. "Yes, I would agree, this is sound advice, and the summarization of this city's condition does make sense. It would make a good tactical example to observe one's enemies for their methods. And you have certainly demonstrated your own to us in the past, so we should apply ourselves wisely."

He leans back as he contemplates this move.

"If we only deliver a standard complement of troops into the area, holding back some of our more elaborate armaments, we should still be able to take it fairly easily. Regardless of how potent they think themselves to be relative to each other, they will not compare as favorably to ours. Therefore, I think a single division of standard formation ground troops would do nicely. All we need, in this case, is to counter three Houses and their militias. The rest can be used for crowd control, or to counter anything unexpected, like those conjurations you mentioned, if they should try anything. We should place a firm line up by their temple for this point. And so, we need to collect portal indexes for multiple way-lines within their city for a rapid deployment. This should be fun to watch. We have never done it this way before."

"Indeed!" Nemelle chuckles. "My understanding is Kaliya and Ayene have been coordinating the development of that new large-scale deployment array of conveyors out at Bahlaie in recent times. I will check on their progress. But, if to use that, we can deploy masses of troops into the field to completely overwhelm them."

"Good, pass the word that we need a solid coverage to draw a line in their city. Our primary objectives must include the defense of anything on our side, and a quick victory over the most obvious targets."

◆◆◆

"Ayene, how is the indexing program coming?"

"Tedious, but moving forward. The hard part is to make excuses to all those people down there why some otherwise unknown individual, who looks Drow on the outside, but doesn't behave as one, is setting up weird tripod devices all around their streets and then doing something that sends random flashes of blinding light all over the place," she giggles.

"Those poor people… Just wait until WE pop in."

"Not us yet, Kaliya. Thaelyn's going to use normal troops this time. We think that witch, as Relissa likes to call her, is letting this one go as a sacrifice to watch us."

"Yeah, but that witch has no idea what is waiting behind the curtain…or so we hope."

"Maybe. I kind of have my doubts she would not do a little behind-the-scenes investigation. But then, I must also ask myself, what does it matter? Her side simply doesn't compare, and she didn't do enough in this time to make up for it."

"True, but she is still a greater Power, as far as I understand it. So, whether her side can do anything or not, SHE most certainly can."

"And this is probably where the Maker comes into it. I would imagine if Lolth does anything, the Maker will do hers. Ugh, Kaliya, I don't know if I care to be on that battlefront. I still have visions of Azgarén that final day."

"You and me both, and I WAS on the battlefront. You, at least, had a nice comfy seat behind a fake glass wall, care of Navina, and the news team broadcasting the whole thing."

"Nice and comfy, until YOU decided to take on that guy personally, even after Darumon basically said…DON'T!" she sneers playfully.

"Yes, but I felt it was inevitable. He needed a target to vent his rage at defeat. Well, I gambled I could do it, based on a few things Thaelyn said once. He wouldn't expect anything as potent as a Celestial, and he might not expect something like ME out there. Fortunately, between his underestimation of my capacity, and his weakened state, it worked in my favor."

"But was it simply a gamble, like to say a calculated risk, or were you simply out there to show off, you little tail-yanker."

"I guess I have to say yes. In the end, I felt it was reasonable to try, maybe also necessary, and also to thoroughly demonstrate my father's vision."

"Yeah, your father. I think it was said he lost his horns with that… vision. And he, in his poor state of health…that's not the sort of thing you should do to a man like that."

"Oh, he's still alive, so it couldn't be as bad as that. Besides, it finally opened up his science faction to full investigation, and that made all his life's efforts worth the suffering he went through."

"Within reason, at least, if not for Darumon chasing you guys all over the place. Anyway, we're collecting these indexes and programming them into the array. We should be done in another couple of days… once we verify all the configurations. Then we make history…again. Wow, a full-scale invasion of a city, even a small one, with thousands of troops appearing out of portals simultaneously."

"Yeah, and they complain about a few flashes here and there as we simply set things up. One thing we definitely need to do is bring those people up a few notches on their lighting choices, so we don't have this horrible difference."

"Just introduce them to electricity. Those candles, or whatever you call them, don't cut it."

The two of them pause to look out onto the field from the command center window. The Bahlaie Research Center, which once served to develop some of their most advanced technology during the Azgarén Emancipation, was still at work developing new technologies, but now on a more official level for modern day applications.

In a newly constructed terminal building on one side, were rows upon rows of Gateway nodes, much like those used elsewhere as part of their public transportation network, but here designated for military use as part of their new operations. Each conveyor chute was individually programable, and was being assigned one of a large number of sequential indexing choices from an army of spooks in Drow disguises who were currently in the city below making one after another portal index in long lines through their streets.

These were called way-lines, rows of portal exit points to unleash whole armies of troops in rapid succession. In the darkness of the Drow city, it would likely blind most of the population who might be standing around outside. As for the rest, one obvious weapon was simple light itself, to say nothing of actual weapons like swords. But it was unlikely they could fully depend on this. Even if blinded, the enemy Houses would fight back with whatever they could muster. And in the case of those diehards who were not expected to convert, it might come down to the simple choice of allowing them to die as warriors, since it was highly unlikely that they would find a place for themselves in the modern world of Tae'Eladar.

"Matron Mother, has the Spider Queen said anything since the time of that meeting? I'm getting nothing out of it from my own sessions."

The first daughter of House Oussund was reporting to her mother. She had been growing disturbed lately by the continued lack of response from their goddess. The second daughter was equally agitated, and the extended lull was causing both of them to feel as though they had been abandoned. And this naturally led them to ask if it was only part of this test, or something deeper.

"Halcyrl," the elder woman declares confidently. "I am quite sure this will pass, once we clean out the refuse that seems to be building up around us."

"But of course. I simply would like to hear a small word or two to ensure we are serving as we would be expected. This is to say, the Spider Queen might have something specific in mind, and surely, if we are also a part of this test, we would want to know if we are proceeding appropriately."

"Ah, do you hold doubts, my daughter? I think, if there were any errors in our ways, she would tell us of such."

"Yes! Of course she would! Indeed, this must surely be an indication. Very well. Then I should return to my duties. Oh, by the way, have you made any new decisions on this plan of yours? We cannot give that…refuse…too much opportunity to build up, you know. The more we offer, the more deeply rooted they become."

"Indeed. I will be arranging a special service at the temple in the coming days. Once it is complete, we will know who we have around us."

"It sounds so encouraging," she smiles contentedly. "Good, then, I will be on my way."

The younger woman bows and departs from the Matron Mother's

personal chamber and makes her way through the halls to another part of the House. There, she meets with her next-younger sister, the second daughter.

"Shyntune! We need to speak."

The other woman, younger by less than a decade, was sitting at her vanity combing her hair when the call came through the door. She abruptly turned to answer it.

"Halcyrl? What did she say about it?"

"It's supposed to be a special ritual she is planning at the temple, probably a trap to ensnare the others out there. The trouble I'm having right now is who will she be calling on to actually ensnare anything. The Spider Queen is still silent…silent and cold, like she's left us alone to something. And this worries me. Left us alone to what?"

"Do you want to speculate, or do we simply admit to ourselves that rubbish in the streets isn't so much rubbish? The stronger it gets, the colder the shrine gets. It cannot be a coincidence."

"But Shyntune, if we are saying the shrine is so cold because something happened somewhere, and she left us as the result, how do we explain our mother and her position? She seems very confident this is still part of a master plan, and she has always been right…well, mostly."

"Halcyrl, HER master plan, not anyone else's. What did she say about that meeting recently? She believes they could ALL be turning conspiratorial. How do you turn most of the Greater Houses conspiratorial unless you have something worthy enough for them to listen to? And then, if SHE is no longer answering our prayers at the shrine, where does SHE fit into what the others are listening to? It cannot be the same thing, but it could be related to a hidden reason of why."

"So, what do we do about it? We can't simply go outside and start asking questions. We're too well-known…our faces, our clothing… Um…" she frowns unexpectedly.

"Yes, Halcyrl, you just answered your own dilemma. Disguises. Then we sneak out. We'll go together, it might be safer if we watch each other's backs out there. Who knows what is happening that's turning everyone else? But if the real answer is out there…" she points at a nearby window, "…that's where we need to go for it."

"All right, I can see no other recourse. Because if she is hoping to pull out this next test, or trap, or whatever you might call it, I suspect it could backfire. If the others are joining together in something, we may find ourselves in a civil war soon, and I don't want to be caught in the middle of that."

They now team up and go to one of the servant's quarters. There, they inquired of the lead house servant, one with which they were very familiar, and asked for a set of commoner's clothing. And although this might normally sound like an odd request coming from a pair of elder daughters in one of the top-ranking houses, it would not actually be the first time.

The house servant nods and calls them inside her room, checking the hallway for any observers. Then, she pulls out an old trunk from under her bed, where she keeps a selection of random clothing. The two young women examine and choose several pieces to assemble a very lowbrow disguise to use outdoors. Of course, they also equipped a set of daggers for personal protection, but they were hoping not to have to use them. Once they were satisfied with their sufficiently peasant-like appearances, they snuck out of the House through a rear servant's access.

Out on the street, they began to simply wander around, not knowing specifically where to go or who to talk to. They strolled along in the general direction of the business section and commoners' quarters, thinking one of them could help, since the stories seemed to be emanating mostly from that area. Going to one of the other greater Houses might not necessarily help, if they treated commoners anything like their own mother did.

Along the way, they saw only a few people walking around, including some workers setting up tripods around the streets. As they observed this unusual activity, the worker began studying a strange panel on top of the unit, then touching something and stepping back a pace. The next thing you know, they were nearly blinded by a brief flash of light as the unit erupted in some form of energy burst.

"What in all the abyss was that!" Halcyrl grumbles as she rubs her eyes to regain her vision.

"I don't know. I've never seen anything like it, and I don't think I like what I see. Do we try to ask?"

"Um…well, we did come out here to learn something. And that is definitely something to learn about, assuming it relates to anything else."

"All right, but go carefully."

The two of them gingerly approach the male worker as he collects his equipment and moves to another location a few steps further along. The two women continue to study him as he again sets up his tripod.

"Wait!" Halcyrl calls. "Before you do that again, um, what is it you are actually doing?"

The man, who was actually a spook in a Drow disguise, turned to respond. This would not be the first time he would need to answer such questions as this one.

"Ah, but of course!" he announces confidently. "This is to record the application of arcanic releases in the local environment to coordinate their dispersal positions at regulated intervals and elevations to be later applied as a delivery network to accommodate the specific activation of transverse insertion nodes whereby the aforementioned arcanic releases can leverage the bypass of the relational matrices of spatial anomalies, and thereby provide the convenient arrival of anticipated byproducts."

Halcyrl found herself unconsciously nodding as she listened to the excessive rambling of technical jargon, none of which made any sense to her. Shyntune simply stared blankly at the man, wondering how he could even conjure up so many words in one breath.

The two of them rolled their eyes at each other, silently wondering if they wished to inquire further. But it was Halcyrl who came back into focus first, as this clearly was an unknown, and perhaps also unknowable sight to be seen on their streets.

"Um, one moment. Although that was a truly fascinating explanation, and I have no idea what you just said, but um, how does this relate to anything else around here? For instance, did someone order this application of, um, arcanic whatsits, and to do the thingies that deliver stuff someplace?"

"Ah, you want to know where it came from? Are you familiar with the High Mage Master Sornorvir at the academy, perhaps?"

"Yes, actually. Did he order this?"

"No."

"Well then, why did you ask me about him!" she growls. "Then, if not him, who else is there? You need someone with authority, right?"

"Indeed, you do. Oh, most certainly. But you said you know that man?"

"Yes, I do…well, not personally, but one of our House members was a student under him."

"Ah, but of course, that would explain it. So, um…which House do you two ladies actually come from, and why are you dressed like that?"

"Uh oh…" Shyntune moans softly. "Halcyrl, you blew it."

"Yeah, and that was a very clever play he made. We walked right into it."

The two of them suddenly felt very vulnerable out on the street. They both began scanning their surroundings, almost expecting something to come jumping out at them.

The man examined their reactions and knew these two young women were probably not supposed to be where they are right now. And there could only be a few reasons for this, most of which did not fit the expected patterns of their game plan.

"Ladies, calm yourselves a moment," he resumes softly. "You want to talk? We can talk. But if you want to know what this is, this is where we may have a problem, and right now it's centered on where you come from, and most importantly, why you're dressed like someone who doesn't come from there."

"Why?" Halcyrl asks tenuously. "What does it matter?"

"One easy way to answer that is if you really were commoners, as you appear, you might already know who we are. We've already had a good many of them come up to us, and for those who did, and who KNEW who we were to begin with, the answers were easy. But I think most of those are answered by now. And here we have you, apparently new on the street, with knowledge of someone a normal commoner would not likely hold knowledge of, like that academy master. Only someone from one of the larger Houses might know him or have a former student from there."

"Yes, this was clever of you to reveal us. And so efficient, too."

"It's simply a test to secure our positions. Many people are becoming aware of our operations by now. The only ones who are NOT aware are those who do not choose to ask those questions you seem to be trying to ask right now. This becomes a weakness; one we need to watch for."

"All right, so we're asking questions we might not be expected to ask. Why is that a weakness? If virtually the whole rest of the city knows who you are by now, why would we, who might come from one of the Houses, be a weakness?"

"Would you like to tell me which House you come from?"

The two women pause to glare at each other. They hold their stare for an extended moment and slowly turn back to the man, but remain silent for another moment longer. He studies them carefully.

"Yes, that might be an answer in itself," he nods. "You must be from one of the top three, am I right?"

"Um, why would you say that?" Halcyrl wonders innocently.

"Oh, please, don't reinforce it with that sort of response. For this much, I might actually say you're Number One itself."

"Damn you," she curses silently. "Just who are you that you can pick us out so easily?"

"Someone who is a bit more intelligent than that Matron Mother of yours would care for, if I'm guessing right."

"He's got that much right," Shyntune notes. "She would simply hate this one…and a male on top of things."

"Yes," Halcyrl winces as she studies him. "This does burn a little, but I'm trying not to let Mother get inside there to make my words for me."

"Do you actually oppose your mother?" the man asks.

"It's not that we outright oppose her…we dare not. But her decisions lately, plus the complete absence of the Spider Queen to say otherwise, leaves us feeling a little uncertain. We're wondering if there is a connection between the two, and if her recent decisions could lead to even bigger trouble for our House."

"Uh huh. Should I ask what sort of plan she has in mind next after that recent meeting she called to blame everyone out here for turning against you?"

"Um, you know about that?"

"It's probably a little obvious by now, depending on where you come from, and who you know, that there is something going on. It may also be obvious a lot of people are involved. And so, she would surely want to bring things back to her side, right?"

"Yes, she would."

"Unfortunately, we already hit a threshold. It will not be going back to her side. The real question is how do YOU feel about it?"

"We would not like to get between a riot and a war. She is planning something at the temple, some sort of ritual to expose the faithless, or something. But we don't hear ANY words from the Spider Queen on whether this is right or wrong, and based on what she claimed from that meeting, we're concerned she is dragging our House into something with no easy way out."

"This much you can be sure of, and it will likely end in battle. But perhaps we can work a compromise. How many of you might be willing to hear an alternate perspective?"

"I think most of our House listens too deeply to the Matron Mother," Shyntune responds. "We, and our two other sisters, tend to band together. Halcyrl and I are the two eldest in the House, but we all tend to think in similar terms. Halcyrl and I made sure of it as they were growing up. Also, we have a little influence with the first son, and he has more with the rest on that side. But our mother clearly holds some very hostile perspectives that don't play well with anyone else. She is constantly abusing the servants, and continually berates just about everyone outside the House, including most of the other Houses. I'm not at all surprised they would turn on her...or any of us. I'm simply surprised they haven't done so already."

"It's because of Despana and Torduis," Halcyrl offers. "You know how those three are. The Matron Mothers of those two are close friends to ours. And between the three of them, I think no one else CAN turn against anything."

"This is unfortunate," the man states. "If not for this, our work might be easier. All right, if you can be sure of your two sisters, maybe also that first son, this is at least something. The rest may go down in flames, but to save even a few people is better than none at all."

"What are you planning on doing?" Halcyrl asks.

"The world is changing, ladies. And you need to change with it... those of you who can learn to do so. This isn't a choice, it's a demand. And every Drow city is involved, not just this one."

"Everyone?!" she blasts. "In all the abyss, so even if mother wanted to take things back, she couldn't!"

"Not if every one of our cities is changing together," Shyntune groans. "I swear! She is so very wrong if she thinks she can...fix... this. But who is behind all this, and why? And what does the Spider Queen have to say about it, or does she?"

"Ladies," the man states. "If you want to know the answer to those questions, the only thing I can say is to go to House Deghym. They're our local contacts in this city, and through them, we've managed to convert every House from Four down the list. And most of the commoners as well. The only ones not cooperating are the top three."

"Uh oh..." Halcyrl moans. "Deghym, you say? Who do we speak to? The Matron Mother, I suppose, right?"

"She's one, or one of the daughters, like Malafay."

"Good, all right, we can do this...I hope. Shyntune, let's go. We need to know what's happening, for our own safety, at the very least, even if mother doesn't care to hear about rubbish in the streets."

The two young women now hurry off to find the Deghym House, while the man returns to his work.

They run through the streets, searching for the House of Matron Mother Luariina and Malafay. They passed several neighborhoods, some of which were unfamiliar even from their earlier escapades outside their House. They eventually came upon a likely candidate, and on checking the signpost outside, they were able to identify the name Deghym. So, they trudge up to the door and halt, trying to build up enough courage to actually knock.

"Um…" Shyntune wonders. "You ARE going to knock, right?"

"Well, maybe you would like to knock this time?"

"Oh, no, you're the firstborn, so this is your job."

"Me?! But why can't you do it. I mean, after all, I might want my younger sister to enjoy the pleasure of knocking once in a while."

"Oh, that's very generous of you, but um, unfortunately I sprained my wrist the other day and I'm trying to avoid using it until it can heal."

"Oh, great! I swear! Sure, Shyntune, why not use a foot then."

Halcyrl then steps forward and knocks firmly on the door. The two of them now wait.

In a short moment, the door unlatches from the inside and opens just a crack to allow a house servant to peek through. To her, it appeared as two more commoner women standing outside.

"Yes? Can I help you somehow?"

Halcyrl responds, "We were told to visit here to learn about those men out there with those funny things that measure arcanic stuff to determine the future development of things that go boom, or something."

"Huh?" she frowns humorously.

"Yes, I suppose that didn't come out right. He also said to speak with someone here, like either the Matron Mother, or a daughter named Malafay, about changes to the world that are occurring in every Drow city. Is this correct?"

"You were told to come here by one of those workers? How interesting. Where do you live? I thought I heard we had most of the people informed by now."

"Yes, so we hear, but I guess we missed something, so here we are. I think we should hear the story, because it sounds like we're almost to the point where we NEED to know, or we might be in trouble for it soon."

"Yes, I suppose this is true. All right, if one of those men sent you here, I guess it must be safe to let you in. Please enter."

She opens the door wider to allow the two women inside, then closes it behind them.

Much like with Malafay in the Arabarn House, this one was also nicely appointed in the entryway. There was a chandelier providing a bare essence of light for anyone with eyes to see by, and it also had decorations of drab artwork on the walls for them not to be able to see.

The house servant led them to one of the parlor rooms, where she bade them to have a seat. She then went in search of Malafay, rather than bother the Matron Mother with a couple of common visitors. In several moments, Malafay arrives to join them.

"Greetings, ladies, I'm Malafay, third daughter of the House. May I know your names?"

The two sisters glared at each other, unsure if they wanted to give out their real names, as they might be recognizable. So, Halcyrl tries inventing something new.

"Um, well, I'm, um…Dil…anna…rae, and this is my sister, um…"

Halcyrl glares at her younger sister a moment as she struggles to come up with a viable combination of elements the elven culture so often used to formulate names.

Malafay studied them, realizing rather quickly, and also by that ludicrous example already given, that these two were hiding something.

"Wow, really?" she emits enthusiastically. "And that almost sounded real…almost, if not for the fact you couldn't pronounce it well enough even for a child first learning to speak."

Halcyrl glared at her, but quickly realized she wasn't prepared for something like this.

"All right, fine. My name is Halcyrl, and this is my sister, Shyntune. Do you know these names?"

"Yes, if placed together in the same sentence, you are from House Oussund. How very strange to see you here, and especially dressed like this. Why?"

"We sometimes like to go outside to see how the other half lives. Our Matron Mother would never approve of it, but the two of us like to escape from time to time."

"Escape?" Malafay muses intriguingly as she sits down across from them. "What do you do out there?"

"Well, sometimes visit taverns, have a drink, and watch people."

"Meet any men?"

"We've seen a few here and there."

"Uh huh...I'm sure you did," she grins.

Halcyrl glares at Malafay for the curiously overt expression. She then glances at Shyntune for her opinion, and saw she seemed equally mesmerized.

"I, uh..." she resumes. "That is, WE...were sent here by one of those men in the street doing something weird. He said we could learn more about it here."

"Oh, he did? Did he say anything else about it to you? For that matter, did he even know who you are?"

"Oh, he made a fantastic play to reveal us before we had time to speak. He tricked me when I asked who ordered that work out there by mentioning the High Mage over at the academy, whom I know by name as Sornorvir. Of course, this blasted my cover away as a commoner who shouldn't know his name OR have someone in their House who was a student there."

Malafay burst out giggling at the depiction as Halcyrl shook her head in frustration.

"Yes, we came up with that one fairly quickly as we suspected we might have spies watching us. You can never be too sure who you can trust in a society so well known for stabbing people in the back."

"Indeed, this much I must admit. So, does this mean you might tell us what you're doing out there, or should we simply go home and wait for it to come knocking on OUR door?"

"What about your mother? Where is she in all this?"

"Planning some sort of trap at the temple to catch all you little rabblerousers who don't know when to return to your holes like good little peasants," she huffs playfully. "Meanwhile, the Spider Queen is completely absent for any comment on whether she likes or dislikes anything we are doing. But in the absence of saying no, the Matron Mother thinks she is doing exactly as she is supposed to be doing. However, that man out there said you hit some kind of a threshold, and with support in every other Drow city out there, to change the world somehow, and people like the top three Houses are going down in flames for it. Well, we don't want to go down in flames, even if the rest of our House does."

"All right, I suppose this is fair. You are rebels from the start, it would seem, if you like to sneak out to play on occasion. Who else is there in your House like this?"

"We can probably bring our other two sisters, but I can't guarantee anyone else. We may hold some influence with the first son, Wodirahc, and he MAY be able to convince others, but this gets tricky after a while. And I can't speak for Despana or Torduis at all."

"As I might expect. Very well, this is better than nothing. Maybe an opportunity will arise later with them. For now, we can start with you. First, what do you know, if anything, about the stories going around in the streets?"

"Mostly that our mother regards them as rubbish, and no one seems interested in talking to us, not even the servants. Even though Shyntune and I have somewhat better relations with them than she does, they still seem very tightlipped."

"They could simply not know as much, living on that side of town, or else they fear her too much, even if going through you."

"Possibly, on both counts."

"Then let's start with this. Does your House ever send up any warriors to the surface for their little raids?"

"Not as much. The lower Houses do this, but our mother regards this as beneath her personal concern. Let others clean the refuse, not any of us, so she says."

"Yes, I might expect this as well. It sounds so much like her. All right, the first thing you need to know is there is a wall up there blocking our path and the warriors simply turn around on the order of guards who maintain that wall, telling them to go home and not come back. But we keep sending them back anyway."

"Well, isn't that convenient!" Halcyrl barks. "And who is it that keeps telling them to go back if they only hit a wall and get orders to turn away?"

"The Spider Queen."

"Oops!" Shyntune yips softly.

Halcyrl was immediately stifled for a response. She simply stared blankly at Malafay.

Malafay continues, "Next is we are told to do this since the very early days of arriving here in the Underdark. Do you know how long ago that was?"

"Um, let me think..."

Halcyrl starts mumbling silently to herself, and tries counting on her fingers, but the number seems to elude her.

"I don't know, the teachings we receive don't give us an accurate figure."

"How about ten thousand years?"

"What?!" she shouts. "Ten THOUSAND?? That's like a one…with, um…or maybe a ten…and then…well, the 'thousand' part after that."

"Yeah, something like that," she smiles. "The trouble is the number you can't count up doesn't exist in our teaching books. It was lost, or maybe forgotten, or maybe simply ignored after this long time. Who knows, but the way things work for us, it was more likely covered up."

"Covered up?"

"Yeah, with such statements as telling us to go up and constantly hit a wall, even though someone tells you NOT to. That sort of thing."

"Uh huh…how nice."

"Furthermore, even in the old days, before that wall even existed, here is where we go up, and according to the stories, we're supposed to be fighting those awful warriors up there who are just standing around waiting for someone to kill them."

"Um, are you joking with that part, or actually serious?"

"Well, think on it a moment. Use that House Oussund head of yours. Surely you got a good enough education to lay claim to that prestigious birthright. If you're a warrior who is supposed to be tough enough to march through something as tricky as these tunnels down here, would you simply stand around for a bunch of backstabbers to do what they do best?"

"I hear something in that statement, Halcyrl," Shyntune states flatly. "They shouldn't be simply standing around, and shouldn't be so fragile that we can kill them so easily."

"Yes, I see it," she admits. "And this likely goes in step with that same line to go up and hit something that isn't there to hit."

"And once again, it falls on the Spider Queen," Malafay concludes. "In other words, she must really hate something up there that she first orders us to go up and hit stuff that dies so easily, and then to keep us doing it long after they finally put up a wall to stop it."

"But what were we hitting that died so easily?" Shyntune asks. "Especially if there was no wall in the beginning."

"Commoners. Farmers, merchants, simple people who were not only unarmed, but had no idea we were coming for them. Then bam, dead bodies, all to make her happy, and our people come back to a celebration feast for the great deeds our proud warriors made to save our people."

"Uh huh, and all that just to make her happy. And that, probably compounded by you using the word backstabbers several times by now."

"Do you know what the word 'murder' means? It's when you go out and kill something for personal gain, or spite, or some other wicked ambition. And although in our culture, this is just a convenient way to the top, in others it's a high crime. I'll bet none of us even knows what our full lifespan is because none of us ever see it. But in THEIR culture, they have serious laws to protect people from such things."

"Uh huh, so they see us as criminals by now, I suppose."

"Oh, to say we are criminals is an understatement, with ten millennia of history behind us. That wall is only recent. But here is where the Spider Queen comes in. She is the one with the hate, and she spills it over into our laps the feel it the same. Our ancestors, who were once said to be driven down here to fester, were in fact driven down here because WE turned so hateful that we offended everything else out there, including our brethren elven kind and our native pantheon of gods, known as the Seldarine. We became outcasts, due to our greed and pompous attitudes that we should own everything."

"That sounds a lot like mother, actually," Halcyrl notes.

"She could be a shining example of the Spider Queen and HER attitude. If not for these tunnels out here being such a bother to navigate, they might have marched on us for real a long time ago, and some of them may have tried, only to turn back for all the other hazards out there."

"Yes, I suppose I could accept that."

"Also, at one time, they counted as many independent nations, and not very well organized, so they might not necessarily care as much to make the effort. And besides, I would imagine they had better things to do than dig us out of our own grave."

"A grave? This is where we are, a grave?"

"It sure feels that way sometimes. We have nowhere to go, and often don't bother to try. But up there, we have the surface world, with a sun shining down to warm the land, a sky to gaze up at, and vast stretches of open space to spread out and sow new seeds."

"You make it sound a little dreamy," Shyntune muses.

"It most certainly would be, if you can get past the part of the blinding light, which we lost the ability to tolerate being in this hole for so long."

"Light…oh dear. That man, he was doing something that involved a bright light, and giving us this really crazy explanation of what it was meant for. What was he actually doing?"

"Marking portal exits in our streets for all those poor fragile warriors who got tired of simply standing around waiting for backstabbers to kill them. Now they're coming to fix it," she grins brightly.

The two sisters felt the blood rushing out of their faces, as they glared at Malafay and her poignant smirk. They turned to examine each other, then slowly to gaze at the exit, silently contemplating if they could run fast enough to escape the city on their own.

"Do you want to hear more?" Malafay wonders openly. "Then listen up. Here's the deal. Throughout most of that history, they just didn't care about us, if only for those infernal raids we kept sending up killing nothing more than civilians. This made them angry, but for all the difficulty in doing anything about it, they instead chose to build those walls to keep us out. But no thanks to that witch we call a goddess, we never learned to STOP doing this, and neither did she bother to tell us what THEY were doing on the other side of it, like evolving a society that goes out and rescues entire civilizations from doom, and fights gods in the process. Now, what do you think the Spider Queen would say to that if those people should ever turn their sights on us down here for any reason?"

"Oh dear..." Halcyrl moans reflexively. "She might be at a loss of words, I think."

"I'm sure you're right!" she chuckles. "But here is where the next part comes in. This isn't our home world. Our kind...all elven kind, left that behind all those thousands of years ago to come here and find new homes. But this world didn't belong to us. It belonged to the humans, and was owned by another goddess who was raising THEM for a special reason, that one I just mentioned. Then we came into it and started making wars. Boom, we got banished, while the rest of them, who behaved a bit more politely, were allowed to stay. This became that new civilization."

"Nice. So, we are actually responsible for our own banishment and this grave we live in now."

"Right. But now that they have grown up...and I mean they grew UP!" she gestures an exaggerated thumbs-up. "They are turning their sights on us now, for real this time. They united the world up there, all of it, one big nation now, and very organized. But we're still in this grave...festering, just like the Spider Queen wants. Well, she's silent for a reason, as she's the one being banished now."

"They can banish a goddess?"

"The one who owns the place will probably be the one to banish her officially. She was never allowed to be here in the first place. She stole us away from our old gods, caused us to defile our original faith, turn hostile to everything else, and, well, here we are now."

"And THIS is our real history?" she yelps. "Ooh! Yes, I think our mother is in big trouble now. What kind of army are they sending?"

"My last word was a single division for this little city of ours. If all we have are the top three Houses, that should be more than enough, plus crowd control for the masses of confused people, and whatever they throw out of the temple."

"Um, I don't know that term. What is a division?"

"They say it counts as about ten thousand professional soldiers, fully outfitted in adamantium and mithril, both magically AND divinely enchanted, and containing elements like frontline soldiers, mages, archers, and priests for support. The sort of thing we never had a chance to actually see due to that wall up there."

Both Halcyrl and Shyntune stared blankly at Malafay, having both gone into shock at the depiction of what the surface world calls an army. Such an arrangement seemed fantastical for the sheer assortment of troops, to say nothing of the numbers they were able to field.

"And this is for just a…little…city, like ours?" Shyntune wheezes.

"Yes, and as I understand it, the Spider Queen is probably watching and intentionally letting us go as a sacrifice tactic in preparation for the larger ones she might actually fight for."

"Oh!" Halcyrl blasts angrily. "So, she's silent because she's letting us go as a tactic?! All right, that does it! Shyntune, we need to get the other girls together and rebel. I am NOT going to sit around while an army of unstoppable fragile soldiers invades our streets in arcanic doohickies that deploy measured thingamabobs for delivering boom products. Is there anything you can tell us to help save our overly pompous House Oussund?"

"Take up a new religion?" Malafay smiles and shrugs innocently.

Halcyrl glared at the woman, almost thinking it was a joke, until it dawned on her she might actually be serious.

"Um, how?" she asks tenuously.

"Ah, I'm so glad you asked. Come with me and I'll show you our new shrine room. It's just this way."

Malafay rises from her chair and begins to lead the others into the shrine room, where she would introduce them to their original gods.

◆◆◆

Sometime later, the two sisters returned to their House, once again using the rear servant's access, and ducking into the lead servant woman's room to change clothes again. They left a series of careful instructions with the woman, to be quietly shared with the others, while they went to see about any other possibilities they could muster.

Shyntune went in search of the other two daughters to bring them into a meeting in the militia quarters, where Halcyrl went to call Wodirahc into a brief conference, ordering him to summon up the other heads of the House militia. Once the gathering was assembled, Halcyrl positioned herself for a presentation. But being inside their own House, she had to choose her words very carefully.

"I would like everyone's attention," she commands. "Our House is the largest and most prominent one in the city, first on the Council, and with the greatest level of authority this city has to offer. Between us, and Houses Despana and Torduis, we can be said to hold enough authority to rule this city, commanding all the others to follow our glorious lead, and our Matron Mother, who is most surely never wrong in her rule. But recently, we have been hearing curious, if also perhaps preposterous stories circulating in the streets outside. While this might not normally be a concern, not for our House, it was enough to compel the Matron Mother to hold a special meeting of the Council to see if there may be any form of conspiracy occurring out there."

She pauses to study their faces before going on.

"Now, the Matron Mother may hold her personal opinions, and these opinions tend to overshadow the true ambitions of others, where she feels her authority must rise above the rest. But one thing that was stated during that meeting is that such an attitude might also ignore a potential threat that is more potent than it appears. Especially if one does not give it enough credit to begin with."

Wodirahc listened and studied Halcyrl's face as she spoke. And knowing his sister as he did, along with the Matron Mother, as she tended to be, he felt there was a hidden message in this statement. He directed himself to listen more intently.

Halcyrl continues, "One of the more important factors in the meeting was to identify where these stories are coming from, and how they could be influencing so many people out there. And it does seem to be creating a kind of movement, to which the Matron Mother is regarding as a potential uprising, if one could ever believe such a thing. Furthermore, she has taken the opinion that it could be affecting one or more of the other Houses out there. Here is where she has generally concluded, based on HER opinions in that meeting..." she glares briefly at Wodirahc for emphasis, as she was trying to relay this to him, as much as anyone else, "...that whoever is responsible must be put down in the traditional manner she likes to see played out."

She pauses again to examine the reactions of her audience.

"Unfortunately," she continues. "One other statement was made in that meeting, which she did not seem to take to heart. It does not matter as much WHERE it comes from, but that it might hold enough daring to make the attempt in the first place, and this is in the shadow of the three most powerful Houses in the city. Now, we, here in this city..." she again rolls her eyes to meet with Wodirahc, "...might not know all the answers to this, but one thing is sure. If this is causing so many people to rise up and band together for any reason, it cannot necessarily originate within the city. Not when you factor in the authority of the top three Houses, and what they impose on the rest. So, where could it come from? This is where one suggestion came into play about it being external to the city, maybe with motivations to take possession of the city. But surely..." she chuckles conspicuously. "Who would dare offend us in our own homes? Unless they felt themselves truly powerful enough to actually succeed," she concludes more seriously.

"Sister Halcyrl," Wodirahc interjects cautiously. "I am hearing certain insinuations here that suggest we might come under attack by someone, where we may find it difficult, maybe even impossible to win the battle. But to what end? Simple conquest?"

"This would depend on the rubbish stories the Matron Mother seems so intent on ignoring out there. After all, in HER opinion, we should rule, no one else. But it would seem there is a movement occurring out there. And if it is external to THIS city, and with enough motivation AND confidence that it could win, where did IT come from, and what OTHER city, or cities, might be involved that WE, who never go outside OR communicate with anyone, might not otherwise know about?"

"Uh oh...all right, I think I'm getting the picture now. What are your instructions, then?"

"Simple. Keep your eyes open and don't take anything for granted, as she does. Her superiority complex could have our house going down in flames before we even knew who set the fires. So, if you see something you can't fight, don't fight it. You might live longer."

"But wait, I need to ask this. Are you saying we should surrender? Will they take us prisoners or something? And then what?"

"Wodirahc, I am not here to tell you to set down your weapons and be slain like she would suggest for all those misbehaving peasants out there. Or like those other Houses, where she might order a cleansing to meet with her approval of authority. If there is a force out there planning a move against us, it could be they hold a significant advantage, especially if they come from somewhere we do not otherwise expect, and perhaps using combat techniques, or even equipment we are not able to counter. The world outside our walls is largely unseen to us. If this represents a change of authority, we might find ourselves coming under it whether we like it or not. So, one might suggest living is better than dying for something that could be described as unworthy in the first place."

"And the Spider Queen?"

"Is not offering any opinions on it, for or against. In fact, she is not even speaking to us by now, which might, in itself, suggest something about this external force and what THEY represent."

"Oh..." he ducks his head and moans morbidly. "I think I would not wish to comment on that. But if you say we should put down our weapons in the face of a superior body, and a cause that might be unworthy, I should not argue with your wisdom, Sister Halcyrl."

"You need to spread this to our full militia," she asserts. "But even more, do you ever share words with Despana or Torduis?"

"Sometimes. We may sometimes plan training exercises together."

"Good, arrange one...soon! And share these same words with them. But do so carefully, as they might not be as wise to listen."

"I understand, Sister Halcyrl."

"Thaelyn!" shouts an anxious voice at his office door. "I have some rather unexpected news, and this will surely affect our plans for that first city."

Thaelyn was at his desk when the door burst open, and the form of an excited female charged in.

"Nemelle, you certainly seem energized today. What happened?"

"A pair of unexpected visitors came to House Deghym a short while ago. I got a call from Malafay on the matter, to brief me on who they were and what was said, and I feel we should involve this in our upcoming battle plan for that city."

"Indeed! Very well, but is this a good thing or a bad one?"

"I would say it is an opportunity, with potential for more."

"Most interesting. And what is it?"

Nemelle brings up a notebook she was carrying with her recent scribblings in it. She begins to reference this as she continues.

"They were two elder sisters, Halcyrl and Shyntune, both of House Oussund, the First House."

"Indeed! And what are they doing out and about?"

"Apparently slumming, by the sound of it," she giggles. "According to Malafay, it would seem these two young ladies have a rebellious side to them, dressing in commoner's clothing and going out to play."

"Oh dear Powers," he covers his eyes. "Please, do not tell me we have more of that sort, and here among the Drow!"

"Yes, I guess you can find this sort in many varied locations. You know, this brings me to reflect on my work during these past decades since my arrival. Do you recall how I asked for help with your Stormhooves and the Night Elves to see if we could make those early infiltrations?"

"Yes, indeed. It was mostly to gather intel, but you also had that notion to begin a subtle campaign to soften attitudes here and there, imposing a little of our culture to replace theirs, and possibly with the potential to see a lingering effect we could tap into when we arrived where we are now."

"Precisely! Well, this could be the result of that effort. And if we see it here, my hope is to find more elsewhere, like those larger cities."

"Very good, keep a watch for it. But what about this one? What did they actually do?"

"They are growing worried down there. The Matron Mother of House Oussund is planning a new test, or trap, whichever you would describe it as, for the rest, this one using the temple to test their faith, I suppose."

"That does not sound good, and especially as the rest are essentially no longer following that faith."

"Indeed! According to these two, their goddess seems to have abandoned them by now, as not even the First House is hearing anything from her. So, our presumption of a sacrifice may be correct."

"Yes, this does fit that scenario."

"The Matron Mother, however, seems undaunted. But hers may be leading the rest into a suicide scenario. Here is where these girls come in. They wanted to know what was occurring out there, for themselves as much as anything. Therefore, they found their way to Malafay after speaking to one of our workers marking portal sites."

"That would be an interesting sight to see. Getting directions from a municipal worker to find the headquarters for a city rebellion," he chuckles.

"Oh, absolutely!" she giggles. "Malafay led them through the story, and ultimately the girls took to our side. Now they are returning home to see about warning others, including the House males, which would be the militia forces. According to the instructions, they will not let on specific details, other than what might be understood if a person with half a mind could simply put together a few bits and pieces that might otherwise be learned if that woman at the top would ever speak of anything beyond her own passion for rule."

"I see," he grins.

"This is to say, if you see something you cannot fight, do not even try. It may not be worth the effort. Simply lay down your swords and surrender. And if whatever is behind this uprising is potent enough to invoke this level of collaboration, it must have a solid foundation, possibly even external to the city where they cannot see the point of origin or what THAT might entail, if it involves other cities or something."

"Nicely stated! This would raise doubt that it is a local issue, therefore, more widespread, and it is only now arriving here. But so far, without any mention of us in it, I suppose, right?"

"So far, yes," she nods. "And further compounded by the LACK of that goddess of theirs speaking out on it. This could then raise suspicion of abandonment, and whatever authority the other side is working with is thereby overriding it."

"Ah, that would be a rub. This would then afford a level of credibility to the equation."

"Now, for our side, I need you to inform our troops to watch for people who might surrender. But they may still need that bit of demonstration of a superior force to surrender to. Can you suggest anything for this?"

"I think I could. We have a number of tactics we can use, and I was thinking of employing one or more of these anyway. But this could pose a curious portrayal with a unique approach."

"Good. Next. As for Houses Despana and Torduis, we do not have a firm answer, but if the top three exchange any form of relational conversation, one element might pass something to another similar one to spread the suggestions."

"All right, good. Then this becomes our plan. And I suspect we should make our move soon, then be on to the next target."

"Absolutely."

Chapter 8

ENGAGEMENT

A week has passed since the last activity occurred down below. Thaelyn was reviewing his troops in the fields at Bahlaie as they assembled for their first advance. A series of large detention halls had been constructed since the time all this began, in preparation to hold what could be tens of thousands of prisoners of war, at least until his people could talk them down and begin their rehabilitation and redemption. The cities would likely need to be evacuated, at least temporarily, of any who would not otherwise convert willingly, and brought to these centers as part of a containment process to force-feed these new philosophies and belief systems.

During this time, he had been developing his own game plan for this first advance, given they may have hidden sympathizers that might be in precarious situations of local threat. Instructions had been given to watch for signs of uncertainty, and allow for the opponents to make their own decisions as to the feasibility of fighting at all.

"We will use the bear tactic as an initial front," he declares to the troops. "This affords us an increased defense, but at a reduced offense. It also reduces the chances of opponent casualties if any are having second thoughts. But we cannot keep this up forever, as we still need a victory. Therefore, we will grant them the time needed to make that initial assessment. If they indeed seem so determined to do so, we will give them their fight. If this results in a loss, so be it, and move on to the next. But I might also suggest a loss does not always equate to a death. We can heal the injured, and this might still turn around for us later. Nevertheless, we may need to admit there could be those who will take death over capture. If so, grant them a good one, as befitting a warrior."

Meanwhile, Nemelle was working with Malafay to pass the word of an imminent attack...a real one this time, not a simple fable. Malafay would then pass the word to everyone else, hoping to clear the streets of anyone simply standing around.

She had called a series of couriers to her House, giving out a large number of personal notes to deliver to the other Houses, from Four down the line, and requesting each of them to send out word locally to the various commoner quarters and neighborhoods to make sure everyone was indoors.

"Ours is the first city to go down," she declares to a family meeting. "I'm a little frightened to see where this goes, but I'm also hopeful for the final outcome."

"We've been spending enough time at the new shrine," Rhyliira notes. "This should help us get through it. The other Houses haven't had as much time with it yet, but hopefully, once this initial conquest is complete, we'll all find a new future for ourselves."

"According to Cardinal Nemelle, we'll be under what they call military law for a while, until things settle. During this time, the people will need to come to terms with the occupation, and the new culture they'll be teaching us. But also, during this time, they'll be working to modify some of our local amenities. She calls it making reforms to our existing way of life, to bring us up to their level."

"Reforms..." Luariina muses.

"Yes..." Malafay emits dreamily. "We'll get schools for our children, much like they have up there. Our workshops will grow into proper industries to provide better lives for more people. They'll teach us their ways, although slowly as we need to grow into it too. We'll get to taste the food they eat, try out the clothes they wear..."

"Um, Malafay," Felynquiri wonders. "I'm not entirely sure if I can see myself in those really small things we saw up there."

"Yes, well, down here in the Underdark, some of that might not work as well anyway. And we can't expect everything to come immediately. Surely, just building some of it will take time. We're also stuck in a hole down here with almost no real room to actually grow...not unless you want to dig out a bigger grave for yourself," she giggles.

"What about simply going back up to the surface?" Alakaere asks. "Wouldn't they want us up there, or allow us to do so if we asked?"

"I'm sure they would have nothing against it, but remember the issue of the light. We'd never survive up there as we are. We'll need to recondition ourselves for it first, and that might take time."

"Yes, I suppose you're right."

"First, they'll teach us about this electricity of theirs, and show us ways to train our eyes by increasing the light levels we're accustomed to. If we can raise that up gradually, transitioning between the two might not be as bad."

"I might still think we will prefer to remain below ground, though," Alyraema offers. "We've been at it for too long. It's a part of us now. Thousands of years, living in a hole, grave or otherwise, and going back up there for anything long term might be a problem. It might be centuries for us to…reform…ourselves enough for that."

"Maybe, but it's a direction we can look forward to. Our exile into this blackness is almost over."

✦✦✦

A messenger was arriving at the door to the Oussund House. A servant woman answers the summons.

"I have a special message here for Halcyrl, daughter of the House."

"Halcyrl? Not the Matron Mother?"

"Correct. This is addressed specifically for Halcyrl. I am told to place it directly into her hand."

"I see. One moment and I will call her for you."

The woman returns back into the House and searches for Halcyrl, who was in her room at the time checking her wardrobe and selecting some of her favorite clothes, thinking she might need to make a hasty retreat when the fight broke out.

"Mistress Halcyrl, there is a courier at the door with a message especially for you. He requires you to take it personally."

"Here we go…" she sighs. "I will be there in a moment."

The woman nods and leaves the room to pass the word.

Halcyrl takes a deep breath. She was both nervous and frightened at what may be coming. But one thing she could not deny, it WAS coming. She left her room and quickly strode down the hall to Shyntune's room, where she was also browsing her personal belongings.

"Shyntune, come with me. I think it's almost time."

"Oh dear. What's happening?"

"A message, and I think it's probably from Malafay. She promised this to us, remember?"

"Right."

They now go downstairs to the foyer and Halcyrl approaches the door.

"I am Halcyrl, first daughter of the House," she announces coolly. "Do you have something for me?"

"Indeed, here you are…" he hands over an envelope made of vellum, which was derived from mushrooms. This was the closest they had to a form of paper. He then bows and departs.

She examines the envelope, hesitating briefly before opening it, then extracting and reading the note itself. Shyntune leans over her shoulder to peek at what it says.

> *"Word is they are preparing now. Be ready.*
> *Friendly bodies will be respected.*
> *Hostile ones given a choice."*

"That sends a shiver down my back, Halcyrl," Shyntune mutters.

"Just remember what side you're on. Get the other sisters, bring them together. I have an idea for mother."

"What sort of idea?"

"Well, she would probably like a nice cup of tea, the poor woman, being so cooped up in her room all day. Maybe if we go up and sit on the roof deck a while, with that pleasant view of the city, it could help her relax a bit," she smiles impishly.

"Halcyrl, I think you're enjoying this too much now," she grins softly.

"Yes, well, my understanding is we'll be coming under new management soon, and she'll be out of a job."

"And this new management?" she raises her brow. "Who will be replacing her?"

"Don't look at me, Shyntune. I may be the firstborn, but according to what Malafay told us, our old way of life is at an end."

The younger sister nods and they part ways, with Halcyrl locating a servant woman for the tea request, and then to visit her mother.

Matron Mother Faerryna was again in her personal chamber, still contemplating her ploy at the temple. In the absence of their goddess responding to any of her calls for opinions, or support of her plans, she was left to consider if she was being tested to devise something on her own. But the notion of an uprising, possibly with multiple Houses on the other side, was starting to grate on her nerves, such that the idea of this test was falling out of favor by now. Maybe a test wasn't the answer at all. Maybe an outright cleansing or military assault would be better. But, who to launch against first? This was the question.

The militia of House Oussund was strong, more than enough to hit anything else successfully, and especially if it was an independent hit, one House at a time. But if to go out against multiple Houses, this would spread her forces thin, such that the tactical side became problematic. She wanted a quick and easy solution, and a prolonged battle on multiple fronts was unfavorable. And yet, if multiple Houses were ganging up, hitting any single target might call the rest into it.

"Mother?" Halcyrl calls gently into the room. "Are you busy?"

"Halcyrl, my daughter. Come in. I am simply sitting here in deep thought of our little problem out there."

"Ah, as I suspected. You know, Mother, you have been spending a lot of time in here with this. You need rest on occasion, a moment to relax. And I had a thought. I would ask you to join me and Shyntune up on the roof deck for some tea. The cool air and view of the city might be good for you, and it could possibly refresh your thoughts. What do you say?" she smiles pleasingly.

"Tea on the roof deck?" she considers deeply. "It's been a long time since I sat up there to look out onto the city."

"Then it is about time to return to an old habit. This would be the perfect medicine for you to find your peace so you can return to your musings with even greater vigor."

"Indeed, do you think so, my daughter? And with you and Shyntune. Hmm..."

"The two of us also like to sit up there. It seems peaceful to the mind. We might spend time reflecting on the history of the city. Have you ever done that?"

"Once, but it seems like a long time ago. Very well, my daughter, you have convinced me. Perhaps you are right. A moment of relaxation would indeed be refreshing. Maybe I could tell you of the city from the early days, before all this rabble came into it."

"Ooh! Yes! I'll have one of the servants bring some of your favorite tea up there."

Halcyrl leaves the room independently, while Faerryna makes her way up to the roof deck. She ascends several flights of stairs to a roof access, where a balcony deck was situated at the top of the House, with a grand view of the city in front of it. A few moments later, both Halcyrl and Shyntune arrived, followed by a servant woman with a pot of fresh tea.

They sat down in a group of reclining chairs while sipping their tea. Both Halcyrl and Shyntune tried desperately to maintain their calm and engage in some simple banter as they gazed out onto the streets below, expecting any moment now for the peaceful scene to be shattered by the sudden arrival of a large invasion force.

Faerryna was clueless thus far, simply enjoying her tea and recalling some of her early memories of a younger city, though the city itself didn't really change much in that time. But in her mind, having been jaded by her aristocratic gluttony, it seemed to have descended into madness, populated by simpletons and disobedient peasants.

On the lands above, Thaelyn and his people were nearly ready to launch.

"We need to establish a line as quickly as possible," he advises his commanders. "Surely, there must be a few guards here and there who are not otherwise aligned with our needs, like those at the gate. We also need containment of the public, at least as much for their safety as for keeping them off the streets. I would imagine we will need to go house-to-house after a while to tally them up, and for as much as I detest the idea of a harsh Big Brother effect, these are, after all, Drow we are speaking of. So, until we can be absolutely sure of full compliance, we may need to apply a heavy garrison, plus a proactive form of law enforcement and observation to watch for any loose elements. We can relax this later after we gain more confidence."

"Of course, my Lord," responds the General. "We'll see to it. This city is a small one. I would expect it'll get worse with the larger ones. And worse still as the numbers build up."

"Indeed, we may need to take these one at a time, so as not to overburden our capacity to process them. We will need a lot of counselors in service here."

"Aye!" he nods.

"Very well, let us be on with it. Load up the first wave."

The lead General and his subordinates each salute and call to the assembled soldiers. This would be a historic moment, both for finally solving the issue of the Drow, as well as to use such a large-scale deployment tactic.

The technicians begin programming the new conveyor chutes with the sequential indexing coordinates. Row after row of soldiers line up and step inside the chutes, then wait for the command to deploy. The General oversees the initial stage, and when the first wave is ready, he gives the order. The technicians hit the activation switch, and hundreds of portals light up simultaneously.

On the streets of the Drow city, the peaceful calm is overwhelmingly blasted by countless flashes of blinding light, illuminating the city like never before in its history. Nearly every street was aglow with the first of many arrivals of heavily armed troops.

Shyntune was taking a sip of her tea at the time the first of these erupted. Her sudden reflex caused her to choke on the liquid, as her eyes were dazed by the flashing lights, even at this distance.

"In all the abyss!" she gags. "What just happened?"

"That was literally everywhere!" Halcyrl intones disbelievingly.

The reactions of the two young ladies, although intended to be feigned, were at least partially genuine. Where once the streets were calm, now hordes of unknown bodies are rushing around, with shouts and calls in a foreign language echoing behind them. Then, seconds later, came another flash, delivering the next wave.

Faerryna's eyes grew large as she gaped at the scene below. This was clearly some sort of action, although what kind was as alien as the people arriving out of it. And it was hardly anything like what she expected of an uprising. She jumped out of her chair with a screech.

"Call the guards! Send out the militia! Defend the House!" she screams and runs back inside.

Halcyrl and Shyntune both stayed on the deck to observe. There was clearly nothing they could do about this, even if they did want to fight. So, they simply held their place and watched.

The alarm rang out throughout the House. Servants were ducking for cover as the warriors grabbed their weapons and rushed outside. They formed up a line in front of the House, waiting and watching their opponents, looking for any sign of who they were and what they were doing. But the sheer numbers were surprising. And then there were the continued flashes blinding them each time another wave arrived.

In Malafay's House, she and her sisters, along with their mother and many others, were also on balconies looking out onto the streets, trying to shield their eyes from the blinding flashes as more troops appeared on the scene.

"Indeed," Luariina nods. "There is no way to fight that. They must have almost limitless resources up there. And here we are thinking we can defeat a few random warriors who are simply standing around waiting for it," she chuckles.

"That has to be the worst of it, and then to see this!" Malafay affirms. "This simply hurts."

"It'll hurt House Oussund more than us, though," Rhyliira adds.

"Them, and also Despana and Torduis."

In the Oussund House, Wodirahc and his warrior troupe had taken up their positions to defend the House. But he silently reflected on what Halcyrl said days before, and this certainly qualified for that statement. He might have been the leader of a large body of defenders, but he was looking at a mass easily twice that, and still growing, forming up in front of him. He glanced cautiously at his men, including several of his brothers and a large body of hired mercenaries.

"This is not going to go well," he mumbles softly. "But I think we should at least give it a test. Let's see how well they fight, for all their numbers."

The Matron Mother had returned to the balcony by this time, after rampaging through the House stirring up the troops. She found her two elder daughters, now joined by the two younger ones, all leaning on the railing, and peering down at the action. Across from them was a plaza, which represented the elite section of town, and opposite the plaza, they could see House Despana on one side, and House Torduis on another, as part of a triad of elite manors. And each of them also had their troops out and moving to engage.

"How is it possible they could number so many?" Faerryna demands. "They're just peasants! Where could they all come from?"

"I don't think these are simple peasants," Halcyrl observes. "First, I doubt peasants would arrive like they did. I think those were portals of some sort. Peasants don't use portals. And then, look at that armor they're wearing. That stuff looks expensive...if you were to ask me."

"Then you think it could be from outside?"

"Well, it sure doesn't look local. Do WE make anything like that? See how it glows? That looks like a strong enchantment. Do we make anything like THAT?"

"Enchanted armor?" she squints to study it. "And shields...and swords! That would indeed be very expensive. And so many of them. That must've cost someone a fortune!"

Wodirahc and his men charged forward, if only hesitantly, but they had to at least make a show of it. They engaged the front line of soldiers on the near side of the plaza. Just like with House Despana on their side, and House Torduis on theirs, the whole plaza was a scene of chaos, with warriors battling soldiers in prolonged contests of swordplay.

The Drow often favored dual-wielding saber-like swords, while the Order troops used a sword and shield style. Nevertheless, the combat was vigorous. And yet, for all the skill the Drow took pride in, they didn't seem to be making much actual progress to cut anything down. The Order troops were countering their attacks with clever parries and blocks. And the shields and armor seemed very effective at denying any form of penetration. In fact, as Wodirahc laid into his most immediate opponent, he was starting to take notice how it didn't even seem to faze his attacker, and neither did it leave any marks on his gear. Furthermore, as the contest progressed, obvious openings were left visible, but his opponent didn't take advantage of them.

"Why don't you fight like someone who wants to win?" he growls.

"Oh, I will, if you want me to," the soldier replies. "But I have orders to give you time to realize who it is you're actually fighting first."

"Huh?"

Wodirahc immediately halted at the unlikely response. He drew back and crossed his swords defensively.

"What do you mean by that?" he asks.

"Would you like to share a few words for a moment?"

"Share words… All right, if you feel a need for it. Who are you and what do you want?"

"We're here to take control of this, and all the other Drow cities out there. You folk have been a bother for a long time now, and it's time to bring that to an end."

"Us folk…meaning to say, you are NOT one of us?"

"To put it to you lightly, we're those fools from above you people think you can plant your blades into whenever your bloody goddess gets an itch for entertainment. Well, after so long a period trying to convince you otherwise, we're tired of the idle banter. You clearly don't know how to listen to reason. So, now we're here to show you who we really are."

"Uh oh…Halcyrl was right. But how did you arrive here so fast?"

"Portals, man. We don't bother to walk any more. You could do it too…if your goddess ever taught you anything about it."

"Oh, and you think she, um…didn't?"

"Unlikely, as she apparently didn't even tell you WE were doing it."

"Yes, I suppose I must admit, that would be rather obvious. This equipment of yours. I don't see any marks on it when I hit your shield with my blade. What is it made of?"

"Mithril, same as my blade. And adamantium for the armor."

"Adamantium? Pure adamantium?"

"Aye to that, lad, the finest money can buy. Plus some heavy enchantments to make it even better."

"Enchanted! Yes, that would answer part of it. And you don't seem weary after that long bout we just had. I'm feeling a bit of a strain by now."

"Aye, maybe so, but our bodies are also enchanted, giving us a bit more to work with than what we were first born to."

"They even enchant your bodies?!" he shouts. "Just what are you up there?"

"A nation of people moving to higher ground and greater deeds. Unfortunately, you folk are falling a bit behind by now. That's another thing we need to fix."

"Fix?" he wheezes. "Then, you're not here to destroy us for all those times we went up to plant blades in you?"

"Granted, you didn't win any friendship marks with us for all that, but we've moved beyond the hate by now, and want you to come back like proper folk should…those of you who can tolerate something other than planting blades in things, that is."

"Something other than…" his voice trails off.

Wodirahc glanced around at the other men who were still in combat. It was obvious the fight wasn't going anywhere if these people were only tagging them along for show. He examined the man in front of him again, who was clearly in a relaxed posture, as if this was little more than a sparring match for him. He then abruptly turned to his brothers and the mercenary troops.

"Hold!" he shouts. "Draw back!"

The fighting came to an abrupt halt as both sides withdrew into a defensive posture.

Up on the balcony, Halcyrl and Shyntune watched the line break apart.

"They've figured it out, Shyntune," Halcyrl whispers anxiously.

"Thank the Protector for that," she whispers back. "But now, look at her…" she points discreetly at the Matron Mother, who was clearly starting to fume.

"What are you doing down there?!" Faerryna screams. "Fight, you fools! Protect the House!"

"Matron Mother," Wodirahc shouts back. "They're using mithril and adamantium…PURE adamantium. Our swords can't cut through that."

"Oh? Then use a dagger and stick it in his ribs while he's standing still. Do I have to come down there and show you myself?"

"Mother," Halcyrl interjects, elevating her voice to be heard down below. "It would actually appear to me that the numbers alone would stand out. Despite the materials used, they must have a sizable force. Fighting all of that might prove a wasted effort. And from what I was watching just now, I might even suggest they weren't fighting at their fullest."

"Not fighting at their fullest?" she screeches. "How can they not be fighting at their fullest?! They're rebels…and peasants, worse than that."

"Mother, the equipment? The cost? Also the portals? I thought we already decided peasants couldn't afford that. And clearly, if they were not even fighting at their fullest, AND matching our own swing for swing, they are NOT peasants, but professional combatants, fully trained and conditioned for warfare. This means, whoever sent them probably has a lot of resources behind them, and a purpose for being here. And that purpose involves launching a full-scale attack on us."

"A purpose! And a full-scale attack? And they simply stand around like idiots? These fools are an affront to the Spider Queen, and SHE is the only purpose here!"

"Well, as for standing around, I might offer a suggestion that they are waiting for US to realize who the idiots really are, if they are so professionally equipped and we do not choose to recognize their potential. This reminds me of that suggestion of a force we might otherwise underestimate for our own belief of superiority."

"Oh, really!" she blasts.

"Yes, Mother, really. There may actually be something out there stronger than our own."

"And the Spider Queen? Surely, it would not be stronger than HER!"

"Naturally, I cannot say what might be stronger than her, but this simply leads me to wonder if she said anything about this…" she waves at the street below. "Again, I haven't heard from her for a long time. In fact, I might even go so far as to say, those rubbish stories you were so offended by, were growing in the streets at the same time her voice faded from our shrine. This is disturbing, to say the least."

"Disturbing!" she shrieks. "How can you possibly say that! Argh! And look at them! They're STILL just standing there!"

Faerryna screams in anguish and glances around the balcony as if looking for something to throw at the troops down below. In the absence of seeing anything appropriate, she glares into the street again. She then starts chanting something unintelligible and weaving her hands in circles.

"Uh oh…" Halcyrl moans. "Move back everyone."

The four sisters step back to give their mother room for some kind of obvious conjuration act. The elder female continues her chanting, and a glow begins to form in front of her within her circular hand movements.

On the ground, Wodirahc and the others gazed up at her in apprehension.

"Lad," the soldier emits tensely. "I might suggest you step back from this. She's likely taking aim at me, for this much."

"You…" he glances at the man. "You're actually telling me to move out of the way of something?"

"Look, my dear Morier, if you need it spelled out, we want the lot of you alive so we can teach you better manners down here. Now MOVE!"

The soldier reaches out and gives a firm shove to push Wodirahc back, leaving the soldier standing there alone in the open to take whatever the Matron Mother had in mind.

"Is he crazy?" Shyntune mumbles. "Mother isn't playing with parlor tricks up here."

Faerryna was finishing up her chant, now with a large orb of dark energy hovering in front of her. She swings her hand around to toss it to the ground, where it impacts right in front of the lone soldier.

Wodirahc and the other Drow warriors all move back, as the impact erupts with a bulge rising out of the ground. It emerges as a huge egg sack, grotesquely pulsing with imminent life. The soldier stares at it, readying his sword and shield for a new fight.

The sack burst open, and from deep inside crawls out a massive spider which stood taller than a man.

"Well now," the soldier croons. "Isn't that lovely! Do you think it likes to play, lads?" he shouts to the others.

The spider lunges at the man, being the closest target available. He dodged and smacked it with his shield to deflect it away. He then rolls off to the side to give himself some distance.

The Spider turns and tries lunging at him again, but this time he counters with his own and smashes it in the face, still using only his shield.

Wodirahc watches, amazed that he's not even trying to kill it, instead seemingly just playing.

Halcyrl and her sisters also watch, wondering what the man was actually attempting down there. As for Faerryna, she was partially amused, but anxiously waiting for her pet to make its killing blow.

The spider seemed a bit dazed after that last one. It turned once again to orient itself and made one more effort, although not as precise after that last hit. Here is where the man ducks under it, using his shield like an umbrella as the spider arrives above him. He then lurches upward, using his enhanced strength to lift the spider and topple it over onto its back. He quickly tosses off his shield and leaps onto the spider's underbelly, then straddling it around the thorax and plunging his sword directly down into it. The creature let out a screech as its life quickly drained away.

The rest of the troops rose up in a round of cheers and applause, while Wodirahc grew pale at the relative ease at which the soldier killed the beast. Halcyrl and her three sisters all gasped at the scene below.

"That's not a good sign!" she blasts reflexively. "Three hits, two of which looked like just batting it away?"

"Uh huh," Shyntune moans. "And without even breaking a sweat."

"Um, Mother, I seriously think we should reconsider that peasant aspect. That wasn't a peasant move. In fact, that was something more than our best warrior move. These people seem to toy with such things."

"Impossible!" she screams. "Just who are you down there, with this preposterous little rebellion of yours? How dare you invade our city and offend the Spider Queen?"

The man pulled himself off the carcass and retrieved his shield. He then looked up at the frantic woman on the balcony above him.

"We're from the surface world!" he shouts back. "You people down here with your preposterous notions of invading OUR lands and offending OUR people, further fueled by your preposterous wretch of a goddess and HER preposterous idea that she holds any proper right to be here in the first place, are about to be corrected, as you never took any of our lessons in the past, so now you will!"

"Surface world!" she gasps and draws back.

"And what's more," he continues. "Your preposterous goddess apparently never taught you better, that we were growing too powerful for you to oppose anyway, especially after we built that wall to keep you out. But I guess she forgot to mention that; didn't she!"

"A wall? What wall?"

"The one your warriors kept hitting for so many centuries every time she ordered you to further offend us with your madness."

"Madness! She is our goddess!"

"No, she's not. You defiled your real gods up there. She took you up because no one else wanted you. And SHE apparently hates all the rest, so you were a perfect fit. You offended us, you offended your elven gods, but now SHE has finally offended us to the point that we're giving her the final heave-ho."

"You can't do that! You're simple males!"

"Aye ma'am, simple males which your FEMALE goddess seems to hate anyway. And we follow the king of the entire world up there. What do you have here, but one wee city we took with barely an effort."

"Mother," Halcyrl emits tenderly. "Are you actually listening to any of his words? A king…of an entire world, owning everything… EVERYTHING! Peasants? WE are the peasants compared to all that. This means, if there was ever a war of any kind, and we were sending up warriors to do anything at all, I think we finally lost."

"Nonsense!" she declares defiantly. "The Spider Queen would never allow any…male…to hold such power. This fool is simply trying to make US the fool. If those males down there won't fight, I'm going to the temple to call up something that will! Come, my daughters, if they think themselves so sturdy as to defeat a simple spider, let's see what else they can fight."

"Um, Mother, I'm actually of the mind this is not a good expense of our efforts. Remember the numbers out there?"

"So we call up even more! They're not even finishing what they started. Just look at them!" she waves a hand at the street below.

"I swear. Not finishing, because they already own everything. What else is there to finish when there is nothing else to fight?"

Faerryna storms back into the House to gather her ceremonial garb. This left the daughters to choose for themselves.

"I'm not going with her," Halcyrl admits. "She's insane. These people are said to be able to fight gods and demons. So, if she's hoping to call up any of those, I doubt it'll be more than a brisk exercise for those people. If you're all in agreement, we need to make our own move."

Shyntune nods and glances at the two younger sisters, who also nod. Halcyrl then leads them off the balcony and down the stairs at a hurried pace, hoping to escape before anything else occurred.

They arrive at the front door, exiting outside, and taking up next to Wodirahc, who was still standing with his brothers. The other men, who were mostly mercenaries, gathered into a separate huddle.

"You there," Halcyrl calls to the soldier. "Can we speak?"

The soldier nods and steps over for a chat. But before they could begin, Faerryna emerges outside in her ceremonial robe. She quickly takes notice of her daughters being outside, but meeting with the foreign army.

"What are you doing, Halcyrl?!" she charges viciously. "Get away from there!"

"Mother, the world up there has changed, it would seem. WE are the only ones who have not...in the ten thousand years since our idiotic ancestors brought us down here to fester in this grave they dug for themselves. Well, I don't like living in a grave. Not when the rest of the world is now travelling to even MORE worlds."

"What foolish nonsense is this now?"

"The sort of foolish nonsense you refused to listen to going around the city. THEY are responsible for it, trying to teach our people the errors of OUR ways. And by now, MOST of the people of this city realize it. You speak of conspiracies? Yes, and every Drow city is in on it by now. Tell that to the Spider Queen...if you can find her again."

"Ooh! You will pay for this, Halcyrl. You were my favorite...you and your sister. We'll just see about that."

"Go ahead, Mother, call up whatever you think will listen to you. I'm sure these super soldiers can handle it."

Faerryna sneers at the younger woman, then marches away.

By this time, the fighting at the other Houses had stopped once the activity with House Oussund started getting heavy. Faerryna calls to the other Matron Mothers, who were seen watching the show from the windows. They draw back and make their own way outside to join her.

Halcyrl turns to the soldier to gain his attention. She studies him for his uniform, which seemed fancier than the rest.

"What are you? You look different from the others."

"I'm a military Captain, Ma'am."

"I see. Very well. Do you have any instructions for a case like this… my mother going to the temple to perform anything?"

"On this occasion, I doubt she can call up anything substantial. But still, we can't have anything ugly romping around. I'm sure you can understand that. Although I doubt there is any way to correct her manners, I'll simply ask this one bit. Do you think YOU can bring it around, or should we take it to the next step?"

"I doubt at this point I can do anything more. I'm now her enemy, so I'll be on the list with the rest of you. It's unfortunate, as she is my mother, and we did have a fairly tolerable relationship. And in a society like ours, as you say, who like to stab people in the back so often, even that much is something."

"Aye, I hear you, lass. Then we need to take that temple and close it off to anything more where your goddess is concerned."

"How do you do that?"

"Our priests are equipped with a special ritual to essentially defile your worship and break the altar. Boom, no more of your goddess. Not in this city, at least."

"And the Matron Mothers?"

"As for them, if they are of such a mind for it, my only choice is honorable death. They can take their own, or leave it to a trial and execution."

Halcyrl lowers her head at the mention, as did her sisters. They glanced at each other for their reactions, but it seemed the same all around.

"We need to share what we know with Despana and Torduis," Halcyrl notes. "They're going to lose theirs as well, so they need to know why. Captain, you're probably going to have to take a lot of prisoners. I don't think some of them will go quietly."

"Fine and good, we expected as much. We'll take care of them, but I suppose it also goes with how well they behave and if we have any more like them," he glances at Faerryna and the others leading off towards the temple.

"I'll do my part, if I can, but I suppose you are right."

The Captain now calls up a group of priests who had been hanging back behind the line. He issues a series of instructions to brief them on the situation and their new directive.

"Can I go along?" Halcyrl asks. "My mother is likely to be extremely difficult to convince of anything."

"I suppose if you like. Just try to keep clear of anything nasty."

"Indeed!"

Halcyrl moves to join the priests, along with the Captain. But before heading off, she quickly turns to find Wodirahc again.

"Wodirahc, you will comply with, and assist these men here. It is likely that everyone here will be taken into captivity for now, until they can bring people in to explain the situation. After that, I'm not sure, but it'll be touch and go for a while, so we need to cooperate."

"Yes, Sister Halcyrl," he nods. "I'll do my best. But can you tell me what to expect? You seem to know something."

"They're here to take us back to join the remainder of the world we once offended. We are part of this world, and they are uniting all of it. We're simply the last to go, and mostly due to being so hard to reach, not only physically with these tunnels outside, but also for our relentless beliefs down here."

"I see."

"You should probably also assist in explaining what we know to the other Houses. Shyntune, you and the other sisters go along. We could use your help. The more cooperation we get, the fewer people will likely be dragged away in chains."

Halcyrl now continues following along the officer and the priests, as the assembly rushes off to the temple to intercept the Matron Mothers before they have a chance to perform any rituals. The rest of the troops begin rounding up the warriors and bringing them up to a line of mages with portal runes to the detention halls.

The Captain and Halcyrl, along with the priests, hurry up to the temple entrance. Faerryna and the other two Matron Mothers had already entered inside and were taking up positions around the altar trying to decide what to do first.

"Mother!" Halcyrl shouts as she passes through the entrance. "I wouldn't do that if I were you."

"Well, Halcyrl, you are NOT me, clearly."

"That's not the point. Captain, please explain to her the situation, not that she might actually listen to any of it."

"Aye!" he affirms. "Madam, we represent the Kingdom of

Tae'Eladar, which involves this entire world, along with four others we have collected together into our authority. And by order of our Lord and King, Thaelyn, and his wife and Queen, Lady Aerlie, this and all other Drow cities are to be annexed into our kingdom from this moment forward, where the people shall be made our loyal subjects and fellow citizens. This is the last and final piece of our world not yet brought into order, and so we are here to see to it."

"And do you think we actually WANT you here?"

"Want us? Likely not. But you're going anyway. Your kind once defiled your ancient traditions, shaming you in the eyes of your true gods and all of us. You further blasphemed yourselves with these continual raids of yours killing our citizens. This gives us every right to put a proper end to it. Also, this world never belonged to you or your goddess. It belongs to another one, who had some rather bold plans for it. And if you fancy continuing to live here, you WILL follow suit, or else be banished entirely from this world. Therefore, as a final closing act of our unification efforts, here we are."

"A final closing act…of unification? Is that how you describe it? Well, let's see how you like this new entry."

"Madam, if you are hoping to conjure up anything nasty, I think it might serve you to know, demon conjuring is against our laws. And right now, this city is, in fact, under military law by order of our king."

"Oh! And do you think I care for your laws?"

"You might, once we throw you in the stockade for a few years. And that's assuming we don't simply execute you for that little bit with that spider you brought up for me to play with. That would also be a criminal offense, and one with murderous intent, which is also against our laws, and with a maximum penalty of death."

"Then why not just go ahead and kill me, if this is your purpose. Why are you simply standing there flapping your jaw?"

"Our purpose is to capture and convert, not outright kill, as your kind is best known for. But in your case, I'll give you a choice. A tribunal in front of our magistrates to decide your fate, or you can attend it here and now on your own. But it is quite clear you will not find a happy home amongst us up there."

He now points assertively at the priests to begin their ritual.

The group of four men, much to Faerryna's distaste, moved forward to the altar, essentially pushing the three women out of the way, and setting a large icon on top of it. The icon was in the form of a crescent moon symbol, which represented the sign of the Protector, the main elven god. The men were High Elves, and this would be their ritual to reunite the Drow back to their original faith.

They circled around the altar and began chanting. Faerryna and the others found themselves helpless to do anything about it, as the energies radiating outward seemed to drive them back. They watched as the symbol began to glow, quickly increasing in intensity to the point where it was painful for the Drow to look at it.

Halcyrl covered her eyes as she tried to observe the activity. The symbol was ablaze with divine light, and a harmonic ringing sounded out within the room. Its presence could be felt vibrating the very air surrounding her.

Suddenly, a shock slammed into the altar, as a pulse of light dropped down from above. This caused the dark altar to shatter into rubble on the ground. The reverberations then travelled around the room to every other symbol and icon representing anything spider-ish, and which otherwise honored their former goddess. The room was soon littered with broken debris, twisted metal, and a lot of squished spider fetishes.

Halcyrl uncovered her eyes, now that the majority of the light had subsided for her to see again. She looked around the room at the mess they made.

"Wow, I think someone upstairs is a bit angry. And I don't want to be the one to clean this up."

Faerryna and the other Matron Mothers all gazed in awe at the result of the action. Everything that represented their unholy faith had been demolished. The temple, other than the structure itself, had been brought to ruin. It was quickly becoming clear their city had fallen and they were defeated.

"What have you done!" she gasps. "She will rip the skin from your bones for this."

"Mother!" Halcyrl tries one more time. "You must be the densest person I know. One, they own this world. Two, their GODS own this world. Three, one in particular is THE goddess who MADE this world, and it wasn't the Spider Queen. Four, SHE didn't want the Spider Queen here in the first place. The Spider Queen is not allowed to be here, not permitted, forbidden to occupy space here, and certainly not welcome to hold followers here. Get it?"

"Not allowed?" Baeffyn wonders distantly. "Then why is she actually here if she's not allowed?"

"She stole her way into it to take advantage of an opportunity with our ancestors who defiled the real gods up there. She apparently hates our old gods, and she wanted revenge."

"Revenge! Why revenge?"

"Something personal, I suppose. I don't know the intimate workings of those people up there…although it might center around men, and THIS god is male…" she points at the icon in front of her.

"People!" Vierryne exclaims. "Are you speaking of THEM…" she points at the Captain. "Because these are gods, Halcyrl, not people."

"Actually no, they ARE people, but on a godlike scale. We just don't know this because we aren't privileged to hold this level of wisdom in this hole of ours. Our ancestors only understood the gods as some mystical…thing…to bow down to as an unimaginably powerful being of unfathomable proportions. But they up there had new knowledge come in with that king of theirs. He is the son of one of them, sent here by the one who made this world, and with the purpose to unite it together in peace, so they can do things like fight other gods, and whatever else is out there offending people like us."

"We are supposed to be FIGHTING gods like her?" she shouts.

"If you listen to our original gods, yes."

"Where did you hear all this rubbish!" Faerryna demands.

"Rubbish?" Halcyrl responds nonchalantly. "First, from all those peasants you never took seriously, Mother. You should try it sometime. They might surprise you with how well educated they really are. Secondly, from House Deghym, where they've been in contact with these people to see it personally. They actually went out there to verify those rubbish statements, which unfortunately, you never considered, since your bigotry would never admit someone could hold more knowledge than you. They have a full civilization up there that's a lot more prosperous than anything we could ever claim in this grave they say we dug for ourselves."

"A grave?" Baeffyn mutters.

"This is how they describe it, and we who groan over our misfortune without ever recognizing what caused it in the first place. Those stories are there for a reason, to TEACH us about that world the Spider Queen never spoke of. Just look at these people here. That's your answer. This is what they made up there. And all we ever got was, 'go up and hit something because it's almost ready to march on us…'. The problem with that is, they were NOT marching on us, ever. Not until we finally made so much noise that they had to silence it."

"And so, they're here now..." Vierryne concludes softly.

Faerryna frowned sternly at her daughter. Despite the explanation, she, with her pompous arrogance, did not care for anyone holding a position above her. She was the Matron Mother of the First House, and this simply felt too good. To be subjugated under another, and especially a male, be it a king or otherwise, was intolerable. Furthermore, to be made a simple citizen of another society, not even a ruling member, was distasteful to her lifestyle.

"A choice..." she mumbles to herself disdainfully.

She begins strolling across the room, examining the shattered remains of their furnishings, as if looking for something. She eventually finds a dagger half-buried in the wreckage of a cabinet. She bends down to pick it up. Along the way, she finds several others, all part of a storage for ritual implements. She gazes at it, silently contemplating what to do with it. But before she can come to any personal conclusions, she turns and glares virulently at her daughter again.

The Captain could see her eyes almost glowing with hatred, so he quickly stepped around in front of Halcyrl.

"If you have in mind to use that against any other person in this room, you'll have to go through me first," he states.

She studies him, recalling that spider, and realizing anything else would be futile at this time. She glances back down at the floor and the other daggers.

"We have others here," she intones flatly. "Baeffyn, Vierryne?"

The two other women strolled over uncertainly and gazed at the pile on the floor. Both of them were in deep thought.

Baeffyn was recalling the statement about the world up there, reflecting on who owned it and what he apparently made.

"A king...the son of a god? The SON of a god! And placed there by a goddess...to rule the world. Do men hold such authority up there?"

"Our goddess seems to hate men, Baeffyn," Halcyrl admits. "This could relate to that revenge thing, who knows."

"To hate men... This is why. And this one...a male, placed there by a female goddess. That might say something, in itself."

Vierryne also stared at the mess on the floor, and similarly pondered those statements.

"Not allowed to be here..." she muses silently. "But she stole her way inside. And then apparently lied and cheated us, while the rest moved forward."

"They say they're able to travel up into the sky by now," Halcyrl offers. "I can barely understand what that is, being down here with no sky. But it sounds like moving forward is only the beginning of what they're doing. And there's no such thing as peasants among them," she glares once again at her mother.

"What do they have?"

"Highly educated people, all of them. They have schools with structured learning to fully educate everyone with everything. And using this, they can advance themselves in ways we cannot even imagine. This would easily put us to shame for what we have down here. We haven't changed in thousands of years."

"Thousands!" she groans and suddenly steps back a pace.

"What will they do to us, Halcyrl?" Baeffyn asks.

"For those who can learn to live in peace with them, they will share what they made and bring us inside. For those who cannot, I suppose they'll be given a choice much like mother's right now. They live in PEACE, no backstabbing or other shortcuts to power. And you learn to adore your family and neighbors, not cheat them."

The woman briefly winces at the depiction, which seemed unnatural by their standards. She then glared at Halcyrl again, passing between her and Faerryna.

"Is this it? The reason why you are trying so hard to explain things? You have already made the conversion, haven't you?"

"I had to, for my own protection and survival, as did my sisters. And do you know what? I actually feel better for it."

"And her?" she orients at Faerryna.

"With regrets, she is too deeply mired in the Spider Queen's ways. I suspect, had this not occurred outside, I might find myself fighting her one day to take possession of our House. I doubt she would let go willingly."

"Maybe. I wonder if my own daughter would feel as much."

She mulled the idea, trying to envision her future within her House, along with her daughters, where one of them would try taking control with the proverbial knife in the back…as opposed to a life where this would vanish. But life versus death was also a motivating factor here, and she cherished hers too much to forfeit it like this. She found herself falling back a step with Vierryne.

Faerryna now found herself standing there alone with a dagger in her hand. It was becoming clear by now that not only her daughter, but her two best friends, if the word friend held as much meaning to the Drow as it did elsewhere, had turned against her favored way of life.

"I see..." she intones solemnly. "Then, this is the end. The end of an Era for us."

"The end of an era that was not meant to be in the first place, Faerryna," Vierryne asserts. "If we defiled our old gods for someone who refuses even to tell us what those people are doing up there, I think that speaks for itself."

"I must agree," Baeffyn nods. "At the very least, to tell us if there is a wall standing in our way."

"So be it," Faerryna accedes. "But I, for one, cannot live in this new Era. Not if it is governed by males and peasants," she spits.

She backs away and brings up the dagger to aim at her heart. She presses it against her chest and takes one final breath before plunging it deep inside. She lets out a soft whine as she spends this last breath, and then slumps onto the floor.

"She had to give one final word..." Halcyrl shakes her head. "To the last with it."

She lowers her head at the scene and turns away. Baeffyn and Vierryne also turned away, as they each considered the viability of their choice.

The priests who were in attendance then moved forward to take the two women into custody.

"You should come with us now," one of them declares. "We are moving everyone who is not already aligned with us to a detention hall for further review."

The women nod silently and follow along, while Halcyrl and the Captain turn to exit the building.

On seeing their sister coming out, Shyntune and her other sisters all breathed a small sigh of relief to see Halcyrl was alright. Furthermore, an assemblage of other daughters from the Despana and Torduis Houses, who had collected with them by this time, also felt a similar sense of relief to see their associated mothers returning outside. But when it became clear Faerryna was not among them, Shyntune felt a shiver run through her.

"Halcyrl..." she calls tentatively. "Is she..."

"She took her own," she admits. "I tried my best, but the more she heard, the less she cared for it. It falls to us now."

"You are the firstborn. Will you take control of our House now?"

"Shyntune, my understanding of their world is they don't do it that same way. We'll need to study their ways and find a new one for ourselves. Until then, let's just try to clean up."

<h1 style="text-align:center">Chapter 9</h1>

<h1 style="text-align:center">INSIDIOUS INTRIGUE</h1>

A month has passed since taking that first city. Efforts have moved on to the next one, increasing the magnitude of their influence as time progressed, thereby hoping to find similar results. In the guildhall, Thaelyn and his team were meeting for a brief update on their progress.

"Still no overt reactions from Lolth," Thaelyn muses.

"Aye," Relissa accedes. "But you know she must be planning something."

"She is clearly holding back," Nemelle notes. "That first demonstration, while it may not have been especially extraordinary, would surely inspire her to contemplate a response."

"Our spies are not reporting anything out of the ordinary, as yet..." Thaelyn asserts. "But then, we are taking this next one cautiously. At some moment, I would imagine she should be reporting the downfall of cities, and the progression of our efforts."

"We're using a few more spooks on this one," Relissa offers. "Can she track those as much?"

"That would be a fine question to ask. Also, that we are not as openly referencing our targets, so we could be virtually anywhere, and doing anything, as far as she knows."

"Aye. But you know, if it were me, after a while, I don't think we can count on this for too long. Maybe the first two, even three, aye. But she'll surely start piping up about it and put those peeps on alert.

We may need to go harder on the military side after a while, just to get it done."

"They tend not to communicate with each other much," Nemelle submits. "And we will generally cut this off as we move forward with our conquests. Other than for a potential lapse in one House or another failing to offer their prayers on a timely basis, she might not even know who is getting hit until well after the fact. But yes, more than likely she will begin to distribute warnings, maybe even to generate one of her famous lies about how and why."

"You may be right," Thaelyn nods. "We will see how this next one goes, and adjust our methods accordingly. But we still have a lot of cities on the list, with the worst ones at the bottom. There are a few in particular which will be especially difficult for their size, and then there is that last one, which we might call their capital."

"Aye," Relissa affirms. "If you can call anything of theirs a capital. They don't make up a proper nation. Each city is like its own state. But that last one..." she rolls her eyes.

"Yes, I have heard a few stories about it," Thaelyn intones intriguingly. "Traveler's tales. That one carries a bit of history behind it. It was once founded by an individual who had a following behind her, but the ups and downs that came after suggests it had a very turbulent ride."

"And a few famous names, too. It'll be a real bugaboo to take that one."

"And no doubt, this is where I suspect Lolth will make her last stand, if she will do so at all."

In the newly captured city below, Malafay and her sisters were discovering new uses for themselves by helping to coordinate a series of developments and new services.

"That temporary Gateway node of theirs is amazing," Rhyliira states. "Just think, instant travel up to the surface. No more tunnels."

"Now, if only we didn't suffer blindness after arriving," Felynquiri responds. "I don't think I'll ever get used to that. But maybe, once that new power station of theirs goes into operation, and they start wiring the place, we'll start to see more light down here, like in the streets and public places. Then, hopefully, we can adapt a little."

"We need to expand the city, too. They had a team of dwarves running through the streets again inspecting some more areas for potential digging. But I'm asking myself, would we really want to stay down here, or do we ever go up with them?"

"For the time being," Malafay offers. "We need to take care of what we have here. We can migrate later. I doubt everyone will want to go up. And some of the larger cities are simply too big to relocate. Besides, I heard a few people suggest there's some benefit to having a city like ours so deep underground. It has to do with the unusual rock formations and cave passageways we have around here. They used a word I never heard of before, and said it could offer us some tourist potential. Spelunking."

"What's that supposed to be?"

"It's a kind of recreational activity to explore caves and underground locations."

"Recreation? People do that?"

"Those on the surface might. And we do have some fascinating formations down here if you can avoid the basilisks and hook horrors. So, we might have some possibilities lining up for us that we didn't even know about."

"What about those crystal caverns?" Felynquiri wonders. "You know, where the crystalmancers go to find materials for their trade."

"That's right!" Malafay perks up. "And once we start using electric light around here, their trade might get cut off. They use that to enchant glowing crystals for many of the public shops and taverns. Even some of the Houses use that."

"Can we use it for anything else? I wouldn't want to see people get tossed out in the street."

"Well, let's think a moment. Those crystals have a natural glow to them, right? And the crystalmancers simply enhance this with a little arcane work. So, if not to use it for light, what else can you use it for?"

"You mean us down here, or them up there? They wouldn't probably see any value in them for the meager light they put out."

"No… But wait a minute! Not for the light, but they sure are nice to look at. Different colors too. And they tend to pulse with that light, like little ripples running through the crystals. What about as a form of artwork? They probably don't have anything like this up there."

"Hey! That's not bad. And it would be something specific to our culture. All right, good. Let's talk to a few people and see if they can try some examples."

"One thing I think we can count on," Rhyliira mentions. "Regardless of whatever trade goods we might see going out, we'll probably have a lot of choices coming in. New types of food, all their toys to play with…can we actually afford all that?"

"That'll be hard for us, unless we can find something worthy to trade outward. But we're just getting started, so let's not get too far ahead of ourselves. First, we need to assimilate the people into this new culture, probably also the new education."

"Um, does this mean WE need to go back to school?" she inquires timidly.

"Well, it probably couldn't hurt. Regardless of how long we might actually live, as compared to any of them, I think we still have a long way to go, so we'll need to prepare ourselves for it."

"We do need to study their language," Felynquiri concedes. "This much is for sure. Ours and theirs have diverged in all this time. We don't even speak the same as our old elven cousins anymore."

"You know, my sisters," Malafay leans forward. "This also brings me to something else, and I think this is very important for us."

"What's that?"

"Our name. Once upon a time, our people were called Ssri. Since then, we seem to have diverged into two new clans, with those Night Elves on one side, and us on the other. We need to give ourselves a new name, especially since the word Drow is so badly tarnished as it is."

"That word is probably the work of our old goddess. For all we know, SHE gave it to us, not anyone else. All right, so what name do we choose instead of this?"

"We should probably think on it a while, but if the others use Night as part of their name, maybe because they still lived on the surface with an actual sky over their heads to see a nighttime, one immediate thought that comes to me is we live in the shadow of the Underdark. What about to call ourselves Shadow Elves."

"It carries a certain ring to it," Rhyliira suggests. "We should bring this up with Relissa and her people and see if they have anything to say."

"Yes, I agree," Felynquiri affirms. "The word Drow should no longer be our name. Those people up there hate it too much, and it simply reminds us of our own shame."

✦ ✦ ✦ ✦ ✦ ✦ ✦

Another week passes and Thaelyn is reviewing a series of reports, along with Nemelle, on their progress with their current target. Relissa is also visiting to offer suggestions.

"This one is proving itself a little more difficult," Thaelyn asserts. "We make one connection, but then something breaks, like a Council meeting, or a temple ritual, to enforce some rule or principle."

"Could it be she's fighting us by now?" Relissa asks.

"Possibly. But we still need to get inside and turn at least some of them around, if for no other reason than to foil her ability to maintain them. Otherwise, we will have a mass of bodies on the other side when we go in with the military."

"Our spooks are dropping lines in their taverns, just like before when I was down there. They can come and go without anyone noticing, and take up disguises and impersonate peeps..." she halts her thoughts as a sudden idea hits her. "Oh jiggers, why didn't I think of that before. Sure! This would work wonders for us!" she grins brightly.

"Uh oh..." Thaelyn moans. "Nemelle, do you recall what I warned you about her? Do you see her face? That is precisely the warning sign."

"Should I try vacating now for safety?" she smiles. "If I hurry, I could transport myself back up to Elysium before anything goes boom."

"Buggers to you two!" Relissa teases. "You'll love this one, I guarantee it. I might even get a new mark out of it...it's been so long."

"Indeed!" Thaelyn raises his brow humorously. "Very well, if this is so good, we should at least listen. We will decide on the mark afterwards."

"Great. Now imagine this. Think back to Azgarén and the Suuden'kai military. Things like those ships out by Sigil, and Kaliya and her team dropping hints."

"Oh dear...yes, this might be worthy of a mark, after all. How would you suggest this in our case? We are not simply speaking of visiting a tavern and spreading rumors here, am I right?"

"Aye, that might be better of Morndindor and the dwarves. Here, we're going inside Houses and impersonating peeps to reveal things directly. Things they are being denied by other means. Like maybe to play a visitor for tea...someone respected, to get in the door and actually have the locals listen. Or if it gets tough, um... Ooh! Here you go. Remember Therinë and the Flame Elves, that priestess we abducted and converted directly, then sent home as a spy. Either that, or a body double."

"Oh dear Powers…"

"Indeed!" Nemelle smiles. "And I like it. It holds a number of possibilities for us. The abduction part, for instance. We could plant a spy right inside their homes, maybe also to pull out other members, if need be, to replace later, and converting them from the inside out."

"Ugh!" he grimaces. "That is even worse! Nemelle, are you trying to join her with that mark?"

"Well, I already found one with that incense, so now that I am no longer a virgin, I suppose I can do it again."

"Now wait one moment, young lady," he wags a finger at her. "What would your Father say to that?"

"Considering the outcome, I think he would approve. I cannot stay innocent ALL my immortal life."

"Someone, help me…" he drops his head. "Why must I have so many difficulties with the ladies in my life?"

"It is because you are such a fabulous man, we need to bestow upon you all of our finer graces."

They share a robust laugh together as they begin devising a new set of plans.

✦✦✦✦✦

"Mother? I just got a new set of instructions from Relissa."

"Indeed, Malafay. And what does she offer on this occasion?"

Luariina and her daughter were convening as part of the recent ideas launched by Relissa and her mischievous intrigue up on the surface.

"They are moving to the next city, but it seems they are having to devise some new methods to foil the locals and their goddess. These may include more deliberate activity by their spooks to impersonate people and drop ideas directly into their laps, rather than spread simple rumors on the streets. If the…ahem…is trying to hide things, they are going to unhide them."

"Uh oh. And how do we fit in?"

"The plan involves a combination of steps, depending on the need. Some might involve esteemed visitors to deliver hidden news, while others might involve actually abducting residents, then converting them and sending them back as spies."

"Abducting?" she winces. "In all the abyss, that sounds devious."

"Relissa said they did this once before in another war to great effect. They were able to convert a whole city, and saved many tens of thousands of lives."

"Really! They must make it a profession to do this sort of thing. But again, our role?"

"Rather than abducting and taking people up there to face...the enemy..." she flutters her fingers. "They thought of bringing them here, with those of us who might be more familiar, therefore a softer blow, and have us share what we know."

"Ah! Yes! That sounds like a workable plan. And here we have a chance to further offer ourselves to aid others. Yes, this holds merit. Very well, when the time comes, we should prepare ourselves for it."

In another Drow city, located somewhere in the Underdark, a new series of exploits are underway. Stories had been passing in the streets for some time now, and this had already stirred up some unrest among the local commoner population. Even a few of the larger Houses were feeling the effect, but their devotion to their faith was hindering the full conversion.

A new campaign had been initiated, as well as advertised, by the local mage academy. The academy was a well-respected city amenity, and although it was populated mostly by males, as the females all tended to take up priesthood services at the temple, these males were more highly revered than your average example. Being well studied in arcane teachings, they might be able to portray knowledge, as gained by magical means, more effectively than the average commoner in the street. This would serve as a starting point. But there was one initial stumbling block that had to be overcome. In order to portray a role, either the original individual had to be converted, or else abducted and replaced by a fake.

In the streets of the city, a series of messengers had been sent out to the various Houses, starting with the lower ranks, and working their way up as Thaelyn's people could feel their confidence levels rise. The message was part of a campaign to bring a new discovery to the Houses, allegedly acquired by reputable sources and disseminated within the Academy, where it was deemed to be of great importance for the various Houses as part of a new scholarly lesson.

On one such occasion, a knock came to the door of one of the lesser Houses, a lower ranking example to serve as a test platform. A house servant answers the door to see a well-dressed Academy scholar arriving as part of the announcement for this new teaching they were distributing.

"You are from the Academy?" she asks. "Are you here for your appointment?"

"Yes, I am. I have arrived with an update to the lesson books used in this House. I must therefore speak to the Matron Mother and her elder daughters, so that they may begin sharing this with the rest of the family."

"Of course. Please come in. I will find one of the daughters and have her attend to you."

She lets the man in and directs him to a parlor room, where he waits for the others to arrive.

The man, in this case, was actually a spook in a Drow costume. The original man he was impersonating was still in custody after refusing to cooperate politely. As such, several spooks could be sent out simultaneously impersonating the same man without concern for overlap, as it was unlikely anyone would notice multiple doppelgangers travelling around the city.

The servant went in search of the eldest daughter to report the news of the visitor. She then gathered up the Matron Mother and her other sisters for a group session in the parlor. When they arrived, the man offered his polite greetings and they all sat down together.

"I cannot recall the last time the Academy came out with new books for our studies," the Matron Mother muses. "Not in my lifetime, at least."

"Naturally," he admits. "But knowledge is not stagnant, and should never be considered complete. Times change, and so do the events around us. And from time to time, it becomes necessary for us to revise our lessons to account for those changes. On this occasion, however, we have discovered a most peculiar series of events that seem to have gone unnoticed until recently. When we began to investigate, first to ensure they were in fact accurate, and later to understand why, after so long a time, they went unnoticed, it became evident to us that someone, somewhere, had either neglected to report this to us, or else it was being intentionally hidden."

"Intentionally hidden? By whom?"

"This became our own question, as from our side of the study, we seemed to be missing some important details. We therefore speculated that the knowledge to associate this discrepancy was not found on our side."

"Your side, meaning the Academy?"

"Yes. Unfortunately, as we continued to investigate, we soon hit a blockage. It almost seemed as though whoever, or whatever might be causing this, was actively pressing it upon us."

"Do we know who it could be?"

"We have a direction, but it is confusing. If we should value our teachings, we should also value the knowledge they convey. And if we are to value any form of this knowledge, we should also value the continued development of knowledge to further understand that which is around us. To do otherwise is to become ignorant, maybe even to become the subject of some influence that would wish to control us through this ignorance."

The Matron Mother and her daughters all frowned at the implications. The wording was carefully crafted to raise suspicion over their situation.

The man continued, "Then, once we began to realize a direction to it, we started to receive threats, and this was offensive to us, being such a respected authority that even the Greater Houses would come to us for our teachings. If our teachings are so highly valued, then our wisdom to interpret these discrepancies should also be valued…but it would seem someone is not pleased by them."

"But who? Who threatened you?"

"The temple."

The Matron Mother reeled back at the suggestion, and privately tried to mull the meaning of it. But being one of the lower Houses, hers did not hold such esteem to know the ways of the greater Houses, who most often submitted priestesses to serve in the temple. This accusation was now intended to raise contention among the ranks, therefore softening the unity of their society.

"And here is where our confusion climaxes," the man continues. "Not only is the temple mostly occupied by members of the Greater Houses, but they tend to rotate their service on occasion, so no one House is always on duty. This would then imply it is not limited to any one House, or perhaps no one House is personally responsible, but some other authority influencing THEM."

"Huh?" she blurts. "What sort of influence could control THEM in such a way? Um, well, I mean…"

"Yes, I know what you mean, and this is part of our confusion, until we began to add these disparate elements together. In order for us to thoroughly interpret what we were looking at, we had to continue our study discreetly, such that this authority, whatever it might be, could not as easily observe us. And from this, we began to write down our notes in a new ledger of teachings for what we found."

He pulls out a smallish book from a shoulder bag he was carrying, and presents it in view.

"The collected works we assembled are cataloged here. These are taken from statements we collected along the way, some of them historical, some more recent. To begin with, it goes like this. Our ancestors first came into the Underdark much longer ago than we first thought. We are interpreting this to simply be an error in recording the length of time, perhaps due to our early settling issues in unfamiliar surroundings, or the lack of anyone paying such close attention to it. But the numbers do seem to add up to a considerable error in someone's calculations."

"By how much?" asks one of the daughters.

"By a good order of magnitude. Some of these numbers do not even match the other records we have in the libraries for events we experienced along the way. This would suggest as much as ten thousand years has passed since then."

This revelation caused the room to draw in a collective gasp at the astonishing figure.

He continues again, "Now, this could be a simple oversight, but when taken together with the rest, I'm almost thinking it could be part of a larger conspiracy to keep us ignorant of something more important. For instance, it is said we have been sending up our warriors during this incredible length of time to strike at those on the surface, believing they were very close to a launch against us, due perhaps to some ancient conflict that drove our people into the Underdark. But the first thing on my mind is…why? Why are we sending them up for a full ten thousand years?"

"He does carry a point, Mother," issues the first daughter. "That's an incredible length of time to send up anything for any reason."

"And worse," he adds. "There has been no record of retaliation in this time. After ANY amount of time, sending warriors up there for ANY reason, and if they had been killing anything along the way, I would imagine retaliation in this time to attack us down here. But there are no significant records to suggest this."

"No significant records," she intones cautiously. "Is there anything besides that?"

"Oh, a few small scraps here and there of a random encounter someone once reported out in the tunnels, but surely not an army launching against us to destroy the city."

"All right, but could this be whatever remained of those people up there after OUR warriors finished with them?"

"This is a good thought, but it leads us to the next problem. We cannot be sure what they do or do not have up there. First, if THEY, up there, were powerful enough to drive ALL of us down here into the Underdark, I doubt they would number only a few meager warriors our people could so easily defeat with a small raid, such as the numbers the various Houses so often send up. They would require a substantial army, numbering at the very least in terms of thousands, likely tens of thousands, and more likely hundreds of thousands, to drive our entire society down here. And this must account for ALL the cities, not just ours."

"Oops!"

"Hundreds of thousands!" the Matron Mother yelps. "How could they possibly have so many?"

"While I am sure this is a fine question to ask, we should probably also ask why they should NOT have this many. They probably represent a large civilization up there, I would think. Therefore, their population count should dwarf what we have down here."

"I, um...see..." she muses tenderly. "And I do not recall anything to specifically describe this before."

"Exactly! It would seem our lessons do not explain to us how a society can grow by such proportions, especially if they have the room to actually grow, as they no doubt have up there in the vast expanses of the surface world."

"And as opposed to us down here," the first daughter considers. "In this very cramped space."

"Furthermore, our warriors are said to go up, hit something that was quite literally standing around out there, as if waiting for someone to hit them, then they retreat back down here, claiming great victory over whatever it was they actually hit. Now, I ask you, would THEY, up there, with such a potent force as to drive ALL of us down here, first of all simply stand around for our own attack, and second, not give chase as ours retreated back home?"

"And oops again!"

"Yes, and this is a particularly substantial oops that no one apparently bothered to take notice of, especially those Greater Houses that are most often the ones sending the warriors up to hit something."

"And ANOTHER oops! What are they thinking over there?"

"This is where we come to that conspiracy, and who might actually be applying it. And it gets worse from here, as NOW there seems to be a wall up there blocking our warriors completely."

"Oh! A wall? Are they now hitting THAT and claiming victory over something?"

"Yes, actually."

The daughter gaped at the man, passing her astonished glare at the Matron Mother and her other sisters.

"I was actually joking with that statement," she mumbles timidly.

"Perhaps, but I am not. The Greater Houses STILL send up warriors, and according to some statements we received, they STILL come back with claims of great victory over something they hit. And here we come to the source of the conspiracy...that authority body who orders our warriors to go out in the first place."

"The Greater Houses..."

"Not precisely. They send them out, yes, but on the orders of the Spider Queen. And further, it is also on her orders to report victories, but never anything about a wall. And furthermore, neither anything about a voice, likely from a guard on that wall, ordering them to return home and not come back. But they do anyway."

"One moment here!" the second daughter interjects firmly. "A guard on that wall shouts, 'go home and stay there', but the Greater Houses keep sending them out anyway?"

"And worse than that," the first daughter offers. "No retaliation, apparently, even for as many times as we keep doing it. You might think they would grow tired of it after a while if they want us to keep away, but we never do."

"Yes! And for how long? How long before they DO grow so tired of it that those countless thousands of REAL warriors finally launch against us?"

"Countless...oh no. But wait... If our warriors only went up to where the tunnels come out on the surface, how far did they actually travel to find anything to hit? Right in front? Was there actually anything right in front for them to hit? Where do they train those warriors up there? We have an academy for ours, do they have one for theirs? I should think they would, and probably NOT right in front of that tunnel."

"Yes, and likely more than one, if they train them in the thousands or more. And then, if we've been doing this for so many thousands of years…you know, I would think by now they ought to know where those tunnels are, and where WE are, that they could launch theirs any time they wanted."

"Yes, probably so, and hordes of them, to finish whatever started the thing that drove our people down here in the first place."

"Mage Master," the Matron Mother wonders anxiously. "Do you have anything to help us understand why the Spider Queen would do this to us? To place us in this situation of such ignorance and jeopardy?"

"I can pass along what we have learned in this time," he admits. "First, she apparently forbids any of the Houses who send up warriors to speak of what they see on their return. This tells me she does not WANT us to know what is up there, and neither does she seem to care what they do, so long as WE think they did something at all."

"That does speak of a conspiracy," the first daughter suggests gently. "Even though I know it is not a nice thing to say about HER."

"Second, if this has been the case for so long, what WERE they hitting even before that wall went up? Because to have that wall in the first place suggests we were hitting something that disturbed them enough to build it."

"Uh oh…" the second daughter intones warily. "So, we did hit something, and rather than chase us down here, they instead built a wall for it."

"We tried to analyze this suggestion once, and have surmised there could be a potential reason, if you should account for the nature of the Underdark, the tunnel networks, the native beasts, and such, being too much of a bother for them. All we had were a few random expeditions finding a way into it, nothing more. They might be an exception, not the rule."

"So, rather than launch a REAL attack, you have a few random people, probably related to whatever we did actually hit, chasing us back, at least as far until it became too hard to find their way, and then they went home. Wow! We must really be a worthy foe if they can't do anything more than that."

"You know," the first daughter notes. "You might have something with that statement. We aren't worthy enough for them to chase down here, certainly not with a big army. Those tunnels might not even allow for a big army to pass through them conveniently to make it worth the effort. Therefore, the wall to keep us out."

"Oh great! Thank you! And those ten thousand years of storytelling we listened to?"

"Something to keep us occupied, thinking we were doing something, when in fact they don't care enough to provide a reason for us to do it!"

"Hold a moment," the Matron Mother asserts. "If this is simply to keep us occupied with something nonsensical, what was the reason we came down here in the first place? I recall something about a war, and being driven down here to fester for something."

"Oh yes, Mother! To fester with tales of hitting something that doesn't care enough about us that they probably think we buried ourselves down here, so why bother. If it were not for US bothering THEM, they might not have built that wall to keep us out. So, I think the reason behind that festering thing must relate to that part about knowledge, or the lack of it, making us ignorant, and therefore someone's fools. And it's all starting to point in one direction."

"And speaking of knowledge," the man concludes. "This might also cause us to wonder what THEY have by now, if ours hasn't changed so much that even the Matron Mother doesn't recall any new books in her lifetime."

"Oh Grand!" the first daughter shouts. "So, if they up there are learning something new on occasion, and we're not... Yes! This would give us something new to think about. We're not worthy to fight because we're so low by now, we're not even a true threat to them."

The man gazes at the discord he sowed and feels a silent mote of satisfaction at his efforts. This would count as one House not as likely to continue their old faith by now. And if it worked as well here, it might work elsewhere. They just needed to join this together with the idea of standing down if they should ever see a true invasion, rather than fighting back.

"These latest results are promising," Thaelyn declares. "And as such, I am thinking of a rapid cascade here, if we can reach a good threshold in this next grouping of cities. We should not give her the time to counteract our efforts."

"This new procedure we are following is certainly encouraging," Nemelle suggests. "We are bypassing her efforts with our own subversive portrayals, using agents she can neither prevent or oppose, and causing enough dissension that they now suspect HER of foul play for keeping them literally in the Under-dark," she grins playfully.

"Oh, Nemelle!" he groans and covers his eyes. "That pun was good enough for a mark of its own. Yes, even this much is a step forward. But next is to bring them into our custody. I think a multiple deployment tactic would be appropriate here for several at once, and place as many as we can under house arrest, if we do not have the detention space for it. Then process them as best we can to explain the new situation."

"We will need a lot of troops for this, plus garrison guards, and over a long duration to ensure we have full containment."

"I am not as worried about the numbers. As for containment, once we reintroduce them to the Seldarine, some portion of that can be offloaded to their new local authority, both legal and spiritual. And then we progress to the next set, closing in on their main. I would also imagine, during this time, as her worshippers are stolen away from her, she should start to lose some of her authority and power. This could weaken her to some degree for the final encounter."

"No doubt, she knows this, and no doubt she will anticipate it. I do not expect that final encounter to go cleanly."

✦✦✦✦✦

"You can't be serious!" screeches one of several women who had been recently brought to Malafay's House. "The Spider Queen is simply using us for her own revenge?"

"She hates men, so it seems," Malafay retorts. "And she also hates our old elven gods, the Seldarine, which is led by a male figure. Our entire culture, therefore, berates males to please her bigotry. I can only guess at the history here, but when our ancestors betrayed the old gods, as well as insulted everything else up there that turned against us for the favor of it, SHE came along and used it for her own. Now, here we are, as we say, festering in this hole. And worst of all, she tells us to go up and hit things that don't even exist by now."

"That don't exist…" asserts another woman. "Meaning to say what? We killed them all off, or they ran away, or…"

"They represent a massive civilization up there, as opposed to our few, relatively feeble cities. We hold a reputation of killing our own off more than anything else. So killing THEM off is a ludicrous suggestion, as our few pitiful warriors probably couldn't kill them off fast enough before they repopulated to kill US off completely."

"Uh oh…"

"Furthermore, they built walls to keep us out, since we were such a bother to them. We were not even worthy to chase down here. But the Spider Queen doesn't tell us about THAT. She forbids us to even speak of what we see up there when we send our warriors up to hit anything. Have any of you been up there? Did you see anything, other than a mass of warriors standing around just waiting for you to come along and kill them?"

"Um, well, actually…"

"Yes, I know, my sister saw the same, and was told the same. Not even our Matron Mother knew the truth, as she only heard what the Spider Queen told her, not her own daughter."

"You're kidding me!" gasps a third woman. "I've never been up there, but one of my sisters has, and our Matron Mother has always believed it was warriors, not a wall."

"Malafay is right," offers the second woman. "I've been up there and seen that wall, and I WAS told to keep silent for it…each and every time. And yet, each time we came home, we had a victory feast. Such nonsense!"

"And it gets worse," Malafay continues. "The entire world up there came together many centuries ago into one big nation, all of them. And we're speaking of humans, elves, dwarves, and even more. Now, ask yourselves this question. For a civilization measuring in the billions of people, would you and your House, and whatever number of warriors you have available, be able to defend against whatever sort of army THAT might actually have available?"

"Um, billions, you say?"

"And let us not forget, as part of what we're trying to share with people like you. Our entire race was chased down here by something, and it wasn't some meager handful of blindmen who could never fight back against one tiny raiding party of a few warriors. And this was many thousands of years ago when we last actually saw anything up there. Now, do you want to know what they built SINCE then? Well, go up to that wall and ask for a tour. I dare you."

"I doubt they would give one to us by now," the first woman considers. "If all we ever do is go up and make a bother of ourselves."

"They might if you stop making a bother and start thinking with your own head. I've been up there and got a tour once. They have built things we don't even have names for, let alone could we compare with them for any sort of war or raiding effort. That wall is simply to keep us out, after we buried ourselves in this hole. But our ineptitude at not taking all those lessons they kept trying to give us has finally worn their patience thin enough that NOW they are taking action. Our city here was the first to go down, and yours is coming up next."

"Coming up? Wait, what do you mean yours went down?"

"We were conquered so fast, there was barely enough time to see it outside the window."

The other women gaped at Malafay as they turned to a nearby window to see if there was anything outside to look at. They approached a balcony and peered down into the street to see a foot patrol of guards marching by. But they clearly weren't Drow, as they used strange lights to illuminate the street in front of them. And the intensity was more than any Drow could handle.

"Um, Malafay, what is it you are actually saying here? They conquered you, and now what?"

"Now, they are educating us as to the errors of our ancestors and what they did up there to get us banished from sight. They are teaching us about our original elven gods, whom we offended when our ancestors turned hostile against them, and they are trying to bring us back to join the rest. So far, we need rehabilitation, but once that's done, our children will go to new schools and learn wondrous new wisdom. And our city will grow and evolve into something befitting a civilization that is now moving beyond this world to find others. Now, would you like to be a part of that, or would you prefer to listen to the Spider Queen tell you to go hit a wall and celebrate a victory over a horde of vicious warriors that don't exist?" she smirks.

The other women all gazed at each other in amazement. It seemed unfathomable to be conquered by something that was now giving you more than what you started with. But if this city was already experiencing it, and this was stated by one of their own, then it had to be true.

The months progressed, with the accelerated interactions hitting inside the Houses this time, rather than trying to work their way in from rumors in the street. This new tactic was proving to be quite effective, especially with spooks doing so much of the work. Many of the cities began to see large population counts turning coat, now that it was clear where the hate was truly coming from and why. The ulterior motives of their goddess were proving to be her own downfall.

The top Houses on their local councils tried to quell the uprisings, but it was quickly becoming obvious it was getting out of hand. And much like with the first city and House Oussund, some were hoping to perform rituals to bring about cleansing actions to set things right again. This is where the military went into action.

Just like before, the city streets erupted in brilliant flashes of arcanic energy, as row upon row of troops arrived through their portals. For those people not yet following the new philosophy, the troops might need to chase them down and manhandle them into compliance, removing them to the detention blocks on the surface where they would be temporarily incarcerated until counselors and therapists could explain the situation, along with their choices.

One by one, a series of cities began to fall, despite the efforts of the higher Houses and their goddess to counter the effect. The wave of conquest was now occupying a broadening swathe of territory throughout the Underdark. And as more of it came under the control of Thaelyn's kingdom, a sense of urgency was building as Lolth revealed this to the final cities still under her control. This would make them all the more difficult targets to convert, as the Houses were now listening to her new storytelling.

"They are moving on us now!" declares one Matron Mother representative in a Council meeting. "Those curs have finally broken through. For all the times our warriors were sent out, they didn't kill enough of them up there to keep them under control."

"The other cities were probably too weak in their approach," asserts another one. "They likely began to slack off, therefore they allowed the surfacers the opportunity to move on them. Such foolishness! I have heard those cities were left to burn, with no survivors to speak of what happened."

"We are becoming few now," argues a third. "This could be the end of our kind! Such folly. They banish us into this pit to fester, and now they come to finish it, not satisfied with us simply festering."

"Indeed," the first one states. "But if this is how it will end for us, we will not give them an easy victory. We will fight to the very last if we must."

"One moment," interjects a fourth. "When you say those others were left to burn, where did you hear this? Did someone go out there and see it?"

"Well, no," the second member responds. "It was actually the Spider Queen herself who told this to us. I was at the temple offering my prayers when She spoke to me."

"I as well," the third one affirms. "I think there were several of us at the temple, all receiving her words."

"I see," the fourth one nods. "And this would surely suggest something did happen. But I think to have eyes looking at it would also be prudent, to see just what sort of damage actually occurred out there."

"You would doubt the Spider Queen at her word?" she winces.

"I would doubt that which I did not see with my own eyes. Burned to the ground? Those cities are much like ours, mostly made of stone. Stone does not burn as easily. And bodies left to rot with no survivors? This forces me to consider a curious principle. Extraordinary claims demand extraordinary evidence. And all we have is a statement, granted a statement given by a goddess, but a statement, nonetheless. Therefore, in answer to this, we must also ask another question, which I feel is very warranted by now."

"And what question is that?"

"Why? Why now, after so long a time of US going up THERE to kill THEM…as if we should carry a special permit to do this, and they do NOT hold as much to retaliate."

"Huh? What are you talking about?" the first one balks.

"Simple. Are we saying the Spider Queen authorizes us to kill them, but they should not hold a right, or a privilege, to fight back? Now answer that question of bodies left dead in the streets, and who is truly responsible for it? Were those cities so foolish to open themselves up to this, or were they so foolish to incite it in the first place? And THEN, what of our goddess telling us to do this for so long? As if to say we are right and everyone else is wrong. What did those warriors actually do up there to cause the surfacers to want to come down here, finally, and after so long a time, that we almost demanded them to do so?”

“Uh oh…” the second one ushers softly. “I think I see a direction to her statement.”

“But this is nonsense!” the first one argues.

“Nonsense?” the fourth counters. “As much nonsense that we can send up our warriors for so many thousands of years and not expect them to finally want to put an end to it?”

“An end…” she retracts subtly.

“Look at it this way. Say someone offended your House, and did so for an extended period, such that, no matter how much restraint you might show for it, holding back your response, eventually you grew weary of it and took action. And then, you would suggest, looking at it from their side, they might say you had no right to take this action. This would infer a level of arrogance even to suggest such a thing!”

“She is right,” the third one notes. “We prompted this, and then we claim they have no right to retaliate…eventually.”

“But the Spider Queen is the authority here!” the first Matron Mother issues. “Shouldn’t hers be the final word?”

“I suppose that statement is subjective,” the fourth one admits. “It may depend on whether you consider any OTHER gods they have up there, and what THEIR ‘final word’ might be. It becomes a contest, ours versus theirs, and whose ‘word’ holds greater significance.”

“I see…” she relents.

“And THEN, our goddess, who tells us to do this for so long, further tells us how it resulted in burnt stone cities, and so many dead, that not even a single survivor might escape to tell us personally. It was HER to reveal this to us, not anyone FROM those cities.”

“No one FROM those cities…” the third one recites distantly.

“And not even travelers who might visit them and return back word to us. Surely, there are such as merchants out there, and this would represent big news to bring home.”

“I believe I see her point now,” the second one asserts. “That evidence she was speaking of. We are told to do something that might have been unwise from the start, perhaps even arrogant to feel we hold any true authority to do it at all, and by someone who might be in contest with others. Then, we are told of a result, but without actual evidence, or eyes to see it. Only her word, the same word that keeps telling us to do something unwise, and in contest with someone we should not be doing it to in the first place."

"I, uh…see what you are saying," the first one admits hesitantly. "But what about those old stories of being banished down here to fester?"

"Banished…by whom?" the fourth member infers. "And for what reason? If she is in contest with someone, and we took to following her due to something…arrogant… This might be cause enough for banishment."

"Oh dear. But she is our goddess! She wouldn't do this to us, would she?"

"I think this follows with the reason for that banishment, maybe also the arrogant thing, especially if she is in contest with someone on the other side. If we do not know what we did up there…and my teachings never spoke of it so precisely, and all we have is her word on things. Goddess or not, my first thoughts are to go out there and see it with my own eyes, maybe to find the answers we are not receiving by other means, and to understand where it actually comes from…and why."

She pauses to glance around the table before continuing.

"Look at us now. We are speaking of fighting to the last. More bodies in the streets? And for what reason? If she tells us to do something unwise, perhaps also arrogant, could it be because she LIKES to see bodies in the streets…any bodies!"

"But that would mean…"

"It could mean all sorts of things," she interjects enthusiastically. "One clear example is how we tend to find our advantage to move up in station around here…at the expense of someone else."

She holds her statement to glare at the other women for their reactions, knowing they likely came into their positions after putting down their predecessors.

The other women also exchanged glances around the table, as the meaning quickly sank in.

"Next," she continues. "We are told to send up our warriors to hit their warriors, correct? Well, one of our House daughters was there with those warriors. Do you know what she saw? She confided this in me once, but the Spider Queen, in all of her wisdom, forbade me to know of this directly, telling my daughter to keep silent. There is a wall up there barring our path. No warriors, just a wall."

"A wall!" the other members cry out collectively.

"Yes, and how curious none of YOU knew about it. And that wall has been there for apparently a very long time, also with a guard telling us to go home and stay there, not to return…again, and again, and again. And yet, it is the Spider Queen telling us to go up and hit something, then to report victory against warriors… Again, and again, and again. Now, who should we actually listen to about cities burnt and no survivors? Why should we claim they made an error to not guard against it, when they likely caused it in the first place by not listening to those guards to stay away? Maybe also, why is that wall up there, and NOT their armies down here, perhaps centuries, if not thousands of years ago, doing the deed?"

"Yes," the third one considers. "Why take so long, telling us to stay away, when clearly, we never listened?"

"Arrogant?" the second one grumbles. "Oh yes! We most certainly are to think we hold any such authority to do anything at all. If all they did was to build a wall…that's a defensive move! And here we might come back to the contest aspect again. Why does SHE tell us to do it in the first place?"

"We do not own those lands," the fourth member asserts. "But if she holds a grudge with someone, and at this point, it will have to be another god, this could hold your answer. If it were people she held this grudge with, I think it would be reciprocal, and that wall would not simply be a wall."

"Indeed! Are we being made to fight her wars for her with people we should not otherwise be fighting wars with?"

"Not on their native soil, at least," the third member accedes. "If she has an issue with another god, I think she should probably take this up with that one directly. Surely, she must have servants near her that would be more appropriate to the need. We would not qualify to fight gods, I don't think. That would be waste of our people, and…um…"

"What?" the first one inquires.

"Well, I find myself compelled to say, it would be a waste of theirs also…for their side of it. If this is a contest between two gods, to have us fighting a battle down here would not solve it on their side. We are simply fighting it…oh dear. Yes. We are fighting it, only because someone tells us to do so."

The other members of the Council all glared at each other for this statement. But before any of them could respond further, the fourth member was speaking again.

"This makes good sense," she nods. "And this simply leaves us speaking of fighting to the last against an enemy that has clearly grown tired of us not listening to their instructions, and NOW is ready to do something about it. But burning to the ground and slaying everything they see? Our goddess once told us to slay everything we see, but if their response was to build a wall, hoping to keep us out…hmm…" she muses conspicuously. "A defensive move? Yes. This might suggest they know something, rather than to simply burn us out of this hole we dug."

"Know something?" the second one wonders. "Maybe to say, to know something…of this contest?"

"Maybe. And now, she tells us to go hit that wall until they grow so tired of us and our insolence that they are finally willing to crawl down into this pit to inform us personally. And if they have attacked every other city out there, it seems clear they know where we are, and have the military power to reach us. But, if the original plan was defensive, is this to say it changed? Or are they hoping to teach us what we do not otherwise know about due to our…arrogance?"

"Uh oh…" the third one relents. "And those stories of burnt cities?"

"They did not come from any of OUR people. And the Spider Queen seems to like telling stories of bodies in the streets. Unless one of us should take the time to go out there and see it ourselves, I think I would be careful of this. Her storytelling is driving us to an ultimate goal here. You mentioned the end of an era, but whose era? Hers, where she tells us to fight something we probably should not be fighting, maybe due to arrogance, maybe also because it was never our fight. Or the end of OUR era…us, our people, who claim we were banished into this hole to fester for something our ancestors did…arrogantly, because she told us to do so. And if the rest of the world up there made any sort of progress in this time, that they can so efficiently come down here now and do…anything, be it burning stone cities, or something else outside our view, and SHE is telling us it leaves bodies in the streets… Ladies, this is suggesting SHE wants us to go down in flames, no less than the rest. Therefore, those stories, to incite it… Arrogantly."

"But wait!" the second member asserts. "What are we actually to do about this?"

"I think, if in all this time we were fighting something, they probably grew so powerful, where after a while our efforts became so much of a bother, that they decided to build that wall simply to keep us out, rather than waste their efforts on us for anything else. Now, we are seeing the result of their growth, after we essentially demanded them to prove it to us. So, if the Spider Queen likes to see bodies in the streets, my suggestion is to deny her this one. In the absence of seeing what they actually did to those other cities, and if we say they only built a wall, not killed our warriors outright, as they clearly hold this capacity by now, they might have other ideas, and it doesn't involve killing. And she isn't happy about it."

"Not happy…simply because of no killing?"

"Maybe those other cities grew wise to her REAL ways, and the surface people are the answer, not the problem."

The various members of the Council meeting all glanced around at each other, while the fourth member silently contemplated her careful play as a spook impersonating the Matron Mother for her House.

"Cardinal Nemelle? Do you have a minute?"

"Ah, Relissa, yes, come in. How are your surveys coming along?"

"We're getting a lot of new work, trying to set up those cities down there to do business our way. But jiggers, this will take a while. New construction, updating their schools, their local workshops, and then I hear they want to redesign their temple. You know, to replace all that old architecture with something nicer."

"Yes, I would need to agree with this most of all. We need to distance ourselves from that old faith and bring a new image into it for a new generation."

"But anyway, I'm actually here for another reason."

"Oh? And what is that?"

"It's, um, you-know-who and her pregnancy. Does she know yet what she's got?"

"Ah, that," she giggles. "Not that I know of yet. Although I would imagine it should not be much longer before she has an exam to study the development of the baby, and they begin to realize she has something more than just one in there."

"Aye, and this should be when? Soon now, I suppose. We're on Month Five, going on Six. She should be doing imaging scans by now, ay?"

"I cannot be sure if she did one already for this period. I heard she went in for one early in the term, to confirm the initial development of her condition. So, I would imagine she should have the next one very soon. If you like, I can ask. But I think she will likely start pointing fingers once she realizes it, and we will all be called in for a little… meeting," she smiles.

"Uh huh, and here's where I go into an early retirement," she chuckles. "Well, if I don't hear of it sooner, call me when you get it on this side."

"I will, Relissa. I suspect we will have a special little celebration for the occasion…assuming there is anything left of the city if she should release another of those screams."

"Oh buggers, please no."

Relissa waved and left the office, while Nemelle returned to her work. She was tabulating up a census tally for their newly acquired population of…shadow elves…and coordinating the production of new ID cards and bureaucratic processing to vassalize them. But this was only an intermediate stage as they adapted to the culture and practices of the kingdom before their final assimilation as full citizens.

The acquisition of new cities was adding new members to the list. But as the list narrowed to the final few, not only was the process becoming trickier to complete without any major losses, but the numbers of people turning over new leaves compounded into the tens of thousands for these last big cities. All except for the final one. That would be the biggest one yet, and not only in terms of population, but also the area it covered. And even worse, the people who ruled the place.

Chapter 10

A CAPITAL PROBLEM

"This one will be our crowning achievement," Thaelyn asserts. "But it will also be the most difficult to simply take by our subversive means. Nemelle's cultural campaign over these past decades may have worked some magic in the others, but this one has been especially stubborn. They have a history of violence on a scale that left a lot of others in the dust. They have seen the rise and fall of powerful despots and potent spiritual leaders, and the conflict of one House against another, often with such devastating effect as to even weaken the surrounding cavern."

"That doesn't sound nice," Relissa shakes her head. "We'll need to see about reinforcing some of that to prevent any more, or else evacuate portions of it if we see it's too weak to stand up."

"Possibly. Some portions appear to be firm bedrock, but others appear to be calcite cave formations. This material is not known for its exceptional strength. We must also see to it they do not perform anything to intentionally collapse something as we make our move. It does not serve us to convert someone, only to see them buried under a collapsed roof. Therefore, I am attempting to formulate a few ideas on how to proceed. No doubt, by now they must realize they are all that remains of their former empire, if you can call it an empire."

"Aye, not much of one, even before we got to it," she chuckles.

"Indeed! The level of brutality of those people makes it nearly impossible for them to form any manner of cohesion, and certainly not enough to coordinate themselves on a mutual effort. It is amazing they can go so far as even to build a functioning city environment. And so, in the absence of this, we might wish to take them piecemeal. The layout of this cityscape might afford us a few avenues to capture portions of it and then hold a line. But we may need to apply our fullest military capacity, including Stormhooves and their advanced weapons to take our territory. And this will likely be where we find ourselves fighting Lolth herself."

"If we are to create a line," Nemelle considers. "We could use some of the natural cavern features to assist in drawing that divide. But still, we do not want them to invoke a collapse of the roof over our heads. The only other possibility is simply to coordinate a precautionary evacuation of the converted population, or as we have done elsewhere, abduct them for forced conversion. Then, reintroduce them once the situation is secure."

"We also have their leaders, which in this case I think are not as likely to be convinced by our efforts. We may need to abduct them altogether and either imprison them, or send them to our penal colony on Shadowfell. Although that is not, in itself, a desirable solution, as these people, along with their goddess, would be especially dangerous, and might actually find a way out of there. And I do not wish to see a return of their malice."

"Although I do not wish to be one to offer this as a suggestion, what about execution, or even assassination?"

"This is possible...undesirable, but possible. I find it unlikely they will convert, so it may come to this. And we certainly have the ability to do so. Whether to place a sniper on a rooftop, or a bomb under someone's chair, many things are possible. But this is so unbecoming for people like us."

"True, but these people go beyond evil, and certainly well beyond the Measure of Balance. I still recall my mother and what she went through. And all she did was hold a difference of opinion with her Matron Mother."

"I am sure she was not the only one. And so, we should carefully map out their streets, neighborhoods, and districts. We should then establish a few hidden offices for our agents. We will use spooks, as before, but we may also need a few actual people to handle portal runes. I might also suggest having laborers ready to build fortifications. We can use our Infinity Shields...they will certainly not be expecting that...and build a wall, maybe also a roof. We can then set up portal incursions just outside to ambush them if they make a rush at us. Here we can use our guns in nonlethal mode to take down and capture people, and then portals to relocate them. This could rob them of their militia rather quickly. All that would remain after that would be their leaders, and they will likely be well behind the lines, and probably retreating by the time we finish with the rest. We may need to give chase after that to finish THEM."

Aerlie was arriving in the medical ward for her scheduled checkup. She was excited on this occasion, because they were planning on making a scan of the baby to visualize it on the screen. This would be like a sonogram image, but conducted by their scanning beam to create a 3D presentation, rather than simply an echo reflection. And although Aerlie and Thaelyn were so far undecided if they wanted to learn the gender of their child ahead of time, this would also provide a clue.

She arrives in the Ward and reports to the examination room, with that same intern who had been working with her since she first discovered she was pregnant.

"My Lady!" the intern elates. "Are we ready for that special moment? Most mothers are very anxious to see those first glimpses."

"I am, but I'm also a bit nervous. I hope everything is alright with the baby and we don't have any complications."

"I think we should be in good order. You have been following your program nicely, and we haven't detected any anomalies along the way. So, let's have you lay out on the table again, and lift up your gown a bit for a clear view."

Aerlie situates herself on the table, and on this occasion was wearing an ensemble consisting of a sleeveless top and leggings, along with a patterned overshirt, all in pale off-whites. The top portion was hooked in the rear to provide access to enclose around her wings, rather than a pullover or a front clasping style.

She lays herself down and draws up her top to reveal her belly, which was showing a prominent bulge by now. The intern makes a quick survey, feeling around the area with her hands to locate the form underneath, checking for position and general size.

"Wow, you feel like you're developing a healthy little one in there. And this is what month now? We're close to six, I think, right?"

"Yes, just about. We're expecting it to go ten, since it's going to be half-elven, and those tend to go halfway between the two sides."

"Well, let's take a look at you under the beam. Just relax a bit and I'll get us started."

Aerlie attempts to settle herself while the intern powers up the scanning beam on the arm attached to the ceiling. The unit comes to life and moves along the track to scan the full length of Aerlie's body. This produces a standard profile image on the screen. The intern studies this briefly before going to a detail scan.

As the intern gazes at the monitor, she quickly frowns at what she thinks she sees. She leans in to examine it at closer range, although her eyes were surely good enough to determine the image even at a distance, and it was not what she might expect out of an elf.

"This is interesting..." she mumbles to herself.

Aerlie was allowing her eyes to drift off into the distance until the intern had something to offer. But at hearing the faint comment, she turned to look at the intern.

"What do you see?" she asks.

"One moment. I still need to do the detailed scan. This will tell us what we're dealing with in there."

"What we're dealing with? I hope we're dealing with a pregnancy."

"Well, yes!" she chuckles disarmingly. "We are, of course, and the computer shows everything on the big scan is looking good. But this thing is being a little dodgy with me today. Hold on."

She now reprograms the device for another scan, this time a more detailed narrow region imaging of only the lower abdomen. The arm repositions itself and makes another run, which results in a more precise and larger image of only the pregnancy itself. There, the intern leans forward again as she examines the image, and soon feels her jaw dropping.

"Great gods!" she wheezes.

Aerlie turned again, more determinedly this time, for the clearly anxious statement.

"What!" she asks urgently. "What's wrong?"

"Wrong? Something is wrong? I'll tell you what's wrong! You're making history! You've got twins in there!"

Aerlie's eyes bulged for the second time, and her breath left her again in a state of shock. Bewildered by the suggestion, she pulls herself up to a seated posture and glares at both the intern and the monitor, which clearly showed not one, but TWO babies in there.

The intern paused to look at the expectant mother and saw the telltale signs of another impending outburst. She cautiously slid out of her chair and took up a position to hide behind the console.

"How in all Creation can I be carrying twins!" Aerlie gasps.

"I don't know," the intern whines timidly. "Not unless…well, maybe unless that blessing from Lathander did something to you."

"A WHAT??" she screeches.

"Um, you did ask for a blessing up there in your home, didn't you?"

Aerlie now gapes at the poor intern, who withdrew even further behind the console for shelter. And as the notion began to manifest itself, she let out another of her Celestial screams.

Once again, it blasted its way through the temple, sending the priests scattering for cover behind altars and statues. People who were attending the service all ducked for cover beneath the pews. Pedestrians on the street all cringed at the sudden outburst. And up in the guildhall, the students were once again shaken out of their class studies.

In his strategy room, Thaelyn and the others, who were still in their conference, were all jolted at the reverberations rumbling through the building.

"Whoops!" Nemelle yips bemusedly.

"Oh jiggers!" Relissa winces nervously. "We're all dead now, I'm sure of it!"

"Great Powers, now what?" Thaelyn straightens up and turns towards the door.

In Aelwyn's office, she also heard the ruckus, and quickly felt a mote of mischief for her role in it.

"And here we go…" she smiles and rises from her chair.

Down the road, in Aristan's office, he was reviewing a new proposal to present to the Council later, when the shrieking rattled his window.

"My goodness!" he exclaims naughtily. "I should have invested in the window industry this year. Their stock prices must be soaring by now."

And somewhere across town, in an exclusive estate neighborhood, Vonafel, who was once more engaged in a hobby craft, heard the telltale signs of her dearest friend raising the roofs again.

"Ah, that must be her imaging scan," she muses intriguingly. "I wonder how that went. Maybe I should go check," she grins.

Aerlie spent her breath yet again, blasting the intern's chair across the room, but fortunately, the intern and the console she was hiding behind both held firm. Although the intern was becoming hard of hearing by this time.

Aerlie was panting as she tried to compose herself enough to again stare at the image on the monitor. It showed the clear portrayal of two twin girls inside there. They were huddled in a tight bunch, as if nuzzling each other for comfort.

By this time, Thaelyn, Nemelle, and Relissa were emerging out of the guildhall into the courtyard, to be joined by Aelwyn on the way out onto the driveway leading down the hill. An assortment of others was also coming out to again see about the disturbance, only to find the initial group proceeding ahead of them. Aristan, for his part, had shared a telepathic message with his wife, and was also on his way down the street, while Vonafel found her way through the Gateway network.

"What do you mean, Lathander?" Aerlie intones warily.

"Um, I thought you ordered something up there," the intern mentions tenderly. "In fact, I think we all did. We all know how embarrassed you were at that little display, so I guess no one wanted to say anything, but naturally, if you see something like that coming down, you have to assume…"

"See it coming down? On the house?"

"Yeah, it was all over INN, a live broadcast…um, well…"

"They put that on LIVE?" she shouts. "Oh dear gods above… Well, all right, I suppose it might be a little hard to miss. But Lathander? What was HE doing up there? Oh, wait. Of course! Naturally, because SHE was involved."

"She?"

"Aelwyn, he's her Father, after all. And SHE is the one who hit us with that crazy incense. Now it makes sense."

"Incense? What do you mean?"

"Well, now, just a moment, because this doesn't sound like something she might do alone. That stuff was said to come from the Drow, which would require an intermediate, and that now points at Nemelle. But even SHE cannot be the end of it, as you still need someone to physically deliver it. Who was working at that time? Let's see, this was during that first city…oh, blast! Yes! And this is just her style. Relissa! But even THAT isn't enough, as I'll bet you had someone behind the whole thing, and that simply leads me to one final person."

Aerlie now jumps off the bed and straightens her clothing as she rushes out into the main temple auditorium. As she arrives on the platform, the priests all glare at her, wondering what new surprises she had in mind. But she simply smiled sweetly at them as she took up a position to await what was surely to be a new audience arriving soon.

The first of these was Thaelyn and his group, including Nemelle, Aelwyn, and Relissa. The three ladies saw Aerlie standing up on the platform waiting for them, and each felt a slight shiver as they knew she had figured something out by now. Thaelyn, for his part, was still in the dark on it. And as they arrived at the steps, Aerlie greeted them with a bright, innocent smile.

"And there you are!" she croons. "My, how nice it is to see all of you…together. Although we're still missing one, but I'm sure she's on her way."

"Aerlie?" Thaelyn raises his brow. "Um, what just happened?"

"Oh, I had my imaging scan today, and good gracious! What a surprise that was."

"Uh huh…so much that it caused you to invoke another shockwave to rival the Spellplague?"

"Well, my dear, you know how excited I am to be having a baby, so I simply needed to share it with the world, a bit like that now-famous live INN report of our coupling that eve. You did know it was broadcast live, didn't you?"

"Live? Oh dear Powers, I was afraid of that."

"Yes, me too, actually. I just learned of it from the intern in there… after she told me Lathander was involved."

"Lathander?" he raises his brow even higher.

"Yes. Apparently, he makes house calls, although I don't recall ordering one. Do you?"

"Um, not precisely."

"But I know someone who might…" she glares with an eerily pleasant smile at Aelwyn.

Thaelyn follows her stare and now raises his brow even higher, as if it could actually reach as far. Aelwyn simply smiled, knowing her role was clearly revealed by now, so all she could do was to accept it.

"Indeed!" he intones suspiciously. "Do we have a bit of mischief occurring here?"

"Oh, but my dear," Aerlie declares. "How could we possibly accuse her of mischief, especially after she drugged us with that strange incense…which had Drow origins. After all, where could she possibly find something like that, right Nemelle?"

Now Thaelyn turns the other way to find Nemelle standing on the other side, trying to hide her grin. His eyes were now bulging and his mouth falling open.

"Really! Her as well? Powers help us, we are surrounded by conspirators."

"But Thaelyn, Nemelle could not be the one to actually provide that stuff. She spends most of her time behind a desk. And I recall this came out of that first city, to which Relissa was working."

"Oh!" he blasts, as he glares at her hiding sheepishly behind Nemelle. "Yes! HER I can expect to play a role. Do we have anyone else?"

"Well, one other name does come to mind…and oh, look, here she is now, along with someone else I'm wondering about…"

They all turn towards the door to see Vonafel just arriving, along with Aristan. Vonafel halts in her tracks as she sees the existing assembly all glaring at her. She briskly glances over her shoulder at the door, wondering if she should just turn around while she still has the chance, but ultimately, she knew she had to come clean.

Aristan also halted, but as he didn't play as much a direct role in anything, he didn't feel quite as self-conscious. He glanced at Vonafel standing next to him, and the two proceeded forwards.

"My dear Vonafel!" Aerlie calls melodiously. "Such a wonderful occasion to see YOU here. Would you like to know of this most joyous of moments?"

"I think I know you well enough to know the answer to that," she smiles cutely. "Let me guess… Twins, right?"

"Oh! Was this a special order?"

"You bet it was, to make up for all your lost time and frustration. You wouldn't do it any other way, so we took the decision out of your hands and just gave you a good time with it."

"And Aristan? Did you play a role of any kind?"

"Me?" he retracts innocuously. "I am innocent, I say! A simple bystander…who offered a few words of advice here and there," he grins playfully.

"A few words of advice?" Thaelyn sets his hands on his hips. "And how do we define only a few words of advice in a case like this?"

"Well, their plan required a bit of refining here and there. And being someone who is as well-versed in bureaucratic matters as I am…"

"Oh! Do you hear this, Aerlie? We needed a bureaucrat to audit this little game."

The group let out a bold laugh, along with the others on the platform and in the pews who were listening. And as they enjoyed the special moment, Hana Laurens from INN was just arriving to investigate the new disturbance. She approached the platform, carefully studying the assortment of people and their curious reactions.

"Um, may I have a few words here? Hana Laurens from the B.T. edition of the Imperial News Network. I hope I'm not intruding on anything personal, but I think a lot of people are wondering what just happened that shook the city again," she smiles gently.

"I'm expecting twins, Miss Laurens," Aerlie announces proudly. "And apparently, we have Lathander to thank for it, as well as a tight circle of very conspiratorial friends who arranged it for us."

"Arranged?"

"Yes, Thaelyn and I were so self-conscious to seek out help, that our…friends," she smirks as she glances around the group, "did the deed for us. They apparently tricked us with some new incense that carried a subtle drug effect, and this likely put us into a condition where Lathander could sneak in and hit us with a double blessing of twins, despite the fact that I'm an elf that shouldn't expect twins to begin with."

"Oops!" she giggles. "Well, under the circumstances, this is a good thing, right?"

"Miss Laurens, I think I can only give my fondest thanks to them for doing what I was too embarrassed to do myself. And Thaelyn, I think you should as well."

"Yes, Aerlie," he admits with a nod. "I most certainly am. Although I am also going to put each of them down for marks on my list. I just need to invent an appropriate category for it."

✦✦◆✦✦

"Twins?" Malafay retorts. "She's an elf, right? And like most of us, she shouldn't normally expect twins, right?"

"Aye," Relissa admits as they speak on the shard-com. "But this is the trick we had to play, to make up for lost time and all the hullabaloo she went through trying for a successful hit. And thanks to your incense, it got us in the door with Lathander to make it work."

"Wow, and again, this is your king and queen."

"Aye, but they're also some of our best friends, so it's all well and good."

"All right, well, give her my best well-wishes for success. This should be a very interesting outcome. Now, what about our movements out there?"

"We're down to the big one, but it won't be easy. We've got peeps out there trying to spread the word, but the ruling Houses are fierce in this one. Also, it seems that goddess is fighting back by giving out a lot of crazy stories. Although, in some cases, we can counter this with conflicting stories. This at least keeps it moving in our direction. But the advance will be tough as we might be fighting our way through the streets."

"I do not envy you for this one. But even if you can only save some of them, I think we can still call it a victory for all the rest you turned around."

"Aye, maybe so. We'll see how it rolls out in the end. But we're fairly sure this is where Lolth gets her final word on things."

"Yes, and I'm curious about how that final word will appear. Very well, good luck with it."

They end the link, and each return to their respective work.

Somewhere beneath the earth, in a massive series of chambers, some of which were natural and others manmade, was a city of exceptional proportions. It was divided into multiple caverns and grottos, linked by passageways representing avenues for travel and trade between districts. The natural divisions made for convenient territorial boundaries amongst the various Houses and their locales, including their respective commoner quarters and militia barracks.

This would be their final possession, the last of their holdings in the Underdark. To capture this would finish an Age-long episode in Tae'Eladar history, beginning with the original arrival of the elven societies, passing through their early growth cycles and wars, the banishment of the Ssri, and everything that came after. Once this final piece of the puzzle was solved, the world could at last move forward into a new era where everyone would know true peace and prosperity.

In one of the grottos, in a secluded corner of workshops and markets, a local business owner was tending to his daily trades. Customers would come and go, as usual, and he kept a careful eye on the street outside, watching for anything unusual passing by. The city appeared calm at this time. There were no bands of militia parading around searching for local disturbances, and none of the authorities seemed interested in anything outside their expectations.

He glances around the scene before turning to find a rear door that led into a storage and utility area. He opens the door and steps inside.

Inside the room was a gathering of agents from Thaelyn's military. These were spies, scouts, mages, and several soldiers for protection. They had arranged to use this space as one of several entry points within the city. It was far to the side of the main action in the city, and might not be as readily noticeable.

"All seems calm out there today," he states softly. "What do you people plan on doing first out there?"

A military captain was stationed in the room as a local commander of their forces for this portion of their operations. He had been examining a series of maps on a strategy table, but turns to meet the shop owner as he spoke.

"See here…" he points at the map. "This cavern seems fairly isolated from the rest, much like several others out there, and no doubt precisely to the liking of the local House to offer protection from anyone and anything outside, as it becomes easily defensible if you only cut off the access at this chokepoint in front," he points to the tight passageway leading into an adjoining cavern.

"Yes, I know many of the Greater Houses do this. We have several of these around the city. Some of them have a history of carving these grottos out intentionally, especially if you consider the longer history of the city, and the wars they had at one time or another."

"That makes perfect sense from the tactical side. But for our purpose, it can prove useful if we can isolate them individually, and convert them. This natural defense can serve to protect our work as we push into new areas."

"Do you actually think you can cover so much territory at one time? This sounds like you would need to move in multiple directions at once, if you hope to take all these grottos before the main city center takes notice."

"We have a large military body to work with, so numbers aren't a problem for us. But being noticed, that can be the issue, depending on how quickly they take notice of grottos turning away from their original worship."

"Yes, and that should be a problem. Word on the streets is they are becoming nervous up in the main city temple. Your work in the other cities is well-known by now."

"We can expect that," he nods. "Especially if your goddess is telling new stories about it. But her stories are mostly to stir up malcontent amongst the higher-ranking members at what we represent to HER, rather than what we are actually doing out there."

"How do you mean?"

"We've heard that some of these stories tell of devastation left behind us, if only to turn the locals with disgust at what we are supposedly doing to your poor unfortunate population that was simply standing around on the streets minding their own business…as if they forgot all the times they attacked us who were simply standing around up above."

"Uh huh…that's a nice little twist."

"Indeed, but turnabout, in this case, is not the same as fair play. We are trying to liberate your people from HER malcontent at everything SHE seems to despise about the world above and your original gods. Recall what we said earlier… SHE is not allowed here, by order of the owner of this world, Maker Kuroku. The Maker and her people, once upon a time, so long ago, once lived in this world. When her people left home to find new pastures and new futures, she joined the Estelar…the gods up there…to represent them. But she never truly abandoned her ancestral home…this world. Then, one day, she decided to refurbish it and seed it with new life. This became the human population, with such as you elves, the dwarves, and others, coming along later to set up their own living space. In time, however, she needed to move forward with her plans to bring it all into harmony, as she desired this for a reason, but that reason required everyone working along a single path of development, and wars were not a part of it."

"Therefore, this king of yours uniting the whole thing."

"Right. But here we are with you, the last piece that needs to be brought into it, and clearly, your goddess doesn't like it. But we think her ire is not simply for the fact that she is a very chaotic figure that cannot tolerate unity and harmony. Rather, we think she holds something personal with the old gods, and with males in particular, to which the Seldarine are governed by one. Here is where our Lord has been trying to conduct a bit of investigation with our native gods to see if anyone might know of the history. And we think we recently discovered something."

"Oh? This should be interesting. What was it?"

"An unrequited love interest."

"You're kidding me! Such a simple thing as that?"

"It wasn't apparently so simple for her. It seems to have driven her into such a frenzy that she turned hostile and tried stealing some of his own Children so she could pervert them with her fanatical madness."

"And so, here we are. You know, this alone might raise my ire for the atrocity of what she's done to our people in this time."

"Yes, but one of our difficulties is we are speaking of a society of beings that, in many ways, are still just people, no matter how high on the ladder they managed to climb. And as such, they still suffer from those same frailties. But how do you explain this to the common man or woman on the street who hold such beliefs that the gods are these infallible creatures that should be above all this?"

"That is a question I don't think I could answer. Everything you people have told me so far seems very outlandish, if not for the fact that you were able to demonstrate some of it to my own eyes. But while I might know who you are, and I might be able to offer my support, trying to convince any of those Greater Houses out there, regardless of your success in the other cities, will probably be a challenge, especially if she's giving out so many new stories to counter you."

"Precisely, and so we must rise to that challenge with our own."

In the city core, in the main Council Hall, a gathering of Matron mothers was assembled to speak on the developing crisis.

"She suspects they are here with us," one member addresses coolly. "Hiding in the shadows and recesses of our fine city...the heathens."

"Does she say where?" asks another. "If we could send out the warriors, perhaps we could cut them down before they have a chance to grow any stronger."

"She did not say. They seem to be cloaking themselves very effectively."

"Such that not even SHE can see them?" she winces. "That sounds frightening."

"Vicaeriia," adds another member. "How can it be that she, a goddess of all things, cannot see such interlopers walking along our own streets? This seems improbable."

"I know, Illiamala. I have asked myself this same question while sitting in the solitude of my home. She is a goddess, and should be All-Seeing. So, either these invaders have somehow risen above that, or she is concealing something from us. And I suspect it to be a test of our own means to discover it."

"I must question that decision. If we should listen to the other stories, we may be the last of us. Would she wish to test us at this point, simply to see if we are worthy? She should instead desire to inform us of everything she can to keep us from falling, like all the rest."

"This makes better sense to me," the second woman asserts. "I would surely hate to think..." she pauses. "Well, no, I would not dare suggest such a thing."

"What thing, Sinbreena?" Vicaeriia asks. "Speak. I am open to ideas here."

"Vicaeriia, this would be an impure thought, and probably offensive."

"Speak it anyway. If it bothers you so much, I think the rest should know of it."

"As you wish. Could it be she is resigning us to our fate? The others have fallen, and it would seem nothing can stop these invaders. So, could she be giving up, maybe sacrificing us for this eventual fate? She barely tells us they are...out there..." she waves a hand figuratively. "And what are we to do about it? What stories does she give about those other cities? How did they fall? What methods did these invaders use against them that was so effective?"

"I am uncertain," she concedes. "At first, she told of fire, burning, mass slaughter, but then this stopped, and I cannot be sure WHY it stopped."

"This is strange," Illiamala wonders. "I recall this as well. It seemed quite certain, but then it ceased, almost as if it held no more meaning to give such tales. Is this because it was no longer meaningful to tell these stories, as if to say, you heard it once, so why bother with another of the same? Or did something change that the story itself no longer holds merit to tell?"

"No longer holds merit?" Vicaeriia muses intriguingly. "Why would you say this?"

"Maybe I am simply pulling ideas out of the air, but one of my house servants, a well-trusted one, came to me once with something she heard in the streets not long ago. Apparently, this same story had been circling for some amount of time, and then argued with another one, that those cities did NOT burn and there was NO slaughter. But rather it was simply a ruse to inspire more hatred and loathing for something that may be outside our view, if only for our lack of actually going out there to see it."

"Ah, interesting. So, the principle here is to go SEE it, and by doing so, to prove or disprove it actually existed in the first place."

"But Illiamala," Sinbreena leans forward. "This is the Spider Queen we are speaking of here, not some simpleminded bard telling fables. If SHE is telling fables, and expecting us to believe them in the absence of going out there and seeing it with our own eyes…and this would further suggest she does not EXPECT us to go out and see it with our own eyes, thereby ONLY taking her word for it, this would be sacrilegious! We are speaking of her lying to us, and she is our goddess!"

"I know, Sinbreena. But when I heard this out of my house servant, I could not help but to ask myself if there could be a mote of truth to it. We do NOT go out there to see things. We do not even see travelers come to town telling stories of what THEY saw out there. So, where do we otherwise get our information, if any at all, about what is happening out there beyond our view? I think I would like to see something with my own eyes to know it is real, wouldn't you?"

"Well, um, yes, I suppose I would desire this."

"And so, here we have some rather fantastic stories of devastation occurring all across the realms, with every other city out there presumably going up in flames. All of them, Sinbreena. That would account for a lot, if my understanding is correct."

"It would."

"This in itself would be a fantastic statement, if only to consider our long history of sending our warriors up there to cull those same heathens so they could NOT do this. Now, where did all THAT vanish away to so suddenly, hmm?"

"She's right," Vicaeriia states. "Which would then suggest something is seriously amiss, either with the original stories of our warriors culling anything at all, or that whatever they culled isn't the same fighting force as what we are seeing down here now."

"And the stories of burning cities?" Sinbreena wonders.

"Much like she said, in the absence of seeing the smoke, where is the fire? The only real question to ask is if there is anyone out there to talk to in order to discover the missing pieces, or do we simply hide behind our city walls waiting for our turn?"

"And therefore, the idea of a sacrifice to our eventual fate? But is that fate the complete slaughter of our people, or is it something else…once again in the absence of seeing those others out there with our own eyes."

"Yes, this is true. But if slaughter WAS the result, I do not want this of our own. Unless I can discover where this misplaced proof is found, I think I would fight against it. However, I am suddenly reminded of something I learned when I was a child. It was from one of my instructors."

"Which one? Someone working for your House, perhaps?"

"No, this one came from outside. I was always under the impression he was a specialist tutor from the academy, but I only saw him once. He gave me a very important lesson, and told me to remember this for the duration of my lifetime, as one day it could save my life, maybe also my family House, and perhaps much more, if I simply applied myself to…philosophize, as he called it…a grander meaning to his words. But he didn't specify what he meant by it. He left it open, and then he was gone."

"What did he say?" Illiamala asks.

The Matron Mother of the city's First House pauses as she closes her eyes to recall that moment in her early life of a stranger dressed in a professional academy robe visiting her House. He called her into a session in the parlor room for what seemed like a brief, but apparently critical lesson. She was the only one in the family to meet with him. None of her younger sisters saw the same man visiting them during their own education period.

"Never take any one word as absolute fact," she reminisces. "No matter where it comes from or how devoted your faith is to this one source, as the telling of any one individual may be colored in such a way as to tarnish the full picture."

The other two women in attendance glared at her, and then each other.

"Vicaeriia," Sinbreena offers softly. "How do you think you would apply this to our current situation?"

"To see it with my own eyes and make my own interpretation. If any of what we have said holds merit, we might be missing something that is being withheld from us…and possibly due to that very same one we placed so much faith into to tell us everything we expect to know."

• • ◆ • •

"If we begin with a coordinated incursion through each of their outward districts," Thaelyn directs to a map on the table. "We could capture a healthy portion of the city, and then close it off to further reprisals, as these chokepoints would make excellent blockades, once we reinforce them with a few of our barrier walls."

"Especially if we use the Infinity Shield projectors," the General advises. "Once those are in place, there will be nothing they can throw at us to get inside there."

"This is one of our best strengths. But we may need to move quickly to install them before that reprisal has a chance to realize we are in the area. We can then either install a common gate through the wall, as we have done on other occasions with these units, or use portals to jump from one side to the other. I think it may depend, at least partially, on how the situation develops."

"Indeed. So, we will order the parts and have them ready. Then, once we arrive, and we can secure the area well enough, we can import them and set them up."

"This may also assist us with the threat of them attacking the cavern roof. If they cannot enter inside to focus on it, we should be secure from them trying to collapse anything on our heads."

"I agree. These passageways look to be small enough that we can obscure their view from a good line-of-sight. Then, as we march forward, we will push our front line ahead of us to the next chamber, and simply repeat, at least until we hit their city core, which I think will be the worst of it. We have a lot of open space in there, and we may find ourselves fighting along a broad front, likely more than one if we arrive on different sides."

"Yes, but while our numbers are not as much a concern, theirs would be, and worse as we are compressing them in the middle. They will find it hard to form up, hard to maneuver, and hard to find advantages if they are being constricted on all sides."

"Absolutely! I would say this could be one of our best advantages, if only for the numbers WE can field, as opposed to whatever they might have on hand, and especially as we will likely be removing some portion of theirs along the way, either through simple combat to reduce their forces, or if we can incapacitate any and use portals to capture them while they're down."

"Yes," Thaelyn nods. "I think our use of portals would be especially valuable here. We can aim for nonlethal action whenever possible, same as before. Who knows, some of them might convert after the fact. But then we come to this…" he jabs a finger at the city center, where a large complex was drawn on the map. "Their main temple."

"This one is big. It looks like the centerpiece of their city."

"It does, and I suppose it is fitting. It is in the middle, along with what we believe to be their council chamber, and a few other things. I personally suspect we will find their top council membership in the area, maybe overseeing the fight in the streets, maybe also consulting with their goddess one last time, and maybe even trying to conjure something to assist their warriors."

"If we take these other locations first, this will also include the local Houses, along with some portion of that same council. How many might actually have the opportunity to be up there at this time?"

"According to this map, we seem to have a cluster of three top-ranking Houses in near proximity to that city center. If we are quick enough to secure the other locations, perhaps to cut off any escape, we could capture their associated Matron Mothers and elder daughters. These are the most likely to be a bother to us. This would then reduce it down to this one set. And although this might not sound as bad as the full complement, let us not take anything for granted for what those three CAN do up there."

"Aye!"

A large supply of equipment was stockpiling in the fields of the Bahlaie Research Center, including fortification components, power units, communications equipment, as well as surveillance and monitoring devices to be distributed around the area. These could be installed early and linked to monitors at various command posts to observe the action at a distance. And since the Drow would not likely have any idea what a camera was, they probably wouldn't know what they're looking at, even if they did see one sitting on a rooftop looking down at them.

Numerous spooks were making clandestine patrols around the city, mostly to keep up a scouting routine to report the action to their command up above. Any serious action at all, whether it might include increased militia activity, the arrival of nonstandard forces on the streets, or the displacement of common citizens who might normally make their rounds, would need to be recorded and analyzed. No one on Thaelyn's side could be sure what Lolth had in mind, other than the occasional bit of gossip they might overhear from their spies in the various Houses.

Adalon was making one more visit to Thaelyn's office as they closed in on their final move against the city.

"…I will deal with her myssself…" she admits. "Thisss has been… A long time in coming. She should be… Expecting me."

"How do you foresee this confrontation of yours coming out?"

"I will bring with me… Reinforcementsss. Ikurin… My ssson. Perhapsss a Gold. Maybe alssso… A Red and a White. I sssuspect… She has gone mad by now. Between the lunacy… Of her original condition… Then compounded… By your relentlessss… And quite impressssive advance… Our observationsss sssuggest… She knows her fate is near."

"Meaning, you might need to simply put her down?"

"I think it is… The only way. Torm and the othersss… Have agreed… She is no longer following… The proper definition… Of the Measure of Balance. And the judgment for thisss… Is resolute."

"I see. I would not wish to argue, and for all the history we have, I cannot personally see an alternative. So, I will simply say, be diligent and be careful. I do not wish to see anything unfortunate come to you, either."

"My thanksss. But I think… You should not fear for me. I have already foressseen my courssse. And then… We shall sssee… The final piecesss… Of our creation… Sssettle into place. I have pondered the future… Of our work here… Thaelyn. And I foresssee… Great thingsss to come."

She smiles as she finishes her statement and turns to leave, gracefully sauntering out of the room, and leaving Thaelyn to ponder a few of his own ideas for the future of their work in this world.

"Kuroku," he mumbles softly to himself. "I think your work is not simply with this one creation. I must also wonder where YOU may travel next."

He now leaves his office and strolls down the hall to the strategy room, where he and his officers would often gather to plan their military advances. On his arrival, he sees the General again, along with a few other high-ranking commanders.

"We have a word from Adalon," he announces on his arrival.

"We do?" the General wonders. "What sort?"

"Lolth seems to be lost in her dementia, as far as she can tell. I think we should not expect anything coherent from her at this point. Our demonstration with the other cities has left a mark on her, and the loss of followers has likely also left a mark by weakening her capacity. Adalon will be gathering up a posse of others to take her down completely, according to the rules of the Measure of Balance. She has the support of Torm and others in this decision, so this becomes a law enforcement action up there."

"My goodness, here we go again. But in HER case, I think I will not shed as many tears for it."

"Indeed. And this will relieve us of that part. Here is where it comes down to the remaining Drow and their reactions. If they simply have orders to fight in the streets, or if any of those ranking Matron Mothers are in the temple at the time, we may need to watch for opportunities on our side. But I will be most interested to see one thing, if I should have such an opportunity," he chuckles softly. "I would like to see the looks on their faces if any of them should behold their All-Powerful goddess fall like a petal in the wind to a group of Draconics."

"Ugh…that might not be a pretty sight, but one worthy of a photo, I suppose."

"Furthermore, this will represent an important moment in our history. I think we should offer an appropriate memorial to it, in some ways a celebration for our success, but also a requiem to all those who suffered during this entire length of time."

"Absolutely, my Lord, I would fully agree to that. And it has indeed been a long time in coming."

Chapter 11

INTERDICTION

The day had finally come, and Thaelyn's forces were assembled and ready. Tens of thousands of troops lined up in the fields of Bahlaie waiting their turn to march on the final Drow city. Portal indexes had been made in the various districts for their initial advance, hoping to secure sections of the city one-by-one before moving on to the city core. The more ground they could secure, the more lives they could possibly rescue from any form of retaliation by Lolth and her more dedicated minions.

Armies of technicians were standing by to assemble the shield walls, once the individual grottos were secure, to cordon them off while the military pressed forward. Secondary rows of troops were also on standby to act as garrisons, mostly to keep the peace and serve as law enforcement and crowd control.

On this occasion, Thaelyn would participate personally, as this was a momentous occasion, and he felt it his duty to be a part of it to symbolize his role in uniting this last element of the world population. He would take up station in one of the launch sites, and move forward as they secured their ground.

"On this day," he announces to the gathering, "we will make our final movement to unite this world in peace. The scourge of the Drow will be ended, and they will discover the prestige of our efforts as we integrate them back into our own. From this moment, our world will be complete, and the future we shall share together will carry us to new worlds and new destinies. But due diligence is still important, as their devotion, no matter how disorganized it might seem by now, must still be taken as a threat, at least until it meets with its own final resolution."

He now turns and signals the beginning of their launch. Row after row of troops file into the gateway chutes for delivery into their respective quarters.

On the streets of the city below, flashes were erupting in several outward districts at once. Local citizens shrieked and ran as military troops arrived in full battle gear, which glowed with its own internal aura enchantments. The local Houses sounded the alarms, and their warriors mobilized as quickly as they could. But in many cases, the Order troops were already bashing down doors to intercept and capture them before they could take their stands.

A line of troops rushed into position at the cavern junction to block off the exit into the adjacent chamber, thereby hoping to seal off the area and prevent any immediate warnings from reaching the city core.

Two divisions were being delivered into each of the outlying zones, the first being the offensive forces, the other the garrison, but both were delivered to capture and contain the area quickly and efficiently. Some of the citizens, those who were already converted, would be granted free movement, but they would need to carry special IDs for the guard patrols to monitor. Others might need to be placed under house arrest until they could be converted, or simply detained until a tribunal could be held, if they refused to cooperate.

As the initial incursions stabilized, the front lines began to push forward. Shield walls were erected in the junctions to offer security for the captured zones while lines of troops marched into adjoining caverns. Again, some portal transit was used, but by this time, the people were catching wise to the invasion, and now they were running.

"Vicaeriia!" shouts an agitated voice.

Illiamala and Sinbreena were both roused out of their respective Houses by shouts in the streets, and the three women met as they rushed outside into a central plaza in the city core.

"Are they here?" she responds concernedly.

"I hear lots of screams," Sinbreena exclaims as she glances around nervously. "And those sounds! Clashing metal, and booming sounds."

"Is this what happened to those other cities?" Illiamala wonders. "Can you see any fire?"

They each try to stretch to see over rooftops and along avenues to the far corners of the huge cavern. And while they could see occasional flashes of light, there was no telltale glow of large-scale burning.

"Get the warriors out there!" Vicaeriia shouts. "Line them up on the street in front of the temple. We need to form a line to hold them back."

"What about us?"

"To the temple! We'll see if we can get the Spider Queen to advise us. Maybe also to send help. Call your elder daughters to assist!"

The three of them rush back to their Houses to call out their respective guards and elder daughters into service. The warriors were already equipping themselves when the noises became apparent, and Vicaeriia and the others summoned up their eldest daughters to join in the temple. The rest would oversee the commotion outside.

The fighting pushed forward through the streets with a vigorous fury. Mages hurled stunning blasts of flash-bang bursts to blind and disorient the natives. This proved to be very effective at disabling the warriors from the other Houses, causing most to fall to their knees in pain and blindness, thus allowing the soldiers to easily grapple them and haul them away. The lines were able to advance forward rapidly this way, as there were less people holding a resistance. But while the lesser Houses were falling quickly, it was the Greater ones that represented the biggest problem. They were already sending out floods of warriors, and while flash-bangs might still prove effective, the Order troops were starting to catch sight of the temple in the city core, and this is where they might need to provide a little demonstration of their fighting capacity in the eyes of the Matron Mothers, who were surely inside by now.

"Keep up the pace, people," Thaelyn orders as he directs a portion of the troop movement. "We are making good progress here. Keep them off balance. Do not let them organize into a tight formation. Keep pushing through."

The front-line soldiers were exchanging blows with the warriors of the larger Houses by now. But by this time, they were being augmented by Stormhooves and their more advanced armor and weapons.

Clearly, the Drow had never seen troops like these before. Not only did they stand head and shoulders...and chest...above the average Drow, and the males were built like mobile bunkers carrying heavy arms that could smash their way through whole lines of enemy forces, it would be their rifles that surprised the Drow the most. These were firing off volley after volley of stunning fire into the crowds of Drow warriors, sending them down in droves.

"What in all the abyss are those!" shouts one Drow warrior. "Is THAT what they used to take down those other cities?"

"It would certainly do the job," responds another. "I'll bet they could smash their way through anything you put in front of them."

"But where did they come from? They don't look human, or anything else we're told is supposed to be up there."

"I know, which means someone hasn't been telling us everything about what's up there."

Inside the temple, Vicaeriia and her two eldest daughters, plus Sinbreena and Illiamala, along with theirs, were all huddling around the altar trying to commune with their goddess.

"Hear us!" she shouts. "We need you, now! They're coming! We can hear them right down the street from us. I doubt our warriors will be able to hold them for long."

An image begins to manifest over the altar. It bore the classic appearance of their goddess, which took the form of a feminine torso with the body of a large spider. To anyone else, it would be a grotesque sight to behold, but to them, it was simply their goddess. But on this occasion, she didn't seem to be behaving quite to expectations.

The image, to a wiser mind, would represent a type of holographic projection, although with more substance to it. But to the Matron Mothers, this was their traditional presentation for their goddess to manifest herself within the temple environment. This is to say, the goddess herself, as a divine being, was believed to be physically present in this manifestation. Therefore, in the classic Age-old belief system of the Drow, this was the mysticism of how they saw it, dating all the way back to the beginning, and well before Thaelyn and any of his teachings of who the Estelar actually were.

The presentation of Lolth over the altar appeared normal enough to their past experience, but her manners were clearly different. She didn't seem quite focused of mind on the situation at hand. Instead, she began cackling wildly.

"Burn!" she screeches riotously. "Burn! Everything, burn…" she cackles some more, appearing lost in some mad delirium. "All because of HIM!" she continues her insane laughter. "I took it away! AWAY! And then threw it back at him. At HIM!"

The women all glared at the apparition, passing their glances amongst themselves as they listened to the incoherent ranting.

"Um…" Vicaeriia tries to draw the attention. "What are you talking about? Who is HE, in all this?"

The apparition could barely respond with a rational reply.

"That man! That MAN! He would not reciprocate!" she crows. "I offered him once, but NO! He was too devoted to HER. He would not turn! So, I took it away!" she now descends into another round of maniacal laughter.

"Vicaeriia," Sinbreena whispers softly. "That sounds personal to me. And entirely unrelated to anything else."

"Yes, but who is she speaking of? Also, what was she offering that he apparently turned away? And then, what did she take of his that she is apparently throwing back at him out of what sounds like spite?"

"I don't know, and further, why is it coming out NOW? Unless we say what is happening outside is the result of that spite."

"Wait a minute!" she whispers urgently. "Are you suggesting that fighting out there is HIM, whoever HE is, coming to take back what she once took as part of this spite thing?"

"That could explain the lack of fires," Illiamala states cautiously. "Maybe your suggestion of seeing something with your own eyes is correct. SHE is describing everything out there as burning, but I didn't see any fires."

"Burning, maybe in a figurative sense, the result of what SHE did to that thing she took, and then threw back, but SHE wants it to burn out of this spite for something."

"Bodies in the streets…" Sinbreena muses. "She WANTS bodies in the streets, a burnt ending of what she took out of spite to deny it back to HIM."

"So, it belonged to HIM first. And then she comes along, offering something, which another SHE was in the way of. That sounds like a personal interest that got turned away. This one wanted HIM, but he was already devoted to another. And as a result, she got angry, stole something that belonged to him, and is using it as a weapon against him."

"That now makes better sense. And WE must be the thing she stole, if WE are the bodies in the streets right now."

"But Sinbreena! Who or what is this HE? A male? Was there a male out there once who watched our people?"

"And she, a female," Illiamala offers. "Who clearly hates males.

Just look at what she teaches us about them. To say nothing of all the rest, like those on the surface. It must be related to that. Our ancestors were supposedly banished from something. But was it banishment, or did SHE do something?"

"Oh no..."

Vicaeriia quickly turns and rushes to the door to peek outside. She could see the fighting getting closer along the main avenue. Now, the warriors out front were engaging the lines of soldiers, but it didn't look good for a victory, only a delay of the inevitable. She returns back to the altar, where the apparition of Lolth was still in her delirium.

"Who are you speaking of!" she demands of the divine entity. "Has he found his way down here and is trying to take us back?"

"So much have they grown...SO MUCH!" she chortles madly. "And THIS! Such a pitiful contrast...so archaic!"

She again descends into her mania as she apparently tries to visualize the extreme differences between the two sides.

Vicaeriia and the others all gazed at each other. She then draws them away from the altar for a close huddle.

"Listen," she asserts privately. "That sounds like a reference to those above, and us down here. I don't know what those warriors of ours were doing up there, if anything, but I suspect it was something other than what we thought it was. Those people outside are cutting us to ribbons. If THAT is what their warriors look like, they must've become something unstoppable. And if ours is so archaic in comparison, it sounds to me like someone..." she glances over her shoulder, "...has been holding out on us. And not simply for the details of what THEY were doing, but what WE were NOT doing."

"Uh oh..." Sinbreena mumbles. "So, we were kept in the past while they moved into something new and different?"

"And likely another aspect of that reference to HIM," Illiamala adds. "And what she denied to US out of spite."

"Great! So, what do we do about it? If SHE is actually the one..."

At this time, before Sinbreena could finish her statement, a disturbance was rising out of the apparition on the altar.

"Aagh!" Lolth screams. "What art THOU doing here! Get away from me!" she shouts in a sudden panic.

The women turned quickly to see the apparition of their goddess seemingly pushed aside out of the projection over the altar, like a body shoved out of view of a camera lens. They hurry back to the altar to watch as Lolth vanishes off to one side, but her shouts and screams could still be heard from somewhere in the background. Then, a rush of other bodies flashes into view as a parade of large dragons advanced across the scene. They entered from one side, passed in front of the projector, and continued off the other side, as they seemed to be chasing Lolth.

The women all gazed into the apparition, now asking themselves what they were looking at, if not an actual body of their goddess manifesting itself over the altar. This view gave a whole new meaning to their form of communication with the divine.

In the window of the projection, they first saw two large silver dragons, a female leading a male close behind. This was followed by a Gold, a Red, and then a White.

"That's bad!" Illiamala moans.

"You think?" Sinbreena shudders.

"What are we looking at?" asks one of Vicaeriia's daughters.

"I'll tell you what it looks like to me, Nedintra," suggests the other one. "But I'm only barely able to imagine what I'm saying right now."

"Speak it anyway, Shi'nae," Vicaeriia directs.

"It reminds me of the Seer's Pool we have back home, and how we can see other people and places. But here, if you could turn it around, where the person you are looking at could look back at you at the same time."

"Like a two-way Seer's Pool? Interesting."

"But this means she's not actually standing there...um, like to say, I'm standing here, and we always thought SHE was standing, or floating, up there. This now says she's probably in a house, or whatever she uses, looking at us through a Seer's Pool, and with us looking back up at her. And then THAT," she points at the image, "is someone invading her house and attacking her!"

"Dragons?" Nedintra notes. "Why are dragons inside there? And how? And do they actually do this sort of thing?"

The screeching inside Lolth's personal home continued.

"Get off of me! Get away! How dare thee attack me!"

"Wretch!" sounds an angry female voice from out of view. "By issue of the Greater Powersss... You have defiled... The Measure of Balance... For the lassst time. Thisss now becomesss... Your penance!"

The sounds of screaming and thrashing continued as the women watched and listened to what was clearly a savage rending of their former goddess.

"Measure of Balance?" Sinbreena muses quietly.

"Greater Powers..." Illiamala considers. "Defiling something, that sounds almost like a policy or a law, and now this...punishment."

"Meaning to say, she DID do something to someone, and probably for that spite thing, and this is what she gets for it."

"But she's a goddess!" Nedintra argues. "Doesn't that mean something? If you're a goddess, you should be All-Powerful, or something. You shouldn't be answering to someone else."

"Greater Powers...other gods," Illiamala recites. "This means, they must have rules, and they probably expect you to follow them. You are NOT so All-Powerful to have it your way. That spite thing isn't allowed."

"And what she did to us," Vicaeriia concludes. "And by comparison, what the others must've done for those people up there, but we did NOT get in here."

"But Vicaeriia," Sinbreena issues worriedly. "What does this actually mean for us? And all those other cities?"

"No fires... Someone we might call HIM taking something back that once belonged to him. And this outside being what he sent."

"Wow!" Shi'nae muses exuberantly. "He must be serious, or angry, or both."

"I would probably imagine both, from what we see up there. Those dragons are the ones to carry out this punishment. So, if this is what dragons do, those Greater Powers not only have rules, but enforcers to those rules."

"Oops! And I recall a few times some of us speaking of trying to steal things from them, like eggs and such."

"Yes, that might not be such a wise idea under these circumstances. Not if they hold the power, and the authority, to attack and kill gods."

The women continued to watch, although the image was empty at this time. However, the sounds in the background were dying down by now, and they could hear voices again.

"Ikurin..." resounds the female again. "We mussst call Thaliel... To clean up for usss."

"Of courssse, Mother. I will sssee to it."

"Kamasssin... Check the remainder... Of thisss domicile. I do not wish... To see any sssurprises. We mussst be sure... To remove... Her ssservants. Lessst they attempt... Any new missschief."

"Of courssse, Maker. We will make... A careful review."

Again the women studied each other's faces as they listened.

"They sound like a thorough group," Sinbreena raises her brow.

"One of them is called Ikurin," Vicaeriia emits. "And the other, his mother. But another one, named Kamasin, addressed her as 'Maker'. What is that, a title? Maker of what?"

The image still showed a blank space, until a moment later when something new appeared in it. It was the face of a mature female Silver. She had arrived in front of the projector on her side and was now looking down at the Drow observers.

"Ah! Ssso… You are ssstill here?" she muses. "Much as I predicted."

The women felt a slight shudder as they found themselves looking up into the face of a frighteningly powerful beast. But again, it was apparently only an image, as they now understood it was not a physical manifestation.

"Predicted?" Vicaeriia whines timidly.

"Indeed, Child. I am a prophetessss… And I foresssaw… You would be here… And ssSTILL would be here… Even after we finished… With that wretch of a Power…" she glances off to the side.

"A wretch? You call her a wretch?"

"Indeed! She once ssstole you away… From your proper godsss. And worssse… Your kind sssubmitted themssselves… To her fiendish hatred. You defiled them… The sssame as she defiled… The Measure of Balance."

"What does that mean?" Illiamala asks gently, unsure if she wanted to inquire from this creature, but feeling it necessary to understand what they just witnessed.

"The Powersss… As sssome call them… Are a sssociety of beingsss… Known as the Essstelar. They govern themssselves… By a rigid ssset of rulesss… Called the Measure of Balance. All thingsss in Creation… Mussst balance… On the polaritiesss… Of positive and negative influence. Sssome take to the positive ssside… To enforce their waysss. Othersss take to the negative… To balance the firssst. But SHE fell… Ssso far into madnessss… That she no longer followed… Any of thisss. Sssuch nonconformity… Is not allowed… As it can bring dissscord… And dessstruction… To the harmony of Creation. And to the Essstelar… Life is a preciousss thing… NOT to be brought into jeopardy… By sssuch frivolousss whimsss."

"Oops!" Nedintra yips. "There's your answer. Rules, punishment…"

"Yeah," Vicaeriia nods. "You said madness? We could hear her laughing insanely, and speaking in terms we did not understand. Something about offering something to a 'him', and then taking something away. We are guessing part of it, but the 'him' part we are not sure of. Can you help us understand?"

"Your proper pantheon…" she responds. "Is the ssSeldarine. The sssame as your brethren… On the sssurface… To which you are sssupposed to belong. But your ancessstors… Once defiled thisss… By turning hossstile… With their greed and their lussst."

"Greed and lust…so that's it."

"They were banished into exile… As punishment for thisss. At the sssame time… You alssso turned… To thisss new one… And away from the old. It was the leader of that group… Where once she held an interessst… But he was previousssly devoted… To another of higher repute. Therefore… She ssstole YOU away… To defile you with her hatred… That she might further offend him."

"Well, that's nice of her!" Sinbreena groans. "We simply became someone's tool of unreturned desire? And what about all this time she was ordering us to send warriors up there to fight someone?"

"A further insssult… To those above… That you refused to learn… From YOUR missstake… As well as… To further fuel her hatred."

"Uh huh…figures. Bodies in the street. So, our accursed ancestors got themselves banished for their greed, but didn't take the hint, and likely because SHE didn't let go of her own."

"Who are you, by the way?" Vicaeriia asks. "Are you part of those gods, or something else? You look like a dragon, but I'm not sure how to interpret things now."

"By my people," she responds. "I am called Kuroku… The Maker of the Draconicsss. We are guardiansss… Of the Measure of Balance… Designed to enforce it… Amongssst they who firssst invented it… And any othersss who may follow."

"Um, Mother," Nedintra suggests quietly. "Yeah, like we said, they must be the ones who keep the gods in line."

"But in thisss form…" she continues. "I am alssso called… Adalon the ssSilver… To people like you."

"Because you appear as a silver dragon?" Vicaeriia notes.

"Indeed. I feel thisss color… Is rather becoming," she chuckles.

"Yeah, uh, how nice…" she smiles uncertainly.

"Vicaeriia of Houssse Helvityl… Sssinbreena of Houssse Orlyana… And Illiamala of Houssse Noqundar…"

"You know us?" Vicaeriia frowns.

"I do. The three of you... Have a choice to make. Vicaeriia... You once held conference... With a man... A ssscholar... When you were a child. You ssspoke of thisss... Only recently. He gave you a lesssson... Of dire advice. Do you recall thisss?"

"A man...him?!" she shouts. "How would you know of this?"

"I am a member... Of the Essstelar... And I carry... The sssame ssSight. But I alssso... Play their gamesss... To manipulate eventsss... Sssuch as to achieve... A desirable outcome. And he was one of those."

"YOU?!" she screeches.

Vicaeriia felt faint and stumbled back a step. And the others felt themselves turning pale.

"I foresssaw you would be here... The Matron Mother... Of the Firssst Houssse... Along with these two. I desired you... To be knowledgeable enough... And flexible enough... To perceive of thoughtsss... And interpretationsss... Beyond what was commonplace... Amongssst your kind... And for ssso many generationsss. Thisss moment... Demanded it."

"Uh huh...sure, if you say so," she accedes feebly. "Um, so what is it I'm supposed to be flexible-izing in all this?"

"You will know... When you ssstep outssside... That door. You should not need... My advice... For thisss much."

Adalon now pulls back and turns to the side, where she finds the controls for the projector, and turns it off, leaving Vicaeriia and the others standing in a pool of their own sweat.

The two daughters turned to gaze out the door. The sounds of fighting still echoed up from the street outside. They began moving forward to peer at the action through the doorway. The rest followed hesitantly alongside them.

The action outside seemed just as vigorous as before, although it also seemed staged, as if neither side was making any real progress, and the invaders were mostly toying with the locals.

"No fires..." Sinbreena states. "And no bodies in the streets."

She glances around the area, and while there were many people rushing this way and that, there did not seem to be a pile-up of bodies left behind them.

"We had more than this out here, didn't we?" Illiamala wonders. "Even from way down the avenue."

"They must be removing them, that's all I can think of. Taking them back, whatever that means."

"Back to join our brethren," Vicaeriia nods. "To whom we are SUPPOSED to belong. That's the whole point of it. Those other cities were captured, not burned."

"All right," Sinbreena offers. "But then, what are they doing to us up there, if they are taking us back? Are we simply joining something, or is it something else, maybe as part of our own punishment for what our ancestors did?"

"I think there is only one way to answer that. We must simply ask, and learn it for ourselves."

Vicaeriia now struts determinedly down the stairs from the elegant temple complex, which rose well above the street level for a proud view of the city. As she arrives near the base, she searches for her House warrior charge, led by the first son, who was found standing behind a row of others giving directions.

"Solaonar!" she shouts.

The seasoned male turns to respond, and sprints up to meet her.

"Matron Mother, this doesn't look good," he ushers anxiously. "Does the Spider Queen have anything to offer?"

"I suppose I could answer yes, if you suggest her clear dementia over a personal desire she apparently went mad over, and then used us as a weapon against him."

"Huh?"

"Yeah, and then telling us to do things to further insult not only us down here, but also those on the surface we offended at one time by our greed and lust for things that probably didn't belong to us in the first place."

"Wait a minute, how does that…"

"And THEN…" she continues unabated. "She fills us with HER hatred for such things as, oh…men, for one thing; our former gods we're all supposed to be worshiping, and our elven brethren on the surface we are supposed to be a part of, rather than festering in this hole she buried us in. How does that sound so far?" she smirks.

"Um…" he flusters. "I, uh…"

"Oh, please! If you have an opinion, feel free to speak it. We just got a first-hand lesson that gods apparently have rules, AND enforcers to make sure those rules are obeyed, right down to a death penalty if you do not. And she just got hers."

The man gaped at her for the outlandish depiction. He glanced at the others in the group, then up at the temple, which seemed calm on the outside. No fires, no explosions, and no demons streaming out the doors. He then turns back to his Matron Mother.

"So, what are we supposed to be doing right now?" he asks tenuously.

"Stop fighting, Solaonar. We are wasting our time with it. These people are apparently here on behalf of those gods we are SUPPOSED to be worshipping, and I guess they want to take us back now."

"Stop fighting?" he wheezes. "But..."

"Solaonar, tell the men to...STOP FIGHTING!" she screams.

Her voice echoed through the cavern, and carried all the way into the street, causing many of the warriors to respond, even without the first son giving the order. The ruckus in the street began to slow, with many of the Drow warriors pulling back. And much to their surprise, the Order troops also stopped and held their positions.

Many of the soldiers glared at the seemingly delicate figure who, like many elven women, represented a shapely, if youthful, feminine form. But the blasting she just let loose on the poor man in front of her gave a whole new impression.

"Bloody hell, man," whispers one soldier to another. "That dame has a set of lungs on her, and not just the part on the outside," he chuckles.

From somewhere behind the lines, Thaelyn and the General had been directing their advance. But on seeing the display up on the steps, they suspected something had just happened. As such, they began to make their way to the front to investigate.

Vicaeriia studied the action down below, and quickly realized she was right. This was not an effort to leave bodies in the street. Not if both sides were willing to stop fighting. She slowly strolled down the stairs a bit more to interact with the troops in front of her.

"My name is Vicaeriia of House Helvityl, the First House in our city hierarchy of governance. Who among you is the leader of this warrior body out here?"

The General and Thaelyn exchanged glances, until Thaelyn simply smiled and nodded to the General, as he was technically the military leader to answer that call. The man steps forward to present himself.

"Here, Ma'am!" he waves his hand. "The name is General Eugan Landers of the Order of Tyr."

"A General? I am not familiar with that title. What does it mean?"

"In a professional military body, it is a top-ranking position to govern all of this you see here, and perhaps more, if we have such a need for it."

"Really! You command all of this?"

"Generally so," he smiles cutely.

Vicaeriia glares at the man for his quirky wit.

"General, generally…uh huh," she shakes her head. "And although I know this is going to sound a little soft-minded, but what are you doing here?"

"Essentially, we are here to finish what we started with all the other Drow cities, and that is to capture them, along with all, or at least as many as possible, of their citizens."

"Right. And this is because of…?" she raises her brow inquisitively.

"It follows with a process, really…" he positions himself to gesture with his hands. "First is to contain the situation for a time until we can find some measure of stability. You know, to secure ourselves from any ill deeds and wrongful behavior out of those who are being detained. But this is mostly a short-term effort until we find the time to explain a few things about why we had to trot all the way down here to conquer you."

"Oh, how thoughtful. And next?"

"Next is to typically vassalize these new holdings, at least for now, until we've had the time to make a few inspections, apply a few reforms, modernize some of your local amenities, add a bit of this and a touch of that…"

Vicaeriia glared at the man with her eyes growing wide. She rolled them to view Sinbreena and Illiamala, only to see they were gaping at the list of improvement efforts he was checking off.

"Most importantly," he continues. "We would need to improve your schools, as surely, being all this time living down here, you might have missed out on a few things."

"Uh huh…missed out."

"And then, once we reach what we might call a critical threshold, we would take it to the next level where we begin the assimilation process. This is where we can officially admit you as full and proper citizens to our kingdom up there."

"A kingdom. So, you have a kingdom up there that wants to conquer us and bring us into it? Um… I, uh, don't want this to sound the wrong way, but do we have a choice in this?"

"Not really. The rest of the world is already a part of it. You're all that's left now."

"The rest…" she wheezes. "The whole…all of it… But how much are we talking about? I don't even have a full idea of what that world actually looks like."

"The lands above are a grand bit more than anything you have down here. At last count, I think we tallied up a few billion people as our full population."

"A few billion!" she shrieks.

"And this accounts for multiple continents on this one world, and not including the four others we took over recently," he smiles pertly.

"Four…other…worlds!" she pants.

"Granted, three of those don't have much on them so far, but that can change, you know," he grins.

"Oh, well, naturally!" she waves it off nonchalantly. "But just how did you do all this? And how long did it take?"

"Oh! Indeed, Ma'am. This didn't occur overnight, mind you," he chuckles. "It took a fair few centuries, to be sure, as we were going slow in order to convince the people up there of what we had in mind, and how good it could be if they all joined up voluntarily. And many of them did, eventually."

"Eventually. And were there any who did not?"

"Aye, there were those who had other ideas. But unfortunately, our Lord and King had a divine mandate by the owner of this world to do it anyway, so their opinions became moot."

"Oh! My goodness, their opinions became moot. A divine mandate, you say? Hmm. The owner of this world. This is interesting. This world has an owner? Is it anyone we know? Not that I might know of such a thing, but what the heck…" she shrugs.

"Well, yes, this might be a bit outside the common knowledge down here, but her name is Maker Kuroku."

Suddenly, Vicaeriia, along with the others in attendance, all screamed and fell backwards. Vicaeriia stumbled and fell to the steps, while the others caught themselves in various positions of collapse.

Thaelyn and the General, along with many of the Order troops, and quite a few of the Drow warriors, including Solaonar standing nearby, all gazed uncertainly at the reaction.

"Um, Madam," the General emits cautiously. "Does this name actually hold meaning to you?"

"Her…" she gasps and turns to gaze up at the temple behind her.

"We saw her," Shi'nae asserts. "Up there, in the temple. We were trying to call on the Spider Queen, but it was strange. Um…"

The younger woman stands up and steps away to give herself some space for her portrayal.

"At first," she poses herself as if preparing for a playact. "Here we are, calling her up at the altar…" she waves her hands in front of her. "And we get this big image of her floating above us…" she raises her hands upwards. "This is how we normally see her, thinking she was visiting us inside here. But I guess this isn't really so. On THIS occasion, she's like…'BURN! Everything BURN…Ha, Ha, Ha!" she grabs her belly for a theatrical laugh.

The General turns to Thaelyn, who is now laying a hand on his brow.

"Dear Powers, not another one," he moans.

"My Lord, don't we have enough of those upstairs?"

Shi'nae continues, "And she's laughing like a drunken madwoman, saying, 'It's all because of HIM…' And things like, 'I took it away, and now I'm throwing it back at him'…"

"Indeed!" the General leans forward. "She behaved this way to you?"

"Oh, absolutely! She was completely gone upstairs…" she points at her head. "But THEN, this is the good part. We're watching her, and then WHAM! She flies out of view. This is where we're getting the impression this manifestation thing isn't so much a manifestation, but some kind of image, like what you might get if you could turn a Seer's Pool inside out. Do you know what a Seer's Pool is?"

"I do, and I can fully understand what you mean by it. A type of projected image, but with a two-way capacity for interaction."

"Right! So, she goes flying off to the side and out of sight, and then we see this crazy rush of dragons! Can you imagine it? Dragons inside whatever she calls a home, and chasing her!"

"Really! Who would expect such a thing?" he feigns sympathetically.

"I know!" she ushers excitedly. "Do they do this sort of thing often?"

"I don't think I would expect to see it often, but to see it at all would be quite a spectacle."

"Anyway, she's like, 'Get away from me!'… And then, 'What are YOU doing here?!'…"

"What sort of dragons did you see in there? Did you get a good look at the colors?"

"Yes! Two Silvers, a Gold, a Red, and a White. All of them looking mean and ready to tear something apart."

"Incredible!"

"Now, the image goes blank, but we can still hear noises. There's like a BANG, and a BOOM, and a CRASH..." she storms across the steps, flailing her arms and making sound effects.

Sinbreena and Illiamala both glared at the girl, and then at Vicaeriia, who simply folded her arms with her head in one hand.

"Vicaeriia," Sinbreena wonders. "Does she do this often?"

"Yes..." she moans softly. "This is why I named her Shi'nae...the foolish dancer. She began when she was young. She took a liking to the frivolity of playacting, and was always something of a jester in the family. I must admit, she can be rather entertaining on occasion."

"Uh huh..."

Shi'nae continues, "...And then there's an AAGH! Get off of me!" she flaps her hands in the air.

"General," Thaelyn muses quietly. "Let us make a special note to ourselves. Do NOT let this young lady come into contact with Relissa up there. I think we would never survive it."

"Indeed, my Lord."

"And this one big Silver starts talking," Shi'nae recalls, now bellowing in a deep simulated voice. "You have defiled the Measure of Balance for the LAST TIME!" she waves a finger in the air. "By order of the Powers so-and-so and what's-his-name and some other, this is now your penance!"

The General and Thaelyn both exchanged bemused glances.

"General, are we recording this display?"

"I suppose we have one or more body cameras in play here."

"Good. Make sure you dispose of them promptly," he smiles. "Before anyone gets any ideas about this."

Shi'nae continues, "This is where we have a bunch of screams and gurgling noises as they finally finish her. Then, this one tells another, 'Ikurin, call such-and-such to come clean up for us'... And then, 'Kamasin, check for stragglers so we don't get any surprises'..."

"Fascinating," the General muses intriguingly. "And this is how they work on their own terms."

"It does pose an interesting perspective for us down here," Thaelyn nods.

"Finally," Shi'nae concludes. "She comes up to her side of that Seer's

Pool thing, and starts talking to US!" she pats herself energetically. "Can you believe it? A dragon wants to talk to US!"

"Amazing! Just think of it," he chuckles privately.

"She even knows us by name...well, our Matron Mothers, at least."

"She does?" he raises his brow.

The General glances at Thaelyn, who is now frowning and leaning forward to catch this latest part.

"We asked what we just saw," she continues. "And here is where she has to explain this Measure of Balance thing, which is totally new to us. I mean, WOW! The gods have this rule thing, and BAM!" she smacks her fist, "if you don't do it right. And also, that we're all actually supposed to be a part of the other elven nations up there, and worshipping the same gods, and how SHE, meaning the Spider Queen, apparently had this thing for some guy who didn't feel the same way, and this is what made her go out and do a lot of bad things, like stealing our people, telling us to do a lot of...stuff..." she flutters her hands casually, "...and apparently making up a lot of stories along the way...."

"Um, Shi'nae..." Solaonar interjects. "Is THIS what happened in there?" he points at the temple. "And therefore, the reason you all came out here to stop this..." he waves a hand at the street below.

"Yeah, but you're not going to believe this next part. We asked her what her name was. She said that people like us might call her Adalon the Silver, because she apparently likes that color. Personally, I like reddened gold, it goes better with my eyes. But that's just me," she giggles. "But more importantly, SHE is this Maker Kuroku, and part of those gods up there. And she must've really didn't like our goddess."

"Her?" he feels his face going pale. "You spoke to her...up there... and she is the one..." he turns to face the assembly of soldiers.

"Yeah, but that's only part of it. She's apparently also responsible for Mother, when she was a little girl, receiving this guy who was supposed to be a scholar from the academy, and giving out a special...lesson..." she air-quotes her statement. "Mother told me about this once. It was to not take any one person's opinion on things, and to keep an open mind that it could be painting a bad picture of something bigger."

"I do not believe this!" Thaelyn roars. "That old lizard did it to us again!"

"I swear, my Lord," the General shakes his head. "She is a crafty one."

"This goes beyond crafty, General! She planned it from the

beginning, and even dropped hints in key places to ensure an easy victory for us."

"So, you know her?" Shi'nae wonders.

"Know her! She works right alongside of us up there, and has been for more than eight centuries as we progressed around the world to bring it into harmony."

"Wow, she must be determined! What actually took you so long to come down here? Did it simply take that long to do the rest, or what?"

"There were a number of complications to deal with, not the least of which was to find a convenient way to arrive and convince your people to listen to us, rather than Lolth. We also had a long period of animosity to resolve, and a number of nations that once existed which were not cooperating as well. Then, when I came into it, we began to bring it together, but yours was difficult due to your location, trying to infiltrate the area, chart our paths, and ultimately to find our opportunities, at least until we found a branch of your fellow Morierea on one of those other worlds we discovered, and they opened up a few possibilities for us."

"More of us? On another world? How in all the abyss did they get over there?"

"Ah, but my dear young lady, that is a story unto itself. Anyway, perhaps I should introduce myself, while we are here. I am called Thaelyn, and I am the king of this world, at least on the surface, and except for a few last-minute details here, I would also say of the Underdark and all your other cities we took possession of. This should complete everything we have here, and will allow us…ALL of us…to finally move forward into a new Era. I simply need to ask if you would wish to submit to this of your own, or if you would like to return to the little exercise we had occurring out here a few moments ago…" he smiles generously.

Vicaeriia and the other Matron Mothers all gazed at each other, along with their associated daughters, and the warriors who were still standing around. They turned to look over their shoulders at the temple one last time, and then panning their view around the city, which looked generally the same, save for the sounds of the soldiers and some abnormal lighting in certain places.

"Sinbreena, Illiamala," Vicaeriia begins. "I think the answer is right in front of us. Even a blind man could see it. And, in truth, I don't think I need to say any more to you on this. Let us simply admit to it by now."

"Yes, Vicaeriia," Sinbreena nods. "Not only is this the beginning of this new Era, but it is the final end of another that probably should never have existed."

Chapter 12

GENERATIONS

"Aerlie, are you sure you do not want that pinch to reduce the pain?"

"Not yet, Thaelyn. UGH!" she moans. "I want to feel what it's like, at least in the…AAGH…beginning. This is a special moment, and I don't want to…ERGH…miss anything."

"Uh huh. Very well, dear. Just let me call on the city engineers again to cordon off the area for any structural damage you invoke," he chuckles.

"Oh! You!" she whaps him across the midsection.

The time was coming, and Aerlie's moment was fast approaching to deliver her twins. She had a gathering of her closest friends to support her, including Relissa and Nemelle, Aelwyn and Aristan, Vonafel, and even Kaliya and Ayene to offer support, among others. Outside, in the medical ward waiting room, was Hana Laurens with her cameraman, waiting to hear from the delivery room, once they had something to offer. And in homes and markets, offices and temples, people were gathering wherever they had video monitors broadcasting the INN news in anticipation of the moment. It seemed as though time had largely stopped as everyone was waiting for the first word of the delivery.

Ankhia Tad'vaal, another longtime friend from the Suuden-Aryku, and a medical expert, had offered to assist with the delivery. This was at least as much for the family friendship, as it was in reciprocation of Aerlie once helping her with her son.

"

"You look like you're getting close, Aerlie," she notes as she examines the contractions. "But it'll get hard from here."

"Yeah, I...OOGHA...recall from the time you had yours. I'm trying to hold out a little long-...ARGH...-er, but I think I'm just about ready for it."

"Are you sure?" she smirks. "You don't want a few more groans and growls first?"

"You know...AAGH... Between you and Thaelyn, I think you're all teasing me now. All right, hit me, I've had enough."

Ankhia reaches around behind Aerlie to the nape of her neck, where she gives a gentle rubbing and pinching action, as part of their divine healing practice to zap the nerves and kill the pain. Aerlie feels the release almost immediately, and begins to relax into the bed.

"Good," Ankhia nods. "Now, we'll take this in sequence, just like we do for the humans whenever they have this. I don't expect it to be any different in your case, other than for the fact that elves don't traditionally do twins."

"Yes, I think it should be fairly routine," she emits smoothly. "After a while, the biology is mostly the same."

Ankhia positions herself at the end of the bed, with several other priests and interns standing by to assist. One of them offers a small amount of a special medicated oil which she takes into her hands and begins applying it to Aerlie's abdomen, rubbing it all around the area to stimulate the muscles.

Aerlie lies there, trying to relax, but finding it difficult for the anticipation. She could feel the oil going into her skin. It tingled and felt subtly warm. She recalled all the times she used this same procedure on so many other women.

"It's so strange," she muses softly. "Me being the one here instead of someone else."

"We all get it eventually," Ankhia reflects.

"Do not forget, Aerlie," Aelwyn offers. "I had mine, and more than once. But I did not have as much difficulty with it as what you are going through."

"I suppose," she accedes. "But being the one under the microscope just feels different. It feels almost surreal, like something I would dream about, but it was never for me."

"It's probably from all those times you tried," Relissa suggests. "But it never happened for you. You just gave up after a while, and relegated it to a fantasy."

"And how many times did she see so many others," Vonafel adds. "Some of whom were also her close friends over the years."

"Maybe you're right," Aerlie admits. "And all the more reason to treasure this one special moment. I wonder what it'll be like to watch them grow up, blossom into adulthood, the things they'll do, the places they'll go."

"That would be a fine sight to see," Aristan considers. "Ours have made some interesting choices in their lives thus far. But in your case, I think I would strongly suggest an emphasis on our new cultural direction for theatrics. You recall our recent additions to the educational courses in our schools, correct?"

"I do. And how you pushed it through the parliament to see those classes expanded with the extra courses."

"Well, yes, but I felt that it could provide for an enhanced level of cultural involvement amongst the populace. I would say the results are rather enticing for how people find interest in social play now."

"Indeed. Like the General down there talking to that one young Drow girl. Oh yes, I heard about that one! But I don't think she would need any class study. She already has it!"

"Perhaps!" he chuckles. "But I am thinking in terms of these representing the royal lineage. I suspect they will probably follow in both yours and Thaelyn's footsteps, and we all know some of his lessons in giving certain impressions to one's opponents."

"Right. And how many times have we seen this? And so, do you think theatrics would be useful here? Well, I suppose. The formal presentation of an image, maybe also to exaggerate certain portrayals…"

"Furthermore, I would delight to see them expand these talents into other areas, whether as a professional interest, or simply a hobby. Imagine, if they could portray themselves on a stage or with music. And as Celestial twins, they would likely make a fabulous pairing."

"It sounds like you want to take over their education all by yourself!" she giggles.

"Well, no, but if I could simply act as a surrogate uncle, that would be fine enough. We are such a close group together; we should each give a little into it. This represents an opportunity to see a new form of life developing. We may not be a full society, but we are certainly unique."

"Yes, we are!"

"Aerlie, are we ready?" Ankhia asks as she continues to study the contractions. "I think the time is arriving."

"All right, Ankhia, let's do it. The whole world is waiting outside, I can almost hear them."

Ankhia makes one more examination of Aerlie's abdomen as she makes swirling motions of her hands to massage the skin.

"Hmm, was it left over right, or right over left..." she muses mischievously.

"Ankhia!" Aerlie snaps playfully.

She now begins a rhythmic motion, along with a soft chanting. This would stimulate the muscles to control the contractions and encourage a determined push to deliver one of the babies. She moves her hands in swirls and circles along one side, then to the other, keeping a minor favoritism to select the first of the two babies to be delivered.

Aerlie could feel the tension building inside, but she had to contain herself with some breathing exercises until Ankhia gave the order. And as Ankhia continued to build up tension, the sensations got stronger.

"Wow, it feels a little different than I expected," she notes to herself.

"Almost there..." Ankhia mumbles. "And now, Aerlie! Push hard!"

Aerlie makes a firm effort to bear down, while Ankhia slides her hands along her belly, encouraging the first baby to follow the path through the birth canal. The motion is smooth and deliberate, resulting in the first of the twins finding their way into the open.

Ankhia steps aside for the interns to take over, gathering up the baby, tying off the cord, and moving it to a side table where they will clean it off and prepare it in swaddling. The process was quick and efficient, a well-practiced maneuver with many hands contributing into it. But almost as soon as the first one was on its way, Ankhia was back to studying Aerlie's belly again. She could see some movement rippling inside as the other one seemed to be getting anxious.

"Wow, this one looks like she really wants out of there!"

"Yeah," Aerlie notes as she could feel the movement. "Such a rambunctious little girl."

"I wonder if this is a sign to come," Thaelyn moans as he rolls his eyes.

Ankhia was back to work, making another set of swirls across Aerlie's body to prepare the next one. As before, she conducts her chant, although this one seemed a bit more ambitious than the first.

"We're still working the first one," admits one of the interns. "And we'll have the next already? This could set a record for the timing!"

Ankhia continues her movements, once again building up the tension, until she feels it is ready.

"Here we go. Push hard."

Aerlie again bears down firmly, and the next baby comes sliding out with seemingly little effort. And once again, the interns take over and tidy up.

"What's the timing on that?" Ankhia asks.

"We got the first at four past ten of the clock, and the next at six past ten. Two minutes apart. Not bad!"

"Nice, and we have two precious little girls, who will surely make trouble for someone as they grow up."

"Thank you, Ankhia," Thaelyn smiles and nods, though he is clearly showing emotion at the experience.

"Do we have names yet?"

"We do. Aerlie and I took some time to choose a pairing of names using our native Celestial conventions, as we feel this is appropriate for who they are."

"Naturally. But which one is which? Or does it matter with twins?" she smiles tenderly.

"Well, surely it will matter as they grow up, but the selection would tend to run as the firstborn, and then the second. And for this, the first will be called Yumenia, while the second will be Nymelia."

"Aye!" Relissa grins proudly. "Those sound like right grand names for a pair of wee tykes like these. And if they're anything like Ailene and Brianne, I'm sure we'll see a lot of fun out of it."

Aerlie relaxes from her endeavor while Ankhia and the interns finish with the afterbirth and general cleaning up. The two babies are then wrapped up in swaddling and presented to the proud parents to coo over.

As they peered into the little faces, they could see their eyes just starting to open up. Thaelyn and Aerlie, as well as Aelwyn and Nemelle, all leaned in to check for their Celestial auras.

"Positive Ordered," Aelwyn smiles. "As if it could be anything else."

"I suppose that might be a given," Thaelyn nods. "And no doubt, much like Aristan mentioned, they will likely follow in many of our own footsteps."

"They do not have the Avariel wings," Ankhia mentions. "But this would make sense to me, as an exobiologist. You would have a much more successful pairing of the limbs in common."

"What about their eyes and hair?" Aristan peers over their shoulders. "We have a tiny bit of hair thus far, and yes, look at that…"

The two girls were showing up the first traces of hair, which was the same nearly metallic golden color as Aerlie's, with some soft silver highlights running through at intervals, representing Thaelyn's color. As for the eyes, as they began to clear, the gathering could see they held a similar topaz blue crystalline glitter, much like with Aerlie, but with flecks of gold scattered around from Thaelyn's side.

Vonafel leaned in to study the colorations, nodding gently as she reflected on her long-deceased friends from her old academy days.

"Yes, they were right. Annah, Deena, Amaree, you were right, girls. And so beautiful they are. Now I can find my rest and join the others. Our work is complete."

✦ ✦ ✦ ✦ ✦

The years passed by, and the kingdom of Tae'Eladar returned to the practice of normal life. The comparatively young spacefaring society was gradually balancing itself with the more experienced Suuden-Aryku, and the people continued to grow with new knowledge and discovery. The future was bright and promising, as they would have nothing standing in their way of pure progress, now that the last of their local societies was combined into the greater whole.

In the city news broadcasting center, a young journalist was setting up for the daily report.

> *"This is Hana Laurens for the B.T. edition of the Imperial News Network. Good evening, everyone. In today's headlines, it's been four years since the last of the Drow population joined the Empire. For the most part, progress has been steady, although the renovations of their cities have proven difficult due to the local geology, and the need to carefully map out the natural bedrock and occasional fracture lines before conducting any new construction work.*
>
> *However, we have recently been informed of the successful completion of a new power station and relay network, which will provide them with electrical power for the first time in their history. In addition to this, with the therapeutic adjustment of their lighting controls,*

it has been reported that we are experiencing, in some locations, at least, a slow migration of our new Shadow Elf population to join with us here on the surface. It is said they still need to make the final adjustment to the native light levels up here, but this is certainly a fine development to return them whence they came after so long a period living in the darkness..."

Elsewhere in the city, life goes on. The streets were packed with shoppers, tourists, and business professionals. Aerlie had returned to her usual work by now in the temple, and Thaelyn to his at the guildhall. And life had gone back to normal for them...mostly.

Up in the royal manor, the twins were under the supervision of the house servants, butlers, and nannies. They were only beginning to prepare for their official school lessons, which would begin by the next season. Meanwhile, the two little girls had already learned a number of lessons simply by watching those around them, and picking things up from their parents and family friends, as well as by using their fledgling Celestial senses.

Today, however, would be a special one. The chefs in the kitchen had just finished a batch of cookies, one of several specialty dishes to celebrate a birthday party coming up later in the day. And the aromas were spreading all around the house.

"Mm, yummy," croons a tiny voice, as a set of eyes peeked around the corner of the hall.

"All right, Nymi, listen. You stay out here and watch for people. I'll go in, grab a couple of cookies, and then we go somewhere and eat them. Got it?"

"Yes, Yumi. And if I see anyone going to the kitchen, I need to flash you, so you can hide."

"Good!"

The two young twins rush off to their assigned tasks. Their objective: That freshly baked batch of cookies currently sitting on the kitchen counter. But even though they were freely available for anyone to go in and take one, this wasn't their plan. Every four-year-old knows that cookies taste better when they're illegitimate!

Nymi takes up a post in the hallway, standing watch well ahead of the kitchen so she might have enough time to warn her sister if anyone was heading in that direction. Yumi, on the other hand, made haste to sneak into the kitchen so she could attend to her covert task.

While Yumi was in the course of her deeds, Nymi stood silently against the wall, looking both ways as she surveyed the area. Then, from around the corner came one of the housemaids. She was on her way through the manor attending to her usual chores when she saw the young girl standing there all alone. This would not normally be an issue, if not for the fact that Nymi was only one of a set of twins that were virtually inseparable. So, the housemaid felt a simple need to inquire where the other one was.

"Nymi," she bends down to meet the girl. "What are you doing out here?"

"Me?" she smiles innocently. "I'm watching for people."

"Oh? Why is that?"

"To see where they're going."

"I see. Where is your sister?"

"In the kitchen."

The housemaid frowns softly at the curious suggestion.

"What's she doing in there?"

"Well, let's see…" she puts a finger up to her temple to focus her psychic perceptions. "Right now, she's trying to move a chair over to one of the counters."

"Oh? Really! Why is she doing that?"

"Because the counter is too high up!" she admits cheerfully.

"Oh, my goodness, how silly of me. But why is she trying to get on top of the counter?"

"To steal some cookies!" she yips excitedly.

"Uh huh…" she moans. "And why are you out here?"

"I'm watching for people," she glances casually along the hallway. "Oh, are you going to the kitchen?" she frowns gently. "Because if you are, I need to flash her so she can go hide," she smiles sweetly.

The housemaid covers her eyes and sighs.

"Oh dear gods, help us all. And these are Celestials. Well, there goes THAT image!"

Down the road from the guildhall, in the Royal Historical Archives, Casarolyn was again giving her presentation on the prophecies of Adalon, with a newly updated memorial display including her most recent verses. And we are not simply speaking of the one discovered at the conception of the twins, but another that came out later at their birth.

It reads…

A trove of gifts, and wisdom true,
Where art meets moral play;
The Twins of Twain shall make their stand,
In such entangled way.

THE END